Thick Fog

An Alexis Parker novel

G.K. Parks

Copyright © 2020 G.K. Parks

A Modus Operandi imprint

All rights reserved.

ISBN: 1942710224
ISBN-13: 978-1-942710-22-6

For my mom and dad

BOOKS IN THE LIV DEMARCO SERIES:

Dangerous Stakes
Operation Stakeout
Unforeseen Danger
Deadly Dealings

BOOKS IN THE ALEXIS PARKER SERIES:

Outcomes and Perspective
Likely Suspects
The Warhol Incident
Mimicry of Banshees
Suspicion of Murder
Racing Through Darkness
Camels and Corpses
Lack of Jurisdiction
Dying for a Fix
Intended Target
Muffled Echoes
Crisis of Conscience
Misplaced Trust
Whitewashed Lies
On Tilt
Purview of Flashbulbs
The Long Game
Burning Embers
Thick Fog
Warning Signs

BOOKS IN THE JULIAN MERCER SERIES:

Condemned
Betrayal
Subversion
Reparation
Retaliation

ONE

The ambulance raced past me, the red of the taillights leaving a streak in my rearview mirror. They were in a hurry. That meant he was still alive. They wouldn't rush if he wasn't. At least, that's what I told myself.

For the briefest moment, I thought about turning around and following them. But I might be wrong. The now distant sirens could have received another call. A different address, a different victim. It might not be him. I swallowed. *Get a grip, Parker.*

Pulling to a stop in front of Mark Jablonsky's townhouse, I jogged toward the open front door. The flashing red and blue lights painted the walkway beneath my feet. A cop stood guard at the entrance, but I didn't care. I held up my credentials, a move I'd perfected years ago, except private security didn't pack nearly the same punch as federal agent. So I retracted the ID quickly and pushed past like I owned the place. Like I was supposed to be here.

"Is anyone else from the Bureau here?" I asked, noting the officers standing awkwardly in the living room. They must have been first on scene.

"Not yet," the cop said.

"They're on their way." I headed for the stairs,

unprepared for what I was about to find.

The first door on the right was Mark's bedroom. I'd been here often enough to know my way around. The sight before me nearly brought me to my knees.

"Oh god." Sucking in a breath, I forced myself to remain upright. The air smelled like copper, and the once white sheets were now spotted and streaked. I took a step forward and then another. The center of the mattress was solid red. The blood had pooled, penetrating through the various layers of bedding. And it was still wet.

How much blood could that be? A liter? Two? How many were in the human body? I should know. Why didn't I know?

Squeezing my eyes closed, I tried to focus. The room spun, but I ignored it. *Focus, do your job, Parker,* Jablonsky's voice said.

The scene had been compromised. I didn't know how many cops and paramedics had tromped through the house, but it didn't matter. All that mattered was they got here in time to save him, but I didn't know if that was true.

I looked down at the carpet, seeing the path the gurney had taken. The wheels carved out a line from the bed to the doorway. The sheets were thrown to the side and left in a ball. I wondered if they'd been like that before the paramedics and police arrived. There was a lot I didn't know, but I did know one thing. The attack happened right here. Jablonsky didn't fight back. I didn't see any blood droplets or spatter to indicate otherwise.

Going to the nightstand, I put on my gloves and opened the top drawer. His gun remained where he left it each night. He didn't even try to get to it. He probably never even woke up.

I went to the window and peered out. No signs of forced entry. The killer didn't come in this way. I knew Mark. He would have made sure the doors were locked before going to bed. None of the windows appeared broken, but I didn't check the back of the house. Too many cops had been in my way, and once the detectives and Feds showed up, I'd be kicked out. So I had to learn as much as I could as quickly as possible.

The phone beside the bed hung by the cord off the table. It needed to be printed, but that didn't stop me from reaching for it. I was almost certain what it would reveal, but I'd been trained to verify facts and not make assumptions. So I carefully depressed the switch hook and hit redial. A moment later, my cell phone rang. I pressed the switch hook again and left the phone dangling. Forensics should start with the phone.

Mark's cell sat on the dresser beside his wallet and credentials. His cash and credit cards were gone, but this wasn't a robbery or home invasion. I felt it in my bones. This was revenge.

I put the wallet down and checked his badge and government ID. They remained. I glanced back at the wallet. Law enforcement would track the charges. Perhaps they'd get lucky.

"You shouldn't be here, Alex," Detective Nick O'Connell said from the doorway. "This is an active crime scene. You should be waiting outside."

I put Mark's badge down. "I know, but I had to see for myself." I turned to look at him. "The asshole who did this called me."

"And then you called me. Glad to know I'm still your favorite," he said, even though neither of us was in a joking mood.

"You're not so special. I called everyone. 9-1-1, you, Heathcliff, Director Kendall. The only person I didn't call was my boss. This is all-hands."

"I know. I called Thompson. He's outside coordinating patrols and setting up a perimeter. The shooter might still be in the vicinity."

"You really believe that?"

"No, but we gotta do something. It's Jablonsky. We have to try."

"Yeah."

O'Connell circled the room. "Shit." He rubbed a hand over his mouth. "Did you find it like this?"

"Uh-huh."

"Did you see him?"

I shook my head. "I saw the ambulance." The thought

I'd been fighting against played through my mind again, and I teetered. "Any word on his condition?"

"No one's said anything to me, but I jumped out of bed and came straight here. You're lucky I remembered to put on my pants." He rubbed his eyes. "I spoke to the officers downstairs, but it just happened. I'm guessing they got here a few minutes before you did. A detective hasn't even been assigned yet. I doubt anyone in the department knows anything at this point."

"Did the responding officers notice anything when they arrived? Maybe they caught a glimpse of the assailant."

"Police cleared the house. The shooter was gone by then." O'Connell watched the phone sway back and forth, inches from the floor. "He probably made the call and ran. He must have known you'd call in the troops." He crouched down, peering beneath the bed. "No casings?"

"I didn't find any."

"He took the time to clean up his brass."

"Does that mean something to you?" I asked.

O'Connell shrugged. "Just an observation."

"Mark's wallet's been emptied. The shooter wanted to make this look like a robbery. But it wasn't."

"I know. Robbers don't call to gloat."

"Nick," I said, "will you take the case? You're the first detective on scene. That makes this yours, and I'll need whoever's handling this to loop me in. Please."

O'Connell was a good cop. He did most things by the book. But he knew me. He trusted me, and we'd been in enough scrapes that he'd bend a few regulations here and there if it served the greater good.

"You know I will, but I'm guessing Lt. Moretti wants to handle this one personally. He and Jablonsky have a history. They go way back. You don't need to worry. Everyone in major crimes will be focused on catching this son of a bitch. We'll get him. I promise."

The sound of sirens grew louder, and I looked out the window. Two government issued SUVs screeched to a stop. Four men in FBI jackets got out of one of the SUVs, and two men got out of the other. A black sedan with government plates parked behind them, and Director

Kendall stepped out.

"Looks like the gang's all here," I said. "More than likely, they'll want to take over since Mark is one of theirs. I don't want this to turn into a pissing match. We don't have time for that kind of nonsense. Mark doesn't..." I swallowed the lump in my throat, unable to continue.

"I'll update them and see how they want to handle this," O'Connell offered. He patted my shoulder on the way out of the room. "Whatever you need to do, you better do it fast."

Casting a final look at the blood-soaked sheets, I marched down the stairs and headed for the back door. Again, no signs of a break-in. The front door was open when I arrived, but if the assailant bashed the door in while Mark was asleep, surely the sound would have woken a supervisory special agent. No, the asshole found another way in.

"Did you check the locks?" I asked the officer standing near the kitchen counter.

"Yes, ma'am. No signs of tampering. The door was locked when we got here."

The word ma'am sent my mind reeling back to the memory of my first partner dying in the back of an ambulance. Aside from his last words, the only other thing etched into my brain from that day was that one horrible word, and right now, that was the last thing I needed to hear from anyone.

I unlocked the door and stepped out onto the patio. The cool night air did little to calm the inner turmoil. Again, I pushed the terrible thought away, refusing to let it fully form in my mind. Once it did, I'd be paralyzed. I had to keep moving. To keep going. I had to stay one step ahead, but I knew I wouldn't be able to outrun it forever. I just needed a few more hours. Then it could crush me.

With shaking hands, I reached into the mouth of the frog statue. Nothing. The hidden key Mark kept inside was gone. I told him to get rid of it. Maybe he finally listened.

"Identify yourself," an FBI agent said.

I turned slowly, keeping my hands where he could see them. I didn't recognize him. But it'd been a while since I'd worked at the OIO, and even then, I didn't spend a lot of time socializing with the other branches of the Bureau. "Alexis Parker."

"What are you doing here?"

"I called it in," I said.

"You can't be back here. You need to wait out front. Someone will need to question you." He gestured at the door, waiting for me to go through it.

"Thank you, Agent Keane," Director Kendall said the moment we stepped into the kitchen. "I'll take over from here."

"Yes, sir." Keane excused himself and rejoined the other members of the team.

From what I could tell, they were establishing a grid. They wanted to flush out the shooter, but knocking on doors and asking questions at this time of night would be met with hostility. However, a federal agent had been shot in his bed. We didn't give a fuck about proper etiquette.

"He called you," Kendall said. "What did he say? Did you recognize his voice?"

"No. I don't know. It happened so fast. One minute the phone's waking me up, and the next I'm being told if I ever want to see Jablonsky alive again, I better hurry. At first, I thought it might be a sick joke. I tried calling Mark, but..." I swayed.

"Take it easy, Parker." Kendall pulled a chair out and waited for me to sit. "Do you want a glass of water?"

"No."

Kendall took a seat across from me. "I know you and Jablonsky remained close even after your resignation."

"Which one?"

The director snickered a little. "Either. Both."

"We're friends. More than friends. Mark's been watching out for me since the first day I set foot in his office."

"That's his job. He trained you." Kendall looked uncomfortable. "Do you know any reason why someone would want to hurt him?"

"You should know the answer to that."

"I know you talk. On occasion, I'm sure he's shared intel

and information with you that civilians shouldn't be privy to. Is there anything I need to know? Now's the time, Parker. Are you working something together? Something off the books?"

"No, nothing like that."

Kendall thought for a moment. "Any idea why the shooter called you?"

"I don't know." I told Kendall about the phone off the hook upstairs. "Maybe I'm on Mark's speed dial."

"Did he use your name?"

"I think so."

"And you were at home when he called?"

"Yes."

"But he called your cell?"

"Uh-huh."

"What exactly did he say to you?"

I put my head in my hands, leaning my elbows against the table, and pressed my palms against my eyes. This was important, and for the life of me, I couldn't remember the phrase he used. Eyewitnesses were rarely reliable. I never thought that would apply to me.

Kendall pulled one of my hands away from my face, forcing me to look at him. "It's okay. What time did he call?"

"Right around three." I reached for my phone and pulled up the call log. "3:02. I was asleep."

"I don't see how this would be relevant, but if it came down to it, could anyone vouch for your whereabouts at the time of the shooting?" Kendall asked.

"James Martin."

Kendall nodded, scribbling it down in the notepad he carried. "Anything else you remember about the caller? His voice? Background noise? Anything?"

"I don't know. It sounded familiar."

"All right. Take some time to think about it. We have a mess here. We need to lock this place down, comb through everything, run a threat assessment, and figure out what's what. You should go home and get some sleep. I'll have plenty of questions for you come morning."

"You can't expect me to sit this one out."

"You're not an agent anymore, and I told you when you quit, I can't reinstate you. Even if I wanted to, my hands are tied, and under the circumstances, I wouldn't want to."

"Sir," I began, but he held up a hand to silence me.

"No, Parker, it's Jablonsky. You can't see this one clearly or rationally. You're too close. You said it yourself. He's more than a friend. He's practically your family. You need to take a step back."

I bit my lip. Regardless, Kendall needed me, and he knew it. "Have you heard anything yet? How is he?"

Kendall looked away. "They rushed him into surgery. That's all I know."

"Did you assign a protection detail to the hospital?"

"Yes."

"Okay." I pushed away from the table.

"I'll let them know you're on your way."

TWO

I paced the waiting room. No one would tell me anything. I wasn't family or an agent. Maybe I should leave. I had to do something, and this wasn't doing anyone any good.

Checking the time, I practically counted the seconds. I hadn't even seen the protection detail. They had been posted outside the OR, as if the bastard might come here to finish what he started. Additional police personnel had been called in to supplement hospital security, but I didn't recognize any of those officers either.

How could this have happened? I tried to think, but my mind wouldn't focus on anything except Jablonsky's condition. Flashes of his bedroom surfaced, and I gasped.

"Don't die. Please don't die," I whispered, my voice a strangled groan. Dammit. I couldn't escape the thought any longer. The fear gripped my insides like a vise, squeezing the air from my lungs and leaving a painful empty hollow in my gut.

I ran out the front doors just before a sob burst from my throat. Swallowing it back down, I found a spot at the end of the curb, sat down, and hugged my knees to my chest. This couldn't be happening. This was a bad dream. One of my nightmares. It wasn't real. I'd give anything for it to not be real. But it was. And I had no idea how the world would continue to turn without Mark.

Who would do something like this? And why would the shooter call me? I had to figure it out. I needed to know. I had to get this guy. The bastard would pay. I'd hunt him to the ends of the earth.

"Think, Parker. Think." I hit myself in the head. I probably looked like a crazy person. At the moment, I wasn't so sure I wasn't. Rocking back and forth, I forced the tears to stop falling. It took every ounce of self-control to tamp down my emotions, an even harder feat since I was exhausted, mentally, emotionally, and physically.

"Alex, sweetheart," a familiar voice said from behind, "what are you doing out here?"

I looked up to see James Martin standing a few feet away. He ran one hand through his hair and held out his other to help me up. I stared at the gauze taped to the inside of his elbow. "I don't want to go back in there. It smells like disinfectant, disgusting cafeteria food, and death."

"With undertones of urine." Martin dropped his hand and leaned against the support pillar beside me. "Hospitals always smell like piss. I'm not sure why, but they do."

"Did you see Mark before they took him into surgery?" I asked.

"No, by the time I got here, they already had him past the double doors with FBI agents standing guard. According to the nurse I spoke to, the surgery will probably take a while. Hours."

"Do you know what happened?"

"Two gunshot wounds. One in the chest. The other in his gut." Martin stared across the parking lot. His expensive sports car stuck out like a sore thumb against the sea of sedans and SUVs. The sky had brightened to a drab gray-blue. "The sun should be up in an hour or so. Do you want to go home and get some rest? I'll stay here with him."

"I can't leave." I licked my lips, and my voice cracked. "I can't lose him."

"I know." Martin sunk onto the ground beside me. "Me

neither. He's my best friend. He has been for over ten years. He was the first real, genuine person I met as an adult. I'd been through a lot of shit with my parents dying and running Martin Tech, but Jabber put everything into perspective for me. He has no problem telling me to pull my head out of my ass. He always has my back. He's always been there for me. He brought me you."

I grabbed Martin's hand and squeezed. Often, I forgot Mark was his friend first. "The person who did this will pay. I'll make sure of it."

"Do you know why this asshole called you?"

"Not yet."

"It's probably good he did. At least it gives Jabber a fighting chance. If he hadn't..." Martin didn't finish that thought.

I ran my thumb over the solid band on his ring finger, the symbol of our commitment to one another. "Do you remember anything the caller said to me? Right now, everything's a blur. I can't think straight."

"You just told me Mark had been attacked and to get to the hospital."

I closed my eyes, recalling Martin tugging on a pair of jeans and a t-shirt before grabbing his car keys while I put on the closest thing, grabbed my gun, and made several frantic calls while racing to Jablonsky's townhouse. I tried to think about what happened immediately before that. "The phone rang, and you handed it to me."

Martin had been wrapped around me. He liked to cuddle, and after his recent bout of separation anxiety, I let him get away with it most nights. A part of me liked to feel safe and protected, and the other part felt trapped and strangled. Right now, either would be preferable to what I was feeling.

"It rang three times," Martin said. "Display came up Jablonsky."

"He called from Mark's home phone," I said. "Even left it off the hook."

"Was he in too much of a rush to hang it up?"

"No, he wanted the investigators to run the phone records. He wanted them to know he called me."

"Why?"

"That's a good question." I shut my eyes, reliving the last few moments of peace before my world turned upside down. The caller's voice played through my mind. His words sending shivers through me. *Sorry to wake you, Alex. But I thought you should know, Agent Jablonsky isn't long for this world. If you want to see him again, you better hurry.*

I knew that voice. I just couldn't place it. I had to think. "He knows me." I dropped Martin's hand and stood. "The bastard called to gloat, just like Nick said. That son of a bitch."

Martin climbed to his feet, swaying and grabbing hold of the pillar while he squeezed his eyes closed.

"Are you okay?"

He nodded. "Probably should have finished the juice they gave me. It's just hard to drink apple in a place that smells like piss."

My gaze drifted to the gauze on his arm. "You donated blood. How did you know you'd be a match?"

He tapped his arm. "Universal donor, sweetheart." He cocked an eyebrow at me. "Didn't you know that?"

"I guess I should have realized it since you're so damn perfect. You're Superman." I wanted to hug him, but if I did, I'd crack. I jerked my chin at the entrance. "We should go back inside in case there's news. How did you get a nurse to tell you anything? They wouldn't say a word to me."

"Did you tell them you're Jablonsky's emergency contact?"

"No."

"Well, that would explain it." Martin took my hand, desperate for the human contact but respecting my need to maintain a barrier and keep my distance. "Come on. I'll see what else I can find out."

I went back to pacing while Martin flirted with the nurses for information. I had to get out of my own head. I had to look at this objectively. Clinically. The caller knew me. A shiver traveled down my spine. This shouldn't be that hard to figure out. I knew the voice. Why couldn't I place it?

I made a lot of enemies in my lifetime. And so had Mark. Obviously, the shooter knew us both. We could have crossed paths during any of the cases we worked together, so more than likely, this tracked back to my days at the OIO. How many arrests did we make? Dozens? Hundreds? Anyone still incarcerated could be ruled out, but that didn't necessarily limit the possibilities.

I'd have to go through my files, starting with the most recent and work backward. Luckily, Mark and Nick had helped move my files out of storage and into my new home office three weeks ago. That would make things easier.

All right. I had a plan. Digging through my pockets, I searched for a pen. In my current state, I didn't trust myself to hold on to my fleeting thoughts. But I couldn't find a pen. Why didn't I have a pen? And even if I had one, what would I write on? My arm? I took a deep breath. I needed to pull myself together.

"Here." Martin appeared with a clipboard, some printer paper, and a pen. "I could tell you needed this."

"Did you read my mind?"

He smiled, though it still looked sad. "Always."

"You should be careful. My mind's a scary place right now."

He snorted. "It's a good thing you can't read mine. You'd never look at me the same way again." He leaned against the wall beside me.

"What'd the nurses say?" I asked, scribbling down my wayward thoughts. I couldn't look up, too afraid of what I'd see in Martin's eyes.

"We should sit tight. It'll probably be six to eight hours before we know anything. They're calling in an expert. Some topnotch thoracic surgeon." He dug out his phone and tapped the screen. "I'm gonna check this guy's credentials. They better be getting the best."

"And the fastest." My thoughts returned to the pooled blood in the center of the mattress.

Martin tapped the screen a few more times, grunting at the information displayed. Obviously, he didn't approve of the hospital's choice of surgeon. He looked up at the clock.

"Let me make some calls."

While he did that, I wrote out a list of things to check, starting with OIO cases before moving on to my private sector gigs. Jablonsky always helped out whenever he could, but ever since I was hired by Cross Security, I'd been relying on their resources instead of Mark's. Still, there was no statute of limitations on holding grudges. Had anyone been released from prison lately? Adding that thought to my growing list, I blew out a breath and worked through a few meditation exercises in the hopes of achieving some clarity. It didn't help.

"Alex?"

I turned to find Jen O'Connell, Nick's wife and emergency room nurse, entering the hospital. She gave me a quick awkward hug, pulling away when I stiffened and didn't return the embrace. She grasped my arm and offered a consoling look.

"Jenny," Martin came up behind her, "what are you doing here?"

She hugged him hard, something I couldn't do, and sighed. "Nick called. He told me what happened. I'm so sorry. Have you heard anything?"

Martin updated her on what he'd been told.

"Let me put this stuff in my locker and check-in. Then I'll see what I can find out. Hang here for a bit," she said before disappearing behind a locked door.

Martin took a seat, and I dropped into the chair beside him. I closed my eyes, analyzing Jablonsky's house and the crime scene from my memory. The only damage to the rest of the house was the front door, which the police bashed in when they entered. The back was undisturbed, even locked. But unlike the front, the back door didn't have a deadbolt, so the shooter could have flipped the lock on his way out.

"Jablonsky used to keep a hidden key in the frog out back," I said. "Do you know if he still does that?"

"I thought it was a turtle," Martin said.

Opening my eyes, I fixed him with the full force of my glare. "Does it matter?"

Martin held up his palms. "As far as I know, it's still there. He never gave me a spare key to his place."

"I used to have one, but that was years ago. Before he moved." I bit my lip and tapped the pen on the paper. "The key's gone. I checked out back, but it wasn't inside the frog or turtle. Whatever it is."

"Is that how the asshole got inside?"

"Probably. There were no signs of forced entry, at least not that I saw." I tapped the pen a few more times, wondering if the assailant knew about the hidden key when formulating his plan or if he just happened upon it once he arrived. A lot of people hid keys under doormats and in fake rocks. That wasn't uncommon. Every fiber in my body told me this was premeditated, but how much planning went into the attack? Was the break-in opportunistic?

Doing nothing was killing me. I couldn't sit this one out. In fact, just waiting for an update on Jablonsky's condition was giving the culprit more time to escape. This asshole didn't have the right to walk free, not after what he'd done.

"How do you do it?" I asked, turning to face Martin.

"Do what?"

"Wait."

He arched his eyebrows while his shoulders bunched. "What else can I do?"

"So you're biding your time? Waiting for him to let his guard down?"

"We're not talking about sitting here, are we?" he asked.

I shook my head and got up to pace. I knew that voice. How did I know the caller? Who was he? I'd give anything for a recording, a playback, something I could listen to over and over. Maybe if I heard it again, I'd be able to identify it. But the shooter didn't leave a voicemail, so the chances of that were slim.

I spun to face Martin. "I can't figure out why he called me." My eyes flicked toward the double doors as another idea formed. "Y'know, he could have killed him." A shudder went through me, and Martin grabbed my hand. "Mark was asleep. As far as I can tell, he didn't wake up. The bastard could have put one in his head." My chin quivered, and my voice shook. I tugged out of Martin's grasp, covered my mouth, and faced the wall, taking slow, measured breaths until I regained control. "He wanted him to suffer."

Martin stood beside me, so close I could feel warmth emanating off his skin. But he didn't touch me. "Are you sure he doesn't want you to suffer too?"

THREE

"Have some coffee," Agent Davis said, placing it in front of me. "I think I remembered how you like it."

"In a cup?" I asked, not bothering to look up as I scoured the reports for tidbits that would help me identity the shooter. Since Davis was a friendly face, Kendall sent him to pick me up at the hospital and bring me to the federal building for questioning. Martin remained, promising to update me the second he heard anything. As of yet, my phone hadn't so much as beeped.

Davis snorted. "We miss you around here, Parker. And now with everything that's happened, we could use you."

"Tell that to Kendall."

"Don't you think I have? But it's a no go. However, this bastard called you, so anything you can tell us is bound to help." Davis ran a hand down his face, his gaze drifting to Jablonsky's empty office. "I'm not the enemy. Help me out here."

"I don't know." I pushed the reports away. "Fuck."

"All right, just take it easy. You know more than you realize."

"Don't do that," I warned. "I had the same training when it comes to handling witnesses."

"Like it or not, Parker, you're a witness. You possess the

intel I need, so whatever it takes to jog your memory or connect the pieces is what I'm going to do. Tough tits."

"What's Jablonsky working on right now?" I asked.

Davis stared out the conference room door. "You know I can't tell you that."

"Well, you wanted my help, so that's where I'd start if I were running this."

"It's Jablonsky. You know how it goes. He supervises everything going on in and out of this office, so it could be any number of things. He's been looking into traffickers and the cartels, allegations of money laundering and fraud involving several judges, and a ring of armored truck heists." Davis searched my face. "Does anything overlap with whatever you've been doing at Cross Security?"

"No."

"Mind if I ask what you've been doing?"

"I don't mind, but Lucien Cross will." Despite my boss's insistence that we avoid law enforcement and cooperating with them, I didn't have the same qualms, which would explain why I was now considered an independent contractor at the company instead of a full-fledged Cross Security employee.

"Tell me anyway."

"I haven't worked on anything like what you described. The last big case I worked was an arson investigation. The bastard burned my apartment to the ground. Since then it's been background checks, cheating spouses, and security overhauls."

"Any chance the arsonist could have gone after Jablonsky to hurt you?"

"Nope."

"You're sure?"

"Completely."

"Anything else?" Davis asked.

"You're starting to sound like a broken record. But no, nothing that would implicate Jablonsky or the OIO. And before you ask, I keep him clued in when and if the situation calls for it, but the last time Mark saved my bacon, it was from a serial killer. And as far as I know, the psychopath is still in prison." Plus, the killer's voice didn't match my recollection of the caller from last night, but I didn't necessarily trust my memory at the moment. "Has anyone checked to make sure? Jablonsky made the arrest. There should be a record somewhere."

"We looked. That was the last case we found where you and he overlapped. The serial killer is in solitary. No visitation. No outside contact. Nothing links last night's shooting to him."

I nodded, though my mind had gone to Mark riding to the rescue. Why couldn't I have done the same for him? Reaching for my phone, I looked at the screen. No news was good news, right?

"Hey, Alex, we'll figure this out. Don't worry, Jablonsky's a tough son of a bitch. He'll pull through."

Blinking away the tears that threatened to fall, I blew out a breath. "Have any arrests been made recently on his current cases? If someone's out on bail, now's the perfect time for them to strike."

"No recent arrests. Jablonsky has us collecting intel and keeping watch, but we always have court cases pending." Davis wrote himself a note. "I'll look into that possibility. Eliminating the agent who built the case is one way to get out of jail."

But something else Davis said struck me funny. "You said he's been looking into the cartels?"

"Yeah, there's been a recent influx of drug activity. The DEA asked us to keep an eye out."

"Focus there."

"Why?"

"Shooting a federal agent in his bed seems like something they'd do. They don't have the same hang-ups as most criminals when it comes to hunting law enforcement officers. They treat it like sport. It stands to reason they might have wanted to halt Jablonsky's investigation before it turned into a full-blown raid, so shooting him would buy them enough time to finish their business and move on before we get our ducks in a row."

"Okay, I'll buy that if you tell me which cartel hitmen have your number memorized. You're not on Jablonsky's speed dial, so the shooter must know your number by heart."

I thought for a long time, but no one came to mind. Even when I'd gone undercover with the DEA, I hadn't crossed paths with anyone that high up in the cartel. I'd been interested in human traffickers and dead mules, not the head honchos. "No one comes to mind."

"Would you tell me if someone did?" Davis asked.

"Yes."

He studied me for a moment before nodding and moving on. "Okay, so let's run through this one more time from the top."

"Let's not." I pushed away from the table, desperate to move, to act, to do something. "Kendall said he ordered a threat assessment. What did that turn up?"

"Not much. As far as we know, Jablonsky hasn't been greenlit."

"So we're assuming the shooter wasn't contracted. Makes sense. A hired hitman wouldn't have called me to gloat. And he wouldn't have shot him in the chest and stomach. He would have delivered a headshot. It'd be simple enough, especially on a non-moving target. Why would he risk leaving Mark alive?"

The look on Davis' face said it all. At best, Jablonsky's chances were slim. The shooter must have figured Mark would bleed out before help arrived. As it stood, no one knew if he'd even make it off the table.

"He doesn't think Jablonsky has a chance in hell of surviving."

"Let's not go there. It doesn't matter what the shooter thinks. All that matters is we figure out who he is, why he went after Jablonsky, and what that has to do with you."

"It might not have anything to do with me."

Davis gave me a 'yeah right' look. "He called you. He told you to show up. Why didn't he wait for you? Obviously, he wanted you there. If he'd just waited, he could have taken care of two birds with one stone."

"The sirens must have spooked him. Police and EMTs arrived before I did. The shooter might be arrogant, but he's careful. It doesn't take a genius to figure out I'd call for help." I stared at Davis. "What makes you think he wants to kill me too?"

"Seems to me if a thug makes a call like that, he has more than one victim in mind."

"I don't know what to say. I have no idea why he called me, but by the time I got there, he was long gone."

"Unless there's no mystery shooter, and you're behind it," Davis said. The look on his face didn't give anything away.

I stopped dead in my tracks. "You better be fucking kidding me."

Davis shrugged. "I'm just stating a fact. Your financials have been all over the place lately."

"So what? That can be explained."

"I'm sure it can," he said, "just like how the only prints we found inside Jablonsky's house belonged to the first responders and you."

"The shooter must have worn gloves."

"I'm sure he did."

If Davis kept this up, he'd be eating through a straw for the next six weeks. "Do you want to ask me something, Agent Davis?"

"No." He didn't ask for an explanation. And I didn't volunteer one.

"Kendall asked about my whereabouts at the time of the shooting. Is my name on your suspect list?"

"Should it be?"

I moved closer until I was standing inches from Davis. "Are the interrogation rooms full? Is that why you're doing this in here?"

"C'mon, Parker, sit down. I'm just doing my job. I want this guy as much as you do. No one who knows you would ever think you could hurt Jablonsky, but you have to admit, it looks weird. You say the shooter called you, but he used Jablonsky's phone. There's no evidence saying anyone else was inside the house."

"The two slugs in Jablonsky's torso say someone else was in the house. As soon as they're removed, you can run the ballistics. I guarantee they aren't mine."

"Why do you think the shooter called you?"

"He called to hurt me." Martin and I had the same

conversation. It was the only thing that made sense. "Or to tease me." I backed away and turned to stare out the window. "I've heard his voice before, but I can't place it."

"That changes things," Davis said, even though I didn't see how. "We should focus on old cases, investigations you and Jablonsky worked together."

"No shit. I thought you said you were already doing that." One of us was several steps behind, and for once, I didn't think it was me.

"We thought Jablonsky reached out to you to get help on a current case and got himself in a bind. We assumed the beef was recent. The shooting could have been a warning. Maybe someone wanted you and Jablonsky to back off of whatever you're working on. Are you sure he hasn't asked for your help on anything?"

"Jablonsky doesn't ask for my help. That scenario works in reverse. And sometimes, he helps even when I don't ask. He always knows when I'm in trouble." I gulped down the bile that burned the back of my throat. How would I survive without him? Shaking off the thought, I returned to the table and pulled out the list I started in the hospital waiting room.

"You recognized the voice." Davis marked out the notes he'd written himself. "Our priority should be evaluating old cases since you said there's been nothing recent. It has to be someone from your joint past."

"Has anyone recently been released from prison? He should be at the top of the list."

"You think someone's holding a grudge?" Davis asked.

"Don't they all hold grudges?"

Davis skimmed the list I'd written. "This is a start."

"I guess." I stared at him. "Look, you have my permission to check whatever you need. Verify my alibi, run my financials, my phone records, whatever, I don't care. Just don't waste too much time. I didn't do this, and I don't know who did. But he's out there, walking around while Mark fights for his life. So either you find the bastard responsible, or I will."

"We're on the same side, Parker. We will get this guy. Your input has been invaluable. And for the record, I know you didn't do it. But I had to ask. I'm sure you understand why."

"Yep, but I don't have to like it."

"I am sorry." Davis made some notes. "Once we have a firm suspect list established and we've had time to make the appropriate calls, we'll have more questions. You said you recognized the guy's voice. So you'll be able to identify it if you hear it again, right?"

"Maybe."

Davis met my eyes. "What's the problem?"

"Everything's jumbled. I can't make any promises."

"Have you slept?"

I shook my head.

"That might help," he said.

"I can't, not until I know if he's...that he's going to be okay."

"All right, I'll get started on this. Just give me a sec and I'll have someone take you back to the hospital and make sure the detail adds you to the approved list as soon as you're cleared."

"Director Kendall said he would take care of it."

"I'll make sure he does." Davis held out his hand, and we shook. But he didn't let go. "You've always worked tirelessly on these cases. I don't have any doubts you'll be working around the clock to figure this out. When you do, call it in."

"Any chance I can convince you to keep me updated on the investigation?" I asked.

Davis shrugged one shoulder. "We'll see." He let go and pushed open the door to the conference room.

"I don't need a ride," I said. "There's no reason to waste an agent's time when it could be better spent looking for the shooter."

Davis nodded and headed back to his desk. Halfway there, he turned around. "Parker, be careful. There's a chance the bastard might contact you again."

"I'll be ready if he does," I said, even though I didn't feel ready for anything.

FOUR

Before returning to the hospital I detoured to my office. I checked my phone every five minutes to make sure I had a strong signal and didn't miss a call or text, but my phone was fine. I just didn't know if Mark was.

Pushing the chair out of the way, I logged into the computer and checked my messages but found nothing except the usual memos and requests. But it was Sunday. Lucien Cross didn't expect his investigators to hold normal business hours on the weekend. So, as usual, the thirtieth floor remained quiet.

I tapped a few keys, opened the databases, and performed a quick check to see if any similar incidents had been reported recently. "This is a waste," I mumbled to myself. The files I needed were at home. But I performed a few more searches and sent a request upstairs to pull whatever footage they could find at the time of the shooting. Jablonsky's townhouse was situated in a residential area, but maybe nearby cameras caught a glimpse of the shooter leaving the neighborhood or arriving.

There had to be more I could do. Cross Security was supposed to be the best. Lucien Cross earned that reputation, so it was time I put it to use.

I looked down at my phone. Even though the investigators didn't hold office hours on the weekend, Cross Security had twenty-four hour tech support. So I grabbed my stuff and jogged up the steps. The level above housed lab equipment, crime scene specialists, evidence collection experts and analysts, and enough computer equipment to make Bill Gates jealous.

A tech greeted me at the front desk. "Ms. Parker," she said, as if she expected me, "what do you need today?"

"A miracle."

"Specifically?"

So I told her about the call I received in the middle of the night. "I know where it originated. It came from a landline, but I don't know who the caller is."

She took my phone and brought up the call log, finding the exact time. "What's the address?"

I gave her Mark's home address, which she entered into the computer along with the date and time. "I already e-mailed a request for nearby video surveillance footage," I said. "Whatever can be scrounged up. Traffic cams, private networks, it doesn't matter just as long as I get an ID on this guy."

"Hopefully, that'll pan out, but I'll do some checking anyway. It's possible the caller had a cell phone on him, even though he didn't use it. I'll see what phones were pinged in the vicinity around that time. It'll take a while to track the data and compile a list of users. In a city this large, we could be looking at thousands of hits. I can't make any guarantees he'll even be in the mix, but it's worth a try."

"I'm grateful for anything you can do," I said, doing my best not to think about the legal ramifications and privacy violations. "E-mail me whatever you get, as soon as you have it."

"Will do."

I turned and headed down the steps. This was a long shot. A needle in a haystack. Our best bet for finding the shooter was stuffed in the closet of my home office. I checked the time again. I'd swing by the precinct and see what Lt. Moretti had planned before going home.

I couldn't help but think I should be at the hospital now. Maybe I should wait on the files. What if something happened during surgery and I wasn't there? I ducked back into my office to call Martin for an update. Before I even pulled out my phone, someone cleared his throat.

"Hey, are you okay?"

I jumped, turning to face the source of the sound. "How long have you been standing there?" I asked.

Cross leaned against the doorjamb. "It doesn't matter." He scrutinized me. "You should have called. I would have gotten started on this hours ago. How are you holding up? Is there anything I can do?"

"You know?"

He nodded.

"Of course you know. You know everything." I slammed my chair against the desk. "Why do you care? You don't even like Mark."

"That doesn't mean I want to see him hurt. He matters to you and James. Therefore, he matters to me and this company."

I snorted, the pieces connecting. "Martin called you."

"We are business partners."

"Not really. You'll just do anything for his R&D on biotextiles."

Cross's expression remained neutral. "Alex, you know you have unlimited access to my resources, to the company's resources, so tell me what I can do."

"I already put in my requests." And now I understood why the woman upstairs had been waiting for me.

"What else do you need?" he asked gently.

On a good day, Cross and I tolerated one another, but we often butted heads. His unexpected kindness sliced through the barrier I constructed to contain the emotional storm raging inside of me. One more sympathetic look from him, and I'd crumble.

"What I need is for Mark to be okay. What I need is for this to be a bad dream. What I need is more time. So unless you have a time machine upstairs, I'm not sure what else you can do." I bit my lip, focusing my efforts on stopping my chin from quivering.

Lucien took a step toward me but kept his hands in his pockets. At least he didn't plan on giving me a hug. I'd probably shoot him if he did because that one move would break me. And I didn't have time to break.

"I'll speak to Amir and see if he has any ideas," Lucien said. "He might have some schematics drawn up."

I looked at my boss. I had yet to figure out when he was joking, but that had to be a joke. However, he said it with such a straight face I couldn't be sure. "Yeah, okay." I moved past him and out the door.

"Hey." Lucien grabbed my arm as I reached to press the elevator button. I gasped, wincing as if his touch had burned me. "Every badge in the city is hunting this monster. They'll get him."

"I'm not sure it'll even matter."

Lucien looked at me. "Mark Jablonsky is an arrogant, egotistical, self-righteous know-it-all, who thinks old-fashioned techniques are the only tried and true way of working an investigation. He's wrong about a lot of things, and when I pointed them out at the symposium we attended, he conveniently ignored what I had to say and insisted on pounding his practices and mantras into me. He's stubborn. Bullets can't kill a man like that. He'll pull through. I'd stake my reputation on it."

For the briefest moment, the thought of hitting Lucien entered my mind, but he didn't say those things out of malice. He said them to make a point. "Do you really think he'll be okay?" I asked.

"I do. And so should you." The elevator dinged, and the doors opened. Lucien put his hand against the door as I stepped inside. "If you need anything, call me. Understand?"

"Thanks, Cross."

He bowed his head. By the time the doors closed, Lucien had disappeared down the hall. This really was an all-hands kind of situation.

* * *

I arrived at the precinct in a daze. It was mid-morning. Under normal circumstances, I wouldn't even be awake yet. Now I felt like I was sleepwalking through one of my worst nightmares.

"Parker," Detective Derek Heathcliff jogged over to me, "how's Jablonsky?"

"Not good."

"I was out on a call when you phoned. O'Connell and Thompson said they got there quickly, but it wasn't fast enough. I should have been there."

"It's not your fault, Derek."

"It's not yours either."

I sighed. "The bastard called me after he did it."

"Shit." Derek rubbed the scruff on his chin. "Have you checked the phone logs?"

"He used Mark's home phone, but I have Cross Security doing what they can." I jerked my chin toward the stairs which led to the major crimes unit. "I thought I'd see what you guys have found in the meantime."

"Yeah, no problem." Heathcliff reversed course, and I realized for the first time he must have been on his way out. "I'll escort you upstairs."

"If you gotta go," I said, jerking my thumb toward the entrance, "I don't want to keep you."

"No, I was actually on my way to the hospital." He led the way up the steps. "Ballistics should be analyzing the slug right about now."

"They removed the bullets?"

"Bullet," Heathcliff said. "I don't know if the FBI split the evidence with us. I've been out all night on a liquor store shooting. I haven't had a chance to get caught up on everything else yet. But that's what I heard as I was leaving. I figured you'd catch me up."

"Just as soon as someone catches me up," I promised.

The major crimes unit was bustling. Lt. Dominic Moretti stood in the center of the room, his hands on his hips, a scowl on his face. Normally, he reminded me of a bulldog with drooping jowls. This morning, he looked like an attack dog, ready to rip someone apart. And from the way the cops under his command behaved, they must have had the same thought.

"Parker," Moretti said, "we need to talk."

"Yes, sir."

He jerked his chin to the side, and I went into his office. Heathcliff went back to his desk, searching the drawers for something he pretended to have forgotten. A few moments later, Moretti stepped inside, slamming the door behind him. The blinds rattled against the window, and I sat up even straighter.

"Thanks for calling." He rested his hips against the edge of the desk. "The Feds suggested we investigate together. It'll increase the chances of finding the shooter quickly. Honestly, I think Kendall just wants to make sure emotions aren't clouding anyone's better judgment." Moretti snorted. "Funny how wrong he is."

"I'm sorry."

Moretti shook away the sentiment. "Thanks for coming in. It saved me making a trip. What do you know so far?"

So I told him everything, which was next to nothing. Unlike Agent Davis, Lt. Moretti didn't interrupt or accuse me of shooting Mark or hiring the hitman. "The voice is familiar. I'm guessing it's someone Mark and I investigated and possibly arrested."

"That'd be my guess. The OIO's supposed to be looking into recent releases and parolees. But if it's someone you and Mark put away, he probably served a couple of years. That would explain the lag between your investigation and this bastard seeking revenge. Did he threaten you too?"

"Not in so many words."

"Be that as it may, you should watch your back. He shot a supervisory special agent asleep in bed. That sends the message he doesn't give a fuck about consequences. And he called you. So he can reach you if he wants."

"I'm not–"

"I know. You're not worried about that right now. But it's something you should keep in the back of your mind. In the meantime, Mark's in our thoughts and prayers, yeah?"

"Yes, sir."

He grunted. "You still with Cross Security?"

"I'm a private contractor."

"What does that mean? Do they have your back on this or not?"

"Cross said he'll assist in any way possible, but he doesn't like involving himself in police matters. I requested a list of cell phone users in the vicinity and any video footage they can find that could lead to identifying the shooter. I'm just not sure how legal it is."

"It doesn't matter. You're a private citizen. You operate under a different set of rules, but for the record, the less I know, the better. I'm just surprised Cross is on board."

"I'm not sure he is, but he's cutting me slack. He and the police don't mix."

"I know. I've heard that about him. What about you? You toeing the company line and staying out of this?"

"Hell no. I'm a private contractor," I repeated. "I do what I want. So I'm gonna be riding your ass for information and making a nuisance out of myself."

Moretti snorted. "Paperwork's on O'Connell's desk. Fill it out. We could use a consultant with personal knowledge of the victim and important details concerning the crime."

"You're not worried I might be biased or more useful as a material witness?"

He glowered at me, and again, I saw the attack dog. "Go sign the damn papers. But this is a two-way street. I keep you updated on our progress, and you disclose everything to me. I don't care how inconsequential you think something is. I want to know about it immediately if not sooner. Do we have a deal?"

"Yes, sir."

"Good." He rubbed his eyes, which were as red and bloodshot as mine. "Get going."

I just made it to O'Connell's desk when my phone rang. It was Martin. "Alex, you need to get back here. The surgeons encountered some complications."

FIVE

"How long are they going to wait?" I asked, staring through the glass at Mark lying in a hospital bed. With the machines, tubes, and coverings, I could barely even tell it was him. Maybe it wasn't. Maybe this was a mistake. This was someone else, and Mark hadn't been placed in an isolation unit in the ICU. But the two FBI agents stationed outside his room indicated otherwise. Their expressions grim as they stared straight ahead, making a point not to look in my direction. "He needs the surgery."

"I know," Martin said. "His vitals have to stabilize, and his stats need to go up."

"So why did they stop? They got one bullet out. Did the doctor decide to break for lunch? Was that the complication?"

"Sweetheart, please."

"No," I spun, my volume increasing, "I don't understand. He's dying, so they stop? What is that? Dying doesn't mean stop. It means work faster. It means help him. Save him."

Martin touched my shoulder, and I shrugged away from him, knocking his hand off of me. "They can't continue until he stabilizes. Right now, he isn't strong enough to survive the surgery. As soon as he is, they'll go back in to remove the second bullet and assess the damage. Until then, we have to wait."

"Make them do something. Buy the damn hospital if you have to."

"I would if that would make a difference, but it won't. If they go back in too soon, they'll kill him."

"And this isn't killing him?" I turned back to stare into the window. They packed the wound and put him in a clean room, but the longer the bullet remained, the greater the chances of infection or other complications. I knew that, even before the doctors went over the facts with us.

"The bleeding's under control for now." Martin took a step closer. His firm chest pressed against my back. "Sweetheart, he just needs to rest and regroup. He'll get there. He has to."

The tears started to fall, and my knees knocked together. Martin pulled me away from the glass, and I fought against him. But he held tight. Eventually, my arms stopped flailing, and I clung to him, my sobs muffled by his shirt. He led me away from the window to a row of chairs. He held me against him while I cried messy tears and silent wails. He shuddered beneath me but never let go.

Exhausted, I cried until my cheeks were sticky and my eyes were swollen. Ignoring the wet mess I made of Martin's shirt, I swallowed only to find my throat sore. We sat in broken desperation. Finally, Martin pressed his lips against my forehead, causing a single tear to run down my face. At least that was the only one. At this point, I didn't have anything else left to lose.

It had been almost two hours. I got up on weak legs and went back to the window to see how Mark was doing. A few unfamiliar men and women in lab coats huddled together outside Mark's room. The protection detail checked each of their hospital IDs before allowing them entry.

"What's going on?" I asked, my voice raspy.

The closest FBI agent turned to me. "His blood pressure and heart rate have leveled out. They've held steady long enough that they might try again."

"Okay." I wiped my eyes, hoping to get my eyelashes

back into normal working order.

"Agent Parker?" the shorter man asked.

I blinked, now even more embarrassed than before about my emotional meltdown. I searched his face. "Agent Darli?"

He offered a tight smile and nod. "I haven't seen you since you and Jablonsky invaded our conference room." He glanced fondly at the ICU room behind him. "SSA Jablonsky's a legend. Legends don't go out like this."

"I hope you're right."

His gaze swept the area, stopping briefly on Martin who was now speaking to Jen and Nick O'Connell. "If you don't mind me asking, would your husband actually buy the hospital?" The real question Darli wanted answered was if Martin had enough money to buy a hospital. Darli and I only worked together once, and he had accused me of some pretty nasty things. But under current conditions, the past now had a lovely rose-tint.

"Martin?" I pointed. "He's not my husband."

"Oh," Darli's gaze dropped to the rings hanging from the chain around my neck, "I'm sorry. I just assumed. He's wearing a ring like yours."

"He likes shiny things. You should see him with a roll of aluminum foil." The flock of lab coats inside Mark's room made some notations and continued their discussion, but I couldn't make out their words through the glass. "I don't think he could buy the hospital, but he'd try if it would increase Jablonsky's chances." Martin had already offered to fly in an expert surgeon, but those efforts had been squelched when he'd been told Mark didn't have that kind of time to waste, except we'd done nothing but waste time for the last two hours. I forced the lump down my throat as the doctors started unhooking things. "Martin. Jen," I called, needing someone to explain what was happening. If they were pulling the plug, I'd go into the room and shoot every single one of them. I wouldn't let Mark go out like this. If he couldn't fight for himself, I'd fight for him.

"It's okay, Alex," Jen said. "They're moving him back to the OR."

"Mark," I called as they wheeled him past, but he didn't

answer. He couldn't. But I wished for a sign he was there, alive, and too stubborn to succumb.

Martin stood beside me, watching them take his friend away. "How long will it take?" Martin asked Jen.

"Probably another six hours. You look like hell. Nick," she turned to her husband, "why don't you get them something to eat?" Another nurse called to her, and Jen apologized, excused herself, and jogged down the hall.

"She's supposed to be in the ER," O'Connell said. His gaze came to rest on me. "I brought the preliminary case file. I figured you might want to take a look at it while we wait. Focusing on work might be good for you." He glanced at Martin, who appeared distracted by something going on at the other end of the ICU wing. "Or we can wait. How about we grab some coffee? According to Jen, the new coffee cart in the lobby downstairs is pretty good. It's my treat."

"Yeah, okay." I nudged Martin. "Do you want to come with us to get some coffee?"

"Go ahead. I'll be there in a few minutes. I just need to take care of something."

"What is it?" I asked.

Martin jerked his chin at a frosted blonde speaking to a nurse. "Renee."

I turned, recognizing the woman from the photograph that used to sit atop Jablonsky's desk when I was still a probationary agent. "Mark's ex-wife?"

"Third ex-wife," Martin said. "I can't believe she showed up." He flicked a glance at O'Connell. "Any idea who's listed as Jabber's in case of emergency?"

"I'll find out," O'Connell said.

"You think the hospital called her?" I asked.

"I know I didn't," Martin said. "But I'll find out who did. I'll meet you guys downstairs."

Sensing this might be important, O'Connell dragged me toward the elevator and out to his unmarked cruiser. He grabbed the files out of the car and flipped pages, handing them to me as he went. "Any chance Jablonsky's ex could be behind the attack?"

"Anything's possible. But it doesn't fit. The caller was a

guy."

"Maybe she hired the shooter. She could have found his name in one of Jablonsky's case files and figured he might want revenge on her ex as much as she did."

"If she wanted to kill him, she should have done it when they were still married. She would have stood to gain a lot more back then. Now all she gets is alimony, like his two other ex-wives."

"Motive doesn't track. When did they get divorced?" O'Connell asked, taking the file from me and leading the way back inside.

"About a year before I became a full-fledged agent."

"Did you ever meet her?"

"Not that I recall."

"But Martin knows her?" O'Connell asked.

"He and Mark go way back. I guess you could say Mark's like his older brother."

"And Jablonsky's like your father, which makes Martin your uncle," O'Connell teased, attempting levity to cheer me up. "Who knew your relationship was so incestuous?"

"Eww." I slapped his arm. "Bite your tongue. I don't interfere in your sex life. So stay out of mine."

"Yeah, yeah." O'Connell stopped at the end of the long line in front of the coffee cart. "Why'd they get divorced?"

After the last twelve hours, I found myself even more protective of Mark. "That's none of your business."

"I'm not being nosy, Parker. I'm working. And since Moretti just hired you to consult on this case, I could use the help." He let out a sigh. "I can always ask Moretti about it. He must know. They also go way back."

"Renee cheated on him," I said. "He worked too much and neglected her. When she threatened to find someone else, Mark promised he'd do better. He'd be home for dinner, that they'd do things together on the weekends, but the job got in the way."

"Job always gets in the way," O'Connell said. "It's unavoidable."

"Renee didn't think so. I think she only did it to force his hand. She wanted him to pick her over everything else. I don't know exactly what happened after that. Martin could probably tell you, but I think they tried couples counseling. It just didn't take." I remembered Mark having a few things to say about it when Martin insisted we give it a try. "But the job always came first, and so she served him with papers." A night spent in a bar years ago came to mind. Mark drunk, sitting across from me, imparting his wisdom. It wasn't until a few days later that I learned what prompted the introspection. "He didn't love her enough," I said. "Even he would tell you that. And a part of him always regretted it. He thought she deserved better."

"That sounds like Jablonsky." O'Connell turned to me. "He's gonna be okay."

"Everyone keeps saying that," I said.

"When have I ever let you down or misled you?" O'Connell asked.

I shrugged.

"Then trust me."

"I'll try."

O'Connell snorted. "Renee Jablonsky," he pointed to a copy of the Bureau's personnel file, "she's listed as closest relative. I'm surprised she kept his name."

"Probably made it easier to cash the alimony checks."

O'Connell skimmed the contents of the file, made sure everything was safely tucked away, and held it under his arm. We inched forward, and I looked around the lobby. The hospital looked like a law enforcement convention combined with a Brooks Brothers photoshoot. It was nothing but a sea of suits and uniforms, a testament to Jablonsky's influence and impact.

"Do you want a cookie?" O'Connell asked as we got closer to the front of the line.

"No."

"Muffin?"

I shook my head.

"Maybe Martin wants something," O'Connell said.

"Probably not."

The person in front of us stepped to the side to wait for the barista to prepare her beverage, so Nick stepped up to the counter. "Two vanilla lattes and a cappuccino, the biggest size you have. And one of each of those." He pointed to the glass-encased pastry tray.

"You must be starving." I watched him fork over a hefty stack of bills.

O'Connell took the brown bag containing a dozen different baked goods. I grabbed the drink carrier and followed him out the door to one of the benches. At least out here I felt like I could breathe again. Martin was right. Hospitals smelled like piss mixed with all the other horrible things I previously mentioned.

O'Connell placed the bag on the bench between us and took one of the lattes from the carrier. He popped the lid and took a sip. "I didn't know if you wanted a latte or cappuccino, but something tells me Martin's good with either."

"Yeah." I sipped the cappuccino, scalding my tongue in the process, but it barely registered.

Biting into a bear claw, O'Connell nudged the bag closer to me, but I didn't make a move for it. "Jen told me to feed you. Do you want my wife to get mad at me? If you don't eat something, she'll make me sleep on the couch. And it has those springs that poke up. Then my back will hurt the next day, and I'll be cranky."

"Nick, stop," I said.

But he didn't listen. "Plus, Heathcliff said you like the big cookies. Are you telling me one of the major crimes detectives sucks at detecting?"

"You all suck at detecting," I retorted, but I took the cookie out of the bag and nibbled on it. "Happy?"

"No." He blew the rising steam from the top of his cup, took another sip, and placed it on the bench beside him.

"Where is Derek?" I asked, remembering he wanted to talk to me earlier. "Did he go home?"

"No, he went to check the crime scene. The techs finished their preliminary examination, but they're going over it again. No one found anything. All the prints and trace were ruled out as contamination due to law enforcement on scene. Several detectives, including yours truly, have performed walkthroughs. Heathcliff wanted to make sure we didn't miss anything."

"He told me he worked last night. Now he's working a

double?"

O'Connell shoved the rest of the bear claw into his mouth and spoke around it. "We're all working doubles, Parker. From the looks of you, I'm wondering when you last slept. Are you working a triple?"

"I got an hour or two before the call came in. I'll sleep once I know Mark's okay."

"Any idea why the shooter called you?" O'Connell asked. "He could have called 9-1-1 or the FBI if he wanted to report his crime and rub it in our faces. How do you think he got your number?"

"Mark's speed dial."

O'Connell shook his head. "I checked. The phone didn't have speed dial. And we didn't find an address book or phone directory in Jablonsky's house. You're probably saved on his contacts list in his cell phone, but the device requires a fingerprint or PIN to access it. And the techs didn't find any blood on the phone, and the only prints matched Jablonsky. I don't think the shooter touched it."

"I don't know."

"Did you notice anything missing from the townhouse?" O'Connell asked. "Maybe you happened to pick something up and forgot to tell us about it."

"I didn't take evidence from the crime scene."

O'Connell looked unconvinced.

"I'm serious, Nick. I didn't. No shell casing. Nothing. I wouldn't compromise the scene. This is too important."

"Yeah, I know," he admitted. "The shooter got in and out clean. No prints. No fibers or hairs. Nothing."

"You're thinking he's a professional."

"I'm thinking he's done this or something similar before."

"Did anything come back on the slug?" I asked, remembering Heathcliff told me ballistics was analyzing it.

"Not yet. But soon."

I blew out a breath. "FBI labs might have gotten it done faster."

"Director Kendall didn't think so. He gave it to us."

"Cross Security could get it done faster," I said.

"Are you offering? It's not unheard of to farm work out

to private labs. Cross has all the accreditation necessary."

"I was stating a fact, but I could ask. I just worry about legal ramifications. Whenever we ID this bastard, I want him to go down hard. Nothing questionable. We need a slam dunk conviction. Private labs might be out of the question, depending on how this bastard's attorney spins things."

Before O'Connell could reply, Martin exited the hospital with Renee at his side. "Go home, Renee," Martin said.

Her eyes met mine, and something ignited in them. She stormed over to the bench. "You're Alexis Parker."

"Yes," I said uncertainly.

Unsure what to do, she stood, gawking at me. Finally, she sputtered, "Were you sleeping with him?"

"Who?" My gaze darted to Martin. "I don't see how that's any of your business, ma'am." Martin ran a hand through his hair and circled, something I only saw him do when extremely frustrated.

"Not James." She threw her hands in the air, exasperated. "Mark. My husband," she said, as if this should be obvious.

"Eww. No."

"Yeah, right." She gave me a cold, hard stare. "Like I'm supposed to believe that." She waved a chewed fingernail in my face. "You're all he ever talked about. This bright-eyed and bushy-tailed hotshot FBI agent. The last thing I remember him talking about when we were still married was how you shot a guy on your first assignment out. How well you handled it. How you would go places. What a bright future you had. You're the reason he always worked late. That is, if you were even working. Or was that just a euphemism? I'm not stupid."

"I never said you were, but you're wrong." I stared at her. "Get off your high horse. You never gave a fuck about him. If you did, you wouldn't have left him."

"You shot a guy?" O'Connell asked, more amused than he should have been.

"Renee," Martin slid onto the bench beside me and put a hand on my thigh to keep me from doing something I'd regret, "Mark would never cheat on you. You know that.

And I suggest you refrain from making such allegations lest you want me to remind you who the cheater in your relationship was. Like I said before, you need to leave. When he's feeling better, I'll let him know you dropped by."

She turned her venomous gaze on Martin, but he just stared at her. Indifferent. Uncompromising. "I loved him, you know," she insisted.

"Is that why you're here? Or were you just hoping you'd get the chance to tell them to pull the plug?" Martin asked.

"How dare you?" she snapped.

"He didn't ask for you. The call you received was a mistake. You don't have power of attorney or any legal rights when it comes to his healthcare decisions. I do. You aren't his next of kin. You're just someone who caused him a lot of pain. Please, don't make this worse. Go home, Renee. Go about your life. Leave us all alone."

"It's a free country. I can be here if I want." She turned back to me. "The nurses said she called it in. She was probably in his bedroom when it happened."

Martin bristled. "Alex is my fiancée. Mark introduced us, so watch what you say." He glanced at Nick, hoping the detective would forcibly remove the woman.

"Ma'am," O'Connell stood, placing his hand on his gun, his badge glistening in the afternoon sun, "I'm Detective O'Connell with the major crimes unit. I'm investigating last night's shooting. I have a few questions for you."

"I...uh...I don't know anything." She backed up unsteadily.

"When's the last time you spoke to Mark Jablonsky?"

She thought back. "A few weeks ago. He called, like he does on occasion. He checks-in to make sure I'm okay."

"Was he worried about anything?" O'Connell asked.

Renee shrugged. "I don't know."

"Did he mention anything to you?" I asked. "Did he say or do anything out of the ordinary?"

She looked at me, confused now that the tables had turned. "Wouldn't you know? Don't you work with him?"

"Not anymore. I resigned," I said.

She let out an ugly laugh, her focus shifting from me to Martin. "Unbelievable." She narrowed her eyes at

O'Connell. "Shouldn't you be asking them these questions?"

"I already have. They've been cleared. You have not." He gestured to a uniform standing watch at the door. "This is Officer Sarcone. He'll take down your information. Where were you last night around three a.m.?"

"Home in bed," Renee said.

"Can anyone verify that?" O'Connell asked, watching Sarcone hurriedly dig out his pen.

"No."

"That could be a problem," O'Connell said. "We might have to speak to you again. Officer, escort her to her vehicle and make sure we are able to get a hold of her should we need to bring her in for questioning."

"Sure thing, Nick." Sarcone offered a tight nod. "Lead the way, ma'am."

O'Connell waited a moment for her to cross the parking lot and get into a luxury sedan. Sarcone copied down the info on her license and her vehicle registration. When she drove away, Nick scribbled the plate number on the top of the folder.

"Hell hath no fury. It's no wonder Jablonsky divorced her," O'Connell said.

"You okay?" Martin asked, giving my leg a squeeze.

"Fine." I met his eyes, seeing fire burning in the green depths. "She really got under your skin."

He removed the last cup in the drink carrier and took a sip. "She has no reason to be here. Jabber doesn't need to see her. It'll upset him, and he doesn't need the added stress on top of everything else he's facing."

"Still don't think she's involved?" O'Connell asked.

"Honestly, I have no idea. But I forgot to mention one thing," I said.

"What?" O'Connell asked.

"The spare key Mark had hidden out back was gone when I got there. The shooter must have found it and let himself in."

"Did Renee know about it?" Nick asked, and we both looked at Martin.

"I don't know," he said. "But from what I recall, Jabber

kept a hidden key at his old house too, probably in the same place. Renee probably knew about it."

"I believe that's called a clue," Nick said.

Or a coincidence, I thought, *except Jablonsky doesn't believe in coincidences.*

SIX

"Do you think Renee's still holding a grudge?"

"I don't know." Martin ran his fingertips against my cheek. "Divorce is ugly, but it's been a long time. I don't see why she'd want to kill her cash cow."

"You're probably right, but we need a look at her financials, just to be certain," I said.

Nick nodded, his phone against his ear as he listened to Moretti. Renee wasn't Jablonsky's only ex-wife, so we had to investigate each of them. Though that hadn't seemed like a priority until Renee confronted me. Now I didn't know. She would have had access to the files Jablonsky brought home with him years ago. She could have gotten the name of someone we arrested from back then, when I was his protégé. Maybe that's why I recognized the voice. But that sounded farfetched, even to me. She would have had to have planned this for years, and that just didn't jibe.

"How well do you know her?" I asked Martin. "It seemed like there's a history between the two of you. What's her story? What do you think?"

"I don't know her that well. We had dinner a few times. Double dates, mostly. She tried to set me up with several of her younger friends and a couple of her nieces. She always thought I just needed to find a nice girl to settle down with."

"I don't think she approves of the one you chose."

"Good," Martin said, but his brow furrowed. "I wish I knew why she showed up here. She hasn't seen Mark in years, as far as I know. He doesn't talk about her or his other ex-wives, except in the context that he wishes they'd get married and stop leaching off of him. At this rate, he doesn't think he'll ever be able to retire."

"That might not be a problem now," I said bitterly. "Who gets his life insurance?"

Martin gave me a funny look. "You."

"What?"

"As far as I know, Jabber's leaving everything to you," Martin said.

"He told you that?" I had no idea. Mark always teased me that I was the daughter he never had. And since he didn't have any kids and no other family, I was it.

"I thought it was obvious." Martin pulled out a copy of the documentation the hospital needed. Among the advanced health directive, living will, power of attorney and other authorization forms was a copy of Mark's will. It was short and to the point. I was the sole beneficiary.

"Shit." I got up to pace. My brain was foggy. I couldn't think through it. Moving around might help.

"How'd you get all that information?" O'Connell asked, covering the mouthpiece on his phone.

"After things went south with Boyle and Carver, Jabber got serious about putting his affairs in order. One night, we got drunk, and he told me I was the only person he could trust. The next day, he had the paperwork drawn up. I have a copy of all his important documents, just in case of anything," Martin said.

"He put a lot on you," I said.

Martin shrugged. "I'd been through it twice before. First with my mom. Then my dad. I guess he figured I could take care of it."

"Still sucks, man." O'Connell squeezed Martin's shoulder. Finally, the person on the other end of the line answered, and O'Connell stepped away.

When he got off the phone, I pointed to the paper in Martin's hand. "Looks like I should be your prime suspect." And now I understood why Kendall and Davis had asked the questions they did.

"I'm not worried about it. Your alibi checked out," O'Connell said. "Right, Martin?"

Martin nodded. "I can get you GPS tracking info to verify if need be."

"That won't be necessary." O'Connell studied the parked cars, as if one of them might hold the answers we needed. "I'm certain of two things. Whoever shot Jablonsky did so with one goal in mind – to inflict pain. And that person wants to make sure you hurt too, Parker."

"Mission accomplished," I said.

"It stands to reason this should track back to an OIO case," Martin said.

"But hell hath no fury," O'Connell said. "I'll admit it's not very likely Renee orchestrated this, but it is an avenue that needs exploring. We can't leave any rock or stone unturned. But I doubt she'd do it herself. She would have had to convince someone else to do it, and since Alex recognized the voice, that complicates matters."

"What did Moretti say?" I asked.

"The LT will dig through Jablonsky's personal life for anything hinky, but you and I should stay the course." O'Connell glanced back at the hospital doors. "Right now, that means hanging out here until he comes out of surgery and the docs give us the good news."

"From your lips to god's ears," I said.

And so the waiting continued. Heathcliff came through the doors and spotted us immediately. He nodded to a couple of LEOs and took a seat in the back corner of the waiting room beside O'Connell.

"Any word?" Heathcliff asked.

"Not yet," I said.

He nodded, but I knew the detective well enough to know something was eating at him. O'Connell noticed too and nudged his colleague with his elbow. "Find anything at Jablonsky's townhouse?" O'Connell asked.

Heathcliff shook his head. "CSU didn't miss anything. I

told them to double-check the back patio and the landscaping. They're on the lookout for the missing key. They took the turtle in to examine."

"Frog," I said.

"It's a turtle," Martin corrected.

"Are you sure?" But it didn't matter. It just bothered me that I couldn't even get that one detail right. If I couldn't figure out what lawn ornament Mark used to hide his key, how would I ever figure out who shot him?

"What else?" O'Connell asked.

"Nothing."

"Bullshit. You work six feet away from me five days a week. What's wrong?"

My ears perked up, and I turned my attention to Heathcliff. Nick was right. Something was wrong.

"It's nothing. We got enough problems," Heathcliff said.

"Spill." I stared at him until he answered.

"I just dropped by my place to change clothes and some kid spray painted *Die, Pig* on my front door." Heathcliff shrugged. "Like I said, it's not important. It's not even a blip on the radar."

"Did you call it in?" O'Connell asked.

"No, I'll handle it myself. No reason to divert resources." Heathcliff wiped his palms on his thighs and leaned forward. "Thompson caught me up on the situation. Have you guys come up with any new leads?"

"Not unless you count Mark's ex-wives." I got up, and Martin tugged gently on my hand. But with one look, he let go, and I continued across the room to stare out the window.

Resting my forehead against the glass, I watched the traffic and pedestrians. For what felt like the millionth time today, I checked my phone, but I didn't receive any messages from Cross Security. It felt like midnight, but it was only midday. I couldn't do this. I couldn't sit here and wait while the shooter got further and further away. But I couldn't leave. My heart jumped – the beginnings of a panic attack.

Turning, I found a TV broadcasting a home improvement show and I focused on that. Or I tried to. A part of me wondered how I had ever been a federal agent when I was this emotionally unstable, but I knew the answer. It was because I understood how to take action. *All right, Parker, pull it together. We got work to do. You can wallow and freak out later.*

Striding across the room, I took a seat beside Martin. "Heathcliff, did anything come back on ballistics yet?"

"Nine millimeter hollow point. Striations don't match any weapons in the system. But it's the same type of ammo Jablonsky had in his carry piece."

"I checked his gun," I said. "It was in the drawer."

"We know the shooter didn't use Jablonsky's gun against him, and that type of ammo is common enough," Heathcliff said. "But that's all we know so far."

O'Connell made a note on a blank piece of paper and tucked it into the file. "Most law enforcement agencies use hollow points. Did they check the bullet for prints? The shooter would have had to load the weapon. He might not have thought to wear gloves when he did it."

"Nothing on it," Heathcliff said, "or what little was left of it. You'd have better luck getting something usable off the casings."

"Which we don't have," I said. "The shooter took the time to clean up the brass, probably before he called me."

"He could be trained," O'Connell said. "Do you think that's why you recognize the voice? Could it be someone else in law enforcement? Someone at the OIO or FBI field office? Or even another federal agency you two worked with?"

"You think one of Jabber's own people shot him?" Martin asked, joining the conversation.

"No," I said.

"Are you sure?" Heathcliff scrutinized me. "The OIO had no problem letting you take the fall for something you didn't do. And from past experiences, we know at least one dirty agent worked in that office."

"We cleaned house," I said. "Before I left, everything was in working order."

"Is it possible Jablonsky found something disturbing and was quietly looking into it?" O'Connell asked.

"He never mentioned anything to me," I said.

"What about you?" O'Connell asked Martin, who shook his head.

"Would he have mentioned it to you, Alex?" Heathcliff asked.

"I don't know, but Director Kendall would know. And he didn't say a word to me about it." I blew out a breath. "This is ridiculous. The shooter isn't law enforcement." But even as I said the words, I wondered if they were true. The shooter knew about Mark's hidden key, had my phone number memorized, and used the same type of ammo as FBI agents. He could have been to Mark's house before. He could have even been invited inside. "Someone give me a sheet of paper."

Martin handed me the clipboard, and O'Connell held out a pen. Under different circumstances, I might have enjoyed this kind of special treatment. Taking the pen, I made a list of every OIO agent I could remember. None of them had made the call. Moving on, I listed the FBI techs we worked with and other office personnel. Still, none of their voices matched the caller. Turning the paper over, I started listing the regular FBI agents I encountered. But aside from coming up with a handful of names, my mind had gone blank. There were so many more men whose names I should be able to put on the list, but we never interacted enough for me to remember them or the way they sounded.

"Is that a suspect list?" O'Connell asked.

"No, the opposite. I know these men can't be the shooter. But a lot more men work in the federal building. We can rule out several dozen potential suspects if it comes down to it," I said, "but that's about it."

"This will help." O'Connell took the paper from me. "Let me call Moretti. I'll have the hospital fax the list over to him."

"Good." I leaned back and closed my eyes. This was progress. Ass-backward progress but still progress.

"Alexis," Martin's tone sent a shot of adrenaline into my system, "that's the surgeon. He must have news."

On shaky legs, I followed Martin. The surgeon nodded

to him, but I couldn't tell anything from his facial expression. Did he have good news or bad? The doctor pushed the door open, holding it for us to follow. Once the door closed behind us, Martin introduced me.

"How is he?" I asked.

"We removed the second bullet. He lost a few inches of intestine, but it shouldn't be enough to cause long-term problems."

"So he'll be okay," Martin said, grasping my hand.

But the surgeon didn't immediately respond. I watched his expression and mannerisms, waiting for the other shoe to drop. "How is he?" I repeated, though my tone sounded a lot more threatening this time. "Is he okay?"

"He lost a lot of blood which caused hypovolemic shock. We treated him. Honestly, he was lucky we got to him so quickly. He easily could have had a heart attack or stroke."

"So what's the problem?" I took a step forward, and if Martin hadn't wrapped an arm around my waist and pulled me against his side, I would have thrown the doctor up against the wall until he answered my questions.

The surgeon swallowed, possibly sensing the dangerous situation he found himself in. "You should prepare yourselves for the possibility he may have some brain damage. We don't know how long or how deprived his brain was from getting enough blood and oxygen. Right now, our best course of treatment is to keep him sedated while he recovers from the surgery. He just underwent a serious trauma, and given his age, it might take him a little longer to bounce back. Once he wakes up, we'll know more. But I don't want to rush it."

"Is there anything we can do?" Martin asked. "I donated blood, but if there's something else, tell me now."

"No, he just needs to rest. And he needs to know his loved ones are supporting him." His pocket buzzed, and he stepped back. "I'll have someone escort you to his room. Stay right here."

"Brain damage," I repeated, watching the doctor retreat down the hall. "Like a vegetable? Mark doesn't even like vegetables."

"No," Martin said. "No. They don't know anything yet."

He pulled out his phone. "I'll take care of this. He's fine. He's out of surgery. And he's going to be fine."

By the time we made it to Mark's room, Martin was already in the midst of a conversation with the head of neuroscience at some research facility. I didn't know how he got the number, and I didn't care. Martin knew not to make promises he couldn't keep. And he said Mark would be okay, so Mark would be okay.

The protection detail recognized us, and since I'd been cleared and Martin was on the list, we were allowed to enter Mark's room. I went inside while Martin stayed in the hallway and spoke on the phone. The tubes and bandages tore at my heart and twisted my stomach in knots. I'd spent more than my fair share of time in hospital beds, but I would have traded places with Mark in an instant.

Leaning down, I reached for his hand but withdrew when I saw the IV tubes. "Don't you dare die on me, Jablonsky. I swear to god I'll never forgive you if you do. And I sure as hell won't forgive myself. It'll be Michael Carver all over again, and I won't survive that. So you get better, and when you wake up, you damn well better be the pain in the ass I know and love." I kissed him on the cheek and wiped at the annoying tears that started to fall again. "Now I'm going to find the asshole who did this and make sure he regrets every decision he's ever made."

Backing away from the bed, I slipped out of the room and took a few deep breaths. Martin hung up the phone and came over to me. But I backed away from him. I couldn't stay here and waste more time. I had to go, and he knew it.

"Be careful," Martin said.

"Always."

He smiled sadly. "I love you. And in case you forgot, I can't lose you. Not ever, but especially now. Stay safe."

"I will." I glanced at his wrist, but he left his watch at home. His watch contained a GPS tracker, just like the charm on my necklace. We weren't the most functional of couples, but after abductions and close calls, it eased both of our minds to track the other's whereabouts. And Lucien

Cross promised this was more secure and reliable than any find-my-friend phone apps. "Are you staying with him?"

"I'm not going anywhere. I'll be here."

"Okay." I walked out the door and updated the boys in blue. Then I got into my car and headed home. O'Connell followed in his unmarked cruiser. On the way, I dialed a number I hadn't called since I left the OIO. When someone answered, I said, "I need to speak to Special Agent Eddie Lucca. It's urgent." The call was redirected, and three rings later, my former partner answered. "Jablonsky's been shot. It's bad. I need your help."

SEVEN

"What do you want me to do?" Lucca asked. "What do we know so far?"

I gave Lucca the Cliff's notes version of the last fifteen hours. "Kendall finally cleared me of suspicion, but no one from the Bureau will tell me much of anything. Davis said Jablonsky was investigating local cartel activity. The shooter could be a cartel hitman, but how would one of them get my number?"

"The Yellow Pages."

"As a general rule, I try to steer clear of cartels and mob bosses. I learned my lesson when it comes to organized crime."

"Have you made any other enemies lately?" But Lucca didn't give me a chance to answer. "Never mind. I almost forgot who I was talking to."

"Hardy har. And no, I haven't made any recent enemies who would do something like this."

"Sorry." He entered search terms into the computer. "Jablonsky filed a recommendation to maintain surveillance on some federal judges. Any overlap there? Pending trials? Recent court appearances?"

"No, I don't think so."

"All right. Hang on." He looked up something else. "It appears the OIO is working under the assumption the shooting is related to an old case the two of you worked. Does that sound right?"

"Nothing sounds right."

"But you recognized the voice."

"I know it, but I can't exactly place it."

"What does your gut say, Parker? You have instincts that defy science and reason. Is this someone you've recently tangled with?"

"No." But I wasn't sure.

"Okay, think back to your old cases. Make a list. When you get it narrowed down to a few possibilities, send it to me and I'll see what I can find on Jablonsky's end. He might be working on something related or recently crossed paths with someone from your joint past. I'll keep an eye on internal memos and track the progress Kendall makes. If I see something worrisome, I'll give you a call. With everything digitized, it shouldn't matter that I'm in D.C. I can still help."

"Thank you."

"Don't thank me yet. You piss off a lot of people, but hopefully, one of them will stick out. Maybe it'll ring a bell, and you'll identify the late night caller."

"That's what I'm hoping for."

"Good luck." He paused. "And call me as soon as you get an update on Jablonsky's condition. I'll be thinking about him."

"Thanks, Eddie. I will."

I spread everything out across the floor. Years of investigations resulted in enough case notes to paper Martin's entire estate and then some. It would take forever to get through every potential, and the worst part was I wasn't even positive the shooter was hidden in this mess. But it was something, and I had to do something.

O'Connell waited for me to get organized before diving in. While I scanned the pages, I told him what Lucca said. "Do you remember anyone in particular having a beef with you or Jablonsky?" O'Connell asked from his seat in my chair.

"I don't know. The assholes who killed Carver are always in the back of my mind."

"Do you remember their voices clearly?"

"Yes."

"So it isn't them," O'Connell surmised. "See, this isn't so hard."

I stared daggers at him. "That's one case out of hundreds."

"It's one less. Keep going." He picked up a file. "Tell me about Gale Barton."

"Money laundering, white collar crimes mostly."

"History of violence?" O'Connell asked.

"Not that I recall."

"Did he ever attempt to buy a judge?"

"No."

O'Connell put the file down, and we moved on to the next one. It took hours, but by the end, we made a list of the messier cases Jablonsky and I worked. O'Connell reread the notes he made. "Shouldn't these people still be incarcerated?"

"One would hope." I chuckled, but it wasn't funny. "Unless, of course, they paid off a judge."

"And the judge hired a hitman to take out Jablonsky rather than face the scary prospect of serving time with hardened criminals he sentenced to hard labor for decades. That tracks."

"Maybe, but what does that have to do with me?"

O'Connell threw down the pen and rubbed his brow. "Absolutely nothing."

"And we're back to square one."

"Hang on," he wasn't ready to give up yet, "even though you're no longer an active agent, do you still receive notifications when someone you arrested is released from prison?"

"I'm not sure. I haven't gotten one of those calls in ages."

"All right." O'Connell had a thought, but he didn't share it. "Moretti said he'd check with Kendall and review Jablonsky's phone records to see if he's gotten any calls like that recently. I'm gonna check in at the precinct and run these through the database and narrow it down a bit. If you want, tell Lucca to do the same. Once that's done, I'll see what kind of recorded material the FBI and the prosecutor's office still have. Tomorrow, you can listen to whatever we find."

"You make it sound so simple."

"IDing the shooter shouldn't be hard," O'Connell said, "but finding him might be."

"Do you want me to come with you? I'm great at database searches. Three heads are better than two, right?"

"I appreciate it, but I need you to do something else."

"Sure, name it."

"Get some sleep."

"C'mon, Nick. I'm fine. I probably got as much sleep as you did last night."

He stared at me. "I'm serious. The next few days will undoubtedly be rough. And I know you. You'll divide your time between the precinct and the hospital. Please, get some sleep. Clear your mind. Everything depends on you remembering this asshole's voice. Without that, we've got nothing."

"Okay."

After he left, I shot a text to Lucca, slumped onto the sofa, and stared at the floor. Twenty minutes passed before I moved again. And for those twenty minutes, not a single thought popped into my head. Apparently, I'd mastered the art of meditation without even trying. O'Connell was right. Sleep would help, but I feared the nightmares.

I flipped on the TV. Within minutes, my eyes closed, and I slept like a brick. And then the phone rang.

Bleary-eyed, I read the display. No name. Just a number. It looked familiar. "Hello?"

"I'm surprised you got to him so fast. I thought by now he'd be dead. But I'm sure nature will take its course, and if not, I'll circle back and finish him off when I'm done."

"Who is this?" I ran down the hall and into the office, grabbing the landline only to put it down and turn on the computer instead. I needed the number traced, and I needed it done now.

"You don't know?" the voice asked, annoyance and anger boiling to the surface. "You should have been thinking about me because I've spent every damn day thinking about you. About what you took from me. How you deceived me. How you destroyed everything I had. Even after all that shit, after everything you did, you haven't given me a second thought, have you? From now on, I'll be the only thing you think about. And I'll be the last thought on your mind before I finally put you out of your misery. By the end, you'll be begging me to pull the trigger."

Plugging in my phone, I switched the call to speaker and hit record on the computer. The quality would probably be shit, but it'd be better than nothing. "Since that's what you want, let's cut the bullshit and fast track this. Who are you? What do you want?"

He ignored my questions. "You should know I'm just getting started. Since you're in such a rush, come find me. I'm ready to play."

Abruptly, the call ended. I cursed and stopped the recording. The phone number belonged to Steve Cooper. "Oh god." Grabbing the desk phone, I called Kendall's private number.

"Parker, what's wrong?" Kendall asked, knowing I wouldn't call his personal line unless it was an emergency.

"The shooter is at Steve Cooper's apartment."

"Shit." Kendall barked orders. "I'll mobilize units immediately." He hung up before I could say another word.

I'd only been to Cooper's apartment once, back when he carried a badge. We hadn't been in touch since that fateful day, and I never knew exactly what became of him. At the time, he'd been staring down several serious criminal charges. We'd both dug ourselves into deep, dark holes, but unlike me, Cooper never crawled out. Cooper had done some bad things, compromised the OIO, federal agents, and open cases, but deep down, he wasn't a bad guy. He'd just made bad decisions due to the circumstances. Truthfully, so had I.

Running down the steps, I got into my car and peeled out of the garage. With any luck, Cooper had a new home with an orange jumpsuit. Who would have thought the safest place for a former federal agent would be behind bars?

One thing was for sure. The caller wasn't Steve Cooper. I would have recognized his voice. But that left a million new questions in my mind. Just like I had done last night, I called 9-1-1 and had units dispatched to the caller's location. Then I called O'Connell, who promised to inform Moretti before getting his ass across town to Cooper's.

Horns blared as I jutted around slow moving traffic. I gripped the steering wheel hard as I took a turn too fast and heard the back tires squeal and bump. Unlike last night, I called Lucien Cross. "The shooter made contact again." I gave my boss details on the call, including the time, duration, and location.

"It's a second data point," Cross said. "We'll compare pings and cross-reference the names. We had thousands of hits on last night's location, so the more times he communicates, the better off we'll be."

"He doesn't use a cell phone," I said.

"I bet my ass he has one, though," Cross said. "I'll send a team to meet you."

"FBI and police are already en route."

"Let's see who gets there first."

Even though I violated every traffic law known to man, I was the last to arrive. Martin's compound was on the outskirts of the city, and with the addition of rush-hour traffic, which I'd done my best to avoid, it still took too long.

Two members of HRT stood outside the front door, shifty-eyed, as they watched everyone and everything. The rest of their team might be inside or scouting the area. I didn't know what they found, but since they weren't inside, I knew the man who shot Jablonsky wasn't here. A patrol car and ambulance had parked in the fire lane. No sirens or lights.

Calm down, I thought. This wasn't an emergency. If it was, the lights would be on. I spotted a Cross Security company car and a four-man tactical team, which Lucien used mainly for bodyguard work, lingering on the sidewalk across the street. They had no official role in this, but Cross sent them in case I needed backup. I waved them off and headed for the front door.

Surprisingly, the HRT members had been waiting for me. They escorted me upstairs to Cooper's floor. Kendall stood in the doorway. His skin gray and clammy. I'd never seen Kendall look like that, not even at agents' funerals or that one time he had the stomach flu. He mopped his brow and upper lip with a folded handkerchief and shoved it back into his pocket. Turning, he nodded to the agents, and they retreated back into the elevator.

My stomach dropped, fear and anger fighting for control of my psyche. I moved forward, unsure if I wanted to run or drag my feet. Kendall moved away from the door and stepped into my path, blocking me from seeing inside.

"Were we too late?" I asked.

"Unfortunately." Kendall put his hands on my shoulders to stop me from maneuvering around him.

"Cooper?"

Kendall swallowed uncomfortably.

"I don't understand. Why is he even here? I thought he was facing hard time."

Kendall let out a breath. "Given the circumstances and Agent Cooper's performance record, he'd been granted leniency. Jablonsky spoke on his behalf. So did I. Cooper received a reduced sentence, but three months in, he was attacked in the shower. His attorney convinced the judge to let him serve out the rest of his sentence under house arrest. He's been here ever since." I pushed past Kendall, but he grabbed my arm. "Parker, you don't want to see him like that. You'll never get that image out of your head."

Despite the warning, I moved to the open door. Cooper's body lay spread eagle on the floor. A once white plastic bag covered his face, secured tightly around his neck by duct tape. The interior of the bag was filled with blood, obscuring his boyish features. He'd been stabbed so many times I could see bone and guts. But the Marine Corps tattoo on his arm gave away his identity.

The bile rose, even as my chin quivered. I slapped a palm over my mouth, afraid I wouldn't be able to contain myself. For a few moments, my vision dimmed, the edges disappearing until I could only see pinpricks of light straight ahead. I'd seen several gruesome crime scenes, but this was the worst. Not even Jablonsky's bedroom contained this much carnage.

A patrol officer stood just inside the doorway. Agent Davis and several other suits stood nearby, doing their best to assess the situation without moving or disturbing anything. But this wasn't just any crime scene. This was personal. And none of them could bring themselves to even look at Cooper.

"Parker," Kendall said, "let's talk outside. I could use some air."

I followed Kendall out of the building and into the back seat of his sedan. Instead of looking him in the eye, I stared over his shoulder and out the window, watching as evidence collection and the medical examiner arrived. I told him about the caller, and we listened to the recording I made.

"What else did he say to you?" Kendall asked. "Did he tell you what this is about?"

"Not really." Unlike the first call, I remembered this one verbatim.

"All right, we already have a trap and trace set up on your phone, but he hasn't attempted to hide his location. He calls from his victims' homes. He wants us to know where he is, so it's pointless."

"He wants us to see his handiwork. He wants to play, that's what he said." I didn't remember any background noise. No screams. No sounds of a struggle. Cooper must have already been dead when the killer phoned. The asshole didn't want to repeat the same mistake he made with Mark only hours earlier. "He said he'd finish off Jablonsky if nature doesn't take its course."

"Son of a bitch," Kendall cursed. "I won't let that happen. I already assigned agents to remain stationed at the hospital around the clock, and Lt. Moretti assigned police officers to assist. No one's getting near Mark without my authorization. Our next step should be getting you into protective custody."

"No."

"Excuse me?"

"You heard me," I said.

"Parker, he threatened you. As far as I can tell, this is about revenge. You don't stab someone that many times unless you're harboring some serious rage."

"Do you think Cooper tried to fend him off? Did you notice any defensive wounds?"

"The ME will let us know."

"Poor Steve." I felt queasy and heartbroken. "What about surveillance?"

Kendall pressed his lips together, waiting a beat before answering. "That's not your concern. Let the authorities handle this, Parker. You're a civilian."

"Yeah, and the only person this asshole's contacted. That makes me more than a civilian. I'm your MVP. Put me in, coach. I'm ready to kick ass." But Kendall didn't respond to my comment.

"Off the top of your head, how many cases did you and Jablonsky work with Cooper?" Kendall asked.

"A few."

"Do you remember crossing paths with anyone violent and crazy enough to do these things?"

Only one name came to mind. "Vito, but he's dead."

"I thought about that too," Kendall said. "Organized crime already pulled records and assured me Vincenzo's empire died right along with him. Every lieutenant and head honcho in his organization either perished in that fire or left the city soon after. They haven't been back since."

"Are you positive? Have you checked everyone and everything?"

"We have, but I'll have Davis look again, just to make you feel better. In the meantime, is there anything else you can think of? Any other reason someone would shoot Jablonsky and filet Cooper?" Kendall must have seen something disconcerting in my eyes because he said, "What are you thinking?"

"Nothing. You're right. Ghosts can't kill people. And you're absolutely sure no one is left to exact revenge on Vito's behalf?"

"Antonio Vincenzo's dead. So is Eli Gates. And so is everyone else in Vincenzo's inner circle. Parker, I know the man once put a hit out on you, but he's dead. No one's left to carry that torch. So who else would do something like this?"

"I don't know." Vito was dead. I knew it for a fact. After all, I killed him in cold blood. But only a handful of people knew that. Jablonsky being one of them. Cooper being another. I didn't believe in coincidences. That secret connected us. And I wondered if that was the reason a man had been viciously slain and another was fighting for his life.

EIGHT

"Derek," I said as soon as he answered his phone, "we need to talk. Can you meet me?"

"When and where?"

I told him we'd rendezvous at Martin's. The Cross Security team followed me home. Cross didn't send them to assist the police and FBI at Cooper's. He sent them to protect me.

While driving, I called Martin and asked if a team of Lucien's goons was keeping an eye on him too. They were. One thing I could say about my boss, he knew how to protect his assets. And after the horrors I'd just witnessed, I had no intention of arguing with Cross's rationale. Right now, we all needed someone to watch our backs. Plus, I liked having the team at the hospital to watch over Martin and Mark should that demented piece of shit show up to make good on his threat.

After pulling into the garage, I went upstairs and monitored the security feed until Heathcliff's car pulled onto the private road. The two company cars sat outside the main garage entrance. One of the bodyguards stepped out of the car when Derek parked behind them.

I opened the front door and waved off the detail before they assaulted a police officer and faced charges of their own. Cross's lawyers had enough to deal with already, especially if he got caught hacking into phone records and private security networks.

"I'm so sorry," Heathcliff said. "I can't believe this bastard was ballsy enough to go after a second FBI agent. Moretti's still at the scene. Half the detectives from major crimes were there. O'Connell said it was a mess. He's never seen anything that horrific."

"Neither have I."

"Shit." Heathcliff exhaled. "I'm sorry."

"You already said that."

Heathcliff looked around. "What's so urgent? What's going on?"

"The asshole called me again. That's how we knew what he'd done to Cooper." I paced the length of the living room. "He blames me. He says I destroyed him. And now he's going to destroy me. Us. I don't know. Everyone who fucked with his life, I guess. Jablonsky, Cooper, me."

"Alex, this isn't your fault."

"I don't know. It might be. I don't know who he is, but I had a thought. And it's crazy. I don't even want to bring this up, but right now, you are the only person in the world I can say this to." I stopped pacing, put my hands on top of my head and tried to remember how to breathe. "I killed Vito." Heathcliff already knew my secret, even though I never admitted it to him. We both knew if I hadn't killed Antonio 'Vito' Vincenzo, he would have done it instead.

"I don't want to hear it. I don't want to know a thing about it." His expression turned to stone, and the sympathy left his eyes. "What does that have to do with this?"

"Maybe nothing, but Mark knows. He covered it up. He destroyed evidence of my involvement. He protected me. And Cooper," I nearly gagged on his name when the gruesome images flooded over me, "he got screwed by Vito too."

"That can't be the only connection between Jablonsky getting shot and Cooper getting killed. O'Connell said you had a list of cases. Surely, the three of you worked on other things that didn't relate to Vito."

"But it makes sense," I insisted. "Who else has the cojones to go after federal agents and enough rage to," I cringed, "maim and mutilate like that?"

"Psychopaths. Serial killers. The kinds of people you mess with on a daily basis."

But I couldn't wrap my head around the possibility that someone else could do something like that. "Aside from a few former SAS operatives and Martin, no one else knows the truth about what happened that night, except you. So stop pretending you didn't know all along. We don't have time to play these ridiculous games. The killer could be coming for you next. Didn't you say someone spray painted a threat on your front door? What if it wasn't some kid? What if he tries to kill you next?"

"Alex, calm down. You're acting insane. Do you honestly think these crimes are about Vito's demise? You think someone from Vito's family is exacting revenge after all this time?"

"I don't know. But what this shithead did to Coop, it was more than just murder. He didn't deserve that. No one deserves that." Tears welled, but I forced them back. "Despite everything, at one time, Coop and I had been friends. And now some animal has ripped him apart. Doesn't that sound like something Vito's people would do?"

Heathcliff rubbed a hand over his mouth. "I thought you recognized the caller's voice."

"Vaguely."

His eyes burned with a rage I only glimpsed on rare occasions. "I recall every single one of those assholes' voices. I could identify any one of them with a single syllable word. Don't tell me you can't do the same. Vito's men threatened your life. They threatened Martin. And Jen. All of us. They killed Gwen." His jaw muscles clenched, and he turned around, slamming his fist against the door so unexpectedly I jumped.

"In that case, I need you to listen to something." I dug out my phone and found the audio recording. Even though I'd already sent it to everyone I could think of, I kept a copy of the audio file on me. I hit play and turned up the volume. "Well?"

"You're wrong," Derek said quietly, his voice lethal. "This has nothing to do with Vito. He's dead. That's someone else." He squinted, and I saw recognition in his eyes.

"You recognize it too."

He hedged. "I don't know, but I'm damn sure this has nothing to do with Vito."

"Okay." But at the moment, it was the only connection I could see, even though from a practical standpoint, it didn't make much sense. "I agree that it can't be Vito or one of his guys, but the killer said I destroyed his life. I took everything away from him. And based on his actions, I can't help but think this ties into what happened that night at Vito's club."

"You can't tell that to Kendall," Heathcliff said. "You could face charges."

"But he has questions."

"That's your guilt talking, Parker. You want to explain this. You need this to make sense. But it doesn't. The killer blamed you, so you want to figure out why. And since doing in that fucker Vito is the worst thing you've ever done, you think that must be it. Sure, it might look feasible on the surface, but it's fucking bonkers. Do you hear me?"

"Yes." Though I didn't agree that was the worst thing I'd ever done, but now wasn't the time to argue. I'd rarely seen Heathcliff this upset.

He strode across the room and grasped my arms, giving me a good shake. "Pay attention. You're not listening. Jablonsky is an FBI agent. You and Cooper used to be FBI agents. This is about a case. A different case."

"How can you be sure?"

"I just am." Heathcliff held tight, as the wheels spun in his head. "We all worked together with Cooper the first time you tangled with Vito. Nick, Thompson, Moretti, me. If it's related, someone else from the task force will be targeted. What about the other agents? Darli, Webster, Sullivan, that one chick who tried to impersonate you?"

"Agent Navate. And for the record, you can't call FBI agents chicks. They don't appreciate it."

Heathcliff tried a smile, but only one corner of his mouth quirked upward. "There's that pain in the ass private detective I know." He let go of my arms, his tone softening. "Think of it this way. If it has to do with that, we know who else this bastard plans to target. Let's make sure everyone is aware of the threat and maybe we'll get some backup nearby to monitor the situation. Does that sound good?"

"Yes."

"Okay." Derek made a few calls and hung up. "That's the easy part. But I'm telling you this has nothing to do with Vito, so we need to focus on the facts. Who else did you, Jablonsky, and Cooper piss off?"

"I don't know." I watched him pensively. "Why do you think the voice sounds familiar to you too?"

"I don't know." He met my eyes. "But I'll be okay. Stop worrying. No one's stupid enough to mess with me." He looked around the empty house. "Well, since you dragged me all the way here, you might as well put me to work. Where do you want to start?"

"Nick and I already went through my old case files and notes, but that was before."

"So we do it again, and maybe something will strike a chord this time."

*   *   *

Heathcliff left around midnight, leaving me with a dozen case files to dissect. Cooper only crossed paths with us on those cases, but they were large, sweeping ordeals with lots of moving pieces. Even though it was a smaller number to examine, a lot of players and potential players were on the field. And since these were all big cases, a lot of other FBI and law enforcement officials had been involved, increasing the killer's potential targets exponentially.

After leaving voicemails for Kendall and Moretti, I took a shower, changed clothes, grabbed some things for Martin, including his watch, and headed back to the hospital. Admittedly, Cross Security took the security part of their name seriously. We drove in a convoy, my vehicle sandwiched between the two company cars. Two men escorted me to the front entrance but remained outside. When I stepped into the sitting area outside the ICU, I spotted another two-man team and mouthed thanks. Randall, a guard who'd protected me before, winked in response.

"Martin," I slid into the empty chair beside him, "what are you doing out here? I thought you'd be in with Mark. Is he okay?" I twisted in the chair, desperate to see into his room, but the blinds were drawn and the room was dark.

"He hasn't woken up." Martin took my hand, brushing his lips against my knuckles before holding my palm against his cheek. I stroked his jaw. "At the changing of the guard, they kicked me out."

"Changing of the guard?" I blinked, taking a moment to process his words. The two FBI agents stationed outside Mark's room had been replaced by two other agents. "When was that?"

"I guess around seven or eight. They said only authorized personnel was allowed inside."

"Kendall upped the security." Four uniformed police officers covered the two doors. "And from the looks of it, so did Moretti."

"Aren't we all on the same side?" Martin asked.

"One would hope. But given the limited amount of evidence we've collected, Moretti might be afraid another agent did this. He wants his guys watching Kendall's guys just in case."

"It can't hurt. But do you think it's necessary?"

After seeing the way Cooper had been torn apart, I didn't know. Rage fueled the killer. And Cooper had pissed off and betrayed the office, his oath, and each of us. He endangered our lives, which would enrage any federal agent worth his salt. Plus, the killer used nine millimeter hollow points, just like the majority of law enforcement officers in this country, both local and federal. "I don't know. I'm too twisted around to know anything right now." I fished Martin's watch out of the tote bag. "Put this on. It'll make me feel better."

He took it, giving me a cockeyed look as he fastened it

around his wrist. "I take it you haven't made much progress since you left."

"Nick and I went through my old cases. Then Derek and I went over everything again. Tomorrow morning, Moretti wants me at the precinct to answer questions, and I'm sure Agent Davis will drag me back to the federal building for another round of interrogations."

"They can't believe you'd do this."

"No. It's not about that." I licked my lips. "The killer called again."

"When?" Martin's eyes grew wide, suddenly far more alert than he'd been up until this point. "What does he want?"

"He wants to destroy me and anyone else who had a hand in destroying him."

Martin's gaze darted to the security team. "You called Lucien. That's why he sent the team. Are they here for me or Jabber?"

"Both, I think. But Cross hates Mark, so I can't be sure they'll step in to protect him. They will protect you, though. You're Cross's golden goose."

"Did he send a team to protect you too?"

"Yes."

"Okay." But the news didn't do much to quell Martin's fears. "Do you think the shooter will attack you next?"

"No."

His brow furrowed. "Don't get me wrong. I'm glad to hear it, but why not?"

"He isn't finished yet. My name's the last on his list. You were right. He wants me to suffer." And I told Martin about the call and Cooper. "I just wish I could figure out who he is. I know him. That much is clear. So why can't I place the voice? On the phone, he couldn't believe I hadn't given him a second thought."

"That almost sounds like an angry ex." He snorted. "I would know. Apparently, so would Jabber. Maybe O'Connell's theory wasn't that far off the mark."

"It's not Renee. She never met me before today. And this asshole, he knows me. Really knows me."

"How? You're always so guarded, even with me."

"Yeah, but you see right through me. I've always hated that about you."

He smirked. "I thought women liked it when men pay attention."

"Not when I lie for a living." A thought tugged at the corner of my mind, just out of reach. I sighed and got up and moved closer to Mark's room. The FBI agents guarding him recognized me.

"Hey, Parker. You going inside?" Agent Hennessy asked.

I glanced back at the nurse's station. Visiting hours were over, but I didn't think anyone would stop me. Martin had given them the paperwork. Apparently, that gave me the same privileges as a blood relative. "Just for a minute. I have to tell him something." I turned and pointed to Martin. "That's James Martin. Do whatever's necessary to have him put on the approved list. Call Kendall if you have to and tell him I said so."

"I'll see what I can do," Agent Hennessy said. "While you're in there, tell Jablonsky we're pulling for him."

Nodding, I braced myself and stepped inside. The only light came from the machines and monitors behind him. I approached the bed, my heart racing.

"Mark, I doubt anyone's told you this yet, but Steve Cooper's dead. The asshole who shot you, he went after Coop. It wasn't pretty. I don't know what's going on, but it obviously has something to do with the three of us. For the life of me, I can't figure it out. So I need you to wake up and help me with this. That's right. I'm actually asking for help, so you damn well better not let me down. You listening, Jablonsky? Cooper's dead. And I don't know who's next. But I have to stop it. Carver and Boyle died because of me. Because I screwed up. Now Cooper's dead because of something I did. Or something we did. I don't know. But I gotta do something. Help me. Please."

The machine beeped, and Mark let out a wheeze around the plastic tube taped to his mouth. But he didn't wake up. I squeezed his hand. For the first time in my life, Mark Jablonsky seemed small and frail.

NINE

"What do we know so far?" Moretti asked. He stood in the center of the bullpen, lingering beside O'Connell's and Thompson's joined desks. "Anything come back on the surveillance footage?"

I hadn't said a word since entering. It was barely eight a.m. Shift change only happened moments ago, and Moretti had already leapt into action. Heathcliff placed a cup of coffee in front of me and took his seat.

"A few rental cars passed by Jablonsky's neighborhood around the time of the shooting. But none of that panned out. We're checking every vehicle that drove past and speaking to the owners, but it looks like a dead end," Heathcliff said.

"Did you run each of them through the criminal databases and also cross them with witness lists and FBI records?" Moretti asked.

"Yes, sir," Heathcliff said. "I even gave them to Parker to take a look."

"None of the names ring a bell," I said.

"Did Cross Security come up with anything useful?" Moretti asked.

"Not yet. The security footage outside Mark's was a

bust, and Cross's team is still working on compiling a list of cell phone users in the vicinity. They had to rerun the list and compare it to the cell phone pings they got near Cooper's place and look for possible matches."

Moretti sighed. "What about actual visuals? Did anyone spot the shooter or report suspicious activity at either location? He attacked Cooper early enough that people were still out and about."

"We're conducting a canvass," Thompson said, "but it's a mixed bag."

"What about at Jablonsky's place? The shooter called to gloat at 3AM. Someone must have noticed something odd happening in Jablonsky's neighborhood at that time. They must have heard gunfire. It should have woken up half the neighborhood," Moretti said.

"Nope," Thompson said, "but officers are still canvassing."

"I spoke to Jablonsky's next door neighbor. Since they share an interior wall, I figured she might have heard the shots, but the neighbor didn't remember hearing anything strange," O'Connell said.

Thinking about the layout of Mark's townhouse, I knew his bedroom was against the exterior wall, farthest away from his attached neighbor, but two shots fired in the middle of the night would be easy enough to hear. "He must have used a silencer."

"Probably," O'Connell agreed.

"Have you figured out how the unsub got inside the townhouse?" I asked.

"We're not sure, but since the deadbolt was engaged when officers arrived on the scene, we're assuming he came in through the back and went out the same way," Thompson said. "It might explain why no one saw anything."

"Did anyone ever find Mark's spare key?" I asked.

"No key," Moretti said. "And we didn't recover any prints off the turtle either."

"The unsub must have known where the key was hidden," I said.

"Or Jablonsky finally got rid of it," Moretti said. "Until

he's awake and can tell us himself, we can't make that assumption. But you're probably right." Moretti turned to Thompson. "Have officers ask the neighbors if any gardeners or landscapers have been working in the neighborhood lately. This wasn't an impetuous act. This asshole planned it, and that takes time and preparation. He must have cased the place prior to the break-in and shooting. Someone must have seen him. Find that person, and get the shooter's description. We're on a clock. He killed last night. He's not done yet."

"Yes, sir." Thompson reached for the phone.

"What about prints? Anything around the doorframes or windows?" I asked.

"Parker, even though the scene was compromised by patrol and paramedics, we dusted everything and found nothing." Moretti shook his head. "Can someone tell me what we got on ballistics?"

No one answered.

"Come on, people, don't be shy. If you know something, speak up."

O'Connell keyed the request into the computer. "Nine mill, hollow point. Severely damaged. No casings at the scene. Striations don't match any weapons we have on file, but like I said, damaged, so forensics is hesitant to insist on that point with any degree of certainty."

"In other words, nothing new since yesterday," Moretti muttered. "That doesn't help us any. Let's shift gears. What about discrepancies and similarities between Jablonsky's townhouse and Cooper's apartment?"

"Different technique," I said. "Same assailant."

Moretti met my eyes, hearing the pain in my tone. "You okay?"

"No, but you saw what that animal did. I doubt any of us are okay."

Moretti nodded, holding up a hand to indicate I had the floor.

"The unsub phoned a second time, right after he killed Cooper."

"Crime scene techs found smeared blood on the receiver and the buttons. Based on the gruesome nature of the kill, your timeline is probably accurate," Thompson said. He didn't look up. We all worked with Cooper and Jablonsky. Even though these were cops and not agents, the crimes hit them hard too. I never bought into the us versus them mentality. We all bled the same. And we all hurt the same.

"The unsub assumed I recognized his voice. He knows me. And he's certain I know him. If anything, he finds it insulting I haven't identified him yet." I thought for a moment. "I don't remember hearing any background noises, but you have a copy of the recording I made. It's just the tail-end of the conversation, but it's all I managed to get. If Cooper was still alive when the killer made the call, we would have heard something in the background. Cooper was a fighter. A Marine. I don't see how this happened."

"We'll find out," Moretti promised. "Did we catch a glimpse of anyone entering or leaving Cooper's apartment?"

"Surveillance feed didn't show anything. The last time Coop had a visitor was three days ago when he had groceries delivered. Nothing since," O'Connell said. "Techs are checking to see if the feed's been tampered with."

"Dammit." I tried to think, but none of the usual techniques for identifying suspects panned out.

"Did the asshole say anything to you that would help us ID him?" O'Connell asked.

"Unfortunately, no. What I don't understand is why he's going to this much trouble to conceal his identity. He wants me to know who he is. He enjoys gloating. Why not take it a step further and tell me who he is?"

"Because he threatened you," Heathcliff said.

"So?"

"So he figures once he eliminates you, he doesn't want any hard evidence linking back to him. That's why he won't tell you his name," Moretti said. "It goes back to what I said earlier. He's smart, and his actions are premeditated. He's been planning this for some time. You must have really pissed this guy off."

"He practically said as much on the phone," I said. "I went through everything, but I don't know. I piss off a lot of guys."

"Comes with the territory," Moretti said. "Kendall's pulling every case file the three of you worked, but I heard you and O'Connell already did that."

"And then Heathcliff and I did it again." I looked at Heathcliff, waiting for the detective to admit the killer's voice sounded familiar to him too, but he kept his mouth shut. "Based on the second call, I'd say our killer already has his next victim in his sights. He's several steps ahead of us. Unless we figure out who's next, Cooper might not be the only fatality."

Moretti blew out a frustrated breath. "Does Kendall know more of his agents could be in danger?"

"That's pretty damn fundamental," I shrugged, "but I'm not an agent. I'm a cooperating witness, so he won't tell me shit."

"You're more than a witness," Moretti said. "Since he's not keeping you in the loop, that will make this harder."

"Yeah, I know."

"Do you have any remaining resources at the Bureau?" Moretti asked. "We're working together, but classified material and internal memos will be a bitch to access without filling out the paperwork and waiting for authorization. And like you pointed out, we don't have time for this."

"I might still have a friend or two, but Mark's our best bet, if he wakes up."

"How is he?" O'Connell asked. "Jen didn't say anything. Has there been any change?"

"As of seven a.m., his vitals were stable, but that's all I know." I hadn't shared the surgeon's news about possible brain damage with anyone. Martin knew, and that was it.

"We'll take care of this without him. The only thing Jablonsky needs to worry about is getting his ass healed," Moretti said. He opened the folder on the desk and read aloud. "Preliminary autopsy findings for Steven Cooper. Cause of death," Moretti paused, "shit."

"What?" My stomach roiled, protesting the sip of coffee I'd just taken, but I forced it back down.

"He drowned in his own blood. That's what killed him."

Moretti reached for a chair and sat heavily. He'd been at the scene, just like O'Connell and Thompson. "The blood inside the bag came from his lungs. He coughed it up, and when the bag filled, he breathed it back in and drowned."

"That's sick," Thompson muttered.

Sick didn't even begin to describe it. "How many times was he stabbed?" I asked.

"Thirty-two. ME reasoned he should have bled out before he drowned, so the majority of the stab wounds were inflicted postmortem. Based on the bruising, they were delivered with extreme force."

"The killer went into a rage," I said.

"It appears so," Moretti said.

"What kind of knife is that?" O'Connell asked, peering at the crime scene photos. "A switchblade?"

"Looks more like some kind of shiv," Thompson said.

"Cooper had been shivved in prison," I said. "That's why he was permitted to carry out the remainder of his sentence under house arrest."

"That could be significant," Moretti said. "O'Connell, I'll need you to look into that."

Slowly, I stood and crossed to O'Connell's desk. The last thing I wanted to see were those photographs, but my personal preference wasn't important. I had a job to do. "What about a pocket knife?" I scanned the notes, but forensics hadn't matched a weapon to the wound tracks yet.

"Could be," O'Connell said. He put a hand on my shoulder. "Let's focus on what we know."

"Which is?" Desperation crept into my tone.

"Plastic bag came from the Stop N' Shop. We found two sets of partial prints on it. We ran them through IAFIS but only matched one set to Roderick Ames, the store clerk," O'Connell said.

"Have we spoken to him yet?" Moretti asked. "We need to make a request for whatever security cam footage they have."

"On it," Heathcliff volunteered, heading out the door before anyone could object.

"There has to be more." I sifted through CSU's attached

report. No prints were found at the scene except Cooper's. My gaze drifted back to the autopsy report. "Coop was trained. Former Marine. Former FBI agent. And the attack happened in broad daylight. I don't see how this asshole got the drop on him, especially when Coop clearly had a home court advantage." I flipped to the attached photos, cringing at the ghastly images. "Did they find any blood at the scene that wasn't his?"

"It'll take time to process, but it's possible. We won't know until everything has been swabbed and analyzed," Moretti said. "The ME noted the knuckles on Cooper's right hand were bruised. He probably got at least one good swing in, but the defensive wounds were at a minimum. I'd say the killer surprised him."

"If Cooper hit him, that might have been what pissed off the killer," Thompson muttered.

"Anything under Coop's fingernails?" I asked.

"No." Moretti let out an exhale. "And we still aren't sure how the killer gained entry to Cooper's apartment. Security cameras in the hallway didn't see anyone exit or enter."

"The fire escape," I said, a memory from long ago surfacing. I teetered, and O'Connell grabbed my arm to steady me. I squeezed my eyes shut for a moment then blinked, waiting for the dizziness to subside.

"Parker, sit down." O'Connell climbed out of his chair and pushed it closer to me. "Did you get any sleep last night?"

"A little." But hospital chairs weren't comfortable and I'd been plagued by sadness, guilt, and fear which wouldn't be assuaged until I identified the asshole responsible. "Did you get the recordings for me to listen to?"

"Yeah." O'Connell glanced at Moretti. The LT nodded, handed out orders to a few other detectives, and went to his office to call Kendall with the updates so they could plot out their next course of action. "I cleared out an office downstairs so no one will disturb you. And I prioritized the files based on your updated list. IT's been running a comparison of the recording you made with the files I requested, but it's been slow going. They've only been at it for about," he looked at his watch, "six hours, give or take."

He eyed me. "Did you remember something else?"

"I'm not sure." But I had my suspicions about the voice. It started when Martin said the killer sounded like a vengeful ex. However, I wanted to do my own comparison before I sounded the alarm. In the event I was wrong, the resulting goose chase would waste valuable time and resources, and with the killer already plotting his next kill, I couldn't afford to be wrong.

O'Connell led me downstairs. "Where do you want to start?" he asked, clicking the mouse at the computer terminal.

I skimmed the case numbers on the files. "The last case I worked with Cooper. The Horvat investigation."

"Correct me if I'm wrong, but Jakov's dead."

"Niko isn't."

"I thought Homeland threw him into some deep dark hole, never to be heard from again."

"Yeah, but I need to make sure." I double-clicked the file and carefully selected an OIO interview. "Even if it isn't Niko, it could be another diehard member of Shade."

"I thought that got disbanded."

I pointed at O'Connell and made a clicking sound. "Yes, which means that Jablonsky, Cooper, and I all played a part in destroying something these assholes worked so hard to build."

O'Connell dropped into a chair beside me. "That does fit."

Unfortunately, the voice didn't match, but I knew it wouldn't. O'Connell told the techs to run comparisons against the rest of the men we arrested from the terrorist cell, just to be on the safe side, and they shuffled those interviews to the top of their pile.

"Strike one," I muttered.

O'Connell shut the door. "Do you think this could have something to do with Antonio Vincenzo?"

"He's also dead, remember?"

"Yeah, but he hated you with a passion, and once Cooper turned on his organization, I bet several people had scores to settle."

"Do you know the details behind the attack Cooper

suffered in prison?"

"Someone stabbed him twice with a sharpened toothbrush. Cooper got the guy into a chokehold, backed against the shower wall, and managed to hold on until he passed out. If he didn't use that guy as a human shield, he might have been beaten to death by the other three guys who took part in the attack."

"Were those Vito's guys?" I asked.

"According to prison records, Cooper's attackers were serving time for gang-related crimes and were affiliated with the Mexican cartels."

Again with the cartels. There was something to that. I could feel it. "So nothing linked them to organized crime or Vito?"

"No, but you never know. Vito had to get his drugs from somewhere. And the cartels have the market on every kind of narcotic imaginable."

"Vito is the gift that keeps on giving, but after jumping to that conclusion last night, Heathcliff pointed out some cold, hard facts to me. I don't think this has anything to do with the dead mob boss. I would probably have identified the voice by now, and Heathcliff said the voice doesn't match anyone from Vito's inner circle. Plus, the OIO had an additional interest in monitoring organized crime after Vito greenlit me. The last I heard, the rest of Vito's inner circle got knocked off or took early retirement somewhere warmer. You should check to see what the police know, but according to the OIO, all those businesses are now under new management."

"It still fits, but you'd know best," O'Connell said. "So who's up next?"

"The DeAngelo Bard case."

"Bard's in prison."

"Yeah, but a lot of people worked for him. He ran a gang, the KXDs, and those guys are a dime a dozen. It could be one of them." I clicked the file, staring at the lengthy list of recorded interviews. This would take some time. "You might as well get back to work. If I find something, I'll let you know."

O'Connell squeezed my shoulder. "Have fun."

TEN

"That's him." I pointed emphatically at the screen. "That's the asshole who shot Mark and slaughtered Cooper." The words cut through me like an icepick. They would never get easier to say. Despite everything, I'd spent most of the morning flashing back to cases I'd worked with Cooper, how he'd saved my life, how he went out of his way to watch out for me, and how he'd come clean in the end. And now he was dead. I couldn't lose anyone else. We had to act fast. I just prayed we could put an end to this before the killer found another victim, assuming Mark pulled through, which was another can of worms I couldn't open right now or I'd be paralyzed.

"It's not possible, Parker," Thompson said. He glanced at O'Connell.

"I'm telling you that's our guy. You need to issue a BOLO."

"Alex, Francisco Steele is currently incarcerated," O'Connell said gently.

"What did the techs say? Did you have them compare the recordings?" I stared wide-eyed in utter shock that two detectives, my friends, weren't jumping into action.

"They said it's possible," O'Connell admitted. "Steele's interview is an 88% voice match to the call you received yesterday. That's probably why you think he's our guy. The caller sounds just like him, but Steele can't be the killer."

"He *is* our guy. Why aren't you listening? Why aren't you doing something?" Frantic desperation clawed at me. I spun. If Nick and Thompson wouldn't do something, I'd go to Moretti. He'd do something. And if he didn't listen, then Kendall would be my next stop. Hell, I didn't need any of them. I could do this myself. Lucien offered me his resources. We could make a citizen's arrest, if need be.

"Parker," Moretti grabbed me before I collided with him, "I just got off the phone with corrections. I verified his inmate number and everything. Francisco Steele remains in custody."

"No," I shook my head, "it's not possible. He's out. He has to be. He called from Mark's and then Cooper's. He knows me, lieutenant. I spent months undercover getting to know him. He's the shithead who did this. I'd bet my life on it." I spotted Heathcliff returning to his desk. "Derek, you remember that undercover case I worked at the strip joint, right?"

"How could I forget?" Heathcliff asked. "I have a permanent bump on the back of my head from those thugs who came looking for revenge."

I hit play on my phone and stared at the detective. "Isn't that Steele's voice? You said last night it sounded familiar."

He pondered the question while taking the phone from me and playing the message two more times. "It could be."

"Can't," Thompson said. "Steele's in prison."

"That doesn't mean he couldn't make a call. Someone could have rerouted it through the landlines or something." Heathcliff blinked a few times. "Steele ran the KXDs with Bard. He planned to decimate the Lords and take whoever remained into the KXDs' ranks. That gives us a lot of potentials to look at. I'll call over to gangs and see if they've heard anything lately about what's been going on."

I stared at O'Connell. "It's him. I betrayed him. I destroyed him. Mark was with me when we made the arrest. That's why he was the first one Steele targeted. The investigation into Bard, Cooper led that. If it hadn't been for Cooper, the OIO wouldn't have gotten involved. I wouldn't have gotten involved. Steele would probably be running the KXDs at Bard's side from some tropical, non-extradition country if it weren't for us. Steele was always Bard's lap dog. He came from a fucked up family. So the gang became his family. He's avenging his family. He's avenging Bard. It's him."

"Okay," O'Connell said, "but since he's in prison, someone else is acting on his behalf. We have to find out who."

"I want to see him," I said. "Face to face."

"I'll see what I can do," Moretti said, but his mind was elsewhere. "Why now?"

"I don't know."

Moretti zeroed in on Heathcliff. "Refresh my memory on the situation. What exactly went down?"

"I stepped in using an alias I established while working narco to back up Alex. Steele groomed her to pass drugs in the strip joint, but being under that long, things were getting out of hand, his feelings for her were getting out of hand. And the situation was only made worse since the PD was running its own op at the same time. Something was about to break off, so I went in to assist," Heathcliff said. "I stepped on Steele's toes and garnered favor with Bard. Steele didn't like it, but he couldn't do much about it. Bard wouldn't let him. Bard owed me."

"You invaded Steele's turf and stole his girl. That's why he hated you," I said. "That's why you nearly had your skull bashed in."

"If I hadn't, you and I both know what Steele expected from you. The OIO never should have sent you into that situation alone." Heathcliff fought to keep his tone neutral, but his hands balled into fists.

"Are we sure Steele's behind this and not Bard?" Moretti asked.

"Steele made those calls. 100%. But he could be acting on Bard's behalf. I don't know if they've been in contact. I don't know what happened after they got pinched." I glanced at O'Connell, wondering if he was going to challenge my conviction with IT's voice comparison assessment, but he kept his mouth shut. Another thought crossed my mind, and I looked at Heathcliff. "Are you sure the spray paint on your door was just some kid?"

Heathcliff shrugged, turning his back to us when someone answered the phone. "Hey, this is Heathcliff in major crimes. I got a favor to ask."

Tuning him out, I said, "Steele killed his mother's boyfriend when he was just a kid. The guy clearly has rage issues." My gut said he personally killed Cooper. I just wasn't sure how.

"And abandonment issues," Thompson said, pulling up Steele's rap sheet. "No wonder he's pissed at you, but he couldn't have committed the attacks. Once again, he's behind bars. You need to get that through your head."

"I'm still not sure how anyone could make the phone calls appear to be from two different landlines when Steele's in prison," O'Connell said.

"Could it be a recording?" Moretti asked.

"No," I said. "Recordings can't react like that."

"What about voice modulation or those computer programs that emulate people's voices?" Moretti suggested. "Perhaps someone's using this as a distraction while eliminating the next target on the list. Maybe they figure blaming Steele is a surefire way to avoid being identified."

"If they copied Steele's voice, they must have spent some time talking to him. We need prison records, visitor logs, call logs, copies of the mail, everything. I want to know who Francisco Steele's been talking to. But this isn't a distraction. This is Steele. I'm positive."

Moretti glanced at me. He didn't say I was wrong, but from the expression on his face, I knew he thought I lost it. However, I'd never been surer of anything in my entire life.

While the detectives worked the angles, determining who on the outside would be willing to do Steele's bidding, I called the prison to verify the facts. According to them, Francisco Steele remained behind bars. I checked the inmate database and found him listed. So I made a request to stop by for a visit.

Despite the correction officer's insistence that Steele wasn't going anywhere, I knew the killer already planned another strike. So I warned Heathcliff to be careful, figuring he could be the next target, and went home to get my files. My notes didn't include every agent who participated in the case, so I dropped by the courthouse to review the transcripts and get names of those who testified against Steele and Bard. Then I headed for the OIO.

Davis met me at the elevator. "Don't tell me you received another call."

"Shouldn't you know? You're monitoring my phone."

"Right." He looked uncomfortable. "Kendall wanted me to conduct the follow-up to yesterday's incident."

"Don't call it an incident. Cooper died horrifically because he used to be one of us." My gaze darted to the office in the corner that once belonged to Sam Boyle and the desk Michael Carver once occupied. "I'm sorry, Davis, but agents who work with me drop like flies. I'm hoping to stop another tragedy before the killer strikes again. So you'll have to pardon my brusqueness."

"Since when are you this polite? You really think the unsub might go after me?"

"You can't be too careful, but you didn't work the Bard case."

Davis smiled in relief. "You know who the killer is."

"Yes, but I hit a snag."

He led me into the conference room, called up to Kendall's office to have the director meet us, and turned his legal pad to a clean page. As soon as Kendall stepped into the room, Davis asked for the name.

"Francisco Steele, and before you ask, Lt. Moretti already told me he's currently serving out his sentence in federal prison," I said.

"That goes back to the drug investigation Cooper led against DeAngelo Bard." Kendall had read up on our joint investigations. "I had Lawson analyze the recording you made. I'll admit the voice on the other end could be him, but I checked with the warden. Steele's inside. Has been since the trial. Surprisingly, he's a model prisoner. Good behavior, works in the laundry, has full privileges."

"How much of that was negotiated on his behalf for the intel he gave us on the cartels and the other gangs?" I asked.

Kendall didn't respond. The prosecutor had offered Steele a generous deal in exchange for information, which Steele happily turned over with one exception. Steele never snitched on Bard, just everyone else. That might have been how he'd gotten so many privileges in prison. Maybe one of them was a day pass to go on a murderous rampage.

"What do we need to know about Steele that isn't in the files?" Kendall asked.

So I told him everything I told the police and everything else I remembered from my months spent undercover. I knew more about Steele than anyone else in the federal building. But despite that, Kendall stuck to his guns. No reinstatements. No favors. I answered all his questions, but he didn't answer any of mine.

"Our top priority is determining who on the outside is carrying out Steele's wishes. I'll have our analysts and techs check the phone lines. The COs and the warden will search Steele's belongings for a cell phone. Contraband is common. He probably had someone smuggle one in, and whoever he's working with on the outside is routing the phone call through the victims' landlines," Kendall said. "That is the most likely explanation."

"Cooper's autopsy indicated the killer went into a rage. Don't tell me that's not Steele."

"We'll look into it, Parker. Thank you for coming to us with this. I'll take it from here. In the meantime, I'll bump up security and have agents assigned to protect the agents and witnesses who testified against Steele. Any one in particular you think Steele might target?"

"Detective Heathcliff, but he's already been warned. Aside from that, the Marshals relocated a stripper, Veronica Kincaid. I don't know if she's still in WitSec, but you should reach out."

"Will do." Kendall nodded to me. "I stopped by this morning to see Jablonsky. I've upped his protection detail, but I made sure they know to allow you and James Martin access to his room."

"Thank you, sir."

"All right. If I need you, I'll let you know. We're monitoring your phone in the event Steele makes contact again. If he does, I expect you'll reach out to us immediately."

"Yes, sir." My inner voice cringed. Kendall wasn't my boss. I didn't need to fall back into that routine, especially when he expected me to walk away and let him handle this. He didn't protect Mark. He didn't protect Cooper, and to be quite honest, he didn't protect me when another agency threw me under the bus and forced me to resign. Annoyed, I pushed away from the table. "Make sure you protect your people this time. I don't want to go to any more funerals."

Marching out of the conference room, I didn't turn around until I stepped into the elevator. As the doors closed, I watched Kendall call everyone to attention. Their top priority was figuring out who Steele was communicating with and how he was getting his messages directly out of the prison and to my cell phone. Funny, the PD was doing the exact same thing. And yet, I didn't think either of them would be successful.

ELEVEN

"Alex," Lucien said, surprised when I stormed into his office, much to his assistant's chagrin, "what are you doing here? What's wrong?"

"Where are we on identifying cell phone pings from the two crime scenes?" I asked. "I spoke to Amir, but he said everything was being directly relayed to you. What are you hiding?"

"I'm not hiding anything." He gestured to the sofa across from the chair in which he was seated. "Please, sit down." He glanced up at his assistant, who remained in the doorway. "Justin, bring us a tray with coffee and whatever happens to be downstairs and a few takeout menus. I also need the files on Ms. Parker's investigation and hold my calls."

"Right away, sir." Justin disappeared before I could protest the offer of coffee and snacks.

Lucien tossed the projection analysis and expense report onto the table and studied me like an exotic creature at the zoo. "Vinnie overheard the paramedics speaking yesterday. I'm sorry for your loss."

"Vinnie?"

"The head of the security team I assigned for your

protection."

"I don't need protecting. I just need to know who's responsible."

He cocked his head to the side. "You shouldn't bite the hand that feeds you."

"It's a good thing I'm not hungry."

He chuckled, amused and in a good mood, which only irritated me further. "I'll save my breath. You know I'm not your enemy, even though most of the time you act like I'm the devil himself. To answer your question, yes, we've compiled a list of cell phone users in the area at the two different points of interest for the times specified. As predicted, the number is in the thousands. The computers finished the analysis an hour ago. I've assigned a team to run those individuals against federal and international criminal databases. I assume, based on his hit list, the assailant must have a record."

"He does."

Cross cocked an eyebrow. "What's his name?"

I didn't ask how Cross knew. He always knew more than anyone else in the room, kind of like Martin. For a moment, I wondered what a meeting between the two of them looked like. Did either of them even have to speak, or did they just read each other's mind and come to some symbiotic mind-meld of an agreement? Shaking off the unexpected and pointless musing, I said, "Francisco Steele, but according to the authorities, he's locked up. They think someone else is doing his bidding."

"You don't believe that."

"I'm positive he's the caller, and from what I've seen at both scenes, that's his handiwork. I just haven't figured out how he's defying the laws of physics."

"What do the police think?" Cross asked. "Do they think he has a protégé?"

"Perhaps. Steele was second-in-line to head the KXDs. The police assume one of his underlings must be behind yesterday's attacks."

"Do they have any evidence supporting their theory?"

"They're working on it. The bag wrapped around Cooper's head came from the Stop N' Shop, so they're hoping to ID the killer that way. They're also checking to see who Steele's communicated with from inside prison."

"And the FBI?"

"The same."

"Both our brilliant federal and local law enforcement agencies can't possibly be wrong, can they?" His words bled sarcasm as he went to the computer and typed. "Steele, Francisco." He read the assigned inmate number, the prison location, and the date of incarceration. "Is that correct?"

"Yes, but I won't believe it until I see it. I want to pay Steele a visit. I'm just waiting for my request to be approved." But since I didn't have a badge, if Steele didn't want to see me, he didn't have to, unless Moretti worked some magic.

"Always best not to believe something until you have proof. After all, that is what our business relies on."

He waited for me to serve up more details, but I had fallen silent, staring at the rug and itching to get up and pace. Finally, I gave in, circled the office a few times, and stared out the window. Unlike my office, Cross had a lovely view.

He cleared his throat, something he did when he was annoyed or uncomfortable, but that nonverbal nudge did nothing to drag me from my reverie. I wasn't sure what to think or do, so I kept my mouth shut until the thought wisps had time to coalesce into something solid, a trick I learned long ago.

"That's fine, Justin. Close the door behind you. I'll let you know if we want to order lunch," Cross said, and I turned just as his assistant stepped out of the room. I hadn't even heard him enter or leave. Cross's assistant was probably a ninja in his spare time.

I gave the tray a glance, but I didn't make a move for the croissants or fresh fruit. Even the mug of gourmet coffee didn't interest me. Cross eyed me as I picked up the top folder and opened it to a printed spreadsheet. The information included names, billing addresses, and cell phone numbers.

"You must have friends at all the major carriers," I

mused.

"Something like that," Cross said.

I dropped onto the couch with the papers in my lap, flipping through them in search of any names or addresses that might ring a bell. I knew the neighborhoods and streets where Bard, Steele, and the KXDs operated. I'd just finished going through the first two pages when Cross cleared his throat again.

"When's the last time you ate?" he asked.

"I don't know."

"I'm ordering lunch. What would you like?"

You sound like Martin, I thought. "Nothing."

"You have to eat."

"There's no point. I haven't been able to keep anything down." I felt something shift in the room, and I looked up from the papers, my gaze falling on the report Cross had tossed onto the coffee table. "You have an appointment."

He made a show of looking at the time. "Not for another hour, but it'll take you at least three times as long to get through all the names on that list, so stop wasting my time. What do you want from me?"

"Nothing."

"Bullshit." He waited, practically tapping his foot impatiently.

"Honestly, I don't know."

"Okay." He sat in the chair opposite me. "Do you think you're Steele's next target?"

I laughed. "Everyone asks me that. The answer is no. He's just getting started. But I have no idea who his next victim will be. I've been going over the victimology in my head. The only thing I know for certain is he wants to save me for last."

"I know. I heard. Though I imagine he'll be the one begging for mercy when all is said and done."

"That's the plan." I snorted, pausing suddenly. "Wait a sec. How do you know what he said? That wasn't part of the recording."

Lucien cleared his throat again.

"You bugged my phone." Not that I was surprised. Actually, what surprised me was the OIO and PD hadn't thought to do it sooner. "When this is over, we need to have another discussion about boundaries and privacy."

"Your safety is my foremost concern. Deal with it."

"In that case, try to care a little less about my safety." But I saw the flicker in his eyes. "Martin put you up to it. Is he a client now?"

"We have an arrangement," Cross said, glee dancing in his eyes, "but that isn't important now either. With the limited time I have available, let's get back on track. You mentioned something about victimology. Let's talk it out."

"Jablonsky was first because he made the arrest. Cooper was second and was brutally slain because he was responsible for opening the initial investigation. He's the one who brought it to our attention. Mark's and mine."

"So Steele's doling out punishment based on his perceived sleight and the roles you each had in his undoing. But the order makes no sense. The last man involved was his first target, and the first man involved was his second target. Theoretically, you're at the end of the list. How long do you think it is?"

"I don't know. Obviously, other agents were involved, witnesses, attorneys, judges, and the jury. I have no idea how deep or invested he is in getting revenge. But I'm certain Detective Heathcliff is on the list. Steele will want him to suffer."

"More than Agent Cooper?"

"A lot more." My stomach flipped as my imagination conjured unsettling images of Derek tortured, maimed, and mutilated. "Any chance you could assign a few guys to keep an eye on him?"

Lucien worked his jaw for a moment. "Detective Heathcliff. That would make him a cop. You know my stance on working with the police."

"They wouldn't have to know about it. Heathcliff would probably refuse outside protection, anyway." Though I hoped Moretti was smart enough to assign a patrol car to sit on him.

"You're sure Steele will go after him?"

"He already tried once when we were undercover. He'll do it again, and this time, he won't miss." I shivered, pulling my legs up so I could hug my knees. Too much violence. Too many possibilities. I didn't care what Derek said. The spray painted message on his front door had to have been Steele's doing, and I told Lucien that.

"If Heathcliff has any cop instincts whatsoever, he'll spot the tail. I'll only assign a team of bodyguards to watch him if he agrees to it. I don't want my guys arrested for stalking. And the police are vindictive bastards. That's exactly what they'll do. So if you want a team to watch over your detective pal, that's a nonnegotiable condition. Get him on board, and you got it."

"Let me make a quick call." Fishing out my phone, I called Derek.

"Hey, I was just about to call you," he said before I could get a word in edgewise. "We spoke to Roderick Ames, the clerk at the Stop N' Shop, and he handed over the hard drives with the security camera footage from the last two weeks. Techs are already analyzing it against facial recognition. I'll give it a look as soon as I get a chance, just in case the computer missed something. O'Connell spoke to IT about the voice analysis, and they think the caller is indeed a match to Francisco Steele."

"I told you so."

"Yeah, I know. I never doubted that. But I'll tell O'Connell you told him so. Forensics also found foreign DNA at the second scene. A few drops of blood, diluted by saliva."

"Cooper punched the killer in the mouth," I said.

"That would be my guess. We sent a swab over to Kendall's people, but our lab's already working on it. Moretti put a rush on it. Hopefully, we'll get something by tomorrow. Steele's DNA is on file, so are most of the gangbangers we scooped up in those raids. We'll find out who's responsible. And we'll have irrefutable proof to back it. We're going to get this guy, Parker. I promise."

"What did gangs have to say?"

"They aren't sure what's going down, but since Jablonsky was shot, the streets have emptied. The corner boys aren't working. No one's around. Everyone's staying inside. Even the KXDs' and Lords' regular hangouts, bars, and strip joints are empty."

"The KXDs and the Lords? Aren't they rivals?"

"Nope. After Bard's arrest, the KXDs started to crumble. And when you and Jablonsky brought in Steele, that was nearly the final nail in their coffin. Neither gang has the power they once did. And they both lacked leadership after the sweeping arrests, but they managed to hold their ground and maintain the status quo in terms of moving product. The Mexican cartel assisted by sending in additional firepower and product and helping them reorganize. They joined forces. They're allies now."

"Desperation makes for strange bedfellows," I said.

"Face it, the cartel needs the gangs to move product, so they stepped in and forced the two sides to play nice."

"Who's running them now?" I asked.

"Gangs believes Bard is still calling the shots from inside prison."

"Has he had any contact with Steele?" I asked.

"We're working on it. Thompson's getting the paperwork together so we can access prison records, but according to the Department of Corrections, Steele and Bard are being detained in separate facilities."

"That doesn't mean anything. They could still talk or pass messages back and forth."

"I know, but we won't have anything solid until we get a peek at the visitor and call logs and see who they've communicated with. Moretti tossed around the theory Bard could be behind the hits, and he ordered Steele to make it happen as a test of loyalty."

"That could be. For the KXDs to stay indoors and stop dealing, the order had to come from the top of the food chain. They wouldn't close up shop otherwise. And the cartels don't care if the foot soldiers get caught or brought in on murder charges, but Bard might. And so would Steele. Flip a coin. The two aren't that different, but Steele called me. He threatened me. That's his doing, not Bard's."

"That's what I told Moretti, which means whoever controls the gang also controls the killer," Heathcliff said. "All right, I'll run with that and see what else I can dig up."

"Derek," I stopped him before he could hang up, "my

gut says you're on the list. You might be next."

"More reason to wrap this up quickly."

"How do you feel about having a few guys watch your back?"

"I already got a few guys watching my back."

"I don't mean other cops."

"Like bodyguards?" He scoffed. "I probably feel the same way you do about that."

"Does that mean I can okay a Cross Security team to shadow you?"

"Fuck no. Moretti already assigned a patrol unit to stay on my ass. I don't need the protection, Parker. I can take care of myself. I'll be fine. Don't worry so much. I'll call you when I know more." He hung up before I could protest.

Cross watched as I angrily shoved the phone into my pocket. My boss did his best to conceal the smug look, but the effort was wasted when he said, "To quote you, I told you so."

TWELVE

I shoved my ID into my pocket as I entered Mark's room. Martin sat with his head resting in his hand while he thumbed his phone. He didn't bother looking up when the door closed.

I sat beside him and traced the tight muscles balled together along his back and shoulders. He turned to look at me, and I kissed him. "How are you?" I asked.

"No change," he said.

"No, handsome, I want to know how you are." I looked down at the phone in his lap that he hadn't let go of. "Is that work? Do you have to go to the office?"

"It is, but I don't want to leave him alone. What if he wakes up?"

"I'm here. I'm not going anywhere."

Martin sighed, running his free hand through his hair and making it stick out at a right angle. "Are you sure?"

"Positive." I massaged the spot on his shoulder that often got sore, but even that did little to alleviate the tension in his body. "After you put out the fires at work, you should go home, take a shower, change your clothes, eat something that doesn't come in a wrapper, and maybe get some sleep."

"What about you?"

"What about me? I'm fresh as a daisy."

"I'm not going to argue. You're beautiful. You always are."

"Now I know you need sleep."

He chuckled. "All right. I'll go in a minute." He shot off a text and tucked his phone away. "Have you had any luck finding this asshole?"

"Some. I know who's responsible. Do you remember the man you pulled off of me that night in my apartment?"

"After you had been reinstated and didn't tell me?" Martin asked.

"Yeah."

"Didn't you and Jabber arrest him?"

"Uh-huh." I was glad Martin remembered those details more than the fact Steele tried to shoot me up with a lethal dose of heroin. "Francisco Steele. He's pulling the strings, but we haven't identified the assailant yet." Another thought crossed my mind. "Or assailants. Right now, we believe members of Steele's gang or former gang might be doing his bidding. I placed a request to speak to him in prison, but authorization takes time. I don't know if he'll even agree to see me."

"He should. He called you twice," Martin said. "Obviously, he has something to say." Anger burned in his eyes. "He wants an audience with you, Alexis. He wants you dead. Taunting and threatening you over the phone isn't nearly as satisfying as doing it in person. You need to be careful."

"Did Cross tell you that?"

Martin met my eyes for a split second before looking away. "Prisons have a lot of security. You will be safe speaking to him, right?"

I didn't say anything. My mind had gone to dark places.

"Alex," he nudged me, "you'll be safe, right?"

"Yes. I'm just not sure Steele can say the same." I licked my lips, my gaze resting on Mark. "I want to kill him for what he's done, and I'm not sure I won't." I fought to keep myself from trembling.

"You're not a killer."

"We both know that's not true. I've killed."

"In self-defense."

"Not always." I inhaled, staring at Mark and willing him to wake up. I'd confess all my sins if that would make a difference. I'd do anything if he'd just open his eyes. "At Quantico, we're taught to respond to threats rationally. We don't shoot to kill because we're pissed off. We shoot back in order to minimize the threat. We shoot back to serve the greater good, to protect the public at large, to protect ourselves, to protect each other. We shoot because the subject gave us no choice."

"You're not a killer, sweetheart. You've taken lives, but you've never had a choice. I know that, even if you don't." He got out of the chair, knelt down, and kissed me. "Are you sure you'll be okay here? I don't have to go. I can stay. Guillot can handle things in my absence."

"No, you need a break. I'll be fine. I need some alone time with Mark, anyway. I'll just bitch and moan until he opens his eyes and tells me to shut up."

Martin smiled, rubbing his thumb against my cheek. "That's one way to get him to snap out of it."

"Did you talk to that neuroscience guy?" I asked.

"I did. I had Jabber's scans sent to him. He took a look. He didn't see anything particularly troubling, but he doesn't want to be overly optimistic either. The human brain is a hard thing to predict."

"Tell me about it. I never know what you're going to do next."

He winked. "Good."

After Martin left, I pulled out the intel Cross had given me and continued scanning the names and numbers. I'd let Cross Security handle the background checks. I just wanted to see if anything looked familiar. As usual, Cross's prediction was right. It took more than three hours to get through everything. I made a list of questionable billing addresses and names, though I couldn't be sure about any of them without looking at a computer or checking my notes. I read the names to Mark, expecting him to speak up if he recognized any of them, but he didn't make a peep.

I just picked up my phone to call Cross with the names I shortlisted when Mark let out a gasp. He wheezed; the machines started beeping. He couldn't breathe. I ran to the door and threw it open, yelling for help.

A nurse raced inside while a doctor sprinted down the hall toward us. He pushed his way into the room, knocking me out of the way. I watched as they checked Mark. The two exchanged words, and the nurse recalibrated the machine. It stopped beeping.

"What's going on?" I asked.

The doctor glanced at me. "His breathing is overpowering the ventilator. We'll take out the breathing tube and see if he can keep it up. He's getting stronger. Hopefully, he'll be out of the woods soon."

I liked this doctor better than the one who told us Mark might be a vegetable. But I didn't trust either of them. The doctor removed the tube from Mark's throat, which resulted in more wheezing, gasping, and a few strangled coughs, but his stats held steady. The nurse and doctor cleared out, and I went back inside, my head spinning.

After making my call, I stared at the monitors until I could see the numbers even with my eyes closed. The steady beeping rhythm meant his condition remained stable. I listened to the sound, memorizing it, until it calmed my nerves. Mark was alive.

I moved the two chairs into a makeshift cot at the foot of the bed, so I could stare at the monitors and watch them without cramping my neck. Then I balled up my jacket and used it as a pillow, hoping to get more comfortable. Eventually, I closed my eyes, concentrating on the sound of the monitors. One random beep and I would jump up and get help. At least, that's what I told myself before falling into an uneasy sleep.

Footsteps in the hallway woke me. I sat up straight and checked the time. 8:32. Mark's vitals held steady. The knob turned, and Martin pushed his way into the room, carrying a large thermos and a white paper bag.

"The doctors just told me Jabber's breathing on his own," Martin said.

I dropped my feet to the floor and leaned forward, resting my elbows on my thighs. "He nearly scared me to death in the process." I ran my fingers through my tangled hair, tugging it back and twisting it into a knot. "At least he looks more like himself without that apparatus taped to his face."

Martin gave Mark's hand a squeeze before sitting in the chair I'd used as the bottom portion of my makeshift bed. He smelled like soap and a hint of expensive cologne. He had shaved and changed clothes. He wore a charcoal gray Henley underneath his leather jacket with dark wash jeans. Not exactly the usual tailored suits he wore to conduct business, but as always, Martin looked like a million bucks.

"Did you get any sleep?" I asked, rubbing my eyes. The color had returned to his cheeks, and his eyes were bright and sharp, despite being bloodshot.

"I lost forty-five minutes somewhere, so I guess so."

"I know the feeling."

Martin had spent a lot of time in hospitals due to his mother's illness and more recently due to my close calls. But until now, I never realized just how much he hated them and how they sucked the life out of him. He reached into the bag and pulled out a set of plastic flatware and handed them to me.

"My stomach's in knots. I can't eat," I said.

"It's just soup, sweetheart. Guillot and I had a working dinner, and I ordered this for you. You love soup." He removed the lid from the thermos, which doubled as a bowl, and handed it to me so he could pour. "You need your strength."

"Thanks." I held the bowl in my lap, letting it cool.

While I ate my dinner and made small talk with Martin, since we both needed a break from the far more serious and pressing issues, one thought nagged at me. Someone attacked Mark and killed Cooper in the first twenty-four hours. Since then, Steele had gone silent. No more calls or threats. Did he get smart and decide not to call in the tips? Or did my request to be placed on the prison visitor list freak him out? Maybe that unexpected move made him rethink his plan and would buy us some time. But even with the police and FBI searching for clues and taking every precaution, I couldn't help but think if I didn't determine who his next target was, we'd be responding to another tragedy by morning. The assailant worked quickly, so why would he slow down now? He wouldn't, and as the seconds ticked by, I wondered when the next call would come in.

THIRTEEN

A member of the protection detail opened the door. "Parker?"

I blinked against the harsh overhead lights. Martin withdrew his hand from where he'd been stroking my hair, and I lifted my head off his lap and sat up. One glance at the monitors told me Mark's condition remained the same.

"What is it?" I asked, my voice gravelly.

"Someone wants to speak to you."

I rubbed my eyes. "I'll be right there."

The FBI agent nodded and closed the door.

I checked my phone, but there were no messages. Did they find another of Steele's victims? "What time is it?" I asked, my head swimming.

"Just after five," Martin said.

"This can't be good." I took a deep breath, wondering who'd been killed. I didn't think I'd survive losing any more friends or former colleagues. After considering locking myself in the bathroom and refusing to come out, I resigned myself to whatever awaited on the other side of the door. By now, it was too late to do anything except find the person responsible. And I would.

Sensing something was wrong, Martin got up to stretch

his legs and followed me out of the room. He probably figured I needed the moral support. The FBI agent pointed to a man waiting near the elevator. I headed for him while Martin lingered near the nurse's station where he could keep an eye on me.

"It's about damn time," Special Agent Eddie Lucca said. He looked me up and down. "I figured you wanted to make yourself presentable. Guess I was wrong."

"Did you come all this way just to bust my chops? What's going on, Lucca?"

"I came to see how Jablonsky is. You never called me back." Lucca glanced into the room I just left. "I'm not on the approved list yet, so how is he?"

"Stable, but it's serious."

Lucca nodded. "I heard what happened to Cooper."

"Yeah."

He watched my expression. "I take it you were there."

"Just for the aftermath. Steele called me from Cooper's phone, but we were too late. Again." I took an unsteady breath. "He's fucking with me. I just have no clue how he's doing it."

"Then it's a good thing I'm here."

"Why are you here?"

"You called and asked for my help, remember? And the great Alexis Parker never asks for help, so I knew you must be in real trouble."

"I didn't ask you to hop on the first flight out."

"It wasn't the first flight."

"You shouldn't be here. The city's a dangerous place, especially for FBI agents. Remember Francisco Steele? He's killing agents. I just haven't figured out how."

"Well, unless you pulled a badge out of a crackerjack box since the last time we spoke, you need me here. So quit bitching and say thank you."

"Careful, boy scout, it sounds like you're looking to break some rules. If you keep this up, they'll take away your merit badges. Maybe more than that. You don't want to follow me down that rabbit hole. Private security is too gray an area for you."

"Aww, Parker, I never knew you cared," he mocked.

"Plus, I'm not officially here. I took some personal time and thought I'd volunteer to help. With Jablonsky out of commission and the Bureau treating you like persona non grata, you need my help."

"You can help from a distance. Steele's on the warpath. You need to go back to D.C. Your wife and kid don't need to lose a husband and father."

"The Marshals moved them to an undisclosed location and are keeping a close eye on them," Lucca said. "That's why I didn't leave the moment you called. I had to take care of them first. They're okay for now. But we have to find whoever's responsible, or they'll never be safe. None of us will."

"Did Steele contact you too?" I asked, realizing I never called Lucca with the update that I'd promised.

"No, but Kendall did. He released a list of potential targets. My name's on it, just like every other agent who worked the case, but since you and I used to be partners, Kendall figures Steele will send someone after me or my family next. Based on the intel we have, I don't disagree."

"Neither do I, which is why you should be at home with your family. I told you I don't want to be responsible for your untimely death. You were lucky to have escaped unscathed the first time we worked together. You shouldn't tempt fate again. I'm sorry I called. I don't have many friends left with access to the reports and files."

Lucca tried not to grin. "I always knew we were friends."

"Only in the broadest sense of the word."

"Regardless, this is our mess. We made it together. We clean it up together." He jerked his chin toward the nurse's station. "Do you need to tell your babysitter you're leaving?"

"Babysitter?" I turned to see Martin watching our exchange and waved him over. "Eddie Lucca, meet James Martin."

Recognition dawned on Lucca's face. "Nice to finally meet you."

"Likewise," Martin said, "though not under these conditions. I thought you transferred to D.C."

"I'm just here to help out," Lucca said. "Alex called, so

here I am. What choice did I have? It's not like she understands the word no."

Martin grinned. "Glad it's not just me."

"Boys, I'm standing right here. And for the record, I'm tired and pissed." I gave Lucca a look. "And don't start that shit. I told you to go home. You're the one who's incapable of listening."

"At least I follow orders."

"Does Kendall know you're here or why you're here?" I challenged. "I doubt he'd see this as you following orders. You're going to lose your job over this. Go home, Eddie."

"Not a chance." Lucca looked at his watch. "We need to get moving. Are you ready?"

"I guess. I just hope you know what you're doing." I turned to Martin. "Call me if anything changes. I'll get back here as soon as possible."

"I will, sweetheart." He gave me a peck on the cheek and whispered in my ear, "It's nice to know you talk about me to your friends." He pulled away, a self-satisfied grin on his face. Despite the circumstances, Martin always handled meeting new people with poise and charm. "Just be careful. Both of you." He nodded to Lucca.

"Will do," Lucca said. "I'll make sure she comes back in one piece."

"Thank you." Martin shook Lucca's hand.

I stepped into the elevator beside Lucca. "I take it you have a plan, boy scout."

"Isn't that part of the code?"

"It's five a.m. I've barely slept in the last two days. And I'm about as emotionally drained as humanly possible, so it isn't wise to piss me off."

"It never was," Lucca said.

"Yet, you do it all the time."

"Fine, I'll tell you my plan. And then you can tell me if it's the same as yours. We head to the prison and speak to Steele."

"Sounds good, but what if he doesn't want to see me?"

"It doesn't matter. I have a badge. He has to see me, and since you just so happened to tag along, I guess that means he has to see you too. See how simple that is?"

I chuckled. "I guess so." And had I not been so exhausted, I would have realized it before asking such an asinine question.

The elevator doors opened, and Lucca glanced at me from the corner of his eye. "We haven't talked much since my transfer back to D.C. But for what it's worth, the Bureau lost a good agent."

"I'm surprised to hear you say that. Cooper's death hit us all hard, but you led the investigation to find the mole at the OIO. I didn't think you still considered him a good agent."

"Not Cooper." We exited the hospital and strode toward the parking lot. Lucca clicked the unlock on the fob, causing the lights to flash on his rental car. "I meant you."

"You know I wanted out. I just didn't realize my time served would come back to bite us in the ass. Kendall won't temporarily reinstate me. He won't even tell me what's going on. I have no idea what kind of progress they've made. I'm working with the PD, but I don't think Kendall's sharing much intel with them either. You have access to the records, evidence collection, old reports, files, databases. You know more about what's going on from the Bureau's side of things than I do."

Lucca stared over the roof of the car, noting the men who followed us out of the hospital. "Are those friends of yours?"

"Just give me a minute." I called off the Cross Security team, promising to personally clear it with the boss as soon as he got to the office. Then I climbed into the passenger seat of Lucca's rental. "Ready."

During the drive, we went over the case. We spoke about the original investigation into the KXDs, Bard, and Francisco Steele, and then we discussed the two more recent crime scenes. Lucca had barely been briefed. For the moment, I possessed more information about the unknown assailant. But he had more details about the cartel and the gang's other out-of-state affiliates.

"The cartel has hitters, but they wouldn't seek revenge. If I'm wrong and the unsub is working for them, then Steele's calls are just distraction tactics to keep our eye off the ball," Lucca said.

"I don't think Steele would agree to that. After we arrested him, he flipped on everyone except Bard. That's the only person he's loyal to. He wouldn't put his ass on the line for anyone else."

"Any idea why he suddenly decided to get revenge?" Lucca asked. "He's already spent over eighteen months in prison. According to what I've seen, he's been a model inmate. He got a sweetheart deal, a reduced sentence, and if he stays out of trouble, he'll be breathing fresh air a lot sooner than he deserves. Why would he jeopardize it now?"

"I don't know. He's crazy. Irrational. He goes after what he wants, when he wants it. He has poor impulse control." I thought about that one evening in Steele's apartment, shuddering at the thought of what might have happened had the phone not interrupted Steele from taking exactly what he wanted from me.

"But he has a firm sense of self-preservation."

"So he'll do just about anything to save himself. That doesn't explain why he's killing federal agents."

"Maybe he figures this is the best time to get what he wants. After all, he has an airtight alibi."

"I don't know," I hedged. "We're missing something. Maybe something happened that set him off."

"Could be."

"Davis told me Jablonsky opened an investigation into drug activity and possible cartel connections in the city. The KXDs were just a local gang, but they got their raw materials directly from the source. Do you think that's what set everything in motion?"

"It all depends on who's orchestrating the hits, but my money's on Steele."

"Mine too."

Lucca looked at me until I met his eyes. Then he turned his attention back to the road. "For all intents and purposes, Francisco Steele thought he owned Alexia Nicholson. He controlled where she worked, how much she worked, if she turned tricks on the side, if she got high, and where she scored."

"I never turned any tricks," I snapped.

"That's semantics. As sexist and disgusting as it is, he believed he had power over you. That's why he tested you and put you into those terrible situations. And you weren't in a position to say no. You had to deliver."

"I also raided the KXD facilities and arrested his ass."

Lucca pointed at me but kept his eyes on the road. "And that's what nearly destroyed him. Steele's not a man who gives up power or control. He allowed Bard to have power over him, but no one else in the gang did. Prisons are different. Inmates control one another. There's an entire hierarchical system within, but typically, the warden, the COs, they're the top dogs."

"Steele wouldn't like that."

"No, he wouldn't, which is why he's acting out. He needs to take back control."

"That's why he's targeting us."

"You, specifically. But yes, that's why he's targeting anyone who participated in his demise." Lucca had always been a better analyst than field agent. Though, I had no intention of telling him that. "We just have to find out how he's pulling it off."

Lucca drove up to the gate, handed his credentials to the guard, and was directed where to park. He pulled the car into an empty space and let out a breath, watching the first rays of sunshine brighten the horizon. He placed his gun in the center console and shut the lid, seeing no reason to take it inside where it would be held by the guards on duty.

After checking to make sure he had his credentials and the necessary paperwork, he tapped the digital clock on the dash with his finger. "What do you think prisoners do at seven a.m.? Eat breakfast? Shower? Play hide the soap?"

"I don't know. We should go inside and find out."

FOURTEEN

Lucca and I waited inside a secure room for the guards to deliver Steele to us. I looked around at the security measures in place, feeling antsy and trapped. Wire and thick metal bars covered the small window. Decidedly, I didn't like prisons.

The door buzzed, and I turned, watching two guards escort a shackled man in a prison jumpsuit inside. The prisoner took a seat at the table and stared up at us while one of the guards secured the bindings and the other stood in front of the door. The prisoner looked up at me, smiled, the sun glinting off one silver tooth, and made a kissy face.

"Who the hell is this?" I asked.

The guard finished what he was doing and looked up. "The inmate you requested to speak to. This is Francisco Steele."

"No, it isn't," I said.

The guard looked at me like I was crazy and turned to Lucca, figuring the two of them could band together against the insane woman. Lucca stared at the prisoner for a long time. "Where's Francisco Steele?"

"I am Steele," the prisoner replied, keeping his eyes glued to me.

"See, this is Steele," the guard said again.

"In that case, you have a big problem," Lucca said. "I suggest you double-check."

"All right," the guard said, "wait here. If you have any problems..."

"Yeah, we know," I said.

Again, the guards went over the rules regarding our interactions with the prisoner. I tuned them out. Lucca liked rules. He could pay attention, if he felt so inclined. I took a seat across from the inmate. The numbers on his jumpsuit matched the inmate number assigned to Steele. In fact, the two did share an uncanny resemblance. They were roughly the same height and weight and had the same hair color, eye color, and skin tone. Even their faces were similarly shaped. But they weren't the same. The unruly facial hair masked the more obvious differences. I didn't know where Steele was, but having a doppelganger take his place must have been part of his plan.

"Who are you?" I asked.

"You don't recognize me, chica?"

I bristled, recalling Steele's pet name for me. "Where is he? He obviously told you to expect us. What else did he tell you?"

The prisoner chuckled before falling silent.

Lucca sat down beside me. "It won't take long to figure out who you really are, so why don't you go ahead and tell us why you took his place? Where's Steele?"

The prisoner didn't break. "I knew you'd come. I wondered why you didn't pay me a visit sooner, chica. We had such a great time together." Again, he made the same annoying kissy face, and I thought about knocking out the rest of his teeth so they'd all be silver.

Instead, I fought to keep my temper in check. "Did you? Do you even know who I am or what I'm going to do to you if you don't tell me where Francisco is?"

He snorted. Of course he knew my name, I'd called in my request prior to the visit, but he seemed familiar. Maybe we had a prior run-in. "You can't do shit to me. You're not a cop or a Fed. You're no one. And you have nothing on me." His gaze wandered over what little of me he could see. "I preferred you in the bikini top and the tiny sequined boyshorts. You sure as shit weren't much of a stripper, but memories of your lap dances still keep me warm at night."

Lucca glanced at me, probably afraid the prison guards would have to tear me off of the Francisco Steele impersonator. But I kept my cool. The more this asshole talked, the more likely he was to let something slip.

"Oh yeah, you liked that, huh? Maybe I should give you an encore performance right here. What was the name of that titty bar? I forget."

"The Black Cat." The prisoner leaned back. "Cheap brews and cheaper whores." He winked at Lucca. "You ever tap that ass? She's a real firecracker."

"Watch your mouth," Lucca warned.

The prisoner laughed. "Did she ever tell you about the night in my apartment? Or the handy in the car on the way back from the club? Bet those things didn't make it into the official report." The chains clanged as he made air quotes around official. "I bet if they came to light, you would have been discredited and I wouldn't be here right now." He glanced at Lucca. "Is that why she doesn't have a badge anymore? Because of misconduct?"

I couldn't figure out why this asshole was determined to prove he was Steele. I wouldn't fall for it, and neither would Lucca. Perhaps this was an attempt to discredit me in front of my former partner or make me question my sanity. But Lucca knew exactly what Steele looked like. He even testified against him in court, except this guy didn't know that.

"Francisco didn't tell you I'd be bringing a friend, did he?" I asked.

"I am Francisco," he spat.

"At best, you're a poor excuse. Francisco's smart and ruthless. And he holds grudges. He wouldn't forget the agents who testified against him."

"I am Francisco," he bellowed.

"So tell me, Mr. Steele," I jerked my chin toward Lucca, "what's his name?"

"I don't remember. There were too many of you. All you

suits look alike."

I gave him an evil grin. "Fine. In that case, why don't you tell my buddy here exactly what happened in your apartment? Don't be shy. I put the entire play-by-play in my report. I'm sure you ought to remember that. After all, you brought it up." I wasn't sure where I was going with this, but I'd do anything to get him to crack and tell me where Steele was.

"I don't kiss and tell, chica."

"We didn't kiss," I said.

"Maybe not, but you let me fuck you every which way." The prisoner stared defiantly at me. "And you begged for more."

I pushed away from the chair. "Is that what Francisco told you?"

"That's what happened." He made the kissy face again, and I shoved against the table, but it didn't budge on account of the bolts anchoring it to the floor.

"Alex, don't," Lucca warned. Before he could say anything else, the guards returned with a manifest. "Well?" Lucca stared at them expectantly.

"This is Francisco Steele." The guard handed Lucca the paperwork, complete with Steele's mugshot. "You're looking right at him."

"If this is Steele, what happened to his tooth?" Lucca asked. "Francisco Steele doesn't have a silver tooth, at least he didn't the last time I saw him." The guard shrugged, which was the least helpful thing he could possibly do. "Do you have a fingerprint scanner?"

"I think so," the guard said.

"Get it," I urged.

"Ma'am, I don't think–"

"That's right. You don't think," I said, exasperated. "And you don't want to think one of your inmate's isn't who he's supposed to be because that means someone screwed up. But this isn't Steele, so you need to fix it. Now get the damn scanner."

"Please," Lucca said, though his please didn't sound particularly friendly.

The guard mumbled something under his breath but

agreed after Lucca threatened to have his boss call a few higher-ups in the BOP and have them sort this out instead. Again, we waited. This time, another prison guard remained in the room, but he didn't speak to us and we didn't speak to him.

The imposter kept quiet. He alternated his gaze from the tiny barred window to me and back again. He tried to remain cool, like this was no big deal, but he was starting to sweat. Eventually, he kept his eyes glued to me, not that I could blame him. He probably hadn't seen a woman in quite some time, and after the switcheroo he and Steele pulled, any hope of an early release, or any other kind of release, just went out the window.

The guard returned with the handheld scanner, forced the prisoner's fingertips against it, and waited for the results to display on the screen. "This can't be right," the guard said. He showed the results to his colleague, and the two stepped into the hallway. Lucca followed to see what was going on.

"Busted," I said.

"Whatever."

"The jigs up. Who are you, and where's Steele? I won't ask you again."

"Fuck off."

I gave him an evil grin. "Is that with two 'f's or a v? I want to make sure I have the correct spelling."

The prisoner glared daggers at me. "You're gonna die, bitch. And it ain't gonna be pretty, and it sure as hell won't be fast. You got a smart mouth. I'm sure we'll find a better use for it before all is said and done."

"If I had a dime." I sat down and leaned back, crossing my arms over my chest as if I had all the time in the world. "So Fuckoff, where's Steele? How long have you been pretending to be him?"

Unfortunately, he was smart enough to keep his mouth shut. So we stared at one another for five minutes. I couldn't make him talk, though several creative attempts came to mind, most of which involved breaking his fingers or similar appendages. But the screaming would bring the guards, and that would interrupt the festivities.

"Parker," Lucca said, "the warden wants to speak to us."

"Funny, I want to have a word with him too." I gave Fuckoff a final look, but he still wouldn't crack. That probably had more to do with him already serving time rather than my ability to intimidate, or at least that's what I told myself as we were buzzed through the sealed doors and met by a different prison guard who led us down a back hallway and up several sets of stairs until we reached the warden's office.

"Warden Schuster's on his way. Have a seat," the guard said. From his tone, I wondered if he thought we were also inmates.

"Thanks," Lucca said. The guard grunted and went out the door.

I leaned closer to Lucca, grasping the arm of his chair when mine teetered dangerously to the side and nearly toppled over. Balancing on the only two stable chair legs, I asked, "Do we know what's going on? Do you know who's impersonating Steele?"

"Luther Vega."

"Vega," I squinted, repeating the name, "he's in the KXDs. I just ran across his name in one of the reports."

"He got arrested prior to the raids. According to prison records, he was released two weeks ago. The guards can't figure out why he's still here."

"He switched with Steele." My voice rose to a higher pitch. "Son of a bitch."

Lucca gestured with his palm that I lower my voice. "I know that. And you know that. What we need to figure out is how this happened."

"It doesn't matter." I thought back. "Steele was on laundry detail. He probably changed uniforms with Vega. They both grew out their hair and beards so they'd look like cavemen, and once they switched clothes, I doubt the guards could tell them apart."

"Or they paid the guards to look the other way," Lucca said.

"Or that." But I didn't care how it happened. There was only one thing I cared about. "If Vega's in here pretending to be Steele, that means Steele's out there. He shot Mark.

He killed Cooper. I have to find him." I knew it. This wasn't someone carrying out Steele's orders. This was Francisco himself.

"He prepped Vega," Lucca said. "Steele expected you to come here. Do you think he knows you're no longer with the Bureau? Vega knows, but that might be because of the request you made or things he heard the guards say."

"I don't know, but it doesn't matter." A sick thought entered my mind. "I have to go. We have to go. Steele's out there while we're in here. Who knows what he'll do while we're distracted?"

"All right," Lucca said, grabbing my forearm before I could bolt from the chair, "just take it easy. We'll listen to the warden, see what he can tell us, get a look at Steele's cell and belongings, Vega's too, and see if there are any clues. Then we'll take it from there."

"Kendall already requested all the information, so did the PD. Let's just go. Someone else can sort out this clusterfuck of a prison."

Lucca looked at me with kind eyes. "We'll make this quick, I promise. One step at a time, remember? We go where the evidence leads."

FIFTEEN

After speaking to the warden, searching Steele's cell, and getting copies of the surveillance footage and details on Luther Vega's release, we left the prison. Since Lucca had to turn all of this information over to Kendall, I didn't have a lot of time to review it. The PD would want to examine it, as well. And as soon as they got authorization and copies, I'd have more time with it. Still, we were on a clock. Steele remained at large. It wouldn't be long before he killed again. If there were any clues here, I had to find them now.

"I told Kendall and Moretti this was Steele's doing, but they wouldn't listen," I said.

"According to prison records, Steele was locked up tight. They didn't know."

"I knew."

Lucca kept his eyes on the road, but his Adam's apple bobbed. "You're not an agent. What you say doesn't carry the same weight it once did."

"They should have gone down there and checked. Why didn't any of them speak to Steele?"

"We beat them to it. Agent Davis had a meeting scheduled for ten a.m." Uncomfortable, Lucca tugged on his collar.

"That's why you wanted to get such an early start. You wanted to make sure I had a chance to speak to him. Rule breaker."

"I didn't do it for you. I did it for Jablonsky and the investigation. Steele called you. He wanted to speak to you. The best way to get more information out of Steele was to let you confront him."

"Except I didn't. Do you think Vega will contact Steele now that we know the truth?" I asked.

"Warden Schuster said Vega's going into isolation until they determine what happened. He won't have any phone or internet privileges and he'll be denied non-essential visitors until he's transferred into our custody and interrogated."

"That will make it more difficult for him to contact Steele, but it's not impossible. After all, he and Steele just pulled off the perfect prison break." Contraband in prisons was common place, and smuggled cell phones were no exception. If Steele could engineer his own escape by walking out the front door with the warden's blessing, I had to believe Vega possessed a cell phone to keep in contact with Steele. But we didn't find a phone or any other contraband in either of their cells. Though, by now, Vega's cell, the one Steele most recently had occupied, had been emptied, cleaned, and assigned to another inmate. It was impossible to figure out if anything in there even belonged to Steele.

"Why do you think Vega would voluntarily switch places?" Lucca asked. "This jeopardizes his future freedom. Two weeks ago, Luther Vega would have been a free man. Now he's facing additional charges, and accessory to murder, especially under the circumstances, will get him years, possibly decades, more time in prison."

"Steele probably didn't give him much of a choice. Vega's a KXD. From what I've seen, their loyalty runs deep."

"On account of the alternative being death," Lucca said. "That's one way to ensure employee retention."

"Do you think Vega will talk?" I asked, figuring he might be offered a plea deal if he provided us with material facts that would lead to Steele's capture.

"Depends on the incentive." Lucca pulled to a stop in front of the precinct where I asked him to drop me off. "It all depends on who Vega fears more, us or Steele. Keep in mind, we don't even know how much Vega knows about Steele's plan or who he wants to target. He might be willing to help us for a reduced sentence and protection, but he might not have anything valuable to offer in return. Steele's careful. He just pulled off the perfect escape. Do you think he'd jeopardize his masterplan by telling some nobody henchman? This isn't a cheesy movie with a dastardly, mustache-twirling villain. Steele's smarter than that."

"Steele is careful, smart, and ruthless, but he has a few personality quirks working against him. Hubris being one of them. His ego might not allow him to keep his perceived genius to himself."

"I don't know, Parker. I'm not sure Steele would share that information with anyone. He doesn't trust easily. It took a lot of time and effort for you to convince him otherwise, and even then, I'm not sure he ever truly trusted you. He wouldn't blab to some KXD foot soldier. They're beneath him. The only person he might tell would be Bard, and as far as we know, they've had no contact."

"True," I conceded, "but if he's holed up in some secret KXD drug den or lab, Vega might know which one. Have Davis speak to Bard. I doubt we'll get much, but Bard prided himself on being all mighty. Something might slip out while he's insulting our incompetence."

"The interview's already set up."

I let out a growl. "Why don't you just tell me everything Kendall has planned and save us both some time?"

"That's all I know. According to Kendall, you suggested he do these things. I thought you knew what was going on."

"Bullshit." But Lucca was the only agent willing to go out on a limb for me, so I didn't argue. I opened the car door. "You're parked in a fire lane. It's a good thing you're not a cop. You'd have to write yourself a ticket."

"Very funny." Lucca leaned closer, peering out the windshield to make sure we weren't being watched. "I'll call you as soon as I know something. Will you do the same this time?"

"Yes. I'm sorry about that. Too much happened in such a short time span, it just slipped my mind."

"I get it."

"Hey, Eddie, I told Kendall we're on the same side. The only thing that matters to me is stopping Steele. I know him better than most. Kendall's ban on sharing intel with me is just slowing down the process. Do you think you can do something about that?"

"I'll do my best to get him on board."

"Thanks." I closed the car door, but Lucca rolled down the window.

"No secrets between us from here on out. Agreed?"

"Agreed."

"Hey, Parker, be careful. We have no idea where Steele is, but he wants you dead."

"Have you looked in the mirror lately? Watch your back and your front." I turned and headed inside.

*   *   *

Lt. Moretti had transformed the major crimes unit into murder central. Every surface was covered with details on the case. Detective Thompson wheeled his chair across the floor to pin another photo to the corkboard.

I cleared my throat, but no one paid any attention. Apparently, that trick only worked for Lucien Cross. Instead, I rapped loudly against the closest desk. "I have an announcement." All eyes turned to me, and I wondered if I should have gone to Moretti with this first. Oh well, too late now. "Francisco Steele escaped from prison. I believe he shot SSA Jablonsky and killed Steve Cooper."

Moretti met my eyes. Thankfully, he believed me. "Does Kendall know?"

"Yes. The FBI's in the process of confiscating prison records."

"We already looked at the prison records. We have everything on Steele. According to Warden Schuster, Steele's still there."

"Steele switched places with Luther Vega." Then I told

Moretti everything I'd learned in the last few hours.

"All right, everyone, listen up. I know we already did this, but now I want everything we have on Luther Vega. He helped Steele escape, so let's get workups on him, Steele, and the rest of the KXDs. We need BOLOs out on Steele. Parker said when he left the prison he looked like a homeless caveman, so we need security footage from the day Steele walked out a free man. Let's get those images blown-up and passed around, along with his mugshot and a few additional renditions. Jacobs, get copies of everything and go talk to Jablonsky's neighbors again. Report back and then rinse and repeat over at Steve Cooper's place and the Stop N' Shop. Maybe we'll get lucky and someone will remember seeing him."

"Yes, sir," Jacobs said.

Moretti picked up the phone and told IT to rerun everything again as soon as the new comparisons were in their hands. "Did someone pick Steele up from prison?"

"I don't know," I said. "I didn't get a chance to look at the footage."

Moretti grumbled to himself. "I'll get on the horn with Kendall and expedite this thing. In the meantime, Thompson, call the DA's office. Update them and make sure we have warrants and documentation for everything and anything. Jablonsky's one of theirs, but this is our case."

"On it, LT." Thompson slid back to his desk and picked up his phone.

"Parker, you probably know Steele the best. Get started on tracking down his contacts. Someone must have seen him or heard from him. Let's make sure we know about it. You also know where the KXDs operated. When you finish coming up with that list, speak to someone in gangs. Tell them I sent you. I want you to run through all the possible locations where Steele might be holed up. Vega's place, crack houses, whatever. Find him."

"Yes, sir."

Moretti barked out a few more commands, but I'd already been given my mission. I pulled out the list I had started the moment I recognized Steele's voice and took a seat behind Nick's desk. He and Heathcliff were conducting a follow-up with Renee to see if she knew anything that could help. That meant I had unfettered access to several databases. But given what happened this morning, I had little faith in the prison system. Still, I couldn't exactly go visit twenty-something inmates and fingerprint them all, though that might be something Lucca could do. For now, I had to trust the information on the screen.

After I completed my list of Steele's acquaintances, I called the office and updated Cross on the situation. Under any other circumstances, I wouldn't read the private security firm in on an ongoing police investigation, but this was personal. And any hang-ups I might have went out the window the moment Steele shot Mark.

"I'll let you know what I find," Cross promised, "just don't tell the cops where you got your intel."

Then I went to speak to the detectives in the gangs unit, and we went over every detail on the KXDs for nearly an hour. But gangs didn't possess any information I didn't already know. Patrol units would check out their previous locations and hangouts again and squeeze whoever they found for information on Steele's whereabouts, but I knew they wouldn't find anything. Steele wouldn't be stupid enough to repeat previous mistakes. He had this planned. Every step. Every location. Every hit. *You know him better than anyone.* Moretti's words reverberated in my ears. I had to figure this out. I needed to build a profile and not just focus on potential future victims. I just hoped it wouldn't be a waste of time.

Back in the major crimes unit, I found a small rolling white board and started with the first phone call, the things Steele said, what he'd done, and the limited number of clues he left behind. He followed the same pattern when it came to Cooper. He did it like that for a reason. He knew we wouldn't be able to catch him. But the game had changed. I just didn't know if Steele realized it.

After killing Cooper, Steele took extra precautions. He knew we were on to him. Federal agents and police officers who'd been involved in the drug raids and the busts were watching their backs. Some had protection. He couldn't strike as easily. He should have saved Cooper for last. *No, Parker, he's saving you for last*, my inner voice reminded me.

"Dammit." I'd gotten distracted again. I had to focus on where he'd hole up until he zeroed in on his next target. So where would he go? Where would he be safe?

I stared at the blank white space on the board. Steele had evaded arrest for weeks before we finally busted him. And he'd been out for almost two weeks before he attacked Mark. Steele wasn't hiding; he was watching.

"Is anyone checking Steele's old apartment building or Vega's place?" I asked.

"Patrol's on it," Thompson said. "Do you believe he'd go home?"

"I don't know where he'd go, but knowing Steele, after spending time in prison, he'd want to live like a king."

"That shitty apartment isn't exactly the Taj Mahal," Thompson said. He clicked a few more keys. "I'll run his financials and check for recent activity. The pittance the prisons give you when they kick you isn't much of anything. So if Steele didn't already have cash stashed somewhere, he'd have to do something to get some. I'll follow the money."

"Good thinking." A thought shot like lightning through my brain. "Steele emptied Mark's wallet and stole his credit cards. Plastic we can track, but cash we can't. He might have repeated the process at Coop's. Good catch, Thompson."

The detective gave me a funny look. "You feeling okay?"

"Not really."

"Figured," he said and went back to work.

Steele knew about Mark's key. He knew Cooper couldn't leave the apartment. He must have been keeping tabs on them. But from where?

Reaching for the phone, I called Jacobs. He was still checking things out in Jablonsky's neighborhood, so I grabbed my stuff and figured I'd head over to Cooper's to look around. If Steele had been watching Cooper, I had to find out from where. He might have left something behind or some clue as to who else he planned to attack.

"Where are you going, Parker?" Moretti called.

"To check on something."

He nodded. "O'Connell go with her."

"Yes, sir," O'Connell said, appearing in the doorway of the conference room. He crossed the bullpen and grabbed his jacket.

"How did things go with Renee?" I asked.

"She doesn't know anything. She never heard of the KXDs or Francisco Steele. That happened years after she and Jablonsky split. What we actually wanted to know was if she'd ever been to his townhouse or if she knew about the spare key or if any of his neighbors had a key or access to his place."

"I doubt she'd know. Martin doesn't even know that."

"Yeah, but we still had to ask," O'Connell said. "When we called her in today, I think we scared the living daylights out of her. She kept apologizing for going to the hospital and the allegations she made. Just thought you'd like to know."

"I don't get it." I eyed him curiously. "You know what else I don't get is why Moretti put two detectives on that. Your time could be better spent elsewhere."

"In that case, it's a good thing he hired a consultant." O'Connell waited until we were out of the building and inside his car before he said, "Moretti wants us to keep an eye on Heathcliff and keep him inside and out of trouble. So we conducted the interview and pulled up the profiles on the KXDs for him to go over again. Steele wants Derek dead. We don't have any doubts about that. It's just a matter of time, so the busier we keep Heathcliff, the safer he'll be. He doesn't do well when he gets antsy, just like someone else I know."

"Derek's not stupid. He must realize what's going on."

"Regardless, he has a job to do. And unlike you, he almost always follows orders." O'Connell looked at me over the rim of his sunglasses. "So don't be a bad influence on him right now. We want to keep him safe, even if that means he stays behind a desk."

"Hey, I would never intentionally jeopardize his safety."

"I know. But I also know he'd do just about anything for you." O'Connell stared out the windshield. "We all would."

"I don't want you to. I didn't ask you to. That's not fair, Nick. Don't put that on me."

"I wasn't. I was just..."

"Fine. Whatever. Look, I'm following orders. See? Moretti told me to find out where Steele's hiding. That's what I'm doing."

"Not by yourself. Steele's dangerous, Parker. You're on the hit list too."

"I can take care of myself."

O'Connell pointed a finger in my face. "That's exactly what I'm talking about. You're a police consultant. You can't make an arrest, so before you go anywhere, you take one of us with you, got it?"

"Yeah, yeah."

"I'm serious. What happens if you find Steele and one of us isn't around to make the arrest?"

I'd probably kill him. But that was a knee-jerk reaction. And too dark of a thought to contemplate, despite the fact it might be the truth. Instead, I bit my tongue before the words left my mouth. "I don't know."

"That's why I'm here."

"Oh. I thought it was because my car's at the hospital."

He chuckled. "That too."

SIXTEEN

I stood inside Cooper's apartment. The scene had been cleared and released. Police tape still hung across the door, but that didn't deter us. We had clearance to be here.

From the living room window, I searched the street below for a vantage point. Then I looked at the buildings across the way to see which windows had unobstructed views. "We should get a list of tenants in that building," I pointed to the only one with a clear line of sight into Cooper's apartment. "Steele might have had a spotter."

"Do you think Cooper left the blinds open?" O'Connell asked.

"Wouldn't you?" A small part of me felt guilty. If I had done things differently, handled matters differently, Cooper might still be alive right now. "These windows gave him a glimpse of the outside world."

"True, but he might have found that depressing." O'Connell went into the kitchen and looked out the window. "Cooper had been sent to a medium security facility. It's not like he'd been in solitary."

"What about the KXDs? Did any of Steele's associates serve time with Coop?"

"Not that I've found. It doesn't look like the attack in

prison had anything to do with Steele's vendetta."

"Do you think Steele knows Cooper had been fired from the Bureau and arrested?"

"I dunno." O'Connell returned to the living room and stood beside me, making a note of the apartment building's address and the storefronts across the way.

I pressed my forehead against the glass to get a better look. At least two of them were empty. One was boarded up.

"It's not fair," I said. "Coop suffered enough. Steele didn't have to kill him." My voice caught in my throat. I held my breath and kept my gaze focused on the street below, waiting to regain my composure. A pedestrian turned the corner, passed the storefront, and disappeared from sight.

Leaving the living room, I went into the bedroom to get a better view of the adjacent street. The boarded-up storefront was situated on the corner. The front faced the living room window, and the side entrance provided a decent view of Cooper's bedroom. I returned to the living room, doing my best to keep my eyes on O'Connell and not the blood spatter on the walls or the stains on the floor.

"I have a hunch. Let's check out that shop." Not waiting for O'Connell's protest, I left the apartment.

O'Connell caught up to me in the stairwell. "The shop is boarded up. Give me a minute to contact the owner. We need permission to check inside."

"Sure, no problem."

We left the apartment building and waited at the crosswalk. Once the walk sign illuminated, we crossed. I scanned the area for surveillance cameras but didn't spot any in the vicinity. O'Connell read the number off the 'space for rent' sign and dialed. While he did that, I circled the shop. The front had been boarded up, except for one corner. I tried to peer inside, but I couldn't see much on account of the sun's glare on the dirty window. So I went around to the side. Instead of flimsy boards, these windows had been papered over and several people had taken the liberty of taping flyers to them.

The advertisements announced the usual services,

discounts, and restaurants. From what I could tell, no one had written anything on them. A few flyers had pull tabs at the bottom with phone numbers, so I grabbed one of each, just in case Steele used this as a means of communicating with his associates, and searched for a break in the paper. The paper in one of the panes had been torn away, allowing me to glimpse the interior.

I cupped my hands around my face and pressed against the glass. From what I could tell, this used to be a dress shop. Naked mannequins and empty clothing racks were shoved against the front window in haphazard piles. Random bits of trash covered the floors, along with a stack of going out of business signs. Just behind the counter, a cot and an army surplus blanket caught my attention, but I couldn't see anything else from here.

"The real estate agency is sending someone with the key," O'Connell said. "Do you want to grab a bite while we wait? I saw a café next to that apartment building you wanted us to check out."

"I'll wait here. We don't want to miss the guy," I said.

But O'Connell wasn't buying it. "Did you see something inside?"

"I'm not sure. Someone might have been sleeping behind the counter."

"Maybe a homeless guy found a way in."

"Yeah, maybe."

"Parker, we have to wait. Moretti wants everything done by the book."

"That's why I need you to get me a cup of coffee. Maybe something iced. One of those blended drinks with whipped cream and chocolate shavings or whatever takes the longest for the barista to make. I don't really care. I'll drink anything. In fact, don't rush. Sit down and eat some lunch. You work hard, Nick. You deserve a break."

"Alex," O'Connell warned, "no."

"C'mon, just go get some lunch. Coffee. Whatever. We don't have time to wait for the key. Steele could already be in the midst of killing his next target."

O'Connell weighed his options. "I gotta hit the head anyway. You will wait right here."

"Yes, sir."

"Okay." But we both knew it was a lie. However, it was good enough to give the detective plausible deniability. I waited for him to enter the café before I tugged on the shop's door. Of course it was locked, but it didn't hurt to check. I pulled out my set of lock picks and went to work. Several people passed me while I manipulated the tools inside the lock, but no one said or did anything. I wondered if they would call the cops.

When the final tumbler clicked into place, I pulled on the handle and stepped into the shop. It was dark, but the brown paper was thin enough to allow light inside. With gloved hands, I flipped the light switch. The harsh fluorescents only emphasized the dusty, abandoned interior. The eighteen naked mannequins watched as I looked for clues.

The cot I spotted wasn't actually a cot. It was a few long benches, probably from the fitting rooms, positioned end to end and side by side to form roughly the same size and shape as a prison bunk. A blanket sat atop the makeshift bed in a heap. One tattered side hung over the edge. I put on a pair of gloves and lifted the blanket, but I didn't find anything except a ripped cushion which had probably been used as a pillow.

Next, I checked the bathroom. A rust-colored stain ringed the sink with splatters against the otherwise bright white fixture. I checked the toilet, but the water in the bowl looked clean. The pipes and faucet looked new, so I didn't think the stains were rust. Blood, perhaps. And if it was blood, was it Cooper's or Mark's?

Since I wouldn't be able to determine that without assistance from CSU, I left the bathroom and checked the only remaining area in the shop – the dressing room. I tugged open the accordion doors.

Bloody clothing filled a dirty plastic bag from the Stop N' Shop. It had been shoved into the corner of the dressing room. I didn't remove the items from the bag, since that would be considered tampering with evidence, but I poked around inside with the tip of my pen. A switchblade sat on top of the pile. CSU could verify it was the weapon used to

kill Cooper, but, in my gut, I already knew that's what it was.

I took a breath, trying to calm my rage. Steele killed Cooper and then came here to relish in the aftermath of his handiwork. He probably tore the paper away from the corner window and watched us scramble to save Cooper and find his killer. I hated myself for not realizing how close I'd been to the predator. I could have ended this, if only I had paid more attention. "Dammit."

I'd been off my game since the first call. I needed to think. To pay attention. This couldn't happen again. "All right, Parker, you have to do better." He must have left some clue behind to indicate his next target. It had to be here. I just had to find it. Resisting the urge to ransack everything, I forced myself to work methodically.

The plastic bag came from the Stop N' Shop, just like the bag Steele had taped around Cooper's head. There was no doubt left. Steele had been there. I called Det. Jacobs and told him to get everything he could out of the clerks and the owner and to search the men's room and anyplace else Steele might have visited in and around the convenience store. He'd been there, so we needed to know what he did and what he bought.

After hanging up, I checked behind every nook and cranny, around the fixtures, and in the vents. Steele didn't leave anything else behind, except his bedding. Carefully, I removed the olive-colored wool blanket from the padded benches and held it up. Nothing. I flipped it over to the other side and shook it out. Still nothing.

I dropped it to the floor in a heap and focused on the torn cushion. It had come from a chair in the dressing room. The cushion had been sewn into the chair, so when Steele removed it, he had to tear it free. Foam stuffing spilled out of three sides, the commercial fabric barely containing it.

My phone rang, and I jumped, dropping the cushion onto the row of benches. Cautiously, I pulled out the device, terrified to check the display. Luckily, it was O'Connell.

"The real estate guy just pulled up. I asked him to meet

me inside the café. You said you'd meet us here, right?" O'Connell asked, playing dumb. "Your coffee is waiting for you."

"I said I'd meet you outside." Hanging up, I picked up the blanket and put it back on the benches and hurried out the front door. I didn't have time to lock the shop again, but I stayed close. Two minutes later, O'Connell and a guy who didn't look old enough to drive came down the sidewalk. "We need to get inside."

O'Connell took the key from the kid, stuck it in the lock, and gave it a turn. After removing the key, he handed it back to the kid and tugged on the handle. The kid tried to step inside, but O'Connell put up an arm. "Sorry. This will only take a minute, but you should wait out here. In case we find something, you don't want to contaminate the scene."

"No, sir," the kid said, shoving his hands into his pants pockets and making the sides of his sports coat pucker outward. He looked like a little boy playing dress up in his father's suit. "I'll wait right here. Give me a holler if you need something."

"Thanks." O'Connell held the door, and I stepped inside. "What does your sixth sense say, Parker?"

"Start with the dressing rooms." I pointed to the accordion doors, which I'd forgotten to close. "Then the bathroom sink." I took a breath. "And lastly, the makeshift bed behind the counter." I bit my lip while O'Connell crossed the room. "I already called Jacobs and told him to be extra thorough. I have no doubt Steele visited the convenience store before offing Cooper."

"He probably wanted to get some snacks and beer." O'Connell knelt beside the bag, opening it and sifting through the contents with gloved hands. "Looks like we found the knife used to stab Cooper."

"I'd call it a murder weapon."

"The bag killed him, but this is a contributing factor. CSU will have to analyze the blood and check for prints."

"Anything else in there?" I asked.

O'Connell glanced over his shoulder at me. "Clothing. A pair of men's jeans, a t-shirt, and a black jacket."

"Anything in the pockets?" I asked.

O'Connell checked each one carefully. "A baggie, empty, but with some white residue."

"It's probably heroin. That's what Steele had been into."

O'Connell called it in, wandering into the bathroom while he spoke on the phone. He came out a few moments later and checked behind the counter. By then, he concluded his call. "Let me tell the realtor we'll need to hold on to the key for a little while."

While he spoke to the kid, I knelt on the floor and peered out the window. It provided an ideal view of Cooper's apartment building. From here, Steele would have seen everything – the police cars, the ambulance, the FBI vehicles, Cross Security's team, and me. I wondered how long he stayed here after killing Cooper, just watching and waiting.

I stood, giving the trash and the crumpled papers in the corners of the room an uncomfortable look. Steele might have jerked off afterward. He had always been unstable. Violence and brutality excited him. It turned him on, so did danger and drugs. And something told me killing only increased the effect. After the way he tortured and killed Cooper, he must have been ready to burst. I shared my theory with Nick when he returned.

"Sicko." O'Connell put his hands in his back pockets and looked around. "I didn't spot any cameras outside the building. I'm guessing Steele didn't get caught on camera, but it might explain how he easily slipped across the street and up Cooper's fire escape without getting seen."

"What about traffic cams? Or the other shops? Even if they only have indoor security cams, they might have caught something through the front windows."

"It's worth checking." O'Connell surveyed the room. "This place is a mess. At least Steele's DNA is in the system. So are his prints. He must have left something behind that will place him here. We just have to analyze everything, but I bet we'll find our proof." O'Connell turned to face me. "Was the door locked?"

"Yes. You can lock it from the inside if you're staying inside, but to lock it from the outside, you have to use a key."

He checked the lock. "I can see that. So how'd Steele get in and out?" O'Connell went down the hall toward the employee bathroom. "Did you check the emergency exit?"

"Only that it was locked." I'd been afraid to open it in case it tripped an alarm.

O'Connell turned the knob. The exterior didn't have a handle, just a thin metal plate screwed flat against it to secure the door. Scratch marks marred the paint around the edges of the plate, where someone pried the door open with a metal object. "These look fresh."

"Guess we know how he got inside."

O'Connell made a note to check the alleyway for surveillance equipment, but I didn't hold out much hope we'd find anything. And even if we did, what would it matter? Steele had been here, but he wasn't here now. And he had no reason to return.

"I wonder if he hung around Jablonsky's place to watch the aftermath," I said.

"Once I sign the scene over, we'll take a ride and check it out. We're getting closer. We'll get him."

"Before or after he kills again?" I spun, sucking in air. "This was supposed to lead us to his next target. Instead, all it did was reinforce my worst fear."

"What's that?" O'Connell asked, his voice hushed, almost like he didn't want to ask the question.

"Steele's enjoying this. He won't stop until he's satisfied. And he won't be until we're all dead."

SEVENTEEN

As far as we could tell, Francisco Steele entered Mark's townhouse through the back door, went up the steps, shot him twice, and left the same way he came in. Nothing indicated Steele hung around afterward. The police had canvassed the neighborhood, questioned Mark's neighbors, and scouted the area. All signs pointed to the shooter being long gone. But we checked anyway. However, without any nearby abandoned buildings, Steele would have had a much harder time finding refuge near the action.

Nick made a few calls to make sure none of the townhouses were vacant or empty the night of the shooting. A few were for sale, but the owners hadn't moved out yet. We showed them Steele's mugshot and the mock-ups the police department made, but they never saw him.

"I know it doesn't feel like it, but we're making progress." O'Connell parked in a reserved space in front of the hospital. "We know who's responsible. The prison is being searched. We're paying extra attention to places inside the prison where Steele and Vega had access, like the cafeteria, the library, the yard, and the laundry room where Steele worked. Moretti assigned a bunch of officers to go over all of Steele's communications, phone calls, everything again. The Feds are questioning Vega, and once they finish with him, I'll take a crack at him. He must know where Steele is or what else he has planned."

"You mean how many federal agents he plans to kill?" I couldn't contain the bitterness. "What about the Stop N' Shop?"

"Jacobs didn't come up with anything new. Nothing on the security footage, and no one admitted to seeing Steele."

"Dammit." I got out of the car and leaned against the door. "What about patrol? They were scouting locations. Has anyone spotted Steele? He was in prison. Shouldn't he be holed up inside a titty bar right about now? Or blowing his load with some whore he found on the corner?"

"You would think, but no one's spotted him yet." He came around the car and put an arm around my shoulders. "Come on, let me walk you in."

"That's not necessary."

"My wife would beg to differ. Plus, I want to see how Jablonsky's doing."

"He's breathing unassisted now."

"That's great."

"Yeah."

Nick gave me a sideways look. "You're supposed to be happy about that."

"I am. It's just...we won't know how bad it is until he wakes up."

"The doctors can only speculate right now. But from what Jen said, his scans are clean. Brain damage usually shows."

"Jen told you?"

O'Connell nodded. "Don't worry. I haven't said anything to anyone." He gave my shoulder a squeeze. "You know how I know he'll be okay?"

"How?"

"Because he has you."

"That doesn't mean shit. Ask Cooper. Ask Carver. Hell, ask Heathcliff. He could probably give you a list of times I've let him down."

O'Connell pulled me tighter into a sideways hug as we entered the hospital. "None of this is your fault. And none of that was your fault. Now you know what's going on. You're in the game, and no one in their right mind would ever bet against what you're capable of. I want you in my corner for every fight, and Jablonsky feels the same way. He'll be okay. Now stop this whole woe is me crap."

"I don't care about me, Nick. I care about him. About all of you. Steele called me. I have to stop this."

"Well, you have help. Plenty of it."

"I know. Lucca said he'd meet me here. He promised to keep me in the loop." I checked my watch. "I'll let you know if there have been any developments on Kendall's end."

"You don't trust the director to share with the department?"

"I'm not sure what he's doing, but he's gone out of his way to make it his mission not to share with me. And frankly, none of us have time for this bullshit."

"I didn't realize your break from the OIO went that badly."

"Neither did I." I pressed the button to call the elevator.

"Go on ahead. I'll meet you outside the ICU in about ten minutes. Maybe the protection detail will speak more freely if I'm not around. I should track down Jenny. I'll be in the doghouse otherwise."

I watched O'Connell head toward the ER while I waited for the elevator. Once it arrived, I stood to the side, giving the man in a wheelchair a wide berth. He smiled at me, and I returned it. At least someone had gotten good news today.

When I stepped out of the elevator, I didn't spot the protection detail. Mark's room was empty. Fear gripped my insides. I checked my phone. No calls from Martin. I gave the area another glance. No Cross Security team either. Where did everyone go? Every worst case scenario played out in my mind as I practically ran to the nurse's station.

"What happened? Where's Mark Jablonsky?" I asked the woman seated behind the counter.

"Hang on one second." She held up her finger, and I thought my head would explode.

"Mark Jablonsky," I repeated. "FBI agents were outside

his room. Where did everyone go?"

She continued typing with two fingers. "As you can see, I'm in the middle of something. You have to wait."

I braced myself against the counter, pressing so hard against it, I wouldn't have been surprised if it toppled over on top of her. "Where is he?" The walls were closing in. "Just tell me."

She hadn't even bothered to look at me. "You should speak to someone at the information center. I'm sure they can assist you. This is the ICU. We don't give out patient information here. In case you haven't noticed, I'm not your personal secretary."

I saw red, and the room spun. "I'd fire you if you were." If I'd been able to breathe and think rationally, I would have exercised more diplomacy, but I was already on edge. "Supervisory Special Agent Mark Jablonsky, I have to know if he's okay. Just tell me. Where is he? It's a matter of life and death."

"Like I haven't heard that one before," she retorted, her eyes still on the screen.

Another nurse came by to drop off a chart. Her smile was met by my most lethal glare. "Alexis, right?" she asked. She reached over the counter and grabbed a manila envelope. "Mr. Jablonsky was moved to our Step Down Unit." She smiled again. "The doctors are thrilled by his progress. Let me get you his room number." She went around the desk and typed the information into the computer and spouted out a number. "Oh, and a man left this for you. He turned it in to the lost and found, but someone down there recognized your name and had him bring it up here. I guess he just missed you."

"What man?" I asked.

"I'm not sure. He was tall, kind of rugged."

That described a lot of men I knew. Taking the envelope, I frowned at the odd shape. Maybe Lucca left me something, but why would he leave it at the lost and found? Opening the flap, I peered inside and pulled out a throwaway cell phone. Almost on cue, it rang.

I stared at it; a cold chill cut through me. Spinning, I checked the area, but no one was watching me. I checked the display, but the number was blocked. No data.

"Ah, perfect timing," she said.

"Who did you say left this?"

"Isn't it yours?" she asked. "The man said you left your cell phone at the coffee cart. He wanted to make sure you got it back."

"Describe him."

"I don't know. Around six feet, maybe a little taller. Fit. Shaved head. Dark beard. Aren't you going to answer that?" she asked.

"Did you get a name?" The ringing stopped.

"No." She turned to the other nurse. "Did he say anything to you, Mildred?"

The unhelpful nurse didn't even look up from the screen. Before she could respond, the phone beeped a text message alert. *Answer the phone, chica.*

Immediately, the phone rang again. "Notify hospital security and the police personnel stationed in the lobby. We need this hospital locked down. Do it quietly," I said.

The nurses stared at me like I was insane, but I didn't have time to explain. Stabbing the green answer button, I stepped away from the desk and searched the hallway for any sign of Francisco Steele.

"Hello?" Every part of me hoped I was wrong.

"Looks like you've had a busy day," Steele said. "At least you finally remembered me. I'm flattered."

"What do you want me to say, Francisco?" I reached into my pocket and sent a text to O'Connell. Steele was close. We needed additional security to Jablonsky's floor, and we needed to lockdown the hospital and search floor by floor until we found the sick son of a bitch. "Do you want me to tell you I never stopped thinking about you? Is that what you want to hear?"

"Don't play games with me, Alex. You can't manipulate me. Not this time. This time, I call the shots."

"Is that what you told Vega?" I wanted to call the authorities or Cross Security and have them run a trace, but I didn't know the burner's number. Without that, they couldn't do anything, and I couldn't pull the number off the phone while speaking to Steele.

"Admit it. That was pure genius. The perfect prison break. No one even knew I was gone."

"I did."

"Only because I told you. If I didn't tell you, you still wouldn't know." The intercom sounded in the background. Steele was still inside the hospital. "But I wanted you to know."

"Now I do. So what's next?"

He laughed. "That's for me to know and you to find out."

"Do you hear yourself?" I asked. "Damn, it sounds like you've been hung up on me this entire time."

"So what?" His voice went from hot anger to cold, calculating revenge. "You're my obsession. You have been since the moment I laid eyes on you, back when you were nothing but a desperate junkie willing to do anything for a fix."

"So why don't you scratch that itch? You know where I am. Why don't you come see me?"

He barked out another ugly sounding laugh. "I intend to."

My phone buzzed in my pocket, and I read O'Connell's reply. Patrol was standing guard at the exits. The FBI agents stationed in the Step Down Unit had been notified and were on high alert, and O'Connell and hospital security were going to start a floor by floor sweep until backup arrived. I finished my check of the ICU and entered the stairwell. Unsure if I wanted to go up or down, but down made more sense. The nurse said the man tried to leave my phone downstairs, so I'd work floor by floor in the opposite direction.

"What the hell are you waiting for?"

"Don't tempt me, chica," Steele warned.

"Why not? Afraid you won't be able to perform?"

He growled. "You know that's not true. You've seen what I can do. And I'm just getting started, but I can't decide who should be next. Any suggestions?"

My limited experience with hostage negotiation kicked in. Moretti was right. I knew Steele, which meant I should know how to get through to him and delay the inevitable. "Francisco, please."

"That's what I like to hear."

"Please," I repeated, letting the desperation eke out, "this is between us. You're pissed at me. Take it out on me. I fucked you over. I sold you out. Tell me what you want."

"This is my game. My rules. You don't tell me what to do."

"Fine. Tell me what to do."

"For starters, keep that phone on you at all times. When I call, you better answer. If you don't, I'll kill another one of your colleagues."

"Yeah, okay."

"You give that phone to the cops or Feds and I'll kill someone. This is between us. And only us. I don't want them in my business. Got it?"

"Yes, just please don't hurt anyone else."

"I never agreed to that." He snorted. "I heard Jablonsky might actually pull through. Don't get your hopes up. I already promised you I'd finish him off, and you should know, I keep my promises, unlike you."

I raced down the steps to the SDU and burst through the doors, expecting to find Steele somewhere on the floor. "I get it. You want to hurt me. So hurt me. Tell me where you want to meet. I'll be there."

"Not yet, but soon. First, I have someone else waiting who needs my attention."

EIGHTEEN

"Wait," I screamed into the phone, but Steele had already hung up. I tucked the burner into my pocket, unsure what I planned to do with it. First things first, I had to make sure Mark was alive and Martin was safe.

I looked around the unfamiliar SDU, immediately spotting Cross's security team. As I headed toward them, I checked the room numbers. 804. 805. According to the nurse upstairs, Mark was in 811.

"We have a situation," I said. "Francisco Steele's inside the hospital." I gave them a description and a brief breakdown of Steele's resume. "Keep your eyes peeled. The FBI assigned a detail to protect Jablonsky, but I want you to make sure they are who they claim to be and they're taking their jobs seriously. Also," I lowered my voice, "if anyone unfamiliar comes near James Martin, and I mean anyone, make sure you put yourselves between him and the stranger. Is that understood?"

"No problem," Vinnie, the head of Cross's team, said. "Lucien wants Martin protected at all costs."

"For once, the boss and I are in total agreement." I nodded to the men. "But for the sake of keeping the peace, let's not mention this to Mr. Martin."

"Yes, ma'am."

I cringed. "Call me Alex or Parker. Never ma'am."

"Yes, ma...Alex."

I looked down at my phone but found no messages from O'Connell. Before storming through the rest of the hospital in search of Steele, I approached room 811. Agent Samuels and a fresh-faced probationary agent stood on either side of the door.

"Samuels." I nodded to him.

"Parker." He introduced me to Benny Kwan. "I heard you have reason to believe the shooter's in the hospital. Anything we should know?"

I repeated the description the nurse gave me. "Detective O'Connell and hospital security are conducting a floor by floor search. Reinforcements are on the way. But I need you to stay vigilant. This guy is unstable and extremely dangerous."

"Is he armed?" Kwan asked.

"Best to assume so."

"Shaved head and dark beard," Samuels repeated. "What's he wearing?"

"I don't know. Honestly, I wouldn't invest too much in the shaved head and beard either. You've seen Steele's mugshots and the mock-ups, right? Those are just our best guesses, but he could look like anyone."

"All right," Samuels said. "We'll keep an eye out. O'Connell knows we're here if he needs help."

"Absolutely, but if you have to step away, make sure someone is guarding Jablonsky at all times."

"I'm aware of protocol, Parker," Samuels said. "Nothing else is going to happen to him."

"Good."

I pushed open the door, and Martin nearly jumped out of the chair, caught red-handed. He'd been reading the medical chart and making notes on his phone. He put the chart down. "He woke up. This morning, after you left. He wasn't awake long. Maybe five minutes."

"Really?" My heart crashed against my ribcage, threatening to shatter. "Is he..." I licked my lips, my voice a squeak. "Do we know if..."

Martin cradled my head in his hands and brushed his thumb against my cheek. "It's too soon to say. He wasn't entirely coherent, but that could be from the sedatives they're giving him. He kept saying the same thing. *Steele. Tell Alex it's Steele.*"

"It's a little too late for that."

"Despite his condition, Jabber's worried about you."

I smiled, biting my lip to hold everything in. "I know. And vice versa." I looked down at Mark, resting peacefully in the bed. "Why isn't he awake now?"

"They are keeping him heavily sedated." Martin rubbed the back of my neck, feeling the tension in my muscles.

"Why didn't you call me? When I got upstairs, I thought..." I swallowed. "You know what I thought."

"I'm sorry. God, I'm sorry." He stole a kiss, hoping that would smooth things over. "I didn't want to call because I knew seeing my name on the display would freak you out. I left a message with Mildred to tell you where we went."

"Mildred's a bitch." I shook that thought away. "Did you see anyone else? A strange man lingering near Mark's room? Or the ICU? Maybe down near the coffee cart?"

"I'm not sure."

I sucked in a breath. "Steele's here. He called me a few minutes ago. He's getting ready to move on his next target."

"You think it's Mark?"

"Maybe, but I think he's going after someone else. If his target's inside the hospital, it could be you or one of the cops or agents keeping an eye out. I don't even know if Steele knows who you are. Everything that happened that night happened so quickly. You never testified. You had no reason to, so you shouldn't be on his radar, unless he's seen us together. It's not safe here, handsome. Honestly, it's not safe anywhere."

"I'm not leaving," Martin insisted before I could even suggest such a thing. "I won't let Steele hurt Mark. If that asshole comes through the door, I'll fucking kill him. Had I known what would happen, I would have done it that night in your apartment when that animal attacked you. I could have prevented all of this from happening."

Martin wasn't a violent man, but I believed him. And he spent enough time training with a tactical team to possess the skills necessary to carry out such a threat.

"My hands have enough blood on them for both of us," I said. "Let's hope it doesn't come to that. In the meantime, I need to find out what's going on. I have to find Steele. I have to stop him from killing someone else. If anything happens, and I mean anything, call me."

He grabbed my arm before I could disappear out the door, pulled me into his chest, and kissed me hard. "Be careful. Jabber's afraid for your safety. And so am I."

"I always come back to you. Remember that." I stood on my tiptoes, kissed Martin quickly, and left him dazed in my wake. "Samuels, hold down the fort. Should anything happen to anyone inside that room, there will be hell to pay."

Two floors later, I ran into O'Connell and hospital security. "Uniforms are stationed at the main doors. Sgt. Rivers took another security team and started at the top floor. I haven't heard a word from him yet," O'Connell said, just as the stairwell door swung open and two uniformed cops and two members of hospital security stepped onto our floor. "Anything?" O'Connell called to them.

"No sightings," Rivers replied. "Did you clear this level?"

"Just finished," O'Connell said before introducing me to Rivers. "Did you check the roof?"

"We did, but there isn't street access. The chopper's on the pad, so he didn't use that as a means of escape. Only places we didn't look are restricted to authorized personnel only." Rivers studied me. "Are you sure Francisco Steele is here?"

"He was five minutes ago, but he said he had to go." I met Nick's eyes. "He's going after his next target."

"Shit," O'Connell spun in a circle, "we have to find him before the body count goes up. Tell me everything you know."

"When we spoke, I heard the intercom in the background. Right after that, he said he had someone waiting."

"The hospital intercom?" Jon, the head of hospital

security, asked.

"Yes," I said. "Can that be heard from outside?"

Jon thought for a moment. "We have speakers in the employee parking garage and our enclosed outdoor picnic area."

"Let's check those out," O'Connell said.

"Those areas are for authorized personnel only. Hospital staff has to swipe an ID to gain access."

"We need to see them anyway," O'Connell said, "and all other restricted areas."

"Whatever you need," Jon said.

"This would be easier if we could check your security footage at the same time. If we spot him on camera, we can follow him," I said.

"Sure," Jon said. "Tom, take the sergeant and his men upstairs and show them whatever they want."

"I'll radio if we find anything," Sgt. Rivers assured us.

We broke into two groups. I went with O'Connell, Jon, and another member of hospital security. For the first time, I noticed the labels on the doors and the electronic locks. Until now, I hadn't paid attention or I just didn't care. We returned to the main level. At the moment, everything looked sinister. Time was not on our side.

The security team led us down a hallway, just to the side of the information desk. With a quick card swipe, we were greeted by a concrete staircase on one side and a single elevator on the other. We took the stairs down to the parking garage.

"What about the morgue?" I asked, recalling it being in the basement of the hospital.

"That's on the other side. You can't access it from here," the security guard said. "This garage is walled in. Entirely separate."

"Does Jen park down here?" I asked Nick, who shrugged.

"These are reserved spaces for department heads, administrators, people like that," Jon said.

The lot was small. It couldn't have had more than thirty-five spaces. We fanned out, searching the subterranean space, but Steele wasn't here.

We left the executive parking garage and checked the employee picnic area. The entirely enclosed square had two doors on opposite sides, six picnic tables, two benches, and several harried hospital staffers. Smoking wasn't permitted, but I found several butts snuffed out on the ground beside one of the benches.

"He's not here," O'Connell said.

"No shit." I gave the area another glance. We asked everyone inside if they'd seen anyone matching Steele's description, but no one had. "He could be anywhere by now."

"The officers at the door are checking everyone who leaves," O'Connell said. "He's not getting out."

I turned to Jon. "Any other ways out of this place?"

"We have several emergency exits and employee only access points."

"If he has someone's ID, he could go anywhere," I said.

"Don't jump to conclusions. Let's check the security cameras. We just need a glimpse of him. Once we get that, we'll get him." O'Connell keyed the radio. "Rivers, have you found anything?"

"Still checking the surveillance footage. We're talking a dozen floors and over fifty cameras. It'll take time."

"Prioritize the main entrance and the ICU. With the number of cops stationed at the front doors, I don't see how Steele could slip inside without someone noticing." O'Connell released the radio, one eyebrow lifting in thought. "Do you think Steele had someone else leave the envelope for you?"

"What about the intercom," I asked.

"Echo?" O'Connell suggested. He held out his palm. "May I see the phone?"

I hesitated. "He said no cops."

"They always say no cops."

"Until I know for sure he isn't watching us right now, I'll hold on to it."

"Your call," O'Connell said, though he didn't agree with my assessment.

We took the elevator up and went down the hall to the security office. From the outside, it didn't look like much. It was situated behind a few labs. The entire floor was authorized personnel only. It housed offices, billing, insurance, and several laboratories for specimen analysis. Security told us to stay close. Only two types of people were allowed up here, the ones in business suits and the ones in scrubs. All of them had IDs and scan strips. Light blue and white were common hospital scrub colors. Security rewound and changed camera angles while we watched the various monitors for any hint as to Steele's whereabouts.

"With all the masks and caps, he could be right in front of us and we'd never notice him," I mused.

"Jen changes clothes when she gets to work. She keeps a spare set of scrubs in her locker in case of anything." O'Connell narrowed his eyes at the main feed. "If Steele got inside a locker room, he could have easily gotten his hands on hospital garb and probably someone's ID card."

"Or he could put on a gown and pretend to be a patient," I said.

"That too." O'Connell turned to Jon. "What do you think?"

"We have several locker rooms, making them easy enough to find. Each department has their own," Jon said, "but they require an ID card to be swiped or an access code entered."

"But it's possible," I said.

"I guess."

I went to the wall and studied the building layout. Everything was written on the schematic. "Does ICU have a locker room?" I didn't spot Steele when the phone rang, but he had to have been somewhere close in order to watch me. And I knew he couldn't have hidden inside a patient room, no matter how he might have been dressed.

"There." O'Connell leaned over my shoulder, pointing at the spot marked employee area on the blueprint.

"He had to be able to see me to know when to make the call," I said. "That's the only place I can think he might have been that I wouldn't have noticed."

"All right. We need to get inside that room." O'Connell held out his hand for the master keycard.

Bewildered, the head of hospital security said, "There's

no way anyone could get inside without an ID badge."

"I wouldn't be too sure about that." O'Connell took the keycard off the desk. "Keep an eye on us from here, Rivers. We don't want anyone getting the jump on us." O'Connell then pointed to a view of the parking lot where four cruisers had just pulled up. "Have two units check around outside while the other two secure the lesser known exits. Do a full 360 degree sweep. Parker says Steele's close, so we go on our consultant's gut. Got it?"

"No problem, Nick," Rivers said.

Without waiting, O'Connell and I ran out of the security office and headed straight for the ICU. With any luck, my gut was wrong.

Mildred remained at the desk, oblivious to the world as she cursed at the computer.

"Where's the locker room?" O'Connell asked, flashing his badge at her. I hung back, not wanting to antagonize the woman into non-compliance.

"Sir," she looked up to find his badge in front of her face, "take this corridor." She pointed. "It's the third door on the left."

"Have you seen anyone come out of there in the last twenty minutes?" O'Connell asked.

"No, not that I noticed."

Since he had the keycard, I let the detective lead the way. He pushed open the door and reached for the light switch. Obviously, he'd been inside a hospital locker room before, probably courtesy of his wife. Four rows of lockers stood in parallel lines. Two were against either wall and the other two were in the center of the room, creating three aisles. Benches sat between the lockers, and several large laundry bins sat at the far end beside a door that led to what I assumed was a bathroom. One of the bins had a hazardous waste symbol. Blood on the edge of the bin caught my eye.

"Nick," I moved cautiously toward it and peered inside, "get help."

NINETEEN

"Can you hear me?" I asked, leaning over the bin and checking for a pulse.

"Anything?" O'Connell asked.

I repositioned my fingers and pressed down harder. "He's alive."

"All right, let's get him out of there." O'Connell attempted to assess the man's injuries before moving him. The only visible wound was the gash at his temple. His neck was red and maybe a little swollen. "Hey, buddy," O'Connell said, "can you open your eyes?" He gave the man a slight shake. "Come on, pal, wake up."

Suddenly, the man gasped, shoving backward and letting out a surprised yelp.

"Whoa, easy," I said. "We're here to help. Just stay still until we figure out how to get you out of there." He eyed us, like a frightened rabbit. "I'm Alex. This is Detective O'Connell. Can you tell me who did this to you?"

"I don't know."

O'Connell keyed his radio, requesting assistance. "Rivers, run the footage backward. I need to know when the last person left the locker room and where the hell he went."

The man in the laundry bin groaned, shifting to the side. He tried to pull himself up but wobbled on top of the pile of dirty laundry. After this, we'd all need a dose of antibiotics and maybe a Tetanus shot.

"Do you remember what happened?" I asked.

"I was at my locker when this lunatic blindsided me with something. It might have been a cafeteria tray." He rubbed his forehead and examined the blood on his fingertips. "Then he wrapped me in a chokehold. I tried to pry his arms off, but..."

"What's your name?" O'Connell asked.

"Mickey Andrews."

"Are you a doctor?" I asked.

"No, I'm an RN."

O'Connell radioed Rivers again. "Deactivate Mickey Andrews ID card, and tell me where it was last used."

"Done," Rivers said. "According to this, he just swiped it at the ER patient intake doors."

The blood drained from O'Connell's face. "Jenny."

I raced out of the locker room, hearing O'Connell's frantic radio call for the nearest units to reroute to the ER. Just as I opened the stairwell door, a medical team, hospital security, and a uniformed police officer came up the steps. "Get to the locker room. Now."

I only made it down two flights of stairs before O'Connell burst through the door at a run, jumping down the last few steps of each flight on his way down. I kept moving. We had to stop Steele before he hurt Jen.

By the time we reached the bottom, O'Connell had caught up to me. We sprinted down the hall, dodging patients and staff along the way. The staff working triage at the ER had no idea what was going on.

"Open this door," O'Connell ordered, his badge in one hand, the other holding his gun down at his thigh. The woman behind the counter hesitated. "Do it."

She pushed the button, and we entered the ER. Individual rooms carved out the two sides. Unfortunately, I'd been here often enough to have the entire layout memorized. Several cops had already responded.

"No sign of Francisco Steele," one of them said.

"He's here," I insisted.

O'Connell requested an update from Rivers concerning Steele's last sighting.

"Andrews' card was swiped at the ER door. The last visual we have is him heading in the direction of the ambulance bay."

"Was he alone?" O'Connell asked.

"Yes," Rivers replied. "According to the timestamp, he has a five minute head start."

We continued our search, passing rooms as we went. The automatic doors to the ambulance bay whooshed open, and we stepped inside. One rig was parked to the side while the paramedics replenished the stock and cleaned the interior, oblivious to our presence.

"Psst," O'Connell whispered, holding up his badge. "Have you seen a man in scrubs and a skull cap come through here?"

"Yeah, he had on a surgical mask too," the paramedic said, hopping down. He pointed to the wide entrance. "The surgeons come out here sometimes to take a break when they are having a bad day. I've never seen one with a mask still on, though."

"Did you see where he went?" O'Connell asked while I edged toward the opening, checking behind the support pillar and anywhere large enough for Steele to hide.

"Outside. He rounded the corner." The paramedic pointed to the right.

"Stay here," O'Connell instructed.

I braced against the edge of the opening, took a breath, held my gun in both hands, and peered around the side. I shook my head. O'Connell got on the radio, hoping Rivers or someone in hospital security could locate Steele on the exterior cameras. But I didn't wait for the response. Steele said he had someone waiting, and I didn't think he'd been talking about Nurse Andrews. Thankfully, the person waiting hadn't been Nick's wife, but the possibilities seemed endless.

"Parker," O'Connell hissed, but I didn't turn around or slow. I had to find Steele. I had to stop this.

The ambulance bay opened to a wide path that curved

around the side of the hospital and led to the main thoroughfare. A chain-link fence ran the length of one side, not connecting to anything. On the other side of the fence were a few metal trashcans.

Keeping my head on a swivel, I went around the fence and checked the cans. This wasn't hospital property. This belonged to the city. It'd be harder to get access to area surveillance cameras. That must have been why Steele went out this way.

O'Connell jogged up beside me. "Any sign of him?"

"No."

The detective peered into the trash bins. "Looks like he ditched the hospital gear."

"Not all of it." The surgical mask and skull cap had been tossed inside. Beneath it was regular trash. I opened the other can and looked inside. "He's still in scrubs."

"Maybe he didn't have anything on underneath them."

"I doubt it." An eerie feeling of déjà vu settled over me. "He didn't drive here. He knows that would be too easy to track."

"If he's on foot, there's still a chance we can catch him." O'Connell spotted another set of dumpsters peeking out from the alley half a block away. "Come on, let's keep moving."

We didn't have time to waste, so we ran, full-out, down the street, only slowing once we reached the mouth of the alley. O'Connell opened the dumpster, finding the scrub top and matching pants tossed inside.

"We're back to looking for a bald guy with a beard." I blew out a breath and kicked the side of the can. "Fuck." I scanned our surroundings. Think, Parker. Where would Steele go? "He must have a way out. An escape route. Maybe he has a car waiting nearby or someone's picking him up."

"We're close to the major transit lines. The closest subway station is two blocks that way." O'Connell pointed. "And the city buses are supposed to stop here every fifteen minutes. He might already be gone."

"It hasn't been fifteen minutes, and the buses rarely run on time." I checked my watch. "The train station makes more sense, but he might not want to get that close to the metro cops. Plus, he wouldn't have tossed his clothes here if he was headed east." I looked around the area. "He told me he had someone waiting – his next victim." I frowned, feeling valuable seconds ticking by. "Dammit."

"Talk it out," O'Connell said, bouncing on the balls of his feet as he whipped his focus from one building to another. "Where is he, Parker? What's your best guess?"

"I don't know. If an agent or cop lived around here, I'd say maybe that's where he went, but I don't see anything residential close by."

"This isn't exactly one of the safer parts of town."

"No, it isn't. But it's too far from KXD territory." I blinked a few times, desperate to recall details from the closed case. Lab locations. Storage facilities. Meeting places. Anywhere Steele might go to hide. "That bar." I pointed to the tiny establishment on the corner.

"It's not open yet," O'Connell said. "That makes it the ideal place for him to hole up."

"It'd also serve his recent voyeuristic fetish." I just didn't know if Steele would waste the time to watch us run ourselves ragged. But this was as much about relishing in our incompetence as it was about killing and torturing. Francisco Steele enjoyed the psychological torture almost as much as the physical. Maybe he even liked it more. "Let's check it out."

O'Connell took the lead, crossed the street, and continued at a fast clip until we reached the bar. The sign said closed, but that didn't mean anything. I went around the building, checking the side entrance. It was locked. No signs of tampering. And as far as I could tell, none of the employees were around. I returned to the front.

"Door's open," O'Connell said. "I already radioed for backup."

We didn't even know if Steele was inside, but this was no time to take chances. I nodded and took up a position at the side of the door. O'Connell held up three fingers, counted us down, and swung the door open.

A bullet impacted against the wood frame, making the entire thing rattle and tremble. O'Connell shoved me to the side just as another shot rang out. This one hit just to the right of where I'd been standing.

"Police. Throw down your weapons," O'Connell ordered. Another bullet flew in our direction. O'Connell hit the radio. "Shots fired at police. Send all available units." O'Connell gave our location, knowing backup was already en route.

We stayed hunkered down, scurrying in a crouch in opposite directions into the bar and away from the door, moving in the direction the shots had been fired. In the dark, I couldn't see who had fired, but it had to be Steele.

The bastard had some balls to shoot at us in the middle of broad daylight. I gripped my nine millimeter tighter, both worried and relieved when no other projectiles flew in my direction. But from the continued reports of gunfire, Steele hadn't stopped firing, which meant he focused all of his attention on O'Connell.

"Nick, take cover," I yelled. Even though I kept heading in the direction the bullets originated, I had yet to glimpse Francisco Steele or anyone else for that matter.

"Parker," O'Connell bellowed, but whatever he said after that was drowned out by the sound of another gunshot. In the enclosed space, it echoed and boomed like a cannon. I jumped over the bar, which acted like a barrier, and that's when I saw him.

Francisco Steele had positioned himself in an alcove at the end of the bar between the l-shaped curve and the swinging aluminum door which led into the kitchen, forming a perfect sniper's nest. Steele was protected on three sides. The only weakness was the opening where the bar and door separated. I couldn't get to him without being spotted, and from here, I didn't have a good angle to return fire.

He remained concealed behind the barrier, lifting his gun overhead and firing in O'Connell's general direction. Since his focus was on the detective, I threw caution to the wind.

"Put your gun down," I said, and Steele turned to stare at me. "I said drop it." I stepped forward, fully exposing myself to him.

"Not this time, chica." He glanced behind him, as if waiting for something. I just didn't know what. I fired right at him. My bullet chipped the top of the countertop, coming close but not quite reaching my target. He gave me a venomous smile. "You have to try harder." He licked his lips suggestively. "Luckily, I'm already hard."

"Stand up."

He kept the smile on his face, but his eyes burned with rage. "I'm not ready for it to end like this. I have so much in store for you. But if you force my hand, I will kill you now. Is that what you want?"

I didn't answer. I edged closer, but Steele turned to aim at me. Unlike him, I didn't have the corner of the bar to use as a bulletproof vest. "You're done. This is over. You're trapped. Give up or die here. It's your choice, Francisco. Frankly, I don't care either way."

"Give up? I'll never surrender. I won't go back to prison." Steele glanced behind him again. "Hang on to that phone. I'll talk to you again soon." He fired in my direction, hitting close enough that the bullet tugged against my open jacket and ripped it backward. I hit the ground hard. By the time I sat up, Steele had vanished.

Where did he go? I pressed one hand against my side while I aimed with my other, searching the area. In that little nook formed by the end of the bar and the open kitchen door, he had the perfect vantage point. And shooting at me had given him enough time to disappear. O'Connell came up beside me.

"He went into the kitchen," I said.

Nick jumped over me and slammed into the kitchen door, gun raised. "Shit."

I pulled myself off the tile floor and followed O'Connell. The kitchen door remained wide open, and in the alley was an open manhole cover. "He's down there," I said, already prepared to climb down.

"Alex, no." O'Connell tugged me backward, away from the hole. "He could have killed you, but he didn't. That wasn't a miss. It was a warning shot. You go down there, he will kill you. And I can't let that happen." He lifted my shirt, exposing the graze that had decimated my jacket, leaving it in tatters but me with merely a scratch.

"No. He's mine. This ends here and now."

Officers ran to us in formation, guns drawn. O'Connell led a team into the sewers. I took up the rear.

Ten minutes later, we gave up the search. The sewer tunnels branched in too many directions, and with no feasible way to track Steele, we'd never find him. Smelly and disgusted, I climbed up the ladder and returned to street level. I failed again.

TWENTY

"Francisco Steele was inside the hospital. We still don't know how he got in, but we will find out," O'Connell declared to the officers clustered around the hospital security office. "Steele slipped past security, made it to the ICU, attacked Nurse Andrews, and stole his ID. According to the surveillance cameras posted on this floor, Steele exited the elevator, hid in the men's room, and waited for an unsuspecting hospital employee to enter the locker room. From there, Steele changed clothes. We got lucky he only wanted to send Parker a message. He could have done anything."

O'Connell rubbed his mouth, pacing in front of the assembled troops and giving each of them the evil eye. Lt. Moretti took over at that point, probably afraid his lead detective was about to lose it. Not that I blamed him.

"From now on, everyone is keeping his and her eyes open. This can't happen again," Moretti said.

"No, sir," came a few mumbled responses.

Moretti ignored them. "The manhunt to find Steele continues. The BOLO's been updated with our latest intel, but we need to know how he got inside. He didn't drive, so how did he get here? These are questions we need answered. Even the tiniest detail might lead to his current location or indicate who his next target is. According to Parker, the threat is imminent. In fact, we might already be too late."

I shuddered. "How's Andrews? Did he remember anything else?"

"The nurse is shaken up, but he'll be okay. He hasn't been able to tell us anything we didn't already get from the ICU surveillance footage." Moretti glowered at the FBI agents who lingered in the back of the room. "Don't you find it convenient Jablonsky had been moved to the SDU and the detail had been pulled prior to Steele stepping foot on the ICU floor?"

The agents didn't say anything. They continued to stare straight ahead. Moretti didn't trust the Bureau not to have leaks, but no one there would help an animal like Francisco Steele.

"He's been watching us," I said, "like he did from the boarded-up shop across from Cooper's apartment. We need to find out when he arrived at the hospital. He might have been here for hours, maybe longer, biding his time and waiting to strike. Originally, I thought, since I went to pay him a visit in prison, he wanted to return the favor, but now I'm not so sure."

"There's a lot we need to figure out. And we have to do it fast. We have patrols and guards set up for a reason. We can't let this happen again," Moretti said, repeating himself.

I leaned my head against the wall and stared at the ceiling. This was my fault. Steele knew where I'd be and wanted to send me a message. *I can get to you anytime I want.*

Turning, I scanned the security logs. No one reported a missing or stolen access card, except Nurse Andrews. I asked the tech to show me the footage from the information desk and the lost and found from earlier. I watched the images flicker in reverse on one of the small monitors.

"Right there." I pointed. "Put that on the main screen."

The tech switched it to the center display, and the LEOs in the room fell silent. Steele dropped the phone off downstairs, but while he was speaking to the woman at the desk, a nurse intervened. He followed her into the elevator and up to the ICU. By then, the FBI and security presence were gone, and he had avoided the cops in the lobby by keeping his distance.

"That's him." I pointed. He wore a baseball cap and windbreaker over a pair of jeans. "Why didn't anyone notice him?"

"He didn't come through the front doors," a patrolman insisted. "We IDed everyone who entered."

"Can you run it backward and find out where he came from?" Moretti asked.

The footage played backward. The tech maneuvered from camera to camera as he searched the footage. "He came from the cafeteria."

"And before that?" O'Connell asked, but I already knew the answer to that question. Steele had changed clothes and his appearance while in a blind spot. We had no way of tracking him before that.

"Sorry," the tech said.

"We need copies of your footage for the entire day. Our system might be able to get a hit off facial recognition, his build, even his gait." Moretti met my eyes. "Actually, make that two copies." Cross Security could get the job done faster, assuming Lucien was still in a cooperating mood.

"What about after he changed into Andrews' clothes?" O'Connell asked. "Did he take any detours or do anything else before escaping through the emergency room?"

"With the mask and cap covering his face, IDing Steele won't be easy," the tech said. "He blends in with the rest of the hospital staff."

"And he kept his mask on," I pointed out. "Show us whatever you have." But that effort turned out to be fruitless. After Steele spoke to me on the phone, he waited just long enough for the coast to be clear before making a break for the exit.

I went back to the previous footage of Steele in the cafeteria. From what we could tell, he sat in the cafeteria eating and reading the paper for nearly an hour and a half. That wasn't behavior I expected to see from a cold-hearted killer.

"Nick, a word." I went out the door and waited for him to follow me. "Do you think he saw us searching the dress shop?"

"It would have been hard to miss the crime scene vans. He might have come straight here once he spotted us poking around."

"Since he can't hide from us, he wanted to make the point we can't hide from him either." I inhaled a shaky breath. "With Martin, Jen, and hundreds of innocent people around, he could have done anything."

"But he didn't," O'Connell said, more for his own benefit than mine.

I clutched the phone inside my pocket. "We don't even know how he got inside. It's not on any of the security feeds. None of the officers or security guards have confessed to falling asleep at their posts, so I don't think Steele came in the front. You've seen the lobby. It's crawling with police and FBI agents, some of which I'm sure are probably on his hit list. I don't think Steele has the self-control necessary to walk past them without doing something heinous."

"You're wrong, Parker. He has self-control. He exhibited it when he didn't kill you."

"That's because he's not finished yet."

"Be that as it may, he's not killing indiscriminately. Mickey Andrews is a testament to that."

"It's all part of his plan."

O'Connell didn't argue, but I wasn't sure he agreed either.

"He'll change his appearance again. It's getting too hot for him. We have his ugly face plastered all over every media outlet and posted throughout the hospital, precinct, and federal building. He's going to do something to change it up," I said. "He's determined to stay one step ahead of us."

"Easiest thing to do is shave the beard." O'Connell narrowed his eyes. "He trimmed it down quite a bit since leaving prison. And from what I recall from the recorded interviews, Steele never used to have a beard."

"No, he didn't."

"He'll get rid of it then. But until we have confirmation of that, we stick with what we know – beard and shaved head. It's the most reasonable assumption," O'Connell said.

I turned my attention to the emergency evacuation diagram pinned to the wall. It showed every route in and out of the hospital. "Check the ambulance bay. Emergencies bypass ER intake and go straight into the ER. Since Steele couldn't waltz in through the front door, maybe he had EMTs bring him inside."

"That's a good thought." O'Connell turned before heading back into the room. "See, this is why Moretti keeps you around."

"Well, it's better than the other reason."

"What other reason?"

I snorted, giving him a wicked look, but didn't say anything. Now wasn't the time for inappropriate jokes. Director Kendall, Agent Lucca, and several OIO and FBI agents I recognized emerged from the elevator and headed toward us. "That's my cue to leave," I whispered. "I'll check into the EMT theory. You got this, Nick?"

"Yeah, just do me a favor. While you're there, check on Jen."

"Will do." I pressed against the wall, allowing the federal agents to pass. "Director Kendall."

He nodded at me. "Parker, anything I should know?"

"Moretti has the facts. I'm sure he'll update you. Jablonsky's safe. And no one else has been seriously hurt. Right now, that's all that matters."

"Indeed."

Lucca hung back, grabbing the crook of my elbow and whispering in my ear, "Wait for me in Jablonsky's room. I'll meet you there as soon as I can. We need to talk."

I stopped by the ER to make sure Jen was okay and asked about patients who'd been brought in. While Jen did her best to get me answers, she cleaned and patched my side. After my trip into the sewers, I wanted to stave off possible infections.

"Alex, you know I can't give out that kind of information," Jen reminded me, "but it's been a busy day. Ambulances brought in several elderly patients and a few kids."

"Anyone in between? Like thirty to thirty-five?"

"Only one that I remember."

"What happened?"

"A car accident. Guy got rolled into one of the trauma rooms, but I didn't see him. The nurse went in to take his vitals and assess the damage. She ordered x-rays." Jen bit her lip. "Give me a second." She waved down another ER nurse. "Emma, what happened with the car accident guy?"

"I don't know. He took off. I assume he must have been drunk or high and didn't want the cops to find out when we ran his blood."

"Did you take a sample?" I asked.

"No, we didn't get a chance. After the initial assessment, I stepped out for a moment so he could change into a gown, and when I went back to his room, he was gone."

"What did he look like?" I asked.

Emma glanced at Jen, who nodded. "Shaved head, disheveled. He kept a towel pressed against the side of his face, so I didn't get a good look at him."

"And you don't know where he went?"

"Nah, but that's not new. We always lose one or two every week," Emma said. "The EMTs probably have his info. Y'know, for billing and insurance purposes. It just depends on the circumstances."

"Thanks." Jen dismissed her, and Emma went into one of the rooms. "Does that help?"

"More than you realize," I said. "In the event you spot anyone matching that guy's description, steer clear, and get help. Nick's upstairs if you need him."

"Are you going to tell me what's going on?" Jen asked, nodding at my side.

"Nothing to worry about. I just got into a bit of a scuffle and took a trip into the sewers. Have you ever been down there?"

"Eww, no."

"Yeah, my thoughts exactly. Oddly enough, not nearly as disgusting as I thought it'd be but still plenty disgusting."

"At least you don't smell and your clothes look clean."

"I had a spare outfit in my car, but I'd love to wash my hair. I just don't have the time."

"You always have a spare outfit in your car."

"That's because I'm prepared."

"Where are you going?"

"To take care of business, but first I have to speak to a boy scout."

She gave me a curious look. "Is that where you get the always prepared thing?"

"No, the scouts stole that concept from me. That's why we're having a conversation." I winked and went upstairs to the SDU, updated Samuels and Kwan, and spoke to Martin while I waited for Lucca.

"Alex," Martin watched as I paced back and forth at the foot of Mark's bed, "you need to relax."

"I am relaxed."

"Liar." He crinkled his nose. "You weren't wearing that an hour ago."

"So?"

"What happened?"

"The short version. Nick and I chased Steele into the sewers, but we lost him."

Martin swallowed and looked down at Mark. "Okay, so now what? Do we move him? Get additional security? What's the plan?"

"Move him?" For some reason, I hadn't thought about that. "Is that even possible?"

"He's out of the woods, so to speak. Obviously, he needs constant monitoring, but it should be feasible."

"When do you think he'll wake up again?"

Martin shrugged. "Hard to say. If they stopped pumping him with drugs, he'd probably be awake now, but unlike you, Jabber would prefer comfortable oblivion to pain."

I smiled. "Pussy."

Martin laughed. "Guess you didn't get your masochistic streak from him. Why? Is there something you want to ask him?"

"Nothing that can't wait. I just figured he might want some say on what we do next."

"For what it's worth, he knew who shot him and what that meant for you. He trusts you to handle it."

"In that case, let's wake him up so he can tell Kendall that." I shook away the anger. "As long as Mark's okay, that's all that matters, unless Steele finds a way to get to him."

"I told you I won't let that happen."

I blew out a breath. We weren't having that argument again. Martin would do what he wanted. He could take care of himself. He'd do what was best for Mark and me. I just had to believe it'd be okay. "Steele scares me," I admitted.

"He scares all of us," Lucca said from the doorway, "but you better not be losing your mojo over this."

"Never." I turned and graced him with a rare smile. "What's going on upstairs?"

"We'll get to that in a minute." Lucca peered into the room, waiting for an invitation. Martin waved him in, and my former partner went to stand at the side of Jablonsky's bed. "How's he doing? From what I hear, he woke up earlier."

"He did." Martin glanced at me, unsure how much to disclose to Lucca. "The doctors are optimistic."

"They're just being realistic," Lucca said. "Jablonsky's the toughest guy I know."

"So what's going on?" I asked.

"We should talk in private."

"I was actually on my way to get some coffee and maybe something to eat. Can I get anyone anything?" Martin asked.

"No, thanks," Lucca said, and I shook my head.

Martin brushed past me, running his hand across the small of my back on the way out of the room.

Once the door shut, Lucca deflated. "All right. You first. According to the cops upstairs, you've had a hell of a day. Steele left you a phone and made contact again. What does he want?"

I gave Lucca the Cliff's notes version. "What's Kendall doing? Did you learn anything from Vega?"

"That's being disclosed to Moretti now. I'm sure you'll get the official word soon enough, so let's not waste time with that. Suffice it to say, Steele and Vega have been planning this since the moment they reunited in prison. I'm not sure why Vega went along with it. I'm guessing he needed Steele's protection and whatever contraband Steele promised to hook him up with. Vega spent the last eight hours at the federal building, and he's coming down hard. He'd give up his own mother at this point."

"Do we know who's on Steele's hit list?"

"Not exactly. Vega named you and Jablonsky, but Steele didn't go into specifics. He just wanted revenge on the bitch FBI agent and her posse."

"I didn't realize I had a posse."

"Don't blow it out of proportion. It doesn't make you cool."

"So what's Kendall's deal?"

Lucca rubbed the stubble on his cheek. "Honestly, Alex, I have no idea. He's acting like you pissed in his Cheerios. Like this is your fault."

"It isn't." But it sure felt like it.

"I know that." He looked down at Mark. "The director's been a bureaucrat for so long, his default setting is to pass the buck. He didn't protect his people. So he needs someone else to blame." Lucca looked up. "Just like what happened when he forced you to resign."

"Careful, it sounds like you stopped drinking the Kool-aid."

"I must have," Lucca pressed something into my palm, "or I wouldn't be giving you this."

TWENTY-ONE

The moment I arrived at Cross Security, I handed over the phone Steele left me. The police and FBI would want it soon enough, so I had to have it analyzed first. Steele had been adamant about not sharing it with the authorities. A part of me didn't want to defy him because I knew the consequences, and the other part knew the best way to find the bastard was to have as many people hunting him as possible. Theoretically, the phone could lead us right to him. I just had to be sure I was doing the right thing.

"We'll check it," Amir promised. He picked up the drive containing a copy of the hospital security cam footage. "How many different camera feeds do they have?"

"A lot."

He tilted his head back and forth. "I should be done with the phone in an hour, but I'm not sure how long it'll take to parse the footage."

"Thanks, just give me whatever you have, as soon as you have it. I'll be in my office. If the phone rings..." I swallowed, fearing what Steele would do if I didn't answer.

"Don't worry. I can redirect it to your office phone. He won't know."

Nodding, I took the elevator down. The exhaustion had

set in, and my legs were tired and achy. I detoured to the break room, brewed a cup of coffee, added cream and sugar and a handful of ice, took it into my office, and plugged the thumb drive Lucca gave me into my computer.

Lucca had copied everything onto the device – the interviews with Vega, the photos taken from inside the prison, and every report Jablonsky and I filed concerning Francisco Steele and the KXDs during our initial investigation. The PD had most of these records, and what they lacked, they'd eventually get. But Lucca expedited the process. Even though I'd written most of the reports or briefed Jablonsky, who then wrote the reports, I had forgotten a lot. Too much time had passed.

"What's a guy got to do to get a cup of coffee around here?" Lucca asked, eyeing the tumbler in my hand.

I blinked, tearing my eyes from the screen. "You're so quiet, I forgot you were here." I pointed out the door in the direction of the break room. "Help yourself. Cross keeps the kitchen stocked. Sandwiches, snacks, coffee, tea, whatever you want."

Lucca kept the retort to himself. Perhaps he was on his best behavior due to the circumstances, but I suspected it had more to do with the two of us being out of sync. He returned a few minutes later with a sandwich, coffee, and a cinnamon roll. Clearing off the edge of my desk, he put his plate down and sat in my client chair.

"Maybe I should join the private sector," he teased around a mouthful.

"You might not have a choice if Kendall finds out what you did."

"I didn't do a damn thing. The police will eventually receive that intel. As far as I'm concerned, you got it from them."

"And the reports Jablonsky and I filed?"

"You kept a copy for yourself."

I looked up at him. "Who are you? And what did you do with Eddie Lucca? The Eddie Lucca I know is a rule-following, company man."

His cheek twitched, and he stared down at his plate and took another bite. I didn't know what triggered the change in Lucca or his sudden dislike for Director Kendall, but now wasn't the time to push. He finished his sandwich and inhaled the cinnamon roll while I read over our case files, making a list of locations Steele liked to frequent.

"Where do you think Steele went after he escaped into the sewers?" Lucca asked.

"I'm not sure, but he said he had someone waiting."

Lucca thought for a moment and pulled out his phone. "What time did you speak to him?"

"It was around five."

"That complicates matters." Lucca dialed, spoke to Agent Davis, and hung up the phone. "Davis is going to have someone e-mail me a list of agents who called in sick or took a personal day today."

"You think Steele kidnapped his next victim?"

"It's possible. After what he did to Cooper, he might have found some benefit to having a captive audience."

"Jablonsky's a captive audience."

"I know." He gulped down the coffee and grabbed his plate. "But he has a contingent of FBI agents guarding his room, not to mention the private bodyguards you assigned for his protection. Steele's not suicidal. He won't make that move unless he has no other moves to make."

Leaving me to contemplate that, Lucca took his plate and mug back to the break room. By the time he returned, I had finished making my list of locations to scout. These weren't necessarily KXD strongholds, though every one of them had some type of connection to Francisco Steele.

"I can't get into his head," I said. "No matter how hard I try, I just can't. I don't know what's wrong with me."

"You can't get into his head because you're stuck in your own," Lucca said.

"How do I fix that?"

He shrugged. "When you figure it out, let me know." He stretched, circling my office.

"All right. Spill." I crossed my arms over my chest. "What's going on with you?"

"Nothing."

"Bullshit. I know you, Eddie. This isn't you." But Lucca wouldn't talk, and I didn't have the energy to convince him otherwise. "I'm sorry I involved you. I didn't know where else to turn. None of my other OIO friends worked this case. You did."

"It doesn't matter, Parker. Kendall would have wanted to touch base with me anyway. He's convinced I'm on Steele's hit list and my family could be in danger. It wouldn't have mattered what you did or didn't do. The end result is the same." He picked up a legal pad and doodled on the page. "Let's go back to the beginning. Cooper opened an investigation into the KXDs. Jablonsky recruited you to infiltrate the gang by going undercover at a strip joint."

"The Black Cat."

He wrote that on the first line. "In the meantime, your cover apartment was in the same building where Steele lived."

"Yep. We were neighbors. He lived above me. I made the approach. Jablonsky chewed me out for being so reckless." A grin tugged at my lips. "It wasn't reckless."

Lucca glanced in my direction. "I remember the briefing we had after that. It was reckless."

"Hey, it got me on Steele's radar."

"Given what's going on right now, that's not a good thing."

"Twenty-twenty hindsight," I said. "Anyway, Steele flirted, he threatened, he fell for my bullshit."

"And he terrified you," Lucca said. "I remember. That was the first case we worked together. While you were poking the beast, I was working behind-the-scenes with Cooper on taking down Bard and coordinating with the DEA on tracking the shipments." He laughed. "You were the biggest pain in the ass I had ever worked with. You did what you wanted. You barely listened to orders. You got yourself arrested in a police raid."

"I called in the tip."

"Yeah." Lucca fell silent.

"Don't stop there. You might as well continue the story. We performed a tactical strike, came under heavy fire, and barely managed to capture Bard. Steele escaped, and if he hadn't resurfaced to get revenge on me and Heathcliff, we never would have found him." My voice grew quiet. "Maybe that's why we can't find him now. We never really knew where he'd go or what he'd do. He kept a lot of things private."

"I almost forgot about the tactical strike," Lucca said. He came around the desk and grabbed the mouse. "You know what else I almost forgot?"

"How to follow rules?"

He grumbled. "The police had a number of undercovers investigating drug sales and gang activity. They had UCs positioned in several locations in that neighborhood."

"And Detective Heathcliff assisted me undercover. What's your point?"

"Steele wants revenge on the people who betrayed him. He went after Cooper because he was in charge of the investigation and testified in court. Jablonsky arrested him. You tricked him."

"What's your point?"

"I testified too because I had been placed in charge of evidence collection. A few of our techs and experts had to provide testimony, but they never interacted with Steele prior to the proceedings."

"You don't think he'll go after them?" I rubbed the kink in my neck.

"They shouldn't be top priorities. Neither should I," Lucca insisted.

"I'm not sure Steele's thinking rationally. He might focus on any one of you, just to be vindictive, but I agree. It doesn't seem as likely. Detective Heathcliff is probably at the top of Steele's hit list. I already warned him, but he won't listen."

"It's not just Heathcliff," Lucca said. "Steele would want to go after all the other undercovers too."

"But most of them didn't break cover or testify in open court."

"What about the bartender at the Black Cat?" Lucca scrolled down the page, looking for the man's name.

"Joe." I remembered the man who'd given me such strange vibes when I first went to work in the club and who I watched get tortured and nearly beaten to death. I wanted to intercede, but I'd been dragged away before I sacrificed my own cover in a poorly executed attempt to save the narcotics officer.

"Joe Aronne." Lucca pointed to the name on the screen. "Is the PD watching out for him too? And what about the barista at that coffee shop?" He pointed to one of the locations on my list. "And the guy at the Stop N' Shop. The PD planted all four of them to monitor drug activity in the area. That included keeping tabs on Steele."

"Shit. That's right. The police had a UC working at the convenience store where Steele always stopped for beer." I grabbed the phone and dialed the precinct. "Hey, Thompson," I said, "is the Stop N' Shop where we spotted Steele the same one he used to frequent before we arrested him?"

"I don't know."

"Well, find out. Ask Jacobs or the guys in narcotics. During the original investigation, narco had a guy stationed at the convenience store. We need to know if it's the same location Steele recently visited."

"All right. Let me check." After a couple of minutes, he came back on the line. "Narcotics keeps a lot of those facts under lock and key in order to protect their UCs." Thompson covered the mouthpiece and shouted something to someone. "Let me look into this. I'll call you back."

"Wait," I said, but he had already hung up. I put the phone down and read the locations on my list. "Dollars to donuts, it's the same Stop N' Shop location. Steele's retracing his steps. He's revisiting his old haunts."

"Correct me if I'm wrong, but didn't Steele pick you up from the hospital after you were attacked in the alley?"

"That could be a coincidence. After all, that hospital has the best trauma center in the city, and that's where Jablonsky is."

"Or Steele's replaying his greatest hits, the remix edition," Lucca suggested.

"Revisionist history?" I asked, but Lucca only shrugged. "All right, so we should assume Derek Heathcliff, Joe Aronne, and the UCs from the coffee place and the Stop N' Shop are on Steele's hit list. Since Steele has an unhealthy fascination with the convenience store's plastic bags and creative ways to use them, his recent visits must serve a far more sinister purpose. He's leaving breadcrumbs for us. I'm just not sure what to make of them."

"Do you think he identified the UC who worked there yet?" Lucca asked.

"I don't know. Shooting the shit with the current clerk or asking what happened to the guy who used to work there might have resulted in a name. Steele's smart. He has connections, and the KXDs have plenty of influence in the prisons. I don't think it'd be hard for him to get the name of the cop who'd been keeping tabs on him."

"Where is that undercover cop now?" Lucca asked.

"The one from the Stop N' Shop?"

"Uh-huh."

"Oddly enough, he's on vacation in Hawaii. His wife's a pharmaceutical rep and she had a conference to attend, so he took some time off and went with her. He'll be back next week."

"Talk about an odd couple. He takes drugs off the streets, and she hands them out like candy."

"Legalized candy," I said. "Who knows, she may only push boner pills and birth control."

Lucca laughed, but a dark cloud settled over him.

"What's on your mind?" I asked.

"Like you said, the KXDs control a lot. They have a lot of influence. They must have gained favor with a few corrupt prison guards. It's the only thing that explains how Steele and Vega switched places so easily."

"First rule-breaking, now cynicism. Stop stealing my main personality traits," I teased, but he was right. "We need to run a check on the prison guards and find out if any of them are working for the KXDs or if they've inquired as to the identities of any undercover narcotics officers. They could be feeding the information directly to Steele and helping him plot his revenge." This was why narco kept their intel guarded, even from other members of law enforcement.

"That's what I've been doing all day, but I haven't found much of anything. They all look clean. Dare I say squeaky?"

"Then we keep looking."

I reached for the phone, just as Lucca reached for his. We shared a chuckle and made our requests with the FBI and PD. Finally, we were getting somewhere. Or so I thought.

TWENTY-TWO

"I give up." I threw my hands in the air. "No money transfers. No weird phone calls. Nothing obvious. Steele never struck me as particularly high-tech. If he has a guard on the take, he kept the payoffs below the radar."

"Nothing on the internet is private. Money transfers, bank deposits, all of that can be traced. Conducting business that way makes it too easy to get caught," Lucca said. "Same with phone calls and text messages."

"It's also possible Steele extorted the guards to cooperate rather than reward them. Something along the lines of 'do this or my boys will kill your family'. Y'know, gangbanger 101."

"What should we do? The police are bringing in all prison personnel for questioning. Obviously, they'll deny it. Unless you have a trick up your sleeve, this won't get us anywhere."

"I know. I hate this. Whatever happened with Bard? You said Davis questioned him. What does he know about Steele's plans for revenge?"

"Nothing." Lucca slouched down and leaned back so he could rest his head against the cushion. "I read the transcripts. Steele and Bard were sent to different facilities. They have not been in contact since Steele's arrest. The

OIO checked prison records, phone logs, the mail, everything. There's no overlap."

"What about visitors?"

"All different," Lucca said.

"The defense attorneys?" I asked.

"Different attorneys. Different firm. As far as I can tell, there's no reason to believe Bard knows anything about what's going on."

"Except he's DeAngelo Bard. He knows everything that happens with the KXDs. He knows what his people do. He wouldn't let them run amok without his blessing."

"Times have changed. The KXDs don't have as much power on the streets. Bard's lost favor without the cartel connection to back his position. The cartel's running the show now."

"Maybe the KXDs' outside operation, but not inside. Bard still has power in the prisons," I said. "A lot of his loyal followers went down the same time he did. So he moved his main operation from outside the prison gates to inside. He's doing a better business now than he was before."

"You're sure about that?" Lucca asked.

"That's what the detectives I spoke to in narcotics said. Bard's people are loyal."

"That's because Bard never turned on them, but the same can't necessarily be said for Steele."

"Steele never gave up Bard or the KXDs."

"No, but he gave up their other connections to save his own skin. He gave up a lot." Lucca lazily pointed at the computer. "The transcripts should be in there. Read them for yourself."

"I read them, but Vega supported Steele, even though by most normal standards Steele betrayed the KXDs by allowing a traitor, me, to take them down. Vega should have told him to fuck off, but he didn't. There has to be a reason."

"You think Bard put the word out to help Steele?"

"I think it's possible."

"Which would mean he'd have to know what Steele has planned, except Bard denies it. And nothing we have contradicts it." Lucca rolled his neck from side to side. "So why does it matter? How does this help us?"

"Let's just assume Bard's full of shit."

"Good assumption." Lucca stared, waiting for me to get to the point.

"The one thing I'm certain of is Steele would never betray Bard. It goes against the dynamics of their relationship. Steele had nothing. Bard's his brother. His father. His best friend. His platonic lover. Bard is Steele's entire world."

"Bard doesn't view Steele in the same light."

"Exactly. Bard's a tough guy who grew up tough, but at his core, he's just running a business and watching out for number one, which means we could incentivize him to cooperate."

"Unless he really doesn't know anything." Lucca let out a lengthy exhale. "There's also another possibility we haven't considered yet."

"What's that?"

"Bard put word out that Jablonsky and the OIO have been looking into the cartel and someone needs to shut that down. Steele had an obvious beef and plenty to make up for after betraying the gang. Maybe Bard gave Steele an opportunity to redeem himself."

"I'm not sure Bard would trust Steele with such an important task. It'd be easier to get some punk who wants to prove himself to take care of business instead."

"It's just something to think about," Lucca said.

Rubbing my eyes, I stared at my scribbles. None of this made a damn bit of sense. "One thing at a time." Since the authorities were exploring the possibility of a corrupt corrections officer, I dug deeper into Bard's background. The gang leader had plenty of enemies – rival gang leaders, law enforcement, the IRS. He also had a lot of associates. But no one in particular stood out. Maybe Lucca was right. Bard wanted blood, and Steele would deliver. No one could argue with that.

"We need to convince Vega to tell us what's what," I said. "He's a KXD. He'd know if the orders came from Bard or if this is Steele acting on his own." And we needed to find out. That would help us determine who else Steele planned to target. Right now, we assumed he only planned to take out his enemies, but if he promised to take out Bard's enemies too, the list of potentials would grow exponentially.

I opened another file. Luther Vega had been a model prisoner. He'd been arrested just days before Bard. He'd been picked up on a traffic violation, of all things. The officer found drugs in the vehicle, and Vega was charged with possession. He'd been given the minimum sentence, but he'd been a frequent flyer at the prison infirmary for his first few months there. "We might be wrong about Bard."

Lucca didn't say anything. I looked up, wondering why the boy scout would waste the perfect opportunity to say something snide, but he had fallen asleep.

"Eddie," I said. He didn't stir. "Lucca," I said louder.

A snore escaped as he shook himself awake. "What? What's going on?"

"Get out of here. You need to get some sleep."

He rubbed both hands over his face. "Yeah, all right." He leaned his head back. "Mind calling and seeing if that hotel down the block has any vacancies?"

"You don't have a place to stay? You didn't check in at a hotel?"

He pulled his hands away from his eyes. "When exactly would I have had time to do that? I came to the hospital straight from the airport this morning."

No wonder he'd fallen asleep. He had to be going on thirty-six hours easy. "Sure, no problem." I reached for the phone. "If you want, you can crash at my place."

"Thanks, but I'd rather take my chances somewhere with room service and a mini-bar. I remember how barren your cupboards are."

"That place burned down not too long ago. Martin and I have an apartment you can use. There are tons of groceries and maybe some home-cooked leftovers. Martin has this weird obsession with keeping us fed. Y'never know what might be in the fridge."

"I don't want to intrude. Thanks, though."

"Sure." I dialed and made a reservation for him. "Give the front desk your name."

"I know how hotels work, Parker."

"Glad to hear it."

He stood, making his back pop in the process. "For what it's worth, I'm happy for you. An apartment, food, and this swanky office, it suits you better than the federal building."

"At the moment, it doesn't feel like it."

"Understandable, but you and hierarchical structure and authority just don't mix." He grabbed the messenger bag he'd been carrying around all day, which contained everything he brought with him for the trip. "I'm glad you and Martin worked things out. I don't know him or much about him, but if he can put up with your shit, he must be a saint. And on your better days, you deserve a saint."

"All the saints are dead, Lucca. I don't want a saint. I prefer the people I care about to stay alive. That includes you."

"I'll do my best."

"Do better than that."

"Damn, you're bossy."

"You should be used to it by now. Or have you forgotten how this works?" I walked him to the elevator. The doors just opened when I heard my office phone ring. "Shit." I ran down the hall and dove for the phone, knocking my keyboard and several folders to the floor. "Hello?"

"I'm not sure if I'm flattered or offended you actually thought I'd crawl into the sewer like a rat. Then again, you must have felt right at home with more of your kind."

"Francisco," I said, relieved Amir had been able to redirect the call, "what do you want?"

"To play."

"Then visit a toy store."

He chuckled. "Still with so much fight, but you'll learn." Music boomed in the background. "Do you remember that club I took you to?"

"Yes."

"You made quite the impression that night," Steele said.

"I hope that kept you warm on those lonely nights in prison," I retorted. "I can't say fondling you was the highlight of my career."

"I always wondered how you moved that much product so fast," Steele mused. Either he didn't hear me, or he chose to ignore me. "That night changed everything." He let out an angry grunt. "How'd you do it?"

"I'm a magician."

"What the fuck does that mean?"

"I never reveal my secrets."

He cursed, growing more irritated by the second. "I could have killed you today. You should thank me for sparing your pathetic life."

"I'll get right on that, just as soon as hell freezes over."

Lucca tapped on the doorjamb. *Cool it*, he mouthed.

I gave him a disgusted look. No, I wouldn't pull my punches. Plus, I needed to keep Steele on the line as long as possible. Amir and the techs upstairs could work miracles. If anyone could get a fix on his location, it'd be them.

"Who was the cop with you today?" Steele asked. "You seemed adamant about saving his pointless life."

"I don't know, just some dick assigned to the case."

"I don't believe you."

"I don't care." Steele would pay for Mark and Cooper. He'd only make things worse for himself if he went after Nick or Jen.

"You should." Steele chuckled again, a sound that made my insides quiver. "Have you seen Hotshot lately? Bet he went into hiding the minute he heard I was out. He knows I'm looking for him."

"Hotshot?" I tried to play dumb, though I knew exactly to whom Steele was referring. Derek Heathcliff wasn't hiding, at least not by choice. But Steele admitted he was looking for him. I just didn't know if he had found him yet. I wrote Heathcliff's name on the pad and held it up for Lucca to see. *Find him.*

He stepped into the break room across the hall, out of earshot of my office, and made the call.

"That cock-block prick narcotics detective, where is he?" Steele asked.

"How should I know?"

Steele didn't say anything for a moment, almost as if deciding whether he should believe me. "Tell him I'm coming for him."

"No."

"No?" Steele said, surprised.

"No," I repeated. "I won't let you hurt anyone else. I'll find you, and I'll end you. I'm not going to sit around and wait for you to call to tell me you've killed someone else. I don't lie down. You should know that by now. And I don't give up. You said you want to kill me, so come get me. Because while you're dicking around, I'm coming for you."

"Let me?" He laughed, a long, belly laugh. "Let me? You're already too late. Or you will be soon enough."

I swallowed, wondering whose life he'd take next. "Francisco, don't do this."

"Then admit it. Admit that I'm in control. This is my game. I call the shots."

Lucca returned to the doorway and gave me a thumbs up. Heathcliff was safe, but that didn't provide any relief. It just left too many other possibilities.

"You're right." The words tasted sour on my tongue. Steele didn't speak for a moment, and the lag in conversation allowed me to focus on the music in the background, loud, thumping rhythms. I checked the time. The clubs were open now. I knew where he was. I just didn't know if it was a trap. "I'm sorry."

"That's better," he said. "So I'll give you a chance, just one, to save him. But you have to get here in time. And if I spot a single cop or Fed, I'll kill them too. The more you bring, the bigger the bloodbath. You better run, Alex. Time's a-wastin'."

"Where are you?" I asked.

He laughed again. "Figure it out." And then he was gone.

TWENTY-THREE

"O'Connell, Thompson," I continued listing possibilities as I ran up the steps with Lucca at my side, "Aronne, Moretti," my voice caught in my throat, but I managed to squeak out, "Martin. Steele said 'he'."

"All right. I'll start with the hospital since so much of the task force had been there. They might still be there. I'll figure out who's missing."

"Yeah, fine." I waved away his suggestion. I didn't care, just as long as we determined the identity of Steele's victim. I burst into the lab and nearly collided with Amir. "Did you get a location? I kept him on the phone as long as I could."

"We have it narrowed to four square blocks." Amir pulled up a map.

"I know where he is." I unholstered my nine millimeter and checked to make sure it was loaded. Of course it was loaded, but that was a habitual action I could never quite shake. "What did you find out about the phone?"

"He's tracking it. He knows where you are, so I cloned it in order to allow you to move freely," Amir said.

"That's how he'll determine if I give it to the cops or Feds." I looked down at the devices. "Give me both of them for now. You have a trap and trace going?"

"Of course."

"Okay." I took a breath, the familiar jitteriness overtaking my senses. "I have to go."

"Parker," Lucca grabbed my arm, glancing at Amir for help, "where are you going?"

"To stop Steele."

"Call the police. Call the FBI. They'll handle it. You're not an agent."

"It doesn't matter. I'll take care of it."

"Where is he?" Lucca asked, but I didn't answer. He looked at Amir. "Where is he?" Lucca repeated.

"Eddie, he said no cops. I have to go alone," I said.

"Don't you realize that's what he wants? He's going to kill you."

"No, he isn't. He would have had better aim when he shot me earlier if that's what he wanted." I ripped my arm free of Lucca's grip and shoved him out of my way. "I have to go. We don't have time for a lengthy debate. I need a head start." I glanced at Amir. "Ten minutes."

The tech nodded, and I ran out the door and jabbed the elevator button. I didn't have time to run down thirty-one flights. The elevator opened. Lucien stood inside, like an elevator attendant, the garage button already illuminated.

"I used my access codes to make this an express trip," Lucien said as he continued to face the panel. "Two security teams will meet you at the location."

"No."

"Steele won't spot them. They aren't cops or Feds, so you're obeying his instructions. But you can't go alone. You don't know what you're walking into."

"You listened to my conversation?"

"Consider it a party line," Cross said. "The teams won't interfere, unless you need help. This is a police matter. You should realize that. What you're doing is stupid. You're interfering in an active investigation. This isn't what we do at Cross Security."

"Good thing I'm only a consultant. Yours and theirs. The cops won't charge me."

"I wouldn't be so sure, but even so," Cross said, "it's

fucking stupid. You are running into this situation blind. Steele's a killer who may have a hostage. Do you even know where he is?"

"I have an idea."

"Any plans on sharing it with me?"

"Why?" I turned to face him. "You already know. The background noise gave it away."

A look of self-satisfaction crossed his face. "Good. We're in agreement. Do you know who he has?"

"No. I told Lucca to find out."

"Speaking of, what would you like me to do with the federal agent upstairs? I'm sure he isn't pleased by your actions."

"Amir's holding him off long enough to give me a head start." The doors opened, and I ran for my car. "Is Martin safe?"

"Yes."

"Keep it that way," I yelled before climbing behind the wheel.

When I parked in the tow-away zone half a block from the club, I wondered how I even got here. The trip was a blur, but it didn't matter. I checked the time. By now, Lucca would have called for reinforcements. They'd storm the building once they organized. I counted on their delayed response time.

But now that I was here, it didn't feel right. This couldn't be the location. The club was too public. No agent or cop would come here unless he was on assignment, right? It was a trap. I could feel it.

I looked around. No sign of Steele or any official vehicles. I entered the club, which was just a dive with live music. I'd only been inside once before. This wasn't exactly my kind of place.

The dim lights and smoky haze concealed a lot from view, but it was still a public place. A man bleeding to death would attract a lot of attention. The bar and dance floor were out. The tables and booths were less obvious. I went past each of them, searching faces for anyone familiar or in distress. Most people leered at me. A few made rather unfriendly remarks.

As the seconds ticked by, I wondered if Steele was tracking the burner and laughing while he cut up another of my friends. The thought sickened me. Even if he wasn't here, he'd want to be close enough to watch. I was sure of it.

Pushing on, I checked the back hallway, finding the offices locked. The last time I'd been here, I'd been lucky enough to slip inside one of them. That wouldn't be the case today. I just hoped the same held true for Steele.

Moving on, I checked the bathrooms. A guy at the urinal gave me an odd look, but he didn't comment as I swung each stall door open. No Steele. No blood, guts, or gore. This had to be a wild goose chase. The bastard.

The ladies' room had a line, two women deep. I didn't care. I pushed my way inside, crouching down and checking beneath stall doors. Nothing.

"Dammit." I exited the bathroom, searching for another place to check. Striding up to the bar, I leaned over and held my phone out. "Hey," I called to the bartender, "have you seen this guy?"

The bartender stared blankly at me, so I waved the phone in his face. He didn't even look at Steele's mugshot. "No."

I wanted to jump over the counter, grab him by the collar, and force him to look at the photo. Somehow, I resisted. I didn't see Steele. I must have been wrong. He must be somewhere else within these four blocks, but not at the club. At least not anymore. Hopefully, Lucca had made actual progress. Steele was probably laughing his ass off while I wasted precious seconds inside the club.

I scanned the room a final time. A metal rig with lights and speakers hung above the dance floor. From here, I couldn't tell exactly what was above, but a man-sized heap hung over the side of the catwalk. Locating an alcove in the corner behind the stage that led to the rigging above, I strode toward it. Halfway there, a man grabbed me from behind and shoved me against the railing and pressed his body flush against mine, constricting my movements.

"You found me. Or should I say I found you?" Steele's hot breath creeped down the side of my face. I moved for my gun, but Steele pressed me harder against the rail, making the metal rungs dig into my thighs and chest. He wrapped both arms around me, pinning my arms to my sides. "If you cause a scene, a lot of innocent people will be hurt, maybe even killed. You don't want that." It didn't sound like a question.

I stayed completely still, my heart hammering in my chest. Every cell in my body wanted to fight, but I resisted the nearly overpowering urge. "I came here, didn't I? You said if I got here in time, I could save him. So let me save him. No one else needs to get hurt, Francisco."

Steele waited, his hips moving ever so slightly to the beat of the music. The sick bastard thought this was fun. He was enjoying every torturous minute.

"Are the cops waiting outside?" he finally asked.

"No." Though, they'd be here soon enough.

"Good. You listened." He licked the side of my face.

"Let go of me."

"We both know what happens if I do, so let's go over the ground rules first." He leaned down, resting his chin against my shoulder. "On the phone, you lectured me about choices, chica. I took that choices and consequences speech to heart. It got me right here." He jerked his hips forward, pressing his pelvic bone harder into my back. This excited him. "I'll give you a choice. You see that rig up there? That lump off to the side, that's one of those FBI geeks. He's alive, but he won't be for much longer. If you want to save him, I'll let you try."

"What did you do to him? Who is he?"

Steele laughed. "I had some fun. Not as much as I did with Jablonsky or the other one in his apartment, but I enjoyed myself. Plastic bags are so versatile. You never know when one might come in handy, and you can get them anywhere. They're even more fun when you combine them with a few cable ties."

I stared at the shape through the haze. It didn't move. "How do I know he isn't already dead? You suffocated him, didn't you?"

"Perhaps." Steele shrugged behind me. "Perhaps not. What'll it be? You can stop me or save him. It's your decision. Think fast."

Without warning, Steele shoved a plastic bag with a pull tie over my head and yanked hard. I tore at the bag, ripping it to shreds before tugging against the thick string. Grabbing the knife from my pocket, I flicked it open and cut the tie off, gasping and turning, but Steele had vanished.

In a split second, I shoved my way across the dance floor, went up the ladder, and out onto the catwalk. Saving a life and stopping a killer were nearly on par, but no one else could save the agent on the rig. I just prayed I made the right choice.

Carefully, I edged across the beam. The lump on the walkway wasn't a sandbag, which had been both my fear and hope. I knelt down, feeling the unsteady footing vibrate up through my knees.

"Whoa, take it easy," I yelled, hoping the man could hear me over the speakers. I didn't need to spook him or we might both fall. "I'm here to help."

Just like Cooper, Steele's latest victim had a plastic bag tied over his head. I cut it loose, revealing Agent Lawson. I didn't know how Steele had gotten the FBI tech genius up here, but it didn't matter. I had to get him down, but first I had to get him breathing again.

"Lawson," I shouted, tilting his head to the side and feeling for a pulse. Everything vibrated so much it was hard to be certain, but my gut said he was alive. Checking his airway, I tilted his head back. "Breathe." I tried a few chest compressions, feeling his weight shift and fearing we'd both crash the twenty-five feet to the floor below. "C'mon." I counted as I pressed down each time. I didn't hear him gasp or notice his eyes open. But when he grabbed my hand, I stopped.

"Parker?"

"Thank god." I rocked back on my heels, nearly toppling over the edge. Grabbing the rail, I let out an uneasy breath. "Help's on the way." Except I hadn't called for help yet. After dialing 9-1-1, I called Cross, who patched me through to his team.

Within seconds, two men joined us on the catwalk.

"How the hell'd he get up here?" one of them asked. I didn't know, but having this conversation twenty-five feet in the air didn't hold much appeal. "Let's get you down and out of the way so we can get him down. What's his condition?"

"I don't know."

"Any neck or back injuries?"

"I don't know."

The team leader held the same expression. "We'll take it from here."

When I reached the ground, the other two members of the first team were on standby. "Where's Steele?" I asked.

"Is your friend okay?" one of them asked.

"I think he will be. He's talking."

"That's good. That's really good. Ambulances are on the way, but Cross is sending his own mobile medical unit in case the paramedics take too long."

"That's great." I searched the area, surprised to find so many people still dancing. How could they be so oblivious? "Where's the other team? Did they detain Steele?"

"They're working on it."

I didn't like what that meant. But before I could ask anything else, the other two members of the security team carried Lawson down the ladder. They laid him on the floor, assessed his injuries, and made certain he was in no immediate physical danger.

"How'd this happen?" I asked as the other two men had the music shut down and the dance floor cleared. The lights came on. I didn't see any visible wounds on Lawson's body. "Didn't anyone warn you about Steele?"

Lawson's cheeks turned red, purely from embarrassment. "I'm a moron."

"A lot of that going around lately." I settled onto the floor beside him. "Start at the beginning."

"Not much to tell." Lawson glanced up at the Cross Security team who had turned their focus outward to monitor for additional threats. "Steele catfished me."

"How?"

Lawson sat up, coughing a little as he took a few breaths. Aside from the embarrassed flush on his cheeks, he looked pale. His lips were purplish, or maybe that was from the lights. "Dating app. She found me online, or he did, I guess, and asked me to meet her," he winced, "him, here. That was before anything happened. Before Jablonsky. We postponed a few times. I didn't think it could be related. I just didn't think."

"Okay. So you came here tonight because you had a date?"

"Yeah, so I'm at the bar, waiting and figuring she got one look at me and changed her mind, when this knockout comes up to me. She apologizes for running late, tells me she had a problem with the equipment, and asks if I can hang around and wait."

"What equipment?"

"Oh, her profile said she's a DJ. So she said the sound system and lights were bugging out. Naturally, I offered to take a look."

"Did she know computers are your thing?"

"Yeah, my job's included on my profile, right along with my Ph.D. in idiocy."

I put a reassuring hand on his shoulder. We all did dumb things from time to time. Hopefully, Lawson learned from his mistake. "Then what?"

"She points me to the speaker system, says she thinks something must have gotten unplugged from above, and she's waiting for the rigging guy to show up."

"So you volunteered to go up there? Did she go up with you?"

"No. That was the weird part. She disappeared while I was checking the connections. The next thing I know, Steele's coming at me. I had nowhere to go. I tried to fight him off, but you've seen what it's like up there. He locked me in a chokehold. I was out before I knew what was happening."

That must have been moments before Steele grabbed me. "I need to know everything."

"That's it, Parker."

"Tell me about the woman. Even if Steele catfished you online, he had some chick stand in as your date. Describe her. What's her name and the handle she used online? Did her profile pic match the woman you met here?" I noticed red and blue flashing lights illuminate the club. The cavalry was here to put an end to this party.

"Sarah, no last name. She was goth. Black leggings, black top with a silver print design, it might have been a middle finger. I'm not sure. Her handle's KillaDJ, but her profile pic was taken of the entire club. You can't make much out." Lawson blinked. "Parker," he clutched my hand, "thank you."

The paramedics rolled in with a stretcher, and they pushed me out of the way while they got to work. Lucca came up beside me while four FBI agents and two police officers pushed their way into the club.

"You're alive," Lucca said. "Wonders never cease."

"So is Lawson, which is all that matters."

"Did you see Steele?"

"We danced, but he left before the song ended."

"You should have had backup. Real backup, not these rent-a-cops."

"Cross doesn't hire rent-a-cops."

"Whatever they are, they didn't stop Steele from escaping. He got away."

"Can't Amir track his phone?" I'd seen Cross's tech work plenty of miracles. By now, he should have Steele's exact coordinates. "Amir will give us the location, and all we have to do is pick Steele up. Easy peasy."

"Not exactly. The signal went dead right after you left. Amir tried to access the phone remotely, but nothing worked. Steele must have destroyed it or pulled the battery. Either way, he's gone. You let him get away."

"I didn't let him get away. I made a choice to save Lawson. Deal with it." Because I sure as hell had to.

TWENTY-FOUR

"Eight men. You had eight men positioned at the club. What happened?" Moretti asked.

Cross glared at me. "Four of them remained with Parker. The second team tracked your suspect on foot. They didn't know he had a car waiting several blocks away. How could they have known that?"

"Two follow on foot. Two follow in the car. It's basic, Lucien."

Cross held up his palms and stepped back. "Quite frankly, this is none of my business. I want nothing to do with any of this."

Moretti squinted in Cross's direction. "I just want to know what happened, son. That's it."

"I'm not your son," Cross snarled.

I looked up, wondering where that came from. I'd seen Cross lose his temper, most of the time with me. It usually involved a lot of throat clearing, slightly raised tones, and plenty of unfulfilled threats. This was different. It was personal.

"So Steele got into a car and drove off. Did they get a plate?" Moretti asked, unperturbed by Cross's uncharacteristic outburst.

"No plate."

"Make and model?" Moretti asked.

"You have that information. They provided it to the officers at the scene. Grey, four-door, with a mismatched right corner panel. It was blue." Cross went behind his desk and sat down. "Anything else? My patience is wearing thin."

Moretti worked his jaw. "Not from you." He faced me. "On the other hand, you and I need to have a conversation in private."

"I'll take you to my office," I said.

"Alex," Cross called before we made it out the door, "when you're finished with official police business, I need a word."

"Yes, sir," I said.

Moretti eyed me as we went past Cross's assistant. "I have a word for him."

"Usually I have two."

Moretti stifled a chuckle. He watched the illuminated light above the elevator, waiting for the doors to open. "Where's the phone? You were supposed to turn it over to us in the hospital, but things got crazy when the Feds showed up. I'm guessing you forgot all about it."

"Would you believe I misplaced it?"

"No."

"How about my dog ate it?"

"You don't have a dog. Cut the Don Adams schtick."

"Steele's tracking it. He gave me specific instructions not to turn it over to the cops. If I do, he'll know because he can monitor its location."

"Why don't you turn off the tracker?" Moretti asked.

"That leaves too many possibilities."

"So you're going to take it home with you?"

I hadn't thought that far ahead. "No."

"We need to monitor it. When he calls, and I know he will, we can track his location. We need that phone, Parker. It's what's best for everyone."

The elevator came, and we stepped inside. Instead of pressing the button for my office, I pressed the button for the floor which housed the labs. "It's already being done."

"By Cross Security." Moretti blew out a breath. "Didn't Cross just say he wasn't helping?"

"Welcome to my world. According to what I understand, I have full use of the resources here. The police department hired me to consult on this case. So what I bring you should be gold, even if it comes from Cross Security."

"I need to contact the DA's office and make sure."

"You should," I said, "but pissing off Steele isn't advisable. The phone is the only connection we have to him. I'm not sure why, but he won't call my phone again. If he stops communicating, we're SOL."

"He's not stupid. He knows we're monitoring your phone. That's why he doesn't want us monitoring this one too. It worries me that he's so desperate to speak to you."

"I'm his favorite person."

"Didn't he shoot at you earlier today?"

"Francisco has an odd way of showing his affection."

"Any idea why he didn't kill Agent Lawson? Frankly, he had him dead to rights. Had you not realized where they were, the FBI tech would be dead now."

"It was a test. Steele wants to see if I'll follow his rules. Saving Lawson's life might have been a reward, or it just served as the perfect distraction for Steele to slip away. But this is far from the end. He'll make contact again, as soon as he picks out his next victim, unless we find him first."

"I dunno, Parker. He could have killed Lawson and left his body on the catwalk. It wouldn't have made a difference. Why spare him? Steele's already proven he's a cold-blooded killer. It doesn't make any sense."

"He didn't kill Nurse Andrews either."

Moretti sucked some air in between his teeth, making a whistling sound. "Andrews had nothing to do with any of this. Wrong place, wrong time."

"Does that matter to a cold-blooded killer?"

"You tell me. You know Steele. You know how he thinks."

"Lawson's just a tech. He rarely ventures into the field, and when he does, it's because he has to collect evidence or hack something. He spoke at Bard's trial and Steele's, basically to explain how evidence was processed. Steele shouldn't have a beef with him. My gut says Lawson would be a low priority target."

"Okay, so he used Lawson as bait to lure you out and get you to play his game. Why didn't he take advantage of the situation? He could have killed you and Lawson. Frankly, I'm not sure anyone at the club would have noticed right away."

"A woman dead on the dance floor might have gotten some attention," I said. "After all, they'd have to dance around me. And that would just be an unnecessary inconvenience." I thought for a moment. "Steele doesn't want to hurt me yet. He has plans. Big ones. Somehow, tonight will factor into them. I'm just not sure how."

"That's why I'm keeping Heathcliff chained to his desk and narcotics has units watching out for their compromised undercovers. It's the best we can do until we remove Steele from the equation. We'll know more once witnesses are questioned and we review the club's surveillance footage." The elevator opened. "I'll do whatever it takes to find Steele, even if it means getting a court order for that phone and every bit of intel Cross Security possesses. Steele's a menace, and he's killing cops. Local, federal, it doesn't matter. He shot Mark for fuck's sake."

"You don't need a court order." I led the way into the lab, spotting Amir immediately. After a brief introduction, he gave me the breakdown on the phone and caller.

"Francisco Steele isn't new to the game. He used a burner phone registered to an alias and purchased with a prepaid credit card, also registered to the same alias. The reason for doing that is to make it harder to flag. The info matches up on the phone and card. It wouldn't have gotten a second look, except Steele's chatty." Amir clicked a key, revealing the list of cell numbers pinged in the vicinity of the first two crime scenes. "He thought he was clever, blocking the number." Amir highlighted it on the screen. "This places Steele in the vicinity of the Jablonsky shooting and the Cooper murder, in case you had any doubts."

"We didn't," I said.

"If Steele was clever, he would have left Dodge after

breaking out of prison," Moretti said.

"That would have been preferable," Amir agreed. He highlighted the name. "He's using the alias Tom Collins."

"Wow, real original," I muttered. "Fuzzy Navel must have been taken."

Amir quirked an eyebrow. He didn't understand the reference. "Tom Collins lives at this address. He's seventy-one. Widowed. No children. He doesn't have a record, and as far as I can tell, he would have had no reason to cross paths with the KXDs."

"Can you get a look at his medical records?" Moretti asked.

Amir's eyebrows knit together in consternation. "Is this a trick question?"

"What are you thinking?" I asked Moretti.

"That either Steele pulled a name out of a hat or off a bar menu and just happened to steal this guy's identity, or the septuagenarian has a chronic pain condition and can't afford his medication."

"Or he's an opium addict."

Moretti shrugged. "You said he's widowed. He could have been buying for her if she had a terminal disease. Doctors and pharmacies have been cracking down on painkillers. Mr. Collins might not have had much of a choice."

I'd never heard anyone make the argument for putting more pharmaceuticals in the hands of people, but it was possible. Anything was.

"I don't know, just something to consider," Moretti said. He looked at the screen. "I'll need everything you have on Tom Collins, the real Tom Collins. We'll put him under investigation, figure out what's what, and if he's harboring a fugitive."

Amir clicked a few buttons, and the printer whirred to life. Moretti scooped the pages off the tray, memorizing the guy's driver's license photo, vehicle registration information, and address.

"After you left," Amir said, "I ran the burner phone's records."

"My burner phone?"

"It's clean. The first time it was used was when Steele called you in the hospital. After he called the second time, I pulled the number and traced the burner he's using. It didn't take much effort to access his phone records."

"I don't want to hear any more until I get a warrant," Moretti said. "I need to call this in anyway. Parker, you good here?"

"What about the phone?" I asked. "Do you still want it?"

The lieutenant sighed. "Keep me informed. The next time he reaches out, I'm your first call. Not the Feds. Me. Got it?"

"Yes, sir."

"All right," Moretti said, though he was far from pleased, "forward the information on it to me, along with the basic info on Steele's phone. I don't want the records. I'll get those from the phone company just as soon as a judge signs the order. But I want everything else."

"Okay," Amir said.

"Should you discover anything solid in the next few minutes that you think I need to know without knowing the specifics, I'll be in the lobby. If not, I'll see you bright and early tomorrow morning at the precinct, Parker. Don't be late."

"Lucca might join us. That is, if he drags his ass out of bed in the morning. Kendall asked him to help Davis debrief Lawson. And knowing Lucca, he'll have to write his report afterward. I'm not sure he'll be up bright and early."

"Whatever, just as long as he shares, I don't care." Moretti nodded at Amir.

As soon as Moretti left the lab, I took a seat in one of the empty rolling chairs and rubbed my hands together, surprised to find they had stopped shaking after everything that happened in the club. Obviously, my body was too exhausted to bother with the residual shakes that usually accompanied situations like this. "You were just about to tell me something," I nudged.

"Steele's burner texted Agent Lawson several times over the course of the last four days. From the intimate language used, I'd say the FBI tech has some explaining to do." Amir held out the sheet, and I skimmed the messages.

"Lawson said he was catfished." I pointed to Steele's flirtatious texts. "This backs his story." I checked the dates and times. "Steele texted Lawson before Jablonsky was attacked."

"Does that change your timeline?" Amir asked. "I thought it might."

"Not necessarily." I didn't know exactly what to make of it. Did Steele plan for Lawson to be his first victim but grew impatient? "Did you share this with Lucca?"

"He happened to be standing here while I was reading it," Amir said. "He probably saw it."

"Good." That meant my former partner was operating with all the facts. It'd make it easier for him to debrief Lawson and get an accurate statement. "What about the rest of these calls?" Two dozen different numbers were listed on the page. "Who are these people?"

"Connections." Amir clicked a button, and the row of monitors on the wall filled with photos and bios. "The top two screens show members of the KXDs. The two screens below them are suspected gang members. The third screen over is a cartel hitman. The rest we're still working on."

"But you were able to identify every number?"

"Except for these three." He pointed to the highlighted numbers on the last screen. "Those are unregistered. I can't get the data on them. The only information I have is when Steele called. From the call duration, they didn't speak long. Less than a minute each time. It's not much to go on."

"What does it mean?"

"I'm not sure yet."

"What about those two screens?" I pointed to the ones in the middle.

"Businesses," Amir said. "He ordered pizza. Called for a taxi. That third one is a dry cleaner. The one below that is a laundromat. And the last six are various Stop N' Shops."

"He has an obsession with those stores." The bag he put over my head had the same logo as the bag he used on Lawson and Cooper. "We need to find out why." I pointed to the businesses. "Print that out. I'll give it to Moretti."

Amir printed off the page, and I went down to the lobby. The KXDs had used laundromats and other businesses to conceal their illegal activities and labs. Even though these locations hadn't been explored during the initial investigation, it was possible Bard's empire had been larger than any of us realized. Perhaps Steele wanted to get things going again. Maybe that's why Bard gave him resources and his blessing. Or that was just another of my hairbrained theories.

While I updated Moretti, a familiar town car stopped in front of the building and Martin stepped out with his personal bodyguard, Bruiser, in tow. A Cross Security vehicle pulled up behind them, and two of the guards got out. Martin didn't even act like he noticed. At this point, he was probably used to having an entourage of armed men following him around.

"Parker," Moretti waved his hand in front of my face, "you good?"

"Yeah, just distracted."

He followed my gaze to the man entering the lobby. "All right. I'll get some people started on this. We have a mess of interviews to get through too. If I need you, I'll call you. You do the same. But after these last few days, I hope it'll be a quiet night."

"Me too."

Moretti stopped Martin a few steps before he reached me. "Make sure she gets some sleep."

"Will do," Martin promised. As soon as the police lieutenant was gone, Martin quirked an eyebrow at me. "What was that about?"

"Who knows? What are you doing here?"

"I have to talk to Lucien. I need his help."

TWENTY-FIVE

"You made sure this was okay?" I sounded like a broken record.

"Yes, sweetheart. The FBI wanted to move him anyway after what happened at the hospital today. This will be safer," Martin said. He looked at Cross. "Without your medical team, this wouldn't be possible. Thank you, Lucien."

Cross nodded. "Anything I can do. You know that."

I stared at my boss, wondering who this imposter was. "Are you sure you have everything Mark could possibly need?"

"And more." Cross offered a smile, a rare sight, at least when it came to our interactions. "Transport will move him from the hospital to one of my safe houses. We already have it outfitted with a hospital bed and monitors. The FBI has been notified. They will supply their own protection detail. Should any complications arise, a twenty-four hour nurse will be right there, along with two doctors trained in multiple disciplines and prepared to provide any emergency life-saving care he might require."

"The safe house isn't that far from the hospital. We could get him back there in a matter of minutes, if need be," Martin said. "In the meantime, the FBI will keep a dummy detail in the SDU and a decoy in Mark's hospital room in case Steele tries again."

"You really think that'll stop Steele?" I asked.

"I'll assign a team to keep watch on the building. After what just happened, we have a more accurate picture of who Francisco Steele is and how he operates," Cross said.

"What just happened?" Martin asked.

"I'll tell you later," I mumbled, turning my attention to Cross. "Are you sure about this? You practically told Moretti to go screw himself. Now you're volunteering to assist the FBI. That doesn't make any sense."

"Alex," Martin scolded.

"No, she's right," Cross said. "I have been giving you mixed signals."

"You always do," I said.

Cross hid his chuckle in a cough and cleared his throat. "When this first happened, I offered you my services. That includes this. But helping you isn't the same as helping the police."

"I'm consulting for them on this case."

"And I will enjoy seeing the looks on their faces when they get a Cross Security invoice for the work you've done, but I will not volunteer my services to them. Everything goes through you. Whatever you want to give them is your business. And whatever you need from me is your business. It isn't theirs."

"So I'm a go-between?"

"That's my only condition," Cross said. "That is what I wanted to speak to you about earlier."

"How does that work? FBI agents and Cross Security are guarding Jablonsky. The two have to communicate if Steele discovers the location," I said.

"Should that be the case, we will defer to law enforcement and assist in a limited capacity," Cross clarified.

"Like at the club when you let Steele walk?" I asked.

"We didn't let him walk. He got away. There's a difference. The teams were there to protect and assist you. They scouted the exterior but failed to identify a threat.

Steele wasn't armed, not in the traditional sense, and he didn't look like the photos we have on file."

I never saw him. "What does he look like now?"

Cross reached for the phone. "Justin, bring in a printout from the dance floor."

A moment later, Cross's assistant came in with said item in hand. Steele had shaved, just like O'Connell predicted. He wore a tight black t-shirt that said "Security" in yellow on the back. He looked like a club bouncer.

"After he left the club, he changed clothes. On those crowded streets, we lost sight, and by the time we made him again, he had already gotten into the car."

"Why did your team wait so long? They could have grabbed him after the bag trick. By then, it must have been quite obvious who he was and what he wanted."

"I promised to protect you, and we rendered aid to Agent Lawson. My people stayed inside with you. That's their job. The other team was outside waiting, but his wardrobe change slowed them down. I assure you, that won't happen again."

I tamped down my internal grumbling. I could argue with Cross until I was blue in the face, but it was a waste of time. Lawson survived. So did I. Those were the two most important factors.

"Steele has to be stopped," I said.

"I agree," Cross conceded. "As I've said several times already, I'm willing to help."

Martin stared at him. "You protect Alex at all costs. That's what we agreed to."

"I didn't agree to that," I piped up, but neither man looked at me.

"Once Jablonsky is under your roof, so to speak, you will do whatever it takes to protect him too. Is that understood?" Martin asked. "Or do I need to take my business elsewhere?"

"It will be handled to your satisfaction," Cross promised. "Nothing has changed, with the possible exception of law enforcement forcing my security team to back down."

"All right," Martin said, "let me make a few calls and get the ball rolling." He pressed his lips against my temple before stepping out of Cross's office.

"You can't protect me," I said.

"The hell I can't," Cross retorted. "History will not repeat itself here, especially in regards to my client's wishes."

"Client?"

Cross cleared his throat again and busied himself with straightening his desk. "Yes, client."

"You finally signed Martin," I said bitterly. "Congratulations."

"We are not adversaries, Alex. You said you don't work for him. And obviously, he came to me to provide protection for you, much in the same way you asked me to provide protection for him. The difference is I didn't make you sign a contract. You get these perks because you work for me." He cocked his head from side to side. "More or less."

"I don't like it."

"Too bad." Cross waited, but I didn't say anything else. "I am the best at what I do. My people are the best. That includes you. So you should be reassured nothing will happen to Mark Jablonsky or James Martin. You have my word on that. And James has my word nothing will happen to you."

"Your word better be good." Turning on my heel, I left his office. As usual, my loyalties were pulled in too many directions – the police, FBI, Cross Security, Martin, Jablonsky, and even Lucca. I didn't want to make enemies with any of them. We were in this together, but lines had been drawn. Kendall started it. Cross ended it. And I didn't know where that left me.

It took some time, but Martin made calls and arranged Mark's move. Since Mark left him in charge with legal documentation, Kendall was willing to play ball on this. The cynical part of me figured it had to do with the numerous background checks and investigations that had been conducted over the years in regards to Martin due to our relationship and my status at the Bureau, but I could be wrong. Perhaps Kendall actually was a good man, the man I thought he was before he accused me of shooting

Mark and refusing to read me in on the case. That was just protocol, but it stung. However, I couldn't let a bruised ego and hurt feelings stand in the way of what was best for Mark. And Steele could get to him if he really wanted to. He could get to any of us. He proved it tonight.

"Hey," Martin said from my office door, "Mark's been moved. I'm on my way over there. Are you coming?"

I turned off the computer. For the last hour, I'd been staring at the list of businesses Steele had called, hoping to make heads or tails out of them. I wouldn't put it past him to have dialed these numbers just to have us chase our tails, but Moretti was all over it. And since Lucca had seen most of this information, the OIO was too.

"Yes." I tucked the tracked burner phone into my desk drawer and pocketed the cloned phone. If Steele checked to see where I was, he'd get the address of the office building. Cross Security only took up three levels, which meant I could be anywhere inside the building. It'd take time for him to discover I wasn't here.

I followed Martin to the elevator. Cross had a car waiting for us in the garage with tinted windows. Steele would never recognize it, and if he was watching, he wouldn't see us inside.

"Every precaution," I said.

"Every precaution," Martin repeated, wrapping an arm around me. Initially, I stiffened but eventually gave in and nestled against his shoulder. "You're angry."

"I'm tired and irritable." I ran my hand over his abs and around his side, hugging him. "Now's not the time for this conversation."

"I love you."

"I know. That makes it more difficult to be angry."

"I'm sure you'll manage."

"Girl's gotta have a talent."

"You have plenty of talents. This doesn't have to be one of them."

"But I'm so good at it."

He laughed for what felt like the first time in days. I closed my eyes and fell asleep until the car stopped. Martin nudged me, and I sat up. We were in an underground garage. I looked behind us at the gate. That would make it more difficult for Steele to gain access.

We got out of the car and followed the two members of Cross Security to the elevator, where one of them inserted a keycard into the panel and pushed a button. *Not bad*, I surmised. When the doors opened, two FBI agents blocked our entry into the large, converted room, which looked like it could be its own miniature wing in the hospital.

They checked our IDs and verified our identities with a fingerprint scanner, which meant Kendall wasn't taking any chances. About damn time. He'd lost a former agent, nearly lost the best tech the Bureau had, and things were still iffy when it came to his top supervisory special agent.

"Go ahead." The two agents stepped to the side, allowing us out of the elevator alcove and into the safe house.

I looked around. Exposed beams and pipes ran along the ceiling. The floors needed to be redone, but the shiny white medical equipment and hospital bed distracted from such things.

Mark's room had been sectioned off. A few chairs and a small sofa had been placed in the vicinity, probably on Cross's request to accommodate Martin. A nurse stood beside the bed, checking each of the lines and the readouts. Once she was convinced everything was hooked up properly, she recorded the information on her chart and stepped out of the room. The other end of the apartment had been partitioned off into separate bunk-like rooms for the two doctors. Additional accommodations were close by for the security team, and a full kitchen sat against the back wall.

"Any idea how many of these places Cross has?" I asked Martin.

"You work for him. Why don't you ask?"

"Because you're his favorite."

Martin grinned. "I'm everyone's favorite."

I rolled my eyes and spoke to the nurse about emergency situations and worst case scenarios. When I was done quizzing her on almost everything except a meteor strike or alien invasion, I ducked into Mark's room, surprised to find it sans Martin.

Poking my head out into the hallway, I found him going over the same things with the doctors that I'd just gone over with the nurse. Sometimes, it was scary how alike we were. Surely, that must be a sign we spent far too much time together.

"Steele left me a present," I said, taking a seat on the small sofa beside the bed. "He's jerking me around. He nearly killed Lawson today." I stared at Mark. "Any idea why he'd target Lawson?" I waited. "Yeah, that's the same conclusion I reached too." I sighed. "You need to have a talk with him. Lawson, not Steele. He's online dating. You'd think an FBI tech would be smarter than that. And to top it off, he got catfished. How does that even happen? Online dating is scary enough, but to not run a background check on the woman, that's just downright stupid."

Mark made a sound, or at least I thought he did, so I shut up, straining to hear if he'd do it again. His vitals hadn't changed. More than anything, I needed him to be okay. I needed him back with us.

Martin stepped into the room and squeezed onto the couch beside me. "Do you want to talk about it now?"

"I appreciate you wanting to protect me, but a protection detail will just get in my way. And someone's going to get hurt. I can take care of myself. I have to. Steele nearly killed someone else tonight. He's watching my every move."

"All the more reason to have Cross Security shadowing you."

"No. He'll get confused. He'll think they're cops, and he'll lose his temper. Do you understand?"

"What I understand is a killer gave the love of my life a phone and thinks he can tell her what to do and where to go."

"You know I don't let anyone dictate terms."

"From time to time, I'd prefer if you were a little less headstrong."

"Ditto."

A grin tugged at the corners of Martin's mouth, and he leaned in and kissed me. "I will worry less if a Cross

Security team is following you."

"And I'll worry more. About me. About them. About what Steele's going to do next. I'll be distracted. Do you want that?"

"No." He sighed. "I'll tell Cross to follow your lead, but give careful consideration to your actions. They affect me too."

"I'll be okay."

"Promise?"

"Anything for you, handsome."

He snorted. "Liar."

I shrugged. "I still can't believe you signed with Cross. You're business partners. That's not kosher. Haven't you realized Cross has his own agenda? I don't know what it is. I thought it was signing you, and then I thought it was getting access to your R&D. But I'm not sure anymore."

"Let me worry about Cross. You have enough on your plate." He combed his fingers through my hair. "I haven't seen you this exhausted in a long time."

"Again, ditto."

"Have you eaten today?"

"A little. You?"

"Does coffee and pastry count?"

"Sure."

"Then yes." He lost himself in my eyes. "God, you're beautiful."

"You're delirious from hunger and sleep deprivation."

He nuzzled my neck before pulling back for a real kiss.

Mark made a gagging noise.

I shoved Martin away, jumping off the couch and crouching beside the bed. "Mark?" I turned to Martin, frantic. "Get a doctor."

"No doctor," Mark said through gritted teeth. He opened his eyes. "The two of you should get a room that isn't this one. You're making me sick."

My jaw dropped, and I stared open-mouthed at him.

Martin stood beside the bed. "You're awake. Thank god."

"Debatable." Mark groaned.

"You're okay? Do you remember what happened?" I

asked.

"Francisco Steele," Mark said. "Son of a bitch shot me. I saw him walk away. He left the phone dangling, taunting me, knowing I couldn't call for help. He spoke to you, didn't he?"

I bit my lip, fighting back my emotions. "Yes."

"The police are searching for him. Moretti has all of major crimes on it. The OIO and FBI are assisting," Martin volunteered.

"Lucca came to help." My chin quivered.

"Steele wants you dead," Mark said. "All of us. We destroyed him. He's getting payback."

"I won't let him." A tear fell. I had so much to tell Mark, but I didn't want to break his heart by telling him about Cooper. Not yet. "He went after Lawson tonight, but we stopped him."

"Hey, I'm okay, Alex. Come here. Give an old man a hug." I put one arm around his collarbone and rested my head on his shoulder. He clutched my arm, and I fought to keep the tears from falling. "Don't start blubbering or I'll start blubbering," he said.

"I won't, but don't you ever scare me like that again, Jablonsky. I'll kick your ass if you do."

I held on to Mark. He didn't protest, but when he groaned, I tried to pull away. But he held tight to my arm. "Steele wants revenge. He wants you," he whispered. "He won't stop until he finds you."

"I know, but Steele's the one who needs to worry."

Mark let go of my arm, and I withdrew, wiping my eyes with the back of my hand as nonchalantly as possible. His eyelids fluttered. "God, I'm tired."

"It's okay. You need to rest," Martin said. "We'll be right here when you wake up."

Mark fought against his heavy lids. "Marty, I love ya, but if I have to wake up to your face one more time, I might just decide not to wake up. Go home. Both of you. The two of you look worse than I do."

"How would you know? You can't see yourself," I teased. "How's your head? Is anything fuzzy? What's eighteen times five?"

Jablonsky glared at me, though it was that teasing glare I hadn't seen in far too long. "Do I look like a calculator?"

"The doctors want to check you out first, and then we'll go," Martin said, watching as the nurse and one of the doctors appeared in the doorway. "Do you think you can stay awake for a few more minutes?"

"Only if they hurry," Mark said.

While the doctors asked questions, Martin and I stood unobtrusively in the corner and watched. "He's tired and in pain," I said. "I thought they wanted to keep him sedated."

"Different doctors. Different recommendations."

"You knew he'd wake up?"

"I suspected, but I didn't want to get your hopes up."

I leaned my head back against Martin's chest, glad his arms were tight around my waist supporting me from collapsing into a puddle on the floor. "Do you think he's okay? He seems okay. He remembers us and what happened."

The doctor finished the exam. We said good night to Mark and went into the hallway. "We'll keep monitoring him, but he's not exhibiting any signs of brain damage," the doctor said. "His last scan didn't show any lesions or bleeds. We just need to make sure he doesn't start to decline."

"What are the chances of that?" I asked.

The doctor hedged. "Minimal."

"You'll call us if there's any change, right?" Martin asked.

After making sure everyone had a number where they could reach us, we left the safe house, met the two members of the Cross Security team in the elevator, and had them drive us to our apartment. My car remained at the office, and Martin's was at the hospital. If Steele tracked either of us, he wouldn't know where we were. I just worried he'd search property records and find my new address. Even though that was a concern, I couldn't stop smiling. And neither could Martin.

TWENTY-SIX

"Do you want something to eat?" Martin stared into the fridge. "I could put a pot pie in the oven."

"You bought frozen dinners?"

"Not exactly. Jen brought food for us, but I had Marcal bring it back to the apartment. He's going to the store tomorrow. Do you want frozen dinners? I'll add them to the list."

"I don't know." Admittedly, takeout and frozen food had been my primary means of survival before we moved in together. "I haven't had much of an appetite. I don't think cardboard and plastic will improve that."

"You should take it out of the box and remove the film before you eat it," Martin teased.

"Good tip."

Devious thoughts ran through his mind. "You always think so."

I rolled my eyes at the double entendre. Seeing Mark awake and alive had cheered us up and knocked Martin's mind back into the gutter. Though he'd claim his comment was entirely innocent and I had the dirty mind.

Not bothering to allow him to participate in the conversation, I went into the bathroom. "I just want to shower and go to sleep. In the last three days, I've only slept eight hours."

"Seven. It was seven." He yawned. "If I had more energy, I'd join you."

"I knew it."

"What?"

"Nothing. Ignore me." Truthfully, I was glad to have the time alone. I closed the door, peeled off my clothes, and removed the bandage from my side. The two inch graze was merely a scratch. The bullet barely touched me. Steele didn't want to hit me. He just wanted to hold me at bay.

While I lathered up, I tried to figure out what Francisco's next move would be. He wanted me to suffer, but he didn't physically hurt me. He had plenty of opportunities these last few days, but he hadn't taken advantage. He wanted to draw it out. Was it a taunt? What made him so certain I'd play his game?

After washing off the last of the suds, I turned off the water and wrapped myself in a towel. I dried my hair, put on an oversized t-shirt and pajama shorts, grabbed my nine millimeter off the bathroom counter, and padded into the living room. The lights were out, except for the small light over the kitchen sink. I took the cloned burner and my personal cell phone out of my bag and carried them into the bedroom.

Martin sprawled out on the right side of the bed, so I took the left, positioning my gun on the nightstand beside me. I routinely locked and bolted the front door, but I didn't remember doing it. So I got up and checked. Then I checked the balcony. Even though we were twenty-one stories high and didn't have a fire escape, now was the time for extra precautions.

"Everything okay?" Martin mumbled, facing away from me.

"I just wanted to make sure the doors were locked."

"Did that," he said. He started to roll over, stopping midway and letting out a hiss.

I scooted closer, so he wouldn't have to move to feel me against him. Most of the time his shoulder didn't bother him, but spending days on end in hospital chairs always took their toll. He flattened out on his stomach while I massaged his tight muscles and planted kisses against his left shoulder blade.

Within five minutes, he relaxed. His breathing grew slow and steady, and I stopped rubbing his shoulder. Resting my cheek against his back, I closed my eyes. Steele remained a threat, but I couldn't think about that now. Mark woke up without having his cognitive functions impaired, and Lawson survived his ordeal at the club. Today was a win.

But the more I thought about it, the less certain I was. Mark was lucky. Steele wanted him dead, and he wanted it to be slow and painful. So I couldn't chalk that up to anything except divine intervention.

Lawson was another story. Steele sought him out, baited his hook, and lured him to the club. But Lawson wasn't a big fish. Lawson was just better bait, bait Steele used to lure me to the club. He wanted to see me. Touch me. Taunt me. It was foreplay for whatever came next. I just couldn't figure out what that would be.

A noise roused me. Shuffled footsteps on carpet. I opened my eyes. Martin lay beside me, facing me. Behind him a figure lurked in the shadows, holding a bloody knife in his hand. I reached for my nine millimeter.

"I told you you'd pay," Steele said.

I grabbed the gun off the nightstand, but Steele vanished. I looked at Martin. His skin was gray and cold. His throat cut open, dried blood caked around the wound.

I screamed, jolting myself out of the dream. Martin lay on the bed beside me. "Alex, what's wrong?" he asked. He pulled me into his arms and held me against his chest. "It's okay. I won't let him hurt you."

Settling against him, I tried to relax. But something didn't feel right. Our bedroom didn't look right. Somehow, I ended up on the other side of the bed. The furniture was different. Everything was different. This wasn't right.

Again, I heard muffled footfalls. Steele stared at me from over Martin's shoulder. My gun in his hand. He fired. The bullet went through Martin before ripping into me. The impact woke me, leaving a residual memory of the sudden onslaught and full of panic.

I jumped out of bed, flipped on the lights, and grabbed my gun, aiming as I swept the room. My heart banged against my sternum. Martin blinked awake, groggy and confused. In my haste to check him for injuries, I practically molested him. He was fine. It was a nightmare. Two horrible, connected nightmares that I couldn't shake.

Throwing open the closet door, I searched inside. I checked the bathroom, every closet, and the entirety of our apartment from top to bottom. The balcony was next. When I pulled the curtain, I expected to find Steele standing on the other side. That expectation resulted in a scream when the glass reflected my own silhouette back at me.

"Sweetheart?" Martin ran to me.

I held up a trembling hand. "It's okay."

"The hell it is." He waited for me to lower my gun before he pulled the curtain closed. "What's wrong? What happened?"

"Nightmare, but it was so real. I thought I woke up. But he was still there." I did my best to breathe through my nose, but it was too late. I was hyperventilating. I reached out and ran my hands over Martin's bare torso. No gunshots or stab wounds. "You're okay." I dragged my fingertips up his chest and held on to his shoulders, letting my thumbs brush against his neck. "You're okay."

He realized I needed him to say it. "Yes, I'm okay." He tried to embrace me, but I backed away. I hadn't checked the front door yet. Crazed, I peered out the peephole. The brightly lit hallway appeared empty. Cautiously, I unlocked the door and inched it open, pressing my face into the tiny slit.

"Alexis, stop." Martin waited for me to ease away from the door and make sure it was bolted before collapsing against it. "Slow your breathing, sweetheart. We're okay. Everything's okay. I won't let him hurt you." But he looked terrified.

"You said that last time," I managed between gasps.

"What?"

I shook my head. "The first time I thought I woke up, you said that. Then Steele shot us both."

He rubbed a hand over his mouth. "You know that was a dream. This isn't."

"Are you sure?"

He looked at me with kind eyes, though his green irises appeared to be laughing at me. "Do you want me to pinch you?" Tentatively, he took the gun from my hand, put it on the coffee table, and hugged me, walking us backward until we reached the couch. "Slow, deep breaths. In and out."

"It's been a while since we've done this," I said, still gasping.

"Shh, don't talk." He rubbed circles on my back. "I'm right here. I'm not going anywhere." He made the effort to calm his own breathing, so I could follow it like a guide.

As I relaxed, the exhaustion returned with a vengeance, fueled by the dissipation of the sudden adrenaline dump. Martin stretched out beneath me on the sofa, and before I knew it, I'd fallen into a dreamless sleep, free of night terrors and premonitions.

The next time I opened my eyes, it was morning. Martin kissed the top of my head. "Alex," he said softly, "don't you have to leave for the precinct soon?"

"Hmm?" I just wanted to settle in and sleep through the next few days.

"Last night in Cross's office, you mentioned Moretti. Aren't you supposed to meet him?" He kissed me again. "I know you're tired. Do you want me to call and tell him you'll be late?"

"No, I have to go. I have to find Steele. I have to stop him." Sitting up made the room spin, so I waited for it to settle before I moved again. The clock on the wall said 7:23. I had time. "Are you going to work?" I asked, my head magnetized to Martin's shoulder. If he moved too quickly, I'd crash into the couch cushions.

"I'm not sure. I want to drop in on Mark and see how he's doing. Depending, I might put in a few hours at the office. I barely put in an appearance Monday, and I didn't even bother yesterday. If I don't show up soon, the place might explode."

"Don't say that."

"I'm sorry." He carefully peeled his shoulder away,

pulling a knee up onto the couch so he could sit sideways and face me. Surprisingly, I didn't fall face first into his lap, not that he would have minded. "You haven't had a nightmare like that in ages. Do you want to tell me about it?"

"It was stupid." I blinked, suddenly more awake. "But I want you to do something for me."

"Name it."

"Take my backup and carry it with you at all times."

"Alex, I don't like guns."

"Neither do I, but you know how to use it, and I just...I need you to do this."

"I have Bruiser and Cross's team, not to mention the security personnel at MT."

"James, please."

He ran his thumb across my cheek. "You're that freaked out?"

I nodded.

"It must have been one hell of a nightmare. You normally don't want me around sharp objects or projectile weapons."

"I want you safe."

"Same goes for you." He watched me closely, analyzing every twitch and move I made. "The first time you dealt with Steele, you were so on edge. You were afraid, just like last night. I hate to see you like that. It scares me, Alex."

"It was a rough assignment. Undercover always is."

"That's all it was?"

I didn't like the early morning interrogation. "He tried to kill Mark. He," I forced air into my lungs, "slaughtered Cooper. He could have killed Lawson last night if he wanted. And he was in the hospital. He could have killed you. Jen. Nick. Anyone. Everyone. He wants to kill Derek. It's just a matter of time until he strikes again or we catch him. I don't know which will happen first. I don't want to think who else I might lose."

"Hey," Martin took my face in his hands, "that won't happen."

"You don't know that. It's part of his game. He's messing with me. Toying. Playing. The reason he's done all of this is because of me." I grasped one of Martin's hands. "Don't tell me that isn't true. I know it is. This is about me and the way I screwed him over. Now he wants to return the favor."

"Did he ever force himself on you?" Martin asked.

"No."

"Alex, if..."

"No," I repeated, "he thought he had a chance, that I'd give in, but it never happened."

"Okay." Martin swallowed. "I heard some FBI agents talking. They figured that's why Steele's so obsessed with you."

"He's obsessed because he couldn't have me. Kind of like you." I quirked an eyebrow at him. "C'mon, that's the only reason you took me to dinner almost every week for an entire year. If I'd slept with you the first day we met, we wouldn't be together now. You would have lost interest. I would have been just like every other woman you'd ever met."

"I beg to differ. You're not like anyone I've ever met. You're special. Even a psychopath can see that."

"Flatterer."

"I remember what it was like when you came back from that assignment. The way you slept at the edge of the bed, skittish, ready to run or fight. It makes sense now. You had to protect yourself from him because he wanted you."

"He still does, but not like that. Well, like that, but not in a romantic sense. He wants to dominate me. Control me. Exude his power."

"And he didn't want that before?"

"It was different. He wanted to coerce me. He didn't want to force himself on me. He wanted to build, I wouldn't call it trust exactly, but something akin to that. He wanted to earn my loyalty and affection by trading in a commodity he thought I needed."

"Which was?"

"Drugs."

Martin frowned. "Except you're not an addict."

"Alexia Nicholson, my undercover persona, was supposed to be. So Steele figured out what she desired and made sure he could supply it. He tested her...me. Whatever. He wanted to earn that loyalty, to make me feel like I owed him, so I'd do whatever he wanted. Give him whatever he wanted. And he wanted me to think it was my idea, but I could see through his game. He was playing me."

"While you were playing him."

The words permeated into the recesses of my brain. "He's repeating the pattern. He only knows one trick. He wants me indebted to him again. That's why we were able to save Lawson. He wants me to think he's playing fair. That he's given me a choice. An opportunity. He wants me to be grateful. He wants me to believe I have some control. A choice. That's what he said. I had to make a choice."

"He should realize after everything he's done, you'll never be grateful, not with all the threats he's made." Martin snorted. "That's no way to woo a woman, especially you."

"It's his way. He did it after we first met. He had his guys attack me, so he could save the damsel in distress. He wanted me ingratiated to him, like now with Lawson." I remembered the threats. The violence. Steele's temper. It was the same Steele. "He hasn't changed. The stakes are higher now because he knows me. Before he didn't. Before it was easier."

"Sweetheart." Martin brushed my hair back, and I flinched. He could see it in my eyes that I was back in that shitty apartment with the job at the strip joint, gathering evidence and living in constant fear.

"He had to kill someone to prove his point. To show me what he's capable of. He meant for it to be Jablonsky, but the old bastard's just too stubborn, thank god. So he went after an easier target. He killed Cooper for no reason other than to prove he could. And he spared Lawson's life for the same reason. But he already had Lawson lined up as part of his plan. Saving Lawson was the key. He knew I'd do it. He knew I'd follow his instructions to a T and I'd choose saving a life over apprehending him. It's all part of his plan."

"What plan?" Martin asked.

But I didn't answer him. I knew Steele had more in store for me. It'd all come down to a choice. Steele was the same guy, just less concerned about revealing his crazier and more violent tendencies. But his goal remained the same as it was when we first met. He wanted me to submit to him, completely and freely. This would be my choice, except he'd make sure the odds were in his favor. I just wasn't sure how extreme he'd go to force my compliance.

TWENTY-SEVEN

When I entered the bullpen, Moretti caught my eye. The major crimes unit had been taken over by navy blue windbreakers. The Marshal service must have heard a fugitive was on the loose and decided to throw in their two cents. This was no longer about locating the man who killed a former federal agent and put another in the hospital; this was a manhunt. The Marshal in charge had written on the large whiteboard at the front of the room. Fugitive Recovery Task Force. Quick, somebody call Tommy Lee Jones.

I sat down at the empty desk next to Heathcliff's, but I didn't spot the detective. O'Connell and Thompson were whispering and working on leads while the Marshals laid out the same set of facts we'd gone over a dozen times.

"The foreign blood and saliva found at the Cooper crime scene matches the DNA we have on file for Francisco Steele," the Marshal said.

I tuned him out, searching the room for familiar faces. Agents Davis, Samuels, and Keane huddled together in the opposite corner of the room. Unlike their police counterparts, they didn't exchange whispers or take notes. This wasn't new. This was a waste of time.

"Psst."

I turned. Heathcliff inched open the conference room door, careful to remain hidden behind the blinds. He jerked his chin, indicating I should join him, and disappeared into the dark room. Getting up as nonchalantly as possible, I edged along the desk. When the coast was clear, I slowly opened the door.

"Francisco Steele is an active gang member with close ties to the Mexican cartels." The Marshal launched into a diatribe about the cartel, and I ducked into the conference room and pulled the door closed behind me.

"Hey," Derek greeted, rubbing his three-day-old beard. "The Marshals arrived at seven and took over our bullpen. I've been hiding in here ever since."

"You did all of this since seven a.m.?" Intel covered the entire front wall. Photos and string broke up the monotony of brightly colored post-its. A couch sat against the far wall in the rectangular room. Derek's jacket was balled up, and one of the cushions hung halfway off the side. Takeout containers spilled out of the trashcan next to the mini-fridge. But at least the coffee looked fresh.

"No, this took a little longer." He went to the pot and held it up.

"Thanks." I gave the couch another look. "Does Moretti know you've been sleeping here."

"He should. He's been in and out for the last two days."

"Any reason for the sudden change of address?"

"Moretti assigned a detail to follow me. But if I don't leave the precinct, they can focus on actual police work. So I'm staying put. It shaves a lot of time off my commute. Plus, someone has to stay on top of things here."

"And the lieutenant's okay with that?"

Heathcliff handed me a mug and refilled his. "OT's been approved. I could use the extra money. It's an all-around win." He held his mug in both hands and stared at his handiwork. "Not that having Francisco Steele loose on the streets is a win for anyone."

"He almost killed Lawson last night."

"I heard." Heathcliff pointed to a neon green string and color coordinated post-its. "Patrol brought in 'Sarah' this morning. She's a lady of the night, who turns tricks for the KXDs. Steele got in touch with her four days ago. He paid her a couple hundred and gave her these." Heathcliff searched one of the boxes piled on top of the conference table and pulled out an evidence bag. He handed the bag to me, and I read the name on the credit cards.

"These are Mark's."

"Yep."

"What else did she say?" I asked.

"Not much. She needed the money. Didn't hurt no one. Didn't do nothing wrong. Y'know, the usual."

"What about the online profile?"

"She didn't know anything about it. That was entirely Steele. IT contacted the dating site. We served the company with a court order and got KillaDJ's log-in information. It links back to the burner phone Steele used to contact you."

"So he's KillaDJ." Not that I had any doubts. "What about Bard?"

"What about him? He's locked up tight. When questioned by the FBI, he denied having any knowledge of Steele's escape or revenge plans. We asked Sarah about it, but she said she hasn't seen or spoken to Bard in over a year."

"Who's running things on the outside now?" I asked.

"Diego Guzman runs the girls, makes sure none of the johns get too out of line, and that they pay up. Gangs heard of Guzman, but he's middle management. As far as we can tell, Bard's still finding ways to call the shots. Guzman and several others are keeping everyone in line and their suppliers down south happy."

"How do the cartels feel about Francisco Steele?" I asked.

Heathcliff shrugged. "You want my honest opinion?"

"Always."

"The Marshals are wrong. This isn't about the cartels or the KXDs or Bard."

"So what's your take on this?"

"Steele busted out and is making everyone's life miserable because he wants to prove he can. Steele always had to be the biggest badass. Getting locked up knocked him down a few pegs. You saw his prison record. He behaved. Good behavior, that's what every report said, right up until the time he flew the coop. He wasn't vying for an early release. He had to keep his head down and mind his business because no one inside trusted him. He's a rat. Rats don't survive in prison."

"Was he ever attacked?"

"Not officially."

"Threatened?" I asked.

"He's a big guy and a known killer. They aren't that easy to threaten."

"What did Vega say?"

"Steele's the one who did the threatening." Heathcliff put his mug down and hooked his finger around a red string, following the length to the right side of the wall. He tapped on a photocopy. "Vega got his ass handed to him on a daily basis. Steele offered protection in exchange for a favor, but if Vega reneged, Steele would make his life a living hell. I won't go into the specifics. It's a little too gruesome for so early in the morning."

I skimmed the statement to get the gist. "Didn't Vega realize the protection would end as soon as Steele escaped?"

"I guess he didn't spend a lot of time thinking about the future."

"What about targets? Lucca said Vega named me and Mark."

"It was a short list. Cooper wasn't on it. Neither was Lawson."

"Who else was on it?"

Heathcliff puffed out his cheeks and blew out a breath. "Tough to say, really."

"You?"

He nodded. "Don't freak out."

"I'm not." I braced myself for whatever else was to come. "Anyone else?"

"Joe the bartender and Vee. Those are Vega's words."

"Officer Aronne and Veronica Kincaid?"

"That'd be my guess."

"No other OIO or FBI agents?"

"Not that Vega recalls."

"Can I talk to Vega?"

"Ask Deputy Marshal Douche. He's running the task force now, but I don't think it'll help. At four a.m. this morning, Vega started howling like a banshee. He didn't want counsel. He wanted help. Begged for it. Was willing to say or do anything to get it."

"Help?"

"Pain meds. He said he was in pain. He was running a fever, vomiting, diarrhea, nasty stuff. We called in some medics. He got transferred to the hospital. They have him hooked to IVs. They might have knocked him out. There's not much else we can do except wait for him to ride it out and finish detoxing. DA isn't happy about the turn of events. Everything he said was said under duress."

"He didn't tell us anything we didn't already know."

"I guess not," Heathcliff said.

I studied him, wondering if this had anything to do with why Derek hadn't gone home. Again, I thought about the spray paint on his front door. "Are you worried?"

"Mainly about you and Joe. The witness is in WitSec, so that might be how the fugitive recovery team got wind of this. Kendall contacted them about the increased threat. But they'll take care of her. That is their specialty. We just have to focus on taking care of our own and finding Steele."

"Steele won't kill me. He wants to drag out the torture. He's getting off on it. He'll only end this when he's no longer having fun."

"Speaking of getting off, we found Steele's semen, saliva, and skin cells inside that vacant dress shop." Heathcliff stared into my eyes. "He's working himself into a lather. Don't fool yourself, Parker. This is about you. He's fixated on you. You can't let your guard down, even for a second."

"You're one to talk. He's already brought you up in conversation. He wants to know where you are."

"The same could probably be said about Joe. The KXDs nearly killed him the first time. I should have done more to help. You wanted to, but I stopped you."

"ESU was on the way. You made the right call."

"Did I?" Heathcliff rested his hips against the table. "At the time, you didn't think so."

"It would have been suicide. The second we moved in, they would have killed Joe and then us. I wasn't thinking straight. You know me and suicide missions." I crossed my middle and pointer fingers. "We're like this."

He swallowed, and I regretted my choice of words. Heathcliff's partner committed suicide years before I met him. He hadn't been paired with anyone since.

"Sorry," I mumbled.

He didn't say anything, his attitude shifting to the stoic, no-nonsense Heathcliff. The way he morphed into different people, shutting off his emotions or turning them on, blew me away. It's why he'd been perfect at undercover work, and it's what had gotten him into hot water with Steele. Briefly, I wondered if I even knew who the real Derek Heathcliff was.

"Overnight, patrol brought in every person and raided every business Steele contacted," Heathcliff said. "He wasn't at any of the locations. But we found a car matching the description Cross Security gave us. Forensics is analyzing it now. I don't know if anything's come back yet." He pulled out his phone and sent a text to O'Connell. A moment later, he got a reply. "They are still analyzing it. So far, a partial print came back as a match to Steele's right index finger. The print was found on a plastic Stop N' Shop bag tucked beneath the passenger seat."

"What is Steele's deal with that convenience store?" I asked.

Heathcliff left his phone on the table and went back to the wall, following a blue string to an array of photographs. "It appears the Stop N' Shop is a front. This one location in particular."

I leaned closer so I could read the address. It was the same one Jacobs had visited. "What about the other five locations Steele phoned?"

"They were clean. Perhaps Steele warned them, but since we found cash and guns here, I'd say this is the Stop N' Shop where Steele stops and shops."

"That would mean he didn't know which convenience

store was the right one." I let that thought bounce around in my brain for a while. "Was he on the security cam footage?"

"Maybe."

"What does that mean?"

Heathcliff flicked a printed photo from the footage. "Just what I said."

I bent down to get a better look. For the first time since stepping into the dark conference room, I realized the lights weren't on. "Guess we're running dark on this one."

"We want to keep it in-house if we can. The Marshals are focused on tracking Steele, his cartel and KXD connections, and addressing the issues with the prison. As far as we're concerned, that well's already run dry. We can't waste more time on it, but they can."

"Good." Narrowing my eyes, I examined the photograph. "Is this the best angle we have?"

"Yes."

"It could be him."

"Hard to say for certain. The clerk didn't ID him. Neither did the store manager."

"Did you run backgrounds on them?"

Heathcliff stared daggers into my back.

"I take it they don't have any known ties to Steele, the KXDs, or anyone else who could be involved," I said.

"That would be correct, but we're holding them anyway. A lot of shit went down in the rear storeroom. The manager and clerk said that door was always locked. The overnight guy had a key and did the restocking."

"Where's the overnight guy?" I asked.

"In the wind. We issued a BOLO. We'll find him."

I examined the photos taken of the storeroom. "That's a lot of cash and guns."

"Almost a million, all in twenties. A case of automatic rifles, and two cases of handguns, nine millimeters. No serial numbers on any of them. Ballistics only tested a couple so far, but they came back clean. They aren't in the system."

"That's where Steele got the gun he used to shoot Mark."

"That'd be my guess."

I dropped into a chair, my brain overloaded with too many new facts to process. If it hadn't been for Cross Security, we might not have gotten any of this information, at least not this quickly. "So Steele has access to cash and guns."

"It looks that way."

"But we don't think Bard had anything to do with it?"

"We can't prove he did."

"Do you think the KXDs would help Steele after he turned over evidence on so many of their connections?"

"The ones on the outside don't know that he did. Even if they heard rumors, those would just be rumors. Whispers on the street say Steele's telling the KXDs he wants to get revenge on the pigs who put Bard away. They're practically falling over themselves to help him."

"How do you know that?"

"I asked around."

"No wonder we haven't been able to find Steele. He's liquid with lots of firepower."

"Moretti spoke to Kendall late last night. We're certain the KXDs are still getting their supplies and product from the cartels. The guns look like a fresh shipment. Kendall thinks Jablonsky's investigation triggered something, but I think it's a coincidence."

"Mark doesn't believe in those."

"And I don't believe in ghosts, but that doesn't mean I'm not haunted." Heathcliff took another sip of coffee. "Steele escaped a little over two weeks ago. He didn't catfish Lawson until Saturday. He shot Jablonsky Sunday and killed Cooper. If that was his plan all along, why didn't he bust out of prison, grab a gun, and go take care of business? Why the delay?"

"He had to gather intel. He had to figure out where his targets would be most vulnerable." I squinted at the timeline, following the various paths and photos. "The first time someone spray painted my front door was seventeen days ago."

"The day Steele got out of prison. You think he did it?"

"I don't know, but the more I think about it, the more likely it seems."

"Why didn't you say anything?"

"I thought it was a punk kid. I'm not one to sound the alarm. We have enough on our plates. And that was before we knew Steele was on the loose." He swallowed a mouthful of coffee, slamming the mug down harder than he meant to. "I washed it off. The next day, he broke a window. I found a baseball inside my apartment. Again, I thought it might be the kids in the neighborhood. I filed a report and had the window fixed. A few days after that, all four of my tires were slashed."

"Derek..."

"I didn't think it was that serious. No direct threats. I had no idea it could be him. After the stunt with my tires, I set up a few pinhole cameras in the halls, had one facing the backyard, and found somewhere else to park my car. The problem stopped until Sunday." He bit the inside of his cheek. "I could be reading too much into this. It could be the neighborhood kids. Steele has us all so twisted around I might be jumping to conclusions here."

"You think he started harassing you the moment he got out of prison."

"Timeline fits, and he didn't have to do any research. He already knew where I lived. I might have just gotten lucky to have been at work when he came sniffing around. My schedule's been unpredictable these last few weeks."

"Have you told Moretti about this?"

He nodded, a flicker of his personality resurfacing. "Didn't you see the teeth marks on my ass?"

"I wasn't looking at your ass. I'll have to make more of an effort in the future."

"Ouch." He snickered. "Techs are scouting the area, but they haven't found anything. There aren't any security cams nearby. It's a safe neighborhood, usually. I know they won't find anything."

"What about a canvass?"

"I asked around after each incident. I'm not a total moron. Plenty of people want a piece of me, so when shit happens, I take precautions."

I bit my tongue before saying, *Like sleeping in the conference room.*

"I asked my neighbors if they'd seen anyone, but they hadn't. They would have told me if someone had been lurking outside my door or messing with my car. He did it when no one was around or paying attention. Late at night or early in the morning. I've been working a lot of nights lately and pulled a few doubles. He had plenty of opportunities to mess with my stuff, just not many chances to mess with me," Heathcliff said.

"He might have done the same to Mark." I dug my phone out of my bag and called Martin. "Hey, is Mark awake? I need you to ask him something."

"He's barely coherent, Alex. I'm not sure how helpful he'll be."

"That's okay. Just ask if anyone vandalized his house or if anything weird occurred in the last two weeks prior to the shooting."

"Hang on."

Heathcliff gawked at me, and I realized I hadn't told anyone the good news. "Mark woke up last night for a few minutes." Just saying those words made my voice crack.

Derek smiled. "That's a relief." He glanced at the closed conference room door. "When you get a chance, you better tell Moretti. He'll want to hear the good news."

"I will."

"Alex, are you still there?" Martin asked, and I picked up the phone and took it off speaker.

"I'm here."

"Mark said the screen on his back window had been cut."

"Did he say anything else? Do you know when that happened?"

"No."

"How is he doing today?"

"It's early. The doctors said he didn't sleep well. They want to incrementally increase his pain medication until they find a level that's tolerable without knocking him flat. I told them to go ahead."

"Should he be in that much pain?"

"He's missing three inches of intestine and has a hole in his chest."

"You're right. I'm not awake enough to think straight."

"Are you okay?" Martin asked.

"Just busy. New developments."

"Anything I need to know?"

"Not yet."

"Okay," Martin said, "I'm heading to the office now. The medical staff said they'd send me updates every hour, and if something changes in between, they'll call me." He hesitated. "I don't know. Maybe I should stay."

"Go to work. You need a break." I turned away from Heathcliff and whispered, "I love you."

"I love you more."

When I turned back around, Heathcliff was digging through a box. "Someone cut the screen on Jablonsky's window." He flipped to the photos taken of the townhouse. "The one in the photo isn't torn."

"Jablonsky might have replaced it or fixed it." I closed my eyes, recalling the scene. "Mark keeps his windows locked. They don't open."

"But no one would know that unless they tried to force one open from the outside, and you can't do that with the screen in the way."

"Steele wanted to find a quiet way inside. He probably figured the window would work and would be undetectable. And when that didn't pan out, he must have found Mark's spare key."

"Has anything strange happened to you?" Heathcliff asked. "Any attempted break-ins?"

I thought about it, but nothing out of the ordinary had occurred. "Steele can't find me. The last time he did, he got my address off your phone. But my apartment building burned down. He has no idea where I am."

"But he remembered your phone number."

"That hasn't changed." I looked down at the cloned burner. "That's why he came to the hospital and left me a phone. He realized he had no way of getting to me. He couldn't get my details off Mark's phone. Cooper didn't possess that information. Steele had no choice but to go to the hospital and deliver his message. Now he thinks he can track me, except as far as he knows, I haven't left the office since last night."

"How do you think he got Cooper's information," Heathcliff asked, "let alone Jablonsky's?"

"Those are very good questions." Unfortunately, I didn't have any answers.

TWENTY-EIGHT

"What's with the Men's Warehouse convention?" Lucca asked as he entered the conference room. "For a minute, I thought I was still in the federal building."

"They've been at it all day," Moretti grumbled. "First, we had the Marshals, who called the DEA, who probably called Homeland or the ATF, or who the fuck knows at this point." Moretti glared into the bullpen. "They're helping. Can't you tell?"

"Sure," Lucca said, afraid to disagree.

"If you don't have anything useful to add or you plan to mouth off like this one has a habit of doing," Moretti jerked his thumb at me, "then you can sit out there with the rest of them with your thumb up your ass."

Lucca gave me a confused look, and I shrugged. Moretti hadn't slept, which clearly made him cranky. Lucca just happened to say the wrong thing at the wrong time. "Did you get Lawson's statement?"

Heathcliff held it up. "Nothing new. Parker and Cross Security updated us last night. We already questioned Sarah, checked with the dating site, and pinged Steele's phone a few dozen times. It's still turned off."

"Actually," Lucca pulled an evidence bag out of his

pocket, followed by a chain of custody form, "I can help you out with that one. I just need a signature on this."

"Is that Steele's phone?" I picked up the bag containing the smashed cell phone.

"Yep." Lucca took the form back from Moretti and tucked it in his pocket. "Steele's prints are on it. The number matches. We plugged it in, but there's nothing interesting on it. No saved contacts. No personal notes or dastardly plans. We have his call log and text messages, but I'm sure you've already gotten all of that from the phone company."

Moretti held out his hand for the bag. "Where did you find it?"

"Tossed next to a dumpster a few yards from where Steele parked. Have you finished analyzing the car?" Lucca asked.

"We found another Stop N' Shop bag with Steele's prints. Nothing else. Nothing on the bag either. No drugs. No gunpowder. Nothing to indicate where he is or what he's planning," Heathcliff said.

Moretti rubbed his eyes. "All right. I'll be in my office if you need me." His features softened, and he gave me a nod, his eyes twinkling. "Thanks for updating me. Jablonsky will be back in fighting shape soon enough. Let's try to nail this asshole before then, okay?"

"That's the plan," I said.

Moretti clapped me on the back on his way out of the room. And then I told Lucca the same thing I had just finished telling Moretti. Despite the good news, no one felt much like celebrating, not while Steele remained at large. We continued to theorize as to Steele's whereabouts, but we had no leads.

"Considering Steele had been a big deal in the gang, he's a loner. No one knows where he goes or what he does. He just disappears." Heathcliff followed a yellow string across the wall. "It goes back to his upbringing. As a kid, he learned to make himself scarce with the men his mother paraded in an out of their house. His few brief stints in foster care didn't stick. He'd leave and wouldn't surface again for days."

"Any idea where he'd go?" Lucca asked.

"No one knows. There's no mention of it anywhere." Heathcliff turned to face me. "Did he happen to share that information with you?"

I thought back, but Steele had only given me limited facts about his childhood, mostly to illustrate he was a badass who could take care of business. "Unfortunately not."

"Back to square one," Heathcliff mumbled.

"We can't keep doing this." I hoisted myself onto the conference table, the colored strings and papers blurring together. I bumped my heel against the table leg. "We're trying to move in too many directions, but we just keep going round and round in a circle."

"That's because everything we look at is a dead end. The evidence leads nowhere," Heathcliff said.

"So let's figure something else out."

"What do you want to do?" Lucca asked. "I'm all ears."

Heathcliff crossed his arms over his chest. "This ought to be good."

"We don't know where Steele is, but we know he's far from finished. He has at least three more targets on his list. Four, if you count me. We have eyes on his preferred convenience store, and those who might be involved are being held for questioning. That means they can't contact Steele. If he returns to the store, we'll grab him, but I don't think he's planning on repeating previous behaviors."

"He keeps changing things up," Lucca said. "Like with the phone calls."

"Right," I agreed.

"We're monitoring the other businesses he contacted. We have plainclothes cops positioned near known KXD locations, places Steele used to hang out, and the list of businesses you gave us last night. Even if he changes it up, these are familiar places. Safe places. He might show up at one of them, especially if he runs out of places to go," Heathcliff reasoned.

"He hasn't so far," Lucca said.

I stared, unseeing, at the wall. "We know how he got your address, Derek. We still have no idea how he got

Jablonsky's or Cooper's."

"Or if he has yours yet," Heathcliff said.

"What are you talking about?" Lucca asked, so I filled him in on our earlier revelation.

"Cooper's last known address is included in his prison record. The prison guards and warden would have had access to it." Lucca narrowed his eyes. "The Marshals took over that part of the investigation. Just give me a minute."

The boy scout went out the door, grabbing it at the last minute for O'Connell whose arms were full. Heathcliff and I cleared off a section of the table, and Nick put the boxes down.

"Special delivery for Alex Parker," O'Connell said, and I peered inside.

"What's this?" I spotted the Cross Security logo at the top of a few forms.

"Didn't you ask your boss to send this over?" O'Connell removed several files and leafed through the tabs. "This is everything we'd ever want to know about Tom Collins and his wife." He grabbed another stack. "This appears to be stills taken of Steele inside the hospital. There's enough here to make a flipbook."

I reached into the next box. "Business profiles on the Stop N' Shop locations, backgrounds on the employees you have in custody, and hard copies of surveillance photos with persons of interest and times circled."

"And there's more," O'Connell said in a game show announcer voice. "We also have this stunning assortment of CCTV footage tracking Steele from the nightclub to his getaway vehicle."

"Cross has been busy." My boss surprised me. He insisted he didn't want to help the police, but this would have taken all night. I wondered how much of this had to do with Martin.

I sifted through the files. Lucca had a feeling Steele had a corrections officer or two in his pocket, and based on what we knew, the theory tracked. Surely, Cross must have found something.

"Did you find anything hinky with any of the prison guards?" I asked.

"Nothing in their financials. Initial background checks didn't turn up anything substantial. No one's spotless if you dig deep enough, but no one has any immediate or close ties to the KXDs or any gang for that matter," O'Connell said.

"Nothing on the alleged cartel connection either," Heathcliff said.

Finding the proper folder, I flipped it open. "What about the administration and medical staff?"

"We didn't get that far," O'Connell said. "Too many distractions. Wasn't Kendall looking into it?"

"Lucca said they were." I separated the blinds and peered into the bullpen. Things had calmed down since I first arrived. Only a few windbreakers and suits remained on the other side. Those had been my people. Now they felt like an invading army.

I scanned the room. On my second pass, I spotted Lucca just outside the break room with Davis and the Marshal leading the task force. My old partner was on to something.

"It looks like Cross might have had the same idea," O'Connell said. He dissected the file I abandoned. "Here's the financial history and background information for the warden, the medical staff, and the professionals who rotate in and out. Shrinks, clergy, teachers."

"Anything good in there?" Heathcliff asked.

"Interesting, but nothing solid enough to cinch this. We'll have to conduct follow-ups."

I read over O'Connell's shoulder. Two of the doctors in the prison rotation recently had large amounts of money wired into their accounts. The routing numbers traced back to accounts held by pharmaceutical and medical supply companies. Another transfer came from a foreign numbered account. Cross didn't include any additional information, but he highlighted it. This was where my boss had decided to draw the line.

"What do you think, Parker?" O'Connell asked.

"I think these might be kickbacks." I scanned the background checks. "Dr. Via might have something going south of the border, but the only reason I think that is because everyone has pounded the cartel theory into my head since the moment Mark got shot."

"It's a red herring. Ignore it," Heathcliff said.

O'Connell read the profiles again. "We're all jumping to insane conclusions. When I first read this, I thought the doctors might be using the prisoners as patients in human trials, which is all kinds of illegal."

"That could also be," Heathcliff said rather unhelpfully, "but it's best to ignore that too."

"God, we're losing it." I rubbed my eyes and turned to the next page.

Cross's handwriting covered the margins. He even tabbed specific sections. Warden Gary Schuster had taken precautions to hide his tracks but not enough. Schuster's bank account didn't fluctuate, even though he just acquired a brand new luxury SUV and a cruiser yacht. Both were paid in cash and purchased in the last month.

Lucca returned to the conference room. "I know how Steele and Vega switched places."

"Warden Schuster." I held up the page. "Steele paid him to look the other way when he and Vega made the switch."

Lucca deflated, annoyed that I had stolen his thunder.

"Are we bringing him in?" O'Connell asked.

"Agents are preparing to scoop him up," Lucca said. "Our search of the prison didn't yield any results."

"But it's Schuster's house. He could have altered the logs, deleted entries, destroyed evidence." I finished reading the page, feeling the familiar kink develop in my neck. "I told you we shouldn't have wasted our time talking to him."

Lucca glared at me. "He wasn't prepared when we showed up. That preliminary search could have been helpful."

"But it wasn't."

"Shit." Heathcliff dropped one of the files to the table and spread out several photographs. "This is where Steele abandoned the car." Heathcliff pointed to the next photo. "He's walking away. He changed outfits again."

"He must own more clothes than Martin," I remarked.

"No," O'Connell picked up the photo, "he flipped his shirt inside out. See the tag? He alters his appearance enough to slip by, but he's not making huge changes. He probably doesn't have that many resources."

"Who cares what he's wearing?" Heathcliff stabbed at another photo. "This is where we lost him. But this," he pointed to another image, "is where Cross picked him up again. Same guy. Just with a baseball cap and sunglasses. No jacket."

"Tag's still on the outside," O'Connell said.

The timestamp was thirty minutes after the previous photo was taken. "Where is this?" I asked.

"Ten blocks away, east of where he left the car."

"You're sure that's him?" Lucca asked. "Facial rec wouldn't be able to get a hit. Not with the bill of his cap and the glasses. Not enough of his face is exposed."

"Cross Security must have analyzed his height, weight, and gait. Maybe they matched his earlobes. I don't know. I don't question the magic of technology. I just accept it," I said.

Heathcliff placed the final photo in the center of the table. "We need to move on this now. Steele might still be there."

TWENTY-NINE

"Ready?" O'Connell asked.

I took a deep breath and nodded. This was it. He had to be here. This was the last place Steele had been seen, assuming the man with the cap and sunglasses was Francisco Steele and not another doppelganger. After the move he pulled with Vega, I had doubts. My inner voice hadn't shut up since we arrived. *This is too easy.* But I ignored it.

"Ready," O'Connell said into the radio.

The condemned apartment building had been undergoing renovations when the city pulled the plug, deciding it'd be cheaper to demolish the building and start over rather than continue with the costly repairs. Cross had hacked into all nearby CCTV feeds in every direction, something the authorities had also tried, but unlike Cross who disregarded things like warrants and privacy, the authorities had come up blank. Cross Security did not. They spotted Steele going down the steps to the basement apartment, and he hadn't been spotted since.

"Anything we should know?" the ESU commander asked.

"Bard resided in a basement apartment similar to this

one. It makes sense Steele would want to hide in a place like this." I thought back to the raid, which had nearly turned into an ambush. "Stay on your toes. Expect surprises."

"Like rats and cockroaches?" O'Connell asked.

"One can only hope."

We'd analyzed the blueprints on the way here. Aside from the apartments, there were other rooms beneath the building. With a bit of ingenuity, Steele might have the run of the entire subterranean level. So teams were positioned at all the exits and entrances. For all intents and purposes, the building was surrounded. Now we just needed Francisco to come out with his hands up.

A member of ESU stood beside the door with a battering ram in hand. We tried thermals to get a look inside, but the insulation didn't give us a clear view. We could see a heat source in one of the middle apartments, but we couldn't be certain it was human.

Lucca tugged on my shoulder, pulling me back so he could enter ahead of me. "You shouldn't be here, Parker."

"Neither should you." *Or Heathcliff*, I thought. The detective was stationed at the western exit with Thompson and another team. "But this is the job. We all knew it when we signed on."

"Not you. You're a consultant."

"And you're on vacation, so you don't have a leg to stand on," I retorted, knowing now wasn't the time to argue, but Lucca made it so easy.

The officer with the battering ram gave us a dirty look, and we fell silent. Two other members of ESU stood behind him, holding the big guns. After they took down the door, they'd enter, deal with any immediate threats, and we'd follow. This is how it always worked. It'd be fine. The danger to us was minimal, and we had vests. Plus, Steele was just one guy. He didn't stand a chance against twenty armed police officers.

The commander counted us down. The officer pulled back the ram, turned his hips, and slammed it into the door. The door gave way, and rifle fire peppered the air.

The officer didn't even have time to get out of the way

before he was struck multiple times. He went down in front of the door. But the gunfire continued.

Another member of ESU fired blindly into the open doorway while his teammate dragged the downed officer out of harm's way by his collar. At the same time, the other teams made frantic radio calls. They were also under fire.

"Pull back," the commander ordered. "We'll need additional units to this location. We have at least four shooters."

"Wait," I said, "listen." The shots came in a constant rhythm. No pause. No break. They didn't speed up or slow down. No one fired like that.

The commander arched an eyebrow. "They're still firing. We need to set up a barrier." He keyed the radio, asking patrol to block off the streets and keep the neighbors inside their houses. "Have paramedics meet us across the street. I have multiple casualties. Repeat, officers down."

The other two members of the tactical team hauled their downed colleague up the steps and away from the door. He wasn't bleeding. None of the bullets pierced his vest, but that didn't mean he was in the clear. From what I could tell, he was down for the count.

The commander practically shoved me up the steps, but I sidestepped.

"Move."

I held my ground.

He cursed and followed his men. O'Connell and Lucca remained at the bottom of the steps.

"It's automated," Lucca said.

O'Connell pulled his cell phone from his pocket, switched to video mode, and crept toward the bashed in door. He crouched down, making sure to lower himself beneath the rounds whizzing past us and pounding into the retaining wall.

"You better be right. I'm not in the mood to get shot," O'Connell said.

The three of us held our collective breaths as O'Connell stuck his hand in front of the open door. After a few moments, the gunfire stopped. Quickly, he retracted his hand and aimed at the doorway.

I took the phone from him while we backed away from the opening. "Steele rigged it. Tripod. Pull cord." I passed the phone to O'Connell to examine and edged closer.

"Parker, don't be stupid," Lucca hissed, even though he had stopped his retreat and was now directly behind me.

I signaled and dashed across the open door. No shots were fired. Turning on my flashlight, I held it beneath my gun and went in low and to the left. Lucca went in high and to the right.

The basement was cold and damp. The thick smell of gunfire made me choke. I coughed a few times, keeping an eye on my surroundings as I approached the mounted gun.

"Right side clear," Lucca announced.

O'Connell radioed in our findings and provided cover while I checked the weapon. It was an automatic rifle, like the ones the police discovered in the storeroom of the Stop N' Shop. It had been jerry-rigged to start firing when the basement door opened.

"We didn't think about tripwires." O'Connell took the gun off the mount, made sure it was empty, and laid it flat on the ground.

"Steele's full of surprises." I edged deeper into the room. Our suspect had to be here. And now he knew we were coming for him. "Fan out."

I recognized Heathcliff's voice over the radio. He and Thompson found another rifle in front of the western door but no sign of Steele.

The dark made me claustrophobic. Flashes of Steele attacking played on a loop just behind my eyes. I felt along the walls for a light switch. No such luck. In the distance, something clanged.

I spun toward the noise. A shadow darted away from my beam of light before I could make out any details. And then a door slammed.

"Freeze." I held my breath, straining to hear over the thumping of my heart.

Footfalls sounded behind me, and I pressed my back against the wall in search of a defensible position.

"It's me," Lucca said, keeping his flashlight pointed toward the floor to keep from blinding me. "Did you hear that?"

"Yeah. I thought I saw something."

"Okay," Lucca put a hand on my left shoulder, a common technique to avoid confusion and mishaps, "let's check it out."

I didn't know where O'Connell had disappeared. Apartment doors lined the hallway on both sides. A community storage area was set up in the rear of the building. That must have been where O'Connell went. We had to clear the basement in order, or else Steele might slip away.

Lucca twisted the first knob, and it opened. Slowly, we crept inside, turned the corner, and ended up in a kitchenette. I hit the light switch, but nothing happened.

"Electric's out," Lucca whispered.

I approached the counter, crouched down, and peered around the edge. "Clear." I stood, sweeping my beam of light from right to left across the chipped tile floor.

"Parker." Lucca pointed his flashlight toward a can of tomato sauce which lazily rolled across the floor. "Cover me."

I moved behind the counter and aimed outward. I hated the dark. Lucca turned off his flashlight and disappeared into the abyss. What was he doing? Had he seen something I missed?

The can of tomatoes rolled against a rough patch of tile, wobbled, and came to a stop. Another sound, like flesh hitting concrete, replaced the sound of the rolling can. I turned my flashlight toward the noise and caught sight of two people, one much larger than the other.

"Federal agent," Lucca announced, flicking on his light. "Don't move."

A girl who couldn't have been older than ten curled into a ball, hugging a dirty stuffed bear to her chest. She didn't speak. She just stared up at him.

He lowered his gun and let out a breath. "It's okay. I'm Eddie. What's your name?"

She didn't answer him.

"I didn't mean to scare you." He rubbed his palm against his pants leg. "I almost tripped over you, huh?" He looked over his shoulder at me. "Parker, why don't you come say hi to our new friend. She won't tell me her name."

"That's because she doesn't like you." Keeping my head on a swivel, I stepped out from behind the counter and crossed into the rest of the studio apartment. "Aren't you afraid of the dark?" I asked, kneeling down next to her. "I know I am."

She reached behind her and grabbed a dark cylinder-shaped object. I tensed, nearly aiming out of habit, but Lucca put his hand on the muzzle of my gun. She tugged on the top of the object, and light poured out as the cylinder expanded upward.

"LED lantern," Lucca said, in case I couldn't figure it out.

"Do you live here?" I asked her. "Where's your mom and dad?"

She didn't answer, but since she understood what I said about the dark, she had to speak English.

Lucca reached into his pocket and pulled out his phone. He brought up a photo of Steele. "We're looking for this man. Have you seen him?"

She hugged the bear tighter as she leaned forward. She squinted at the screen and shook her head. Okay, that was progress.

"Is anyone else down here?" I asked.

She shook her head again.

"Did you hear the gunfire?" I waited, but she just bit her lip. "Scary, right?"

"Parker," Lucca whispered, inching closer, "she must have already been inside. If she came in after Steele rigged the doors, we wouldn't be having this one-sided conversation."

"Can you show us how you got inside?" I asked.

She shrugged.

"Aren't you supposed to be good with kids?" I whispered to Lucca. "You have one. Do something."

"Give me ten bucks," Lucca said.

I reached into my pocket and pulled out a twenty. He smiled at the girl. "My partner's so gullible." He held the money out to her. "Want to get some fresh air and sunshine? We can get some ice cream at the shop across the street."

She hesitated, suspecting this might be a trap. *Come on,* I thought.

"Parker?" O'Connell called, and I turned at the sound of his voice.

"In here."

By the time I turned back around, my twenty bucks had vanished and she had climbed off the air mattress, the bear against her chest, the lantern in her free hand.

"Get her out of here," I said to Lucca. "And be careful. If you cross into another apartment radio ahead. You don't want to spook Heathcliff or Thompson. And watch out for Steele. He has to be down here somewhere."

Lucca gave me an uncertain look, but the girl wasn't waiting for us to debate. She was on her way out. And since we didn't know where Steele was or what other booby traps might be waiting, Lucca had to protect her.

"For the record, I don't like this." Lucca jogged to catch up. He kept his gun at his thigh and a hand on her shoulder. I just hoped Steele wouldn't hurt a kid, but I didn't know if there were any lines he wouldn't cross.

O'Connell came through the door. "It looks like the landlord did some renovations and never reported them to the city. He carved out a few additional apartments in the basement. I just checked out two identical units off to the right where the laundry room was supposed to be. It's no wonder this place got shut down. Nothing is up to code."

"Any sign of Steele?" I asked.

"Not yet. This would be easier if we could see more than two feet in front of our faces."

"Lucca found a kid. A girl, maybe ten years old. She won't speak. I think the gunfire freaked her out."

"Freaked me out too."

"Well, the dark's doing a number on me, but I'm not bitching about it. Have you heard anything from Heathcliff or Thompson?"

"They found additional apartment units on their side of the building too, but no sign of Steele."

"He's here. He has to be. Let's keep moving. Lucca will

catch up." I shouldn't have sent him out alone, but our priority was getting the girl out. He would take care of it. Plus, we already cleared the path behind us. It should be safe.

As we searched apartment after apartment, I couldn't reconcile the girl's presence in the building. How did she get here? Why was she here? Who was she? Did Steele know she was here?

"Clear," O'Connell said as he checked the kitchen in the fifth unit.

"Clear," I repeated.

We just closed the door when a deafening roar sounded in the adjacent apartment. O'Connell kicked the door in, and we burst inside. Bright white light blinded me, and I threw up a hand.

"Police," O'Connell announced at the same time Heathcliff did.

"Stay cool. It's only us." I lowered my gun and flashlight. "What was that?"

"Another one of Steele's traps." Thompson pointed at the smoking bits of microwave that had been blown around the kitchen.

"I don't see the door," Heathcliff said, crouching down as he examined one of the pieces. "Looks like he removed it, put some kind of explosive, perhaps a grenade, inside, and it went boom."

"Tripwire," Thompson said, holding his flashlight near the ground. The beam of light made the fishing line glisten. "I told you to be careful checking the kitchen."

Heathcliff stood, his right hand bloody. "You wouldn't have seen it either."

"Are you okay?" I moved closer, pointing my flashlight at the various nicks in Heathcliff's arm.

"Fine." He pushed past me. "This must have been where he stayed. It's the only unit that went boom. So where is he?" He stormed into the bathroom, shoved the curtain aside, and opened and closed the cabinets. "Nothing. Dammit."

The radio chirped. "What's your status?" Lucca asked. He must have heard the explosion.

"We'll live," O'Connell said. "Where are you?"

"Second floor. You need to see this," Lucca said.

"How'd you get up there?" From the schematics I'd seen, no one could enter the main building from the basement.

"Ceiling tiles are missing in apartment six. You can climb up the built-in bookcase and push up through a hole in the floor. It leads into a maintenance closet, which had a ladder leading up to the second floor."

"Yeah, great," Thompson said.

"Have you found more booby traps?" I asked.

"Not in the immediate vicinity, but I haven't checked beyond that," Lucca replied. "Just get up here."

I looked at the detectives. "What are you waiting for? You heard the man."

THIRTY

"Where's the girl?" I asked.

"Outside. The paramedics are keeping an eye on her until someone from child services gets here." Lucca gloved up.

"Do you think she's Steele's kid?" I asked.

Heathcliff snorted. "Steele could have a dozen kids running around, but I doubt he'd want one hanging around with him."

"She's not his," Lucca said. "She didn't recognize him from the photo."

"If she was telling the truth."

"She's a kid, Parker, not a hardened criminal," Lucca berated. "You're acting like she's Steele's accomplice."

"From the looks of it, Steele wouldn't need an accomplice. He has everything he could possibly need right here." I crouched down and lifted the flap on an olive green duffel bag, finding two more rifles, three handguns, a roll of twenties, and a few t-shirts, some pants, and a couple of zippered sweatshirts in various colors. A receipt was stuck to the inside of one of the t-shirts, and I pulled it out. "He got these from the army surplus store on Seventeenth. He paid cash for everything."

"What's the date?" Lucca asked.

"I can't tell." I handed him the receipt. "It's faded."

"Techs should be able to enhance it," Heathcliff said, his attention drawn to the maps and clippings taped to the wall. "But we have far bigger problems than that."

"Derek, you need to get that injury looked at. If nothing else, we don't need your blood contaminating the scene."

"I'm fine," he insisted, shoving his hand into an evidence bag. "See? Problem solved." He looked out the grimy window. "Steele picked this building for a reason."

"It's abandoned. No signs of life, except for the little girl. No nearby traffic cams. Not that many security cams either. It's quiet and far enough from KXD territory that we would never have thought to check here," Lucca said.

I peered out the window, fingering the two deep grooves on either side of the sill and examining the fresh dust on my gloved fingertips. "Steele likes to watch his prey. So who was he watching from here?"

"I have a better question," Lucca said. "How did he know we were coming?"

"He didn't," I said.

"Are you sure? He covered the doors with heavy artillery. Six cops were injured during the breach. You don't think that was for us?" Lucca asked.

"It wasn't intentional," Heathcliff offered before I could say anything. "Look at this place. This is clearly his base of operations, so he turned it into a fortress. That's what he does. Everything's a fucking fortress with these people."

"Bard did the same thing," I said. "Not with guns, but he set traps." I met Derek's eyes. "He had his escape route planned. He wanted to be prepared. He's determined to stay one step ahead."

"Assuming he was here when we breached, he couldn't have gotten that far." Heathcliff reached for the radio. "We had the building covered, but with so many downed officers, we were distracted. He could have slipped away."

"I'll call Cross."

While Heathcliff told them to expand the perimeter and start a search for Steele, I asked my boss to check nearby feeds. If Steele had been here, he must have left as soon as the rifles started firing.

"He has a fifteen minute lead," Heathcliff said.

"I don't think he was home when we came knocking." I stared at the duffel bag. "Wouldn't he have taken this with him?"

"Maybe not everything, but he would have grabbed the cash," Lucca said, "unless he really didn't have time."

Heathcliff scratched his beard. "Steele could find another way to get money, but he wouldn't abandon this." He pointed to the collage of articles on the wall. "This is what feeds his mania."

Newspaper clippings covered the wall. Based on the yellowing and fading, these weren't recent. Most of the dates were cut off, but many of the articles had to do with the sweeping arrests that had been made and Steele's capture. More articles detailed the trial, the sentences, and highlighted the guilty.

"Guess Steele likes being a celebrity," I said.

"It's not about Steele." Heathcliff pointed to a newer section of clippings. Based on the degree of fading, they varied in age. "This is about you."

"Me?" I stepped closer to read the headlines.

The other articles detailed FBI investigations Jablonsky and I had worked. Ninety-nine percent of the time our names and faces were kept out of the papers for our own protection and because we liked it that way, but occasionally, Jablonsky's name popped up. The only thing worse were the photographs. A few had been taken when I'd still been at a scene. Unless Steele specifically looked for me, he wouldn't have noticed me in any of the photos. I was always in the background or just on the fringe of a press conference. Obviously, Steele had been looking. He wanted to keep tabs on me. The entire time he'd been on trial and in prison, he'd been watching. Waiting. Planning the perfect strike.

I felt sick. The sight of Heathcliff's hand inside the bag brought up the nightmarish image of Cooper's final moments. Sweat erupted from my pores, and my heart raced. Don't get sick and don't black out. But now I couldn't deny it any longer. This was my fault.

"He's stalking you." Heathcliff stared at the array.

"They're old. Someone had to send them to him while he

was in prison," Lucca said.

"Maybe Warden Schuster handed them off after he finished reading the morning paper," I suggested, "or Steele nicked them from the prison library."

"He's stalking you," Heathcliff repeated. "Don't you get it? Whatever he has planned didn't just pop into his head when he and Vega switched places. From the moment you arrested him, he's been following your career. Following you." He pointed to a more recent article about a missing girl. My last name was mentioned once in the article, but somehow, Steele figured it must be me. I just didn't know how. There had to be a million Parkers in the world, but not that many had been OIO agents. "The reason we can't figure out what he's doing is because he's spent the last eighteen months figuring out what you're doing."

"This is my fault. But how does this change anything? Steele's goals are the same. This just proves it. He wants revenge. He wants to get even. He wants to make me suffer, along with everyone else who played a part in his demise." I tore my gaze away from the wall. "What's different?"

"He knows more about you than you realize," Heathcliff said.

"He's profiling you," Lucca chimed in. "All of us. According to prison records, he spent a lot of time in the library with the law books. He's been figuring out how things work, the Bureau, the police, you. He wants to know how to get away with it. Whatever it is."

"Every prisoner does that," Heathcliff said. "No greater incentive to learning the law than desperation to find a loophole."

"I think it's more than that," Lucca argued. "I think he wanted to figure out how long it takes for us to respond, the circumstances necessary to obtain a warrant, to search a place, access surveillance, make arrests."

"It doesn't matter. We haven't been operating under those conditions. Like you said, I'm not a cop. I'm a consultant. I don't have to follow the rules."

"He knows that too," Lucca pointed out, "which makes him dangerous."

"You think he's setting a trap for Alex?" Heathcliff asked.

"I think so. Under the circumstances, it's safer to assume that's his plan," Lucca said.

"Steele might have some idea how things work, but he's not sure. He has to test it out. Test everything out." I thought about the call from Jablonsky's and the second one from Cooper's, Steele's appearance in the hospital, the burner, his escape, Lawson, all of it. "Steele can't be positive I'll play by his rules or that I'm really out of the law enforcement game. For all he knows, I could be posing as a private eye. He got burned once when I was undercover. He's afraid it'll happen again." I gestured at the clippings. "He doesn't know me – the real me. So he doesn't know what to expect. That's why he's testing me. Over and over. He has to be certain. He won't make a move until he's positive it's the right one. That's why he lured me to the club. Steele had to be sure I'd show up and that I'd show up alone. He wants to make sure I'll play his game."

"And he tracked the phone to make sure you wouldn't turn it over to the police," Lucca said.

"Yep, or he hoped I'd be stupid enough to take it home with me." I stepped closer to the window. "Who do you think he's watching from here? He must have someone or something in his sights. It's not me. This neighborhood isn't even close to where I live or work."

"I don't know. We need to figure out who lives around here – agents, cops, prosecutors, witnesses, rival gang leaders, anyone he has a beef with, or anyone he could leverage to use against you." Heathcliff reached for the radio. "Let me get the ball rolling while we wait for the okay to get the hell out of here."

I backed away from the window. "Careful," Lucca warned. He pointed to the rickety floorboard an inch from my left foot. "This whole building is on the verge of collapse."

A member of ESU poked his head into the apartment. "All clear. No other traps. We're ready to turn it over to evidence collection."

"Okay," Heathcliff said.

"I heard you found a stray."

"Apparently," Heathcliff said. "O'Connell and Thompson are with her. Did you find anyone else in the building?"

"No one, detective, but we found a few sleeping bags and supplies in some of the apartments. Squatters, probably. But they were cleared out when the building was sealed."

"All right. Tell CSU to bag and tag everything." Heathcliff reached for his radio. "Dispatch, I need to know if any cops live in the area. This is a top priority. Get on it."

"I'll call Kendall and do the same." Lucca pulled out his phone as we carefully made our way to the main entrance, dodging the two broken steps on the staircase.

Another thought entered my mind, and I stopped dead in my tracks "No one went in or out the front door. It was still sealed and the basement doors were booby trapped. We still haven't figured out how Steele got out of the building."

"All I can tell you is he isn't here." The ESU officer stared at me. "We swept every floor. Every room. All the doors were locked. It looks like your suspect entered that apartment through the hole in the floor via the ladder left in the maintenance closet. The closet door was bolted from the outside." He pointed down the hall, and I could see the padlock hanging. "Until we opened it up, the second floor apartment door was also locked."

"Steele's a ghost," Heathcliff said. "Guess that means he can walk through walls."

"Then he wouldn't have pretended to be Vega to bust out of prison." Normally, I enjoyed logic puzzles. But not in this case. "What about the window?"

"He wouldn't get very far if he jumped," Heathcliff said.

"Have someone check the window and the ledge outside anyway. He had to get out somehow," I said.

"Hopefully, our little friend can shed some light on it," Lucca suggested. "Maybe she got in the same way Steele got out."

THIRTY-ONE

Heathcliff glanced at the kid. "How does she figure into any of this? She's just a kid. What was she doing hiding in the basement?"

"I don't know." I sat beside Heathcliff in the back of the ambulance and watched the girl as she bounced the bear on her lap, remnants of strawberry ice cream clinging to her cheek.

O'Connell and Thompson kept her sequestered beside the ambulance. They'd found a bench and tried to talk to her. As far as I could tell, she hadn't said a word to anyone.

"How's it going, boys?" I asked.

O'Connell shrugged.

"Come on, sweetie, talk to us." Thompson put his hands on his thighs and leaned closer to the girl. "You're not in any trouble. We're not going to hurt you. We just want to know how you got here."

She shook her head.

"Did someone hurt you?" O'Connell asked.

Again, the headshake.

"Did you come here by yourself?" O'Connell asked. Distrust flickered in her eyes, and she held her bear tighter. "It's okay. We just want to know if you saw this man." He showed her the photo of Steele taken from the hospital surveillance feed. "Was he here?"

"Maybe your friend saw him," Thompson said. He poked the bear's nose. "What's his name?"

"Boo-boo."

"She speaks," I whispered.

"That's a great name." Thompson leaned in. "Can I tell you a secret?"

She nodded.

"My bear's name is Yogi. He keeps me company when I'm lonely so I don't get scared."

She laughed, and I realized she must be younger than I realized.

"Did Boo-boo see this man?" Thompson asked.

She shook her head.

"Would it be okay if I asked him?" Thompson whispered something in the bear's ear.

"He can't talk," she said.

"Not even to you?"

She shrugged.

"Will you tell me what he says?" Thompson asked.

Lucca wandered over, tucking the phone into his inner jacket pocket. "Kendall made an announcement, but no one claims to live around here. He's checking personnel files for everyone not in the office, starting with those with the highest level of risk." He watched as Thompson whispered something else in the bear's ear. "How's that going?"

"She speaks," I said. "Thompson thinks Boo-boo knows something." I met Lucca's eyes, a teasing tone to my voice. "Why didn't you get her to open up to us earlier? Shouldn't you know a thing or two about children?"

"Zip it, Parker." Lucca leaned against the side of the rig, watching as the medic pulled pieces of metal and plastic from Heathcliff's hand and arm with a tweezer.

Heathcliff met my eyes. It was no secret I wasn't great with kids. I wasn't very good with adults either. But Lucca had a baby girl. He should know how to talk to them. "Don't sweat it, Lucca. The only reason Thompson knows what to do is because they're on the same level psychologically."

"How old do you think she is?" I asked.

"Six or seven," Lucca said.

Okay, so I'd been off by a few years. "How does a six-year-old wind up in a condemned building with an escaped fugitive?"

"I don't think Steele knew she was here. She was hidden in that middle apartment downstairs. From the looks of it, he set up shop upstairs. I doubt after his stint in prison he'd choose to remain in a cramped, dark, and cold concrete space. That's why he broke through to the second floor," Lucca said.

"And like you pointed out," Heathcliff added, "she had to have already been inside before he rigged the rifles."

"Shit." I slapped a hand over my mouth, forgetting not to curse a second too late. "Any word on the officers wounded during the breach?"

"Nothing life threatening," the EMT said as she finished pulling the last shard of shrapnel from Heathcliff's wrist.

"Additional units were sent to the hospital to provide protection, just in case Steele tries something," Heathcliff said.

"Okay, good." I climbed out of the rig and stared up at the apartment building. "You're right, Lucca. Steele wouldn't trap himself inside, not after being locked up. He had another way out." Jumping out a second story window wouldn't be lethal, but it would hurt. No, Steele had something else in mind. Another way in and out of that apartment. But what was it?

I crossed the street and stared up at the window. The building had a fire escape on the other side, but that wouldn't have helped, especially when the apartment door had been locked from the outside and nothing indicated Steele had been inside the building except to move straight up from the basement to the second floor apartment.

"He brought the ladder in," I said.

"Probably," Lucca agreed, coming to stand beside me. "I'm guessing he busted through the ceiling and floor to make his own personal trap door."

"He didn't want us to find his lair."

"Now you're making him sound like a cartoon villain."

But I was on to something. "The ceiling tiles in the maintenance closet had been replaced. The hole leading up and into the apartment wasn't obvious. The ladder just rested against the wall. We might not have bothered to move the tiles and go up that way, in which case we would have cleared the building the normal way. The apartment doors were bolted and locked. We might not have checked every unit. Steele probably knew we would eventually but wanted to buy some time. I don't think he wandered around inside the building. He just carved out one space, possibly where the floorboards had rotted through, and picked out his nice new home. Compared to the prison cell, it wasn't half bad."

"That's why he didn't booby trap all the doors."

I touched the tip of my nose and pointed at Lucca. "Bingo."

"Plus, the only reason we'd check this building is if we tracked him here, and if we did that, we'd go in the same way he did. Through the bottom." Lucca smiled. "I told you he was reading up on procedure. He knew we'd check the building's layout, find out the basement was entirely cut off from the rest, and focus our efforts there."

"Good job, boy scout."

He licked his lips, hoping to hide the growing grin on his face. "Despite everything, we weren't half bad as a team."

"Parker," O'Connell called, waving us over, "we got something."

Lucca and I headed across the street. A white sedan with the child services emblem painted on the two front doors parked next to the ambulance. A woman with permed hair and a kind smile knelt in front of the little girl.

"What's going on?" Lucca asked.

"This is Sophie Harrell," the woman said. She smiled at the girl. "You know you caused everyone quite the scare. You can't just run away."

The girl stared up at the woman with a level of petulant indifference that made me proud. She hugged Boo-boo and curled up on the bench, hiding her face against

Thompson's side. Automatically, he patted her on the shoulder.

"Are you sure she ran away?" Thompson asked.

The woman nodded. "She's a runner. Would you mind watching her for a minute while I update your partner?" Thompson nodded, and the four of us clustered together beside the ambulance so Heathcliff could hear while his wounds were disinfected and bandaged.

"What's the deal, Stacy?" O'Connell asked. Obviously, he must have had prior dealings with this woman. From his tone and body language, he trusted her judgment and valued her opinion. If she said Sophie Harrell ran away, then she ran away.

"Her parents died in a bus crash about a year ago. Without any surviving relatives, Sophie was placed in the system. She lives in a foster home with four other kids, but she used to live here." Stacy looked at the building we'd raided.

"Let me guess, in the basement," Lucca said before quickly introducing himself.

"Uh-huh. At the time of her parents' deaths, they had already received eviction notices, so it was right before the city condemned the building." She looked back at the little girl. "I'm not sure she understands what happened to her parents. She was in daycare when the accident happened. The next thing she knew, her things were packed and her life uprooted."

"What happened to her parents' belongings?" O'Connell asked.

"Anything of value was sold and probably put against their outstanding debts. The rest probably got left behind."

"So it's still home," I said, recalling the canned food and the air mattress. "She's waiting for them to come home." That thought broke my heart.

Stacy shrugged. "It's a tough situation. She's run away five times in the last year."

Heathcliff watched me over the woman's shoulder. "How long has she been missing?"

"A day and a half," Stacy said.

"Do you know how she gets inside the building?" I

asked.

"There's an opening in the laundry room. It's too small for an adult. It's almost too small for her, but she squeezes through," Stacy said.

"Can you show us?" Lucca asked.

"Sure. Will your partner mind keeping an eye on her a little longer?" she asked Nick.

"Nah, they're good. If they get bored, they'll get more ice cream."

We tromped through the grass on ground level, and Stacy knelt down to reveal a rectangular square where the exhaust hose from the dryer had once connected. Now it just left an opening big enough for a large raccoon or a small child to fit through. "There." She pointed. "That's how I think she gets inside. The contractors were supposed to have boarded it up."

"That doesn't help us any," I said.

"We'll figure it out," O'Connell promised.

My phone rang, and I quietly excused myself and stepped away from the group. Except it wasn't my phone. It was the burner.

I spun, searching for Francisco Steele. I didn't see him, but that didn't mean anything.

"Hello?"

"I don't remember inviting you over," Steele said.

I scanned the faces on the street. The police were out in force. They had barriers set up and a perimeter. Steele wasn't here, or he was disguised. I looked up, checking the windows of nearby buildings.

"Don't waste your time. You won't find me," he said, and I knew he was watching.

"Since you've been paying my friends a visit, I thought I should return the favor."

"You could have put out some hors d'oeuvres."

"Check the micro."

I bristled. My fists clenching as Steele laughed. I'd kill him.

"I see you brought Hotshot with you."

I turned to see Heathcliff speaking to Thompson and Sophie. "Leave him alone," I growled.

His voice went hard. "That's not how this works. I make the rules, remember? Or do you need a reminder?"

"No, I remember."

"So you intentionally chose to ignore the one thing I told you to do. You can't deceive me, chica. I'm on to your tricks."

"What tricks?"

"What tricks?" he barked. "According to this, you haven't left the business district since I gave you the phone. But clearly, you're not where you should be. Want to explain that?"

"Fuck you."

"Oh, you'll have your chance." He fought to contain his rage. "Very soon, in fact. But first, I'll have to do something to make you understand this is my game. I control what happens. Where you go. What you do. Who lives. And who doesn't. Not you, chica. Me. I let you save that geek last night. That was all me, but only because you were willing to obey. Have you forgotten that lesson already?"

My fists clenched so hard my fingernails cut into my palms. "You're insane."

"Insanity is pretending to be a coked-out whore. Insanity is thinking you can lock someone away for decades at a time without any repercussions. I'm not insane. I know the truth. I control people's fates. Do you have any idea how many people I've destroyed? How many I've saved? They worship at my feet. Beg for my help. I'm a god. Their god."

"You're pathetic. Are you drinking the Kool-aid or just serving it? Let me guess, you started your own church too."

"Find me, and I'll let you worship at my altar. But this is your last chance, chica. I want you to dance for me. You remember the VIP lounge and the back room? Come alone. And I mean alone. I'll be waiting."

"What happens if I don't?"

"You'll see precisely how godlike I am. It'll take the street sweepers weeks to pick up all the entrails."

"Francisco, please." Begging worked last night. I had to hope it'd work again.

"Do what I say and do it now. If you listen, I'll consider

letting you save one more worthless pig's life. But hurry, he's all tied up at the moment and waiting for your performance."

The phone clicked. "Francisco?" I swallowed, my fingers cramping around the phone. "Steele, are you there?" I yanked the phone away from my ear. "Fuck."

THIRTY-TWO

Heathcliff took one look at me and sprinted across the street. "What's wrong?"

I shook my head. I had to get out of here. I had to stop Steele from killing again. The bandages taped to Derek's arm and hand made my head spin. "He knows we're here. He wants you dead."

"Okay." He didn't look around. He stared straight at me. "You need to leave. You saw what he hung on the walls. He wants you. We won't let him get what he wants. *I* won't let him get what he wants."

"I'm not the only one he's after. He's itching for payback. He wants revenge on you too." I studied the windows in the building across the street, fearing Steele could have a sniper rifle trained on us. Could that have been what caused the grooves on the window sill? "He's watching us right now. You need to get out of sight."

"Can't." Heathcliff fingered his belt. "My badge says otherwise." He unclipped the radio stuck to his chest. "Dispatch, any word yet on the address I gave you?"

"Working on it," came the response.

"Well, work faster." He let go of the radio. "I'll figure this out, okay? Right now, you need to duck and cover."

"No." I stared into his eyes. "Steele's going to kill again if I don't do what he wants. I can't let that happen. I won't be able to live with myself if..." I inhaled. "Cooper's dead because this whack job fixated on me. He'll do it again. I know he will. I have to do what he says. I don't have a choice. I have to go."

Heathcliff grabbed my arm. "What does he want, Alex?"

"I'm not sure."

Heathcliff watched me closely, his jaw clenching. "You don't have a lot of time. I won't give you a lot of time. Every second you're alone with him is one too many. And your life matters. You matter to me. Find out who he has and save them. We'll be right behind you." Without warning, he took my face in his hands and kissed my forehead. "Don't die," he whispered before turning and walking back to Thompson.

"Lucca," I yelled, "I need to take off. Give me your keys."

"Is it Jablonsky?" he asked, tossing them to me.

I didn't answer. Instead, I ran to the rental and climbed behind the wheel. Why didn't I drive here on my own? Now things were messier than they needed to be, but I couldn't worry about that now. I had to find Steele. I had to find his next victim.

Reaching for my phone, I dialed Cross. "Steele just phoned. Where is he?"

"Somewhere around here." Cross rattled off the address. "He's moving fast. He must be in a vehicle. Shit."

"What?"

"He killed the phone. We lost him."

"That's okay. I know where he's going." I took a breath. "You're sure he was moving?"

"Positive."

Inner doubt filled me with fear. What if this was a ploy? Steele could wait for me to vacate the area, then double-back, and make a move on Heathcliff while I was distracted and out of the way. "Call Lt. Moretti. Tell him Steele made contact and give him Steele's last known location and his new phone number."

"Okay. Where are you going?"

"Straight to hell."

"Do you want a team to meet you?"

"No."

"Are the authorities going with you?"

"You listened in on the call, Lucien. You heard what Steele said. I can't risk it."

"Tell him to fuck off. This isn't your problem. You're not an agent, anymore. The Bureau should have done more to protect its people. It's not up to you to save them."

"They're my friends. Don't you understand that?"

"More than you realize," he said softly. "Don't be reckless."

"It's the only way I know how to be."

He cleared his throat. "If someone with a badge asks, I will tell them where you went. I won't obstruct justice or conceal material information in an ongoing investigation. My legal team would not approve of such action. And I'm sure Moretti will ask. Whether you want it or not, help is on the way."

"Cross, for once in my life, I'd prefer to do things your way. Keep your mouth shut and the cops out of it. Almeada doesn't care what you do. You pay him enough, so let your lawyer earn his keep."

"You're wrong, Alex. Mr. Almeada cares a great deal what I do."

"Since when?" I yanked the wheel too hard and fishtailed. I had to get to the Black Cat before Steele. "Sorry, I can't talk. I'm driving." I hit end call and shoved the phone back in my pocket.

Unfortunately, Heathcliff and Cross were right. I needed help. Then again, I knew what would happen if I spotted Steele. Putting a bullet through his head wouldn't be legal, but it might be just. Frankly, I didn't have the mental or emotional strength to think through the ramifications. I just knew that's what would happen if I got the opportunity. But Steele would do everything in his power to stay alive. I just hoped his god speech meant he had grown too cocky to consider his own mortality.

I took the turn too fast and jumped the curb. Luckily, the rental was sturdy enough to make it. Slamming on the brakes, I scanned the parking lot. The Black Cat didn't open for another two hours. No one would be inside yet. This wasn't the kind of place where management spent the morning and afternoon prepping for launch. Everyone straggled in, the lights dimmed, the music started, and clothes came off. Not much prep required.

Predictably, the parking lot was empty. I wondered if I beat Steele here. Did that mean he had his next victim in the car with him? Or was his victim somewhere inside? That possibility propelled me from the car to the front door of the titty bar.

The metal gate had been lifted. A note was taped to the door. *Go in and get comfortable.*

Palming my gun, I tugged on the handle, surprised to find the door unlocked. Inside, the music blared and the spotlights lit the stages. I crept inside, expecting to find an army of KXD members or pieces of Steele's latest victim strewn about. I didn't find either.

"This is a bad idea." Letting my gun lead the way, I moved forward. The booths and tables were empty. I slid behind the bar, but no one was there. Quickly, I checked the control booth. So far, so good.

I moved across the room toward the VIP area, which was a series of private booths separated by individual curtains. The first three were empty. Inside the fourth, a black sequined bra and matching boyshorts hung from the chairback. On the seat was another note. *This time, you'll only dance for me.*

"In your dreams." I left the note on the chair and scanned the room for hidden cameras. But Steele wasn't watching.

I checked the two remaining private lounge areas, but I didn't find anything. Steele's latest victim had to be here. Somewhere. This was just like last night at the club. Steele wasn't making this easy.

Leaving the VIP area, I ducked into the back hallway and kicked open the locker room door. My thoughts went to Veronica, the stripper who narced on Steele. Without thinking, I reached for my phone to call Director Kendall. I had to know if her location remained secure, but I forced my hand out of my pocket. Steele said no cops. I couldn't call to ask, not yet. All I could do was hope Heathcliff would take the initiative.

A plastic Stop N' Shop bag caught my eye. It hung from the edge of the mirror, but there was nothing inside. Was this his next murder weapon? Did that mean I beat him here? That I could stop him from killing again?

I left the bag hanging. I wanted to search every locker in the room, but that would take too long. I didn't have the time to open them, even if I had thought to bring a crowbar or bolt cutters, which I did not.

After checking behind the stages, the storeroom, and the bathrooms, I found myself in front of the last door in the hallway. This was where Officer Aronne had been tortured and beaten. Holding my breath, I twisted the knob, only to find it locked.

I tucked my gun into my shoulder holster and dug the lock picks out of my pocket. I didn't have time for this. My insides quivered, and I forced my hands to stop shaking. Every fiber in my being told me I didn't want to see what was behind the door.

When the last tumbler gave way, I tucked away the picks, grabbed my gun, and pressed my back against the wall. The last thing I needed was to get blown away by another of Steele's booby traps. Slowly, I turned the knob and inched open the door. Thankfully, nothing exploded.

The office contained a metal desk and chair. I stepped inside, careful to check for tripwires or other traps. Photographs covered the top of the desk. A few more sat in the print tray of the nearby inkjet. A cheap throwaway phone hung from a cable still attached to the printer.

I picked up the photo, running my gloved fingers over the glossy paper. The ink smudged, leaving a dark trail on the tips of the latex. Spinning, I aimed at the doorway. Steele had to be here. The printing was still fresh. The ink hadn't even dried.

"Francisco?" I called, hurrying into the hallway. Searching left and right, I considered my options. The backstage area was a maze with curtains leading onto the various stages and the hallway jutting off in three different directions. How had I missed him? "Steele?" I tried again.

Silence.

One of the curtains fluttered. Gripping my gun tighter, I went up the three steps to the back of the stage. The curtain moved again. I charged forward, expecting to meet resistance on the other side. Instead, the heavy curtain separated as I emerged onto the main stage.

Shifting my aim from right to left, I did a double then triple take. The stage was empty. Suddenly, the main spotlight came on, blinding me. I shielded my eyes with one hand. Red and white blobs floated in front of my retinas.

I couldn't see him. I couldn't see anything. I took a step back, the light tracking me, keeping me blind. I ducked back behind the curtain, hoping my vision would clear. I peered out the corner of the curtain. He had to be in the control booth, operating the lights. The bastard wanted me to dance for him. He just didn't realize we were about to tango.

By the time I went around the stage, popping up beside the bar and close to the control room, the spotlight had turned off. The alcove behind the bar was empty. Where did he go? I turned, searching the room, feeling like I was chasing a ghost.

Again, I checked the main room, behind the buffet, under the tables, and in the booths. From here, I could see no one had entered the VIP area. Still, with the way the hallway wrapped around the back stage from both ends, Steele and I could play Ring Around the Rosy all day. This wasn't working.

"Francisco," I tried again, "I thought you wanted me to dance for you."

Nothing.

I grabbed a chair and used it as a step to climb onto the high stage. Maybe I could cut him off from the middle. I made it to the curtains when the spotlight turned on again. This time, I spun and fired, taking out the annoying light source. Then I jumped off the stage and ran to the control booth. He wouldn't get away from me this time.

And yet, he wasn't there. How could that be? I would have seen him. There was no cover between the bar and the hallway or the bar and the tables. It didn't make any sense. He couldn't just vanish into thin air. There had to be an explanation.

I leaned over to check the control panel. A few lights illuminated the system. But without clear labels, I didn't know what any of the toggle switches did. Thinking back, I didn't remember anyone ever working the controls. Joe would just turn everything off at the end of the night. Could it be automated?

I stepped out of the alcove and stared up at the rigging. Steele had proven last night he could find creative places to leave his victims, and since the spotlight had followed my movements, maybe he had been up there moving it around. But there was no catwalk or walkway of any kind. The lights were directly attached to the ceiling. What was going on?

Before I could figure it out, the front door opened. With the bright afternoon sun behind him, the only thing I could make out was his silhouette. Clearly, he had a gun aimed at me.

"Drop it," I yelled.

He didn't comply immediately, so I fired a warning shot to the right of his head. It impacted against the metal doorframe, making it clang and rattle.

"Whoa." He held his gun up and to the side. "Take it easy. It's me. It's Lucca."

"Eddie?" I lowered my gun and dashed across the club toward him. "Steele's here. Or he was. Did you see anything outside?" I cautioned a quick glance into the parking lot, spotting Lucca's rental and an unmarked cruiser, which I assumed he borrowed.

"No."

"All right. We need to split up." We cleared the main room again, converging on the rear hallway from opposite ends. I checked the office and the other rooms. No sign of Steele. Eddie did the same, hitting the locker room and bathrooms on his way. We met in the middle, behind the main stage.

"I'll check out back," Lucca said.

I bit my lip and nodded. The photos had just been

printed. I couldn't have missed Steele by more than a few minutes. How did he get past me?

Returning to the office, I looked down at the tray and flipped through the newest photos. They had been taken of Heathcliff while he had been inside the ambulance. Steele was watching us.

Shivers went down my spine. I put those photos down and turned my attention to the ones scattered on top of the desk, finding shot after shot of Joe Aronne. We had a problem. A big one.

THIRTY-THREE

"What do you want to do?" Lucca asked.

"It's either Heathcliff or Aronne. Steele has reason to want them both dead." I looked at the photo of Heathcliff. "Steele was there. He was right fucking there. How did we not see him?"

"Are you sure he didn't have someone else take the photos?" Lucca lifted the phone attached to the printer.

"No, Cross pinged his device. He was in the vicinity when he called me."

"That's who called after the raid?" Lucca glared at me. "He told you to come here. What else did he say?"

So I told Lucca everything.

"Did he leave anything else behind besides the photos?" Lucca went through the stack of glossies on the table. Every single one on top of the desk was of Joe. "This is his target."

"How can you be certain?" I asked.

"Five minutes after you left, Moretti called. Joe Aronne's mother lives half a block from the condemned apartment building. She broke her hip last month, so he's been staying with her." Based on the different outfits Aronne wore, the photos had been taken over the course of several days. "He's Steele's next target."

"What about Derek?" I held up the freshly printed photos. "Steele asks about him nearly every time we talk."

"That's to distract you."

"I don't know." I put my hands on my head and spun in a circle. Lucca had found me by tracking the GPS on the rental. He'd come alone. Heathcliff told him to. We didn't want to spook Steele, and dozens of federal and local law enforcement officers camped out outside the bar would be hard to miss. We tried that once today with less than stellar results, but the cavalry was on the way. "Why isn't he here? Why didn't he do something? Where's his next victim?"

"Are you sure he was here?" Lucca asked. "Did you see him?"

I shook my head.

"All right, let me check the control booth. Once we figure out what's going on, I have to call this in."

"I know." But I had to come up with my next move before that happened. So I called Cross while I wandered back down the hall, rechecking all the areas I'd examined before. The curtain on the main stage continued to flap, and I looked up to see an air vent above. "Dammit."

"Parker?" Lucien asked.

"Has Steele reactivated the phone? Do you know where he is?"

"You should be right on top of him," Cross said.

"Call the number." That was the ballsiest thing we could do. It would tip our hand and let Steele know just how close we were to tracking him down.

"Give me a sec."

I stepped onto the stage and got Lucca's attention, using hand signals so he'd know to listen for the phone. Ten seconds later, I heard it ring. Lucca and I followed the sound back to the printer.

"He was here. There's no doubt that's the phone he used to call me," I said. "When did it reactivate?" I asked Lucien.

My boss gave me the timeline, and I checked my watch. Steele had arrived at the Black Cat moments before I did. He must have unlocked the door, set the photos to print, and left the notes before hightailing it out of there. Lucca and I had searched every inch of the strip joint. The killer wasn't here.

"Thanks." I disconnected. "He didn't stay."

"It's another test," Lucca said. "He must know the police are on the way. The only reason they haven't arrived yet is because Detective Heathcliff's running interference for you."

"That means Steele wants us distracted. We're wasting time. He's on his way to kill Joe or Derek, if he hasn't already. He's hoping while everyone storms the club and searches for him, we'll drop the ball on the other fronts."

"Doesn't Aronne have a detail on him?" Lucca asked.

"He does." I returned to the VIP area and plucked the note off the seat. "Steele wants me to dance for him. Do you have any idea what that means? It has to be a clue, right?" I held the note up for Lucca to read and spotted more writing on the back. *Hotshot's a dead man.*

The blood drained from my face. "It's Derek. He's going to kill Derek. He went out on the raid. He's not protected. Steele just wanted me out of the way, so he could strike without fear of being interrupted."

Lucca grabbed my arm before I could escape. "Breathe, Parker." He plucked the paper from my hand and flipped it over. "Who's Hotshot?"

"Heathcliff. When he went under, he was Eric 'Hotshot' Hall. That's how Steele knows him. That's how he keeps referring to him."

"Okay, calm down."

"Don't tell me to calm down." I tugged my arm free, fighting every instinct which told me to charge into battle with guns blazing. Grabbing my phone, I dialed. "Come on. Pick up." It went to voicemail, and I cursed, hung up, and dialed O'Connell. "Where's Derek? We have to find him. Steele's hunting him."

"He was just here," O'Connell said. "Thompson, have you seen Heathcliff?" I waited for O'Connell to update me. "You just missed him. Thompson said he told him he had to help you."

"Shit." Just as I said that, a blue and white pulled up outside, followed closely by three more police cars.

Lucca put the note down and held out his badge, telling the responding officers who we were and why we were here.

"All right. If you hear from him or see him, find out where he is and get a protection detail on his ass. Steele's planning to strike." Before I could hang up, Lucca took the phone from me.

"Hey, O'Connell, does the PD have eyes on Officer Aronne? I have reason to believe Steele's stalking him. Can you have Moretti call me with his location?" Lucca paused. "Thanks." He hung up and handed me my phone.

"What are you doing?"

"Divide and conquer. The Black Cat is about to turn into police central. Hopefully, we'll find Aronne and Heathcliff before Steele does, but we're not going to do it by waiting around here. Steele didn't leave enough clues behind to indicate where he's going. Frankly, luring you here doesn't make a damn bit of sense. Not when Steele was close enough to snap some shots from his phone." Lucca looked at the photo. "See this," he pointed to a faint overlay, "it's a reflection from a window. Steele had to have been in a neighboring building. CSU should be able to tell us which one."

"Great, get the police started on this. I gotta go. I have to find Derek."

"Don't you think he's on his way here?" Lucca asked. "He told me to find you and help you out. He should be right behind me. Once he gets here, he'll probably be told to leave, but still, he has to get here first."

I licked my lips, remembering my last exchange with the detective. Heathcliff wanted to protect me, which meant he would bring the fight to Steele. I just wasn't sure what the once buttoned-up detective would do now that his inner badass had been unleashed.

"Take care of this and make sure Joe's protected. Keep everyone safe, Lucca. I'm counting on you."

Pushing my way past the uniforms, I got into the rental and maneuvered around the parked patrol cars. "Cross," I said, knowing my boss wouldn't be pleased with my latest request, "I need you to ping Detective Heathcliff's phone. I need to know where he is, and I need to know now."

*　　*　　*

"What are you doing here?" Heathcliff asked, peering into the hallway.

"I could ask you the same thing."

"What happened? Did you get there in time? Who did Steele attack?"

"No one yet. At least that's what I'm hoping." I looked down at the remnants of the washed off spray paint. "Have you lost your mind? You know he's been watching your house. Why would you come here? Did you notify Moretti or your protection detail?"

"What do you think? Moretti and the Marshals set this up."

I stared at him, my jaw dropping. "You volunteered to be bait? Are you insane?"

"Maybe we can ask for neighboring padded cells since you're just as crazy." He gave me that look, the one reserved for his undercover persona. The same look that forced hardened criminals to take a step back. The look scared me, though I wouldn't admit it. I'd seen the same look on Francisco Steele's face and in Antonio Vincenzo's eyes. It was the look of a killer.

"You want him to make a move on you. Why?"

"It's better than sleeping in the conference room or waiting for him to realize there's too much heat on him so he better make you next on his list."

"Don't do that. Don't protect me."

Heathcliff gave me a half-hearted shrug, still the badass. "I can take care of myself, Parker. I can end this. I should have done it from the get-go."

"You don't think Jablonsky or Cooper could handle themselves? You saw what Steele did to them."

Heathcliff jerked his head from side to side, as if annoyed by a gnat. "They weren't expecting it. I am." He held up his bandaged arm. "I'm injured. It gives Steele an advantage, which I'm sure he intends to exploit. He'll underestimate me. This is a good play. It'll work."

"It's suicidal."

"You would know." The conversation frustrated him. "Get out of here. He doesn't need to get confused by having too many targets to choose from."

"Do you hear yourself?" I asked. "You're a cop, Derek. You don't do things like this."

"I've done things like this as a cop. And if he brings the fight to me, I'm gonna finish it. Nothing wrong with that."

"Is this about Vito?"

"Fuck, Alex. That's all I've heard from you these last few days. No, it isn't. But I would have taken care of that too, except you didn't let me. You had to save me from myself. It's time I return the favor. And unlike last time, the law is on my side."

"Derek," I tried again.

"You should go. Steele knows where to find me. You said he wants me dead. So let him come. I'm tired of hiding. I'm tired of wondering who we'll lose next. He will come for you eventually. Give me a chance to stop him before it comes to that."

"This is a bad idea."

"Save your breath. You're not going to change my mind. We've been through too much together. You understand the heartache of losing a coworker, a partner, a friend. Steele broke your heart by attacking Jablonsky. He shattered it to pieces when he killed Cooper. I promise you that won't happen to me."

"It better not." I stepped away from the door. "Be careful."

"You too." He watched me walk down the sidewalk and back to my car.

I'd already called O'Connell and sounded the alarm. Lucca had done the same, and surely, by now the police presence inside the Black Cat must have reached the same conclusions we did. Steele had one of two possible targets in mind.

Parked two cars over were the officers assigned to guard Heathcliff. Another unit remained half a block away, parked beside a hydrant, and a few Marshals disguised in workout gear stretched beside a bench. Steele wouldn't get anywhere near Heathcliff, but if he did, I was certain the detective could hold his own in a fair fight. However, Steele didn't fight fair, so it was best to stack the deck in our favor.

Leaving the detective in capable hands, I drove back to the precinct. I owed Moretti a proper debrief and wanted to know what we had uncovered so far from the Black Cat. I just parked in a reserved space when my phone rang.

Relieved it was my phone and not the burner, I checked the display and approved the video chat request from Lucca. "What's up?"

The camera shifted, and Steele's mug filled the screen.

THIRTY-FOUR

"Missed me, chica?"

"Francisco." This had been the first time I'd seen his face. Stubble dusted the top of his recently shaved head, matching his five o'clock shadow where the beard had once been. His eyes were just as cold and ruthless as ever, but there was something else. A crazed desperation that wanted to claw its way out. "Where's Lucca?"

"Right here." He turned the camera around just for a second.

The screen filled with a close-up of my partner, gagged and bound. Blood dripped down his face, soaking into his collar and onto his left shoulder. Lucca shook his head, squinting his eyes and blinking rapidly, as if trying to tell me something. Before I could figure out what it was, Steele turned the camera back around.

My blood boiled. "Let him go."

"Why?" Steele asked.

"I'll do whatever you want. Just let him go."

"No."

"Francisco, if you hurt him, there's not a place on this earth where you can hide that I won't find you."

He grinned wickedly. "That's what I'm counting on."

The image jostled and flipped, nearly making me motion sick. I might not have realized what I was seeing if it hadn't been for Eddie's scream. Despite the gag, it came through loud and clear. Steele's face filled the screen again. "Game on, bitch."

I ran as fast as my legs could carry me into the precinct and up the steps, sliding my temporary pass into the reader and tugging on the door until the automatic lock released. Taking the steps two at a time, I burst through the two sets of double doors and into the major crimes unit.

"Steele has Lucca," I gasped.

All at once, every detective and agent in the room sprang into action. Within the first minute, they had Lucca's last known location. Thompson had taken my phone and pinged Lucca's cell. Moretti got the coordinates for the cruiser Lucca had driven. The two matched up. And then we were moving.

I climbed into the car and followed Thompson. O'Connell had gone to the Black Cat after leaving the condemned apartment building. He would meet us. Dispatch had notified all units. The Marshals sent teams ahead to form a perimeter in case Steele tried to escape again. Eight police cars with lights and sirens rushed to Lucca's location.

The car had been abandoned near the wharf, not far from the water. Fresh blood covered the back seat. Eddie's blood. I turned away, squeezing my eyes closed and fighting to hold back the tears. This couldn't be happening. He had a wife and daughter. They needed him. He couldn't be dead.

"Fan out," Thompson ordered. "They couldn't have gotten far."

Blood smears coated the back door, and I crouched down. "He was dragged." Moving at a fast clip, I followed the blood trail until it ended abruptly in the middle of the parking lot, near the pier.

"Lucca?" I screamed, straining to hear his response. "Eddie?" I waited. "Answer me."

Thompson clicked his radio. But no one had found Steele or Lucca.

"Detective," an officer jogged up behind us, "we found this beneath the front seat."

"That's Lucca's phone." I grabbed it with shaking hands. The last call placed had been to me. No texts. No messages. No incoming calls. I scrolled through the photos. The newest one on the roll had been taken moments after Steele hung up. It showed a knife shoved into Lucca's torso beneath his ribs.

Thompson grabbed the phone before I could drop it. He looked at the photo and swore. "They have to be close. We will find him." While he barked orders to the officers, a platoon of FBI agents arrived on scene, along with a contingent of Marshals and Lt. Moretti.

The lieutenant passed out assignments, and the search began. Lucca had to be here. Steele couldn't have gotten far. O'Connell, Jacobs, and a few other detectives retraced Lucca's steps from the Black Cat, hoping to figure out where Steele nabbed him. Anything we could find at this point could only help, but we didn't have time to waste. We had to find them now.

I moved down to the water and stared into the abyss, wondering if Steele dumped my partner's body. I checked for blood stains and drag marks but didn't find any. The dark murky water could conceal a body and blood, but it was too soon to jump to that conclusion. Eddie Lucca had to be alive. I wouldn't accept any other possibilities.

Racing back to the abandoned cruiser, I slid behind the wheel, searching under both visors, the center console, and the glove box. Nothing. I leaned down, checking beneath the seats and the mats. Getting out, I opened the rear door. Nothing but blood.

"CSU's on the way," an officer said, as if this should make me feel better. It did not.

I closed my eyes, hoping to shut out the world. I had to think. Shoving the officer out of the way, I got back into the driver's seat and fiddled with the onboard computer. Lucca always entered our destinations into the GPS. Even though this wasn't his car, he probably hadn't shaken the habit.

"Moretti," I hollered, "did you speak to the protection detail guarding Aronne?"

"They didn't see anything, Parker."

"Did Lucca check in with them? When we split up, that's where he was headed."

"They haven't seen him."

My eye twitched as I examined the GPS. "According to this, Lucca arrived at his destination."

"Hey," Moretti grabbed a hold of one of the Marshals walking by with a tablet, "let me see that." He tapped on the screen. "Lucca made it there."

"Steele was waiting for him." I felt sick. "That's why Steele left the photographs. He wanted to lure me there, but I chose wrong. Steele knew who I'd pick. He knew I'd go to Heathcliff. Oh god."

"Easy, Parker."

But I shrugged away from him. "This is my fault." Steele knew me better than I knew him, and now Eddie was paying for it. Shoving my emotions to the side, I focused on what we knew. "Steele watched us raid the basement apartments. From there, he went to the Black Cat and then waited for someone to show up at Officer Aronne's. Somehow, he got the jump on Lucca and brought him here." I looked around, unable to figure out what was significant about this place. Everywhere Steele led me had been a walk down memory lane. But there was nothing special about this place. "He's not here."

"What?" Moretti asked.

"He's not here." I copied down the address from the GPS. "Process the car. Process the scene. Let me know if you find anything." I tapped on my phone, scanning for WiFi networks, but I didn't find any. Visually, I searched for security cams, but nothing popped up. This was a blind spot. Steele must have known that. "Steele switched vehicles. That would explain why the blood trail just stops right there."

"All right. I'll bite. Any idea where he's headed?"

I had no idea. We hadn't found anything at the Black Cat, but maybe I overlooked something. Maybe Steele left a calling card where he grabbed Lucca. Or maybe my mistakes had caused another good agent to lose his life. The pressure in my chest threatened to collapse my heart.

"I wish I knew."

Moretti patted my cheek. "Don't lose it on me, Parker. Lucca needs you."

"Right." I watched officers search nearby containers, walk a grid looking for clues, and question anyone they spotted nearby. *Lucca's not here*, my inner voice said. *Stop wasting time and find him.*

"I'm going to retrace their steps. Lucca tried to tell me something, but I don't know what it was. Maybe there's something at Aronne's or the Black Cat that we missed."

"Go. I'll tell O'Connell you're on your way."

While violating every traffic law known to man, I phoned Cross, hoping he could provide a miracle. But there weren't any surveillance cameras covering the underpass where Steele left the car. And there was nothing near the wharf, which I already knew by checking for networks. Cross promised to check cell towers and run numbers again, but by the time he got anything back, Lucca would be dead, if he wasn't already.

Slamming on the brakes, I shoved the car into park, leaving half of it blocking one of the lanes, and got out. My mind replayed the video. I couldn't see much except Lucca and Steele. At the time, I didn't know where they were, but now I knew they had been in the back seat beneath the overpass. Immediately after making the call, Steele had dragged Lucca from the car, presumably into another vehicle. Where could they have gone? The Marshals set up a perimeter, but it might have taken too long or it included too large of a span. We'd never search everywhere in time.

"Parker," O'Connell waved me over, "we found blood."

"More blood?" I knelt down, eyeing the spatter on the sidewalk. Based on the trajectory, Lucca had been hit hard with something which sent droplets flying several feet in the air before landing. "Scuff marks." I pointed.

"Lucca put up a fight," O'Connell said.

"He needs to keep fighting." I followed the scuff marks to the curb directly in front of an empty parking space. From here, I looked around, wondering where Steele would choose to wait and watch. This wasn't a great neighborhood, so there were plenty of boarded-up buildings. Still, Steele would have to be close enough to cover the distance and launch a surprise attack without Lucca noticing. He couldn't have been more than fifty feet away. That narrowed things.

"We've been asking the neighbors and shop owners if they saw anything," O'Connell said. "No one's talking."

"Big surprise." Steele couldn't have come from the other direction because Lucca would have seen him. He had to have come from behind. "There." I pointed to a few boxes and some pop-up tents in an alley where several homeless had congregated. "Have you talked to them yet?"

"They didn't see anything."

I gave O'Connell a look and went across the street, digging out my wallet as I went. Only two people remained, zipped safely into their tents. Boxes near the front with piles of rubbish and personal property had been left unattended, though I couldn't figure out exactly why.

I tried speaking to the man missing four of his front teeth, but he didn't know anything or see anything. He just wanted to go back to sleep. From his slurred speech and the smells coming from him, I didn't think he was sober enough to remember much of anything. The other person, a younger guy with a dirty beard and bright eyes, remembered someone new near the front, but he thought the guy was a panhandler.

"Did he look like this?" I showed him the closest mock-up we had of how Steele currently looked.

"I dunno. Maybe."

"Is that his stuff?" I pointed to the boxes.

"No, he didn't have much of anything with him, just this jacket." He rubbed his hand against the material covering his chest.

"I'll give you fifty bucks for it."

"Sorry, I need it to keep warm."

"Here, man. How 'bout we trade?" O'Connell emptied his pockets and took off his jacket.

The guy looked at the jacket and the money in my hand. "And I get the fifty bucks?"

"Sure." I held out the money, and he took off the garment. Inside the pocket, I found a familiar old subway token with a hole punched through it and a small metal loop hooked through.

"What's that?" O'Connell asked.

"A piece of Mark Jablonsky's key chain." I forced air into my lungs. "I know where Steele took Lucca."

THIRTY-FIVE

I laid into my horn, which did nothing. If the lights and sirens going off couldn't clear the accident, nothing would.

O'Connell rolled down his window and yelled to me, "Units are on the way. Hopefully, they aren't stuck in this gridlock."

"I'm not waiting." Opening the car door, I filled my lungs and ran, zipping around the stopped cars. An SUV had T-boned a water delivery truck. Large bottles filled the streets. Several other cars had been involved in fender benders, probably in their attempts to avoid the multi-gallon bottles. It was a mess. Until some of the vehicles were moved out of the way, no one was going anywhere.

Dashing across three lanes, I made it back to the sidewalk and spotted a cab on a side street. The woman stepped out, and the cab slowly started to pull away.

"Wait," I screamed. "Stop him."

The woman saw me coming and flagged down the driver. For the first time today, something had gone right.

"Thanks." I shoved my way inside, gave the cabbie Mark's address, told him this was official police business, and I'd pay him five hundred dollars if he got me there in the next five minutes. We might have broken the land speed record.

When we pulled up, I tossed my credit card and business card into the front seat. He could stop by Cross Security to collect his payment or he could go on a crazy spending spree until he maxed out my card. Either way, I didn't care.

"Take off," I warned. "There's an active shooter in the area."

That got him going.

Palming my gun, I crept up to Jablonsky's front door. If I was wrong again, it wouldn't matter. Lucca would be dead, and Steele would have moved on to his next target. The front door hung precariously from the damaged frame. A few boards held it in place. Steele didn't come in this way.

Moving from cover to cover, I went around the house. I didn't have time to waste, but I didn't want Steele to see me until it was too late. As soon as I stepped onto the back patio, I knew they were here. Blood droplets dotted the concrete like a proverbial trail of breadcrumbs. The door remained open. Steele knew I was coming.

As quietly as possible, I slipped inside. The kitchen chairs were askew. Two had toppled over, and one was missing. Lucca had put up a fight. How long had it been since the call? Thirty minutes? Where was my partner?

Aside from the mess, the kitchen was clear. I pressed against the wall and peered into the living room. Lucca spotted me immediately. But he couldn't speak, thanks to the gag. He didn't jerk or move, but I saw fear in his eyes.

Poking my head around the corner, I didn't see Steele, but I saw what had freaked out Lucca. A rifle was aimed at his head. Steele had jerry-rigged it so if anyone tried to come in through the front, it'd pull the cord and squeeze the trigger.

I had to remove that before the police arrived. They'd take down the front door when they breached and kill Lucca in the process. That must have been what Steele planned. He wanted to make me regret every one of my decisions. Thank god for traffic accidents.

Keeping my head on a swivel, I entered the living room.

No sign of Steele. No sign of any other tripwires. Lucca let out a few moaning gasps, but I couldn't understand him.

"Shh," I said as I carefully removed the wire from the door and repositioned the rifle away from Lucca's head before attempting to dismantle the booby trap.

Lucca let out another strangled groan, and I left the rifle on the floor and pulled the gag out of his mouth. He sucked in air, which sounded like a whistling gurgle. The knife remained lodged in his torso. From its position, I suspected it had gone through his liver. The blade might have been the only thing keeping Lucca from bleeding out. His skin was pale and covered in sweat. His eyelids fluttered, but he took a few more ragged gasps. Maybe it was his lungs and not his liver that were in trouble.

"Eddie, hang on. Help's coming." I cut the duct tape which bound him to the chair. "Where's Steele?"

"Upstairs." Lucca's head bobbed, and he fought to keep his eyes open.

"Okay," I glanced up the steps, "let's get you out of here."

I slipped beneath his left arm, cringing when he let out another grunt. "I'm sorry. This is all my fault." I supported as much of his weight as I could and slowly dragged him toward the back door. We made it as far as the kitchen table before I heard Steele bounding down the steps.

Lucca grabbed the table for support while I pulled my gun and spun, but it was too late. Steele slammed into me with the force of a freight train. For a moment, I was airborne. Then we knocked into the back door and tumbled onto the patio.

I landed hard on my back, the momentum carrying us with enough force to flip Steele over top of me. Scrambling to my feet, I searched for my gun, but it was lost somewhere in Mark's kitchen. Steele charged again.

We banged into the wooden privacy fence which separated Mark's backyard from his neighbor's. Steele reached for my wrists, and I kicked him in the stomach. He lost his grip on my hands but grabbed my leg as he recovered. I clawed at the fence, searching for purchase, desperate to remain upright, but he dragged me to the ground and pummeled me.

Stars exploded behind my eyes, and I blinked through the pain, wondering what he hit me with. A heavy object thudded to the ground next to me. Taking advantage of my dazed state, Steele yanked my arms above my head and held my wrists in one of his. He pinned my thighs with his knees and quickly frisked me with his free hand.

"Satisfied?" I spat when he tossed my cell phone into the bushes.

"Not yet." He leaned down, running his nose along my cheek. "But I will be."

I reared up, but he shoved me harder against the ground. "So much fight, just like last time." He turned toward the house. "But no one's coming to save you this time."

"I don't need saving, but you might."

He laughed, that sick sound I'd come to despise. "This is where our game started. It's only fitting it's where it ends." The chain around my neck caught his attention, and he ripped it from my throat, his face contorting in anger. "You belong to me, chica. No one else. I'll make sure of that."

He reached for something in his pocket, and I bucked beneath him. He backhanded me, and I shifted my hips to the side, moving with the blow. The force behind it knocked him off balance, and I slipped a leg free and kicked into his low ribs. His bones gave way beneath my heel, and he howled. I grabbed the rock he'd hit me with and swung, but it glanced off his shoulder.

His eyes blazed fiercely; the pain deadened by whatever narcotic he currently had coursing through his veins. He yanked me up and slammed me repeatedly into the fence, rage fueling his strikes. I fought to hold on as he tore at me, waiting and hoping he'd regain some control.

Suddenly, he took a step back, and I crumpled to the ground. Broken boards landed beside me. And Steele took a deep breath and ran a hand down his face. "Don't make me hurt you, chica."

I stared up at him, my back aching and head spinning. Thankfully, he hadn't done too much damage. He settled on top of me and cradled me against his massive frame, like a rag doll.

I didn't move. I didn't even try. "Is that what happened with Cooper? He made you hurt him?"

"No," Steele said, "you made me hurt him."

"Why did you let Lawson live?" I asked, distracting him as he shifted his hold on me. I didn't fight or struggle. It took every ounce of willpower not to and all of my effort to maintain a steady unemotional tone. But Steele was untethered. Anything could set him off, and until I had the upper hand, I couldn't risk him losing it again. My mind drifted back to Lucca. I had to end this quickly if there was any hope of saving my former partner.

"You did what I said, so I allowed him to live."

"Let Lucca go." Desperation crept into my voice. "You have me. You don't need him. You've won. I'll do whatever you want."

"No. You made your decision. You picked Hotshot over me. You chose him again. You have to pay for that." He forced me flat on my back and adjusted above me, wrapping one hand around my throat while the other moved to my belt buckle. The clasp distracted him, and he looked down to unfasten it.

I reached to the side for one of the wooden planks, squirming beneath him. "You're fucking crazy. Don't you get it? I'm not a coked-out stripper. I'm a cop. Hotshot's a cop. Our job was to arrest you. I don't know how you got out, but you're going back. The warden won't be around to help you escape this time. You're never getting out again."

"We'll see about that." He pressed his forearm hard against my side, hitting a tender spot and causing me to scream. He stopped, cocking his head at me, as if something didn't compute. I could almost see the crazy switch flip in the other direction. "Stop fighting. I don't want to hurt you. Just relax." He let go of my belt and reached into his jacket pocket. He pulled out his kit and popped it open with practiced ease. "You'll feel better in a minute. Then you'll see things clearly." Just as he jabbed the syringe into my hip, I hit him with the broken board.

I pulled back to swing again, but he yanked the board out of my grasp, rocking back on his heels. That's all I needed. My legs were free, his hands off of me, and I wrapped my legs tightly around him, swinging my body around and getting him into a headlock. I squeezed hard, my chest against his back. He swatted at me, and I hooked one arm around his, isolating his shoulder. He slapped at my arm with his one free hand, trying to roll free by jerking from side to side, but I had a firm grip. He couldn't get me off.

He dug his fingers into my wrist, squeezing as hard as he could, but I didn't loosen my hold. If I did, I'd be dead and so would Lucca. Finally, Steele stopped squeezing my arm. He was fading fast. Just a few more seconds, and he'd be out. But if I held on longer, he'd never wake up.

I focused on holding on. He shifted again, practically sitting up while I clung to him. I couldn't see exactly what he was doing, but he pulled something from beneath his pants leg and flopped to the side, crushing my good leg against the ground.

He pressed the muzzle of a snub-nosed .38 against my thigh and pulled the trigger. I didn't feel it, but I heard the gunshot. Did he miss?

My leg muscles nearly went slack, still on fire from the injection, and I focused on keeping them tight around him. I hung on until Steele went completely limp. I waited, counting the seconds, though my heart raced. I didn't have time to wait. I had to help Lucca.

Untangling my limbs from Steele's, I kicked his gun away and nudged him with a broken plank. He didn't move, and I hoped he was dead. I hurried into the kitchen, barely aware of my right leg dragging behind me. Based on the blood trail, Lucca had crawled closer to the door. He lay on his side, not moving. Blood leaked out from around the knife at a steady pace, almost like a rapidly dripping faucet.

"Eddie," I rolled him onto his back, "wake up." I tore off the bottom part of my shirt, wrapping it around the wound. My fingers brushed against his neck. I felt his pulse, but it was weak. "Lucca, come on. I'm gonna get you out of here." Where were the cops? It felt like I'd been trapped in this hell for years, but a glance at the clock showed me it had only been a couple of minutes. I tried to lift him, but I couldn't. "Lucca?"

He sucked in a breath. "Where's Steele?"

"Out there."

He lifted his head just enough to see out the door. "Good." He dropped back against the tile. "Alex, I need you to do something for me."

"Anything."

"Tell my wife I love her and I'm sorry."

"Your wife?"

"Tell her that. Please."

"No," I sunk onto the ground, keeping one hand around the shirt and blade, holding it steady, "do it yourself."

"Parker, don't be a hard ass."

"Tell me what you did." I had to keep him talking. "Whatever it was probably requires jewelry and groveling. I'm not buying some woman I don't know jewelry. And have you met me? I don't grovel." I felt my face getting closer to the ground. "What'd you do?"

"She found out the truth."

"You're gay?"

"No. Just tell her." He closed his eyes.

"Lucca, don't do this to me. I can't. I just can't." I concentrated on keeping steady pressure against his chest. Where was a cop when you needed one? "Stay with me, Eddie. Come on." I gave him a friendly slap to the cheek, like Moretti had done to me, "Open those eyes. Look at me."

Noise sounded from behind, and I heard sirens. "Parker." Lucca's voice sounded distant. "Parker," he said more urgently, "run."

I whipped my head around, spotting Steele lumbering through the door with a gun in his hand. I threw myself on top of Lucca just as Steele fired. Another gunshot sounded, this one in my ear. Lucca held my gun in his hand. Smoke traveled up the barrel, and I stared at it. I'd never noticed that happen except in movies. Steele twitched once or twice on the ground and then went still.

Lucca cursed and dropped back to the floor; the bleeding more profuse. The knife had slipped out with his sudden movement. I pressed harder against his wound, surprised by the amount of blood surrounding us. Steele's shot had missed, impacting above my head, so where did all this blood come from?

Lucca sucked in another shaky breath, groaning and shuddering beneath me.

"Hang on." The sirens were right outside. I heard car doors slamming. And then I yelled as loud as I could, "Help. We're back here."

THIRTY-SIX

Everything moved in a blur, like a dream or just another of my horrible nightmares. So many familiar faces, but not the ones I expected to see. Tactical teams stormed through the front and back doors. Uniformed officers brought up the rear. The tactical team flipped Steele onto his stomach and cuffed him before they even bothered checking for a pulse.

And then gloved hands lifted me off Lucca, dragging me away from him.

"Help him." I watched in horror as they knelt beside him. Their first responder training not much more effective than my own. "Where are the paramedics?"

"On the way," an officer said.

"How long? He can't wait. He's been bleeding too long." I tried to think, every thought coming too fast and too slow at the same time. I couldn't make sense of my own mind. "Cross." I held out my hand for a phone. Cross kept a mobile medical unit on standby. And unlike EMTs, his van was outfitted to handle anything. Concierge emergency medicine at its best. They could save Lucca. "Call Cross."

"Who?"

"Lucien Cross."

The cop gave me an odd look. "Are you okay?"

"Fine." I shook away his question.

"Parker," a voice called, and I turned. O'Connell stepped over Steele, noting the hole in the killer's chest. "How's Lucca?" He peered around me.

"Not good. He needs help."

"It's here." O'Connell turned to the nearest ESU member. "Is the building clear?"

"Yes, sir."

O'Connell hit the radio, and a team of EMTs came in, dragging the stretcher and gurney behind them. O'Connell watched them pack Lucca's wound and load him onto the gurney. At the moment, Eddie remained breathing.

"He's lost a lot of blood." I stared numbly at the puddle on the floor which appeared to be spreading.

"You're wearing most of it," O'Connell said. He cocked his head at the way I stood. "Hold up," he called to the EMTs. "Take her with you."

"I'm fine. Just help Lucca. Please, you can't let him die." I trembled. "He can't die."

O'Connell slid beneath my arm and walked me out Mark's front door toward the ambulance.

"No," I jerked backward, "I can't go in there. The last time I sat in the back of an ambulance, my partner died. I can't." I tried to pull free, but Nick held tight. "No, Nick. Please. Don't make me go. Don't make me live that again."

"You're okay. Lucca's okay. Just go with him, all right? I'll meet you there. Jen will be waiting. I promise, everything's going to be fine."

Nick lifted me onto a second gurney and held me down while the EMT secured the straps. I didn't understand what was going on. But my protests fell on deaf ears. After they tied something around my upper leg, I was loaded into the ambulance beside Lucca.

I fought against the neck brace, pulling it off, so I could watch what was happening. The EMT checked Lucca's vitals, hooked him to a few monitors, and recorded the numbers. He spoke to him, though I wasn't sure if Lucca was still conscious. Then he changed his gloves and turned to face me.

"Do you want something for the pain?"

"What pain?" I asked.

He took my vitals, spending far too long looking into my eyes. But the monitor hooked to Lucca beeped a warning, and he shifted back to the other gurney. My worst nightmare was about to play out again.

Tears welled. "Save him," I beseeched. I didn't want to tell Lucca's wife he loved her and he was sorry. I didn't even know her name. Or did I? I couldn't remember. I always had a rule not to get personal because I didn't want to feel like this. And despite my rules, despite leaving the OIO, despite everything, I was trapped in the exact same hell I thought I left behind.

Tugging the leads off my chest, I fumbled with the straps. I had to get free. My heart beat hard but not nearly as fast as it should, given how much I was hyperventilating. Undoing the last clasp, I swung my legs down and sat up. Part of me wanted to curl into a ball, but that wouldn't help anyone.

"What do you need me to do?" I asked.

The EMT looked utterly bewildered, but he had his hands full. "Hold this." I took the bag and watched as he worked on my partner.

The best thing about Mark's townhouse, it wasn't far from the hospital. We arrived two minutes later. A trauma team waited on the other side. They whisked Lucca away.

Another team came up. By then, I was on the verge of collapse. The numbing fire in my hip seemed to have spread into a pleasant warmth along my nerves. It took away the panic, but even it couldn't numb my breaking heart.

*   *   *

The door opened, and I buried my face in the pillow. A man cleared his throat. Sighing, I looked up.

"How do you feel?" Lucien Cross asked.

"You ever been hit by a truck?" That couldn't even compare to how I felt, but I'd take every ounce of pain and misery I could get if it meant Lucca would survive.

"No." He closed the door and picked up my chart. "Have you?"

I shifted, grabbing the hot compress before it fell off my hip. By the time the doctors realized Steele had shot me up with heroin, it had been too late to do much of anything. So they pumped me full of antibiotics, gave me fluids, and spent a great deal of time cleaning and treating the bullet hole in my thigh. Since it was the same leg Steele injected, they feared the possibility of infection, abscesses, and other complications was much greater. At this point, I didn't care.

"No pain meds?" Cross asked, putting down the chart and examining the x-rays on the lightboard. "That's a bad decision."

"Just like every other one I make."

"You're lucky. Nothing's broken. The MRI doesn't show any permanent damage, just some bruising and inflammation around your spine." He looked at the crappy set of crutches against the wall. "How long will you be on those?"

"I don't know."

"I'll get you a better set. Is your leg still numb?" He touched just below the bandage, and I whimpered. "Guess not." Taking a pill bottle out of his pocket, he put it on the tray beside me. "Shooting up into a muscle won't get you that euphoric rush, but you'll come down just as hard. This will soften your landing. Take one when you can't stand it. And when that wears off, take half."

"Where'd you get your medical degree?" I glared at the unmarked bottle. "Are you dealing now?"

He snorted. "No. Since you're too stubborn to get proper medical care, I had to bring the proper care to you."

"Leave me alone."

But he remained at my bedside. "You look like shit. I'll get you some ice for your face. Maybe if you comb your hair and change your clothes you won't look so bad. Cut-off jean shorts stained in blood aren't a good look. You definitely need to change." He frowned. "Why didn't they put you in a hospital gown?"

"They open in the back, and I'm not in the mood to flash

everyone who enters."

"Do you have a change of clothes at the office?"

"Yes, but I have shorts and a t-shirt in the trunk of my car."

He opened the clear plastic bag and found my keys to the company car. "The nurses said you wanted to sign yourself out."

"I'm just waiting on the paperwork."

"In that case, I'll get your clothes for you. You don't need to traumatize the other patients."

"Who cares?" I couldn't figure out why we were having this pointless conversation. None of it mattered. Eddie mattered. The hospital staff didn't need to waste their time on me. They needed to focus on saving him. "If you want to do me a favor, find out how Lucca is."

"Still in surgery. His wife's been notified. She's on her way."

My chin trembled, and I focused on the physical pain to distract me. "Okay."

"I don't want James to see you like this." Cross checked his phone. "He's still at the safe house with Jablonsky. I'm surprised he isn't here with you."

"He doesn't know yet."

"Well, he might figure it out." Cross fished my necklace and rings out of his pocket and laid them on the tray table beside the pill bottle. "I believe these belong to you. I took the liberty of having the clasp fixed. It was a rush job, but it should hold."

"Shouldn't that be in police evidence?"

"Why?" Cross asked. "It has nothing to do with anything. And you don't want a ring like that placed in evidence. Cops have sticky fingers too."

I rolled my eyes. "Whatever. Do you want to chew me out about getting involved in this and dragging you into the middle of an investigation? If so, go ahead. I don't give a shit."

"It's fine." He stared at the large diamond.

"We're not married."

"I didn't ask."

"Well, we're not."

"Okay," Cross said, "but regardless, James hired me to protect you. You had me withdraw the detail, and now look at you. My client is not going to be happy. My business partner is not going to be happy. And I worked too damn hard to get Martin Tech on board and even harder to get James Martin to sign with me. I am not happy about this. I just have one hard and fast rule, Alex, and that's don't fuck with my business. And this," he gestured at me, "is fucking with my business."

"Sorry," I said, though I didn't mean it.

"Let me grab your clothes and some necessities." Cross checked his watch. "Will you at least try to look presentable?"

"Sure, boss. Whatever you want."

He looked at me again, perhaps seeing how broken I was. "You know, the liver can regenerate, and we can live with a little less than half. That's why liver transplants happen so often. If you have to be stabbed in a vital organ, that's a good one to pick."

But that didn't make me feel any better either.

THIRTY-SEVEN

"Alex," Jen O'Connell entered the nurses' lounge, taking a seat on her husband's lap and giving him a peck on the cheek, "how are you feeling?"

"Fine." If one more person asked me that question, I was liable to jump out the window. "How's Lucca?"

"Resting. Kelly wants to speak to you."

"No." I stared at the soda machine in the corner, wondering if I could crawl inside and hide. Martin gently squeezed my knee, which was propped up on a pillow on top of his crossed legs since he'd been so insistent that I keep my injury elevated.

"Okay." Jen didn't push. "Do you guys need anything?"

"We're okay, honey," O'Connell said. "Thanks for letting us set up shop in here."

"Don't thank me. Thank the hospital administration." She gave her husband a kiss. "I'll meet you at home. Do you think you'll be late?"

"Probably."

"Okay, I'll leave your plate in the fridge." She said her goodbyes and left the lounge.

"Parker," O'Connell waited for me to tear my gaze away from the vending machine before he continued, "Francisco

Steele's dead. Warden Schuster admitted he fudged on the prisoner release procedures. He let Steele escape. He let this happen."

"Sounds like you're building a strong case against him."

"We are." O'Connell reread my statement. "I would have thought Heathcliff was Steele's next target too. You took reasonable action, even if it didn't pan out."

"Eddie didn't think so. He was right. I was wrong." My throat tightened. "That should be me. Not him. Me."

Martin took my hand and pressed it to his lips. He didn't agree, but he was smart enough not to say it. But I was sure Kelly Lucca and baby Grace would agree with me. Eddie was their world, and right now, their world could end at any moment.

"He'll make it, Parker," O'Connell insisted.

"Cooper didn't."

"Alexis," Martin said gently, "stop."

"Did we ever find out how Steele got in and out of the condemned apartment building?" I asked.

"Rope ladder. Forensics found the metal anchors on the floor beneath the window sill. They must have fallen when Steele tugged the rope free from the window after he climbed down."

"How can you be sure that's what it is?" I asked.

"When CSU ran tests on the receipt, they found a charge near the bottom. They're positive that's what made the indentions on the window sill. He probably climbed down the moment we breached. In the chaos, no one noticed him slip away. And the window was shut. We had no reason to think he jumped out."

I scowled. If we'd caught Steele then, Lucca's life wouldn't have been jeopardized.

"We spoke to Tom Collins. He admitted to having prior dealings with Steele. But he thought he was a good guy, just troubled. When Steele got released from prison, he called Tom to pick him up. I think the old man might have been gullible or he saw the wounded adolescent in Steele and wanted to help him. Maybe the guy was just lonely. He gave Steele a ride and some money. But he hasn't seen him since."

"The pre-paid credit card?" I asked.

O'Connell nodded. "We could probably pursue charges, but Collins is clean. He spent the first sixty-something years of his life as a law-abiding citizen. I don't think he had any idea what his dealer was capable of."

"Did he buy the drugs for his wife?" I asked.

"Yeah, a few bottles of oxy. The DA's deciding what they want to do with that information."

"It's a terrible situation," Martin said.

"What about the Stop N' Shop?" I asked.

"I spoke to Luther Vega about it. Told him Steele was dead and offered him a deal to have him moved out of gen pop, so he'd be safe." Nick reached for a file near his feet and held it out to me.

"And?" I asked, having no desire to read.

"And it turns out Bard had an operation running outside the prison with that particular convenience store. They were transporting drugs to the store by hiding them in shipments of imported sodas. They had an entire process going in the back room, which is also where they'd cut the drugs and do deals. People are in and out all the time. No one thought anything of it. Plus, they'd short out the cameras from time to time to avoid getting caught. Steele heard about it, and once he was out, he went there to pick up everything he needed."

"Including guns and cash. Bard must have given the okay." Nothing happened inside the gang without Bard's approval.

"That would be my guess. But you should ask Kendall or Jablonsky. That's what the OIO had been investigating for the last month." O'Connell retracted the folder and put it back on top of the pile.

"That's why Bard gave the okay," I said. "He knew Steele would distract us and draw attention away from that."

"Or he just wanted revenge and knew Steele was a loaded gun," Martin suggested.

O'Connell pointed at him. "That's what I think."

"Either way, it comes down to one simple fact. Steele was nuts. And he put himself on a collision course with me. Everyone who got in his way became collateral damage."

"Not everyone," Heathcliff said from the doorway. I turned to look at the freshly shaven, respectable detective I had grown accustomed to seeing. He met my eyes. He didn't have to say it. He was sorry, just like I was.

We spent another hour going over details. I spoke to Lt. Moretti, Director Kendall, a few members of the DA's office, several U.S. Marshals, and someone from the Dept. of Corrections. Everyone agreed; Steele took his revenge. This wasn't a bigger conspiracy or a cartel hit. This was one delusional man who turned into a monster and fixated on me.

"We found this," Kendall said, handing me an envelope. "It was hidden in a baggie in the toilet."

"I hope you washed it first." Gingerly, I took the envelope and looked inside. "Was this in Steele's cell?"

"Vega's. But the prints on the phone match Steele. He must have placed it there after they switched. Our behavioral analysts know he fixated on you. He couldn't have been without the photos and info for long. They both quelled and fed his obsession. I'm surprised he didn't take it with him. He must not have had time."

I flipped through the images, finding several photos from when I testified in court against him. "Did he take these?"

"We can't say for sure, but that'd be my guess." Kendall let out a breath. "Steele planned this from the beginning. It was just a matter of time. No one could have done anything to stop him."

I shrugged, not sure if I believed it.

"When they're determined like this, they always find a way. You know that, Parker," Kendall said. He looked down at my leg, still propped on a pillow over Martin's knee. "I'm glad you're okay. Have you spoken to Lucca yet? He's been in and out for the last hour."

"No."

"You should."

Anger boiled up inside. "Lucca never wanted to leave. He came back here to help us. To help the OIO. Jablonsky. Me. You. He's loyal. You should have done more for him. You should have fought to keep him."

Kendall assessed me for a moment. "Are you sure this is about Eddie Lucca?"

"Who else would it be about?"

Kendall thought for a moment. "Take care of yourself, Parker." He nodded at Martin and walked away.

I wanted to scream, cry, and hide away from the world. And the damn hole in my leg kept me from pacing, running, and escaping the crushing weight of absolutely everything. Pushing my way off the threadbare couch in the nurse's lounge, I grabbed the fancy crutches that hooked together behind my back that Lucien had delivered and hauled myself up. I had to get out of here. The walls were closing in.

"Sweetheart," Martin said as I clicked back and forth across the floor, "do you want to check on Lucca?"

"No. I don't know. I don't know anything. I just know I can't stay here."

"We can go home," Martin suggested. "You haven't slept in nearly a week. You need to take it easy. You need to recover."

"From the world's worst hangover, I agree." Everything hurt, my insides and outsides. No wonder I was so bitchy. "We have bigger problems. I'm fine."

He looked at me sadly. "No, you're not. We've been here before. And it's a long, hard road ahead. But you'll get there."

"Four weeks. That's what the doctor said."

"I wasn't talking about your leg." He got up, approaching slowly, like one would a wounded animal. "I'm talking about you."

"Let's not talk about me." I hated the sadness and fear in his eyes. "Are we okay? You've been going through so much with Mark and now me. No one's checked in with you. You just got through that rough patch not that long ago. And now this." I didn't know if I had anything left to give, but I'd give whatever I had to him.

"It's sweet of you to ask. Yes, I'm okay."

"Are you sure?" The last thing we needed was Martin's insecurities to return while my demons were running rampant.

"You didn't break me, sweetheart. You came home. You always will, right?"

"That's the plan."

"I'm okay then. I'm just worried about you."

I wasn't okay. I wasn't even close. And at the moment, I didn't know if I ever would be. Martin could see that, and it bothered him, which broke the few remaining intact pieces of my heart.

"You know you can't control everything. You saved Mark and Lucca. You did your best. You just have to make peace with that," he said.

I realized the hollow in my chest had returned. I hadn't felt it in so long. Mistakenly, I thought I was finally free of it, but I was wrong. The pain and emptiness from recent losses was amplified by my memories and shadows of old wounds which would never fully heal. "You shouldn't have to go through this with me again. It's not fair to you."

"We all hurt, Alex. And we're all afraid sometimes. You do what you can to save everyone else. This is how I save you. I just hope you'll let me." He took my chin and turned my head so he could stare into my eyes. "Don't shut me out. I know that's how you deal with these things, but don't do it, sweetheart. Please, I can't lose you. That will break me."

Tossing the crutches to the side, I wrapped my arms around him and breathed in his scent. "Why did this have to happen? Why couldn't I stop it?"

"I don't know. But it could have been worse. We almost lost Mark. I could have lost you. But you're both okay. Heathcliff's okay. Nick's okay. That FBI tech's okay. That's because you saved them. You did that. Losing Cooper, Lucca getting hurt, that's not on you." He let go and handed me the crutches. "Let's see how Lucca is and then call it a night. You've been through a lot these last few days."

"Tell me about it."

When we stepped out of the elevator, I spotted the woman with the honey-colored hair swept into a messy ponytail. She carried a toddler on her hip as she paced in front of Lucca's room. I didn't know if the pacing was from nerves or something she did to soothe her daughter. But it didn't look particularly soothing to me.

"I can't do this." I took a step back. My crutches clicking on the tile.

She turned at the sound, recognition dawning on her face. And she changed course, heading directly for me. Every instinct in my body said to run, but I wouldn't get far like this. Lucca's request came to mind, and I wondered why he owed her an apology. Flashes of Renee Jablonsky entered my mind. Kelly better not accuse me of sleeping with her husband too.

"Alexis Parker?" she asked. She eyed me up and down, particularly the bandage on my leg.

"Uh-huh."

She glanced at Martin, offering a tight, practiced smile. "I'm Kelly. I'm Eddie's wife. This is Grace."

Martin uttered his usual greeting and made a cooing noise at the little girl. The kid giggled and squirmed. Another woman, who looked eerily similar to Kelly, appeared and scooped Grace into her arms.

"Thanks, Steph." Kelly turned back to me. "You were Eddie's partner."

"Yes, Mrs. Lucca."

She chuckled. "You're the crazy woman with a death wish that my husband could never shut up about. I never heard him speak so highly of anyone before or since."

"Are we talking about the same Eddie Lucca? The Lucca I know can't stand me."

She laughed, as if I were making a joke. And then she hugged me. "Thank you."

I pulled back, nearly toppling over in the process. "Mrs. Lucca, this is my fault. I shouldn't have called him. I shouldn't have involved him. If I hadn't...I'm sorry," I rambled, the words pouring out. "How is he?"

"The doctors say he'll be right as rain in a few months. He should be out of the hospital in a matter of days. At least he'll get some time off or actually stay behind that desk, like he said he would."

I didn't say anything.

"You kept him safe. All this time. When we were here,

you kept him safe. You made sure he came home to me every night. And you brought him back to me now too." She dabbed at her eyes.

"It's my fault. I put him in that position."

She shook her head. "He would have come anyway. He loves Agent Jablonsky and you. I was mad at him for leaving. We had a fight. It was stupid. So stupid. He loves this. How can I fault him for that?"

"He loves you. All he ever talks about is you and your daughter, even when I tried very hard to keep him from sharing personal details, he still brought you up all the time. He wanted to make sure I told you that. And that he was sorry. I told him he better tell you himself."

"And you made sure he did." She squeezed my hand, which would have been trembling had I not been gripping the crutches. "He might be awake. Do you want to see him?"

"I don't want to impose."

"He wants to see you." She wiped her eyes. "Please, it'd mean so much to him."

Slowly, I followed her back to Lucca's room and poked my head inside. He opened his eyes, probably from the racket I was making. "What happened to you?" he asked.

"Steele shot me."

"You just didn't want me to get all the attention." He gestured to the flowers and fruit baskets around the room. "Which one's from you?"

"Shut up." I moved closer, awkwardly dropping into a chair while making a mental note to send a get well gift to his room as soon as we left the hospital. "You saved my life, Eddie. How can I repay you?"

"Gift basket."

"Besides that."

He shook his head. "You came back for me. We're even."

*　　*　　*

A few weeks later, someone knocked on my office door. I looked up at the Cross Security receptionist. "Ms. Parker, there's an FBI agent here to see you."

"Send him in," I said, expecting to see Mark.

Lucca stepped into the doorway. "What happened to your crutches?"

"Lucca?" I got up from behind the desk and hugged him.

"Ouch." He winced, rubbing his abdomen. "Do you want to kill me? I got stabbed and lost a chunk of my liver, remember?"

"Sorry." I stepped back with my palms raised.

He shrugged, a devious twinkle in his eyes. "I guess it's only fitting. You only hug me when I get transferred. The last time was when I got transferred to D.C."

"Where are you going this time?" I asked.

"Back to the OIO. Apparently, a former agent told the director off and got him thinking. Pair that with recent events and Jablonsky's recommendation, and D.C. finally listened."

"So you're back?"

"I'm back." He grinned. "Kelly's happy. She likes living here. She has more friends. We got Grace back into her old play groups. Though, at that age, I doubt they remember who their friends are."

"Who knows?"

He gave me a funny look. "You don't look happy about this."

"Did you come to offer me a reinstatement?" I asked.

"No." He glanced pointedly at the furniture in my office. "Why would you want that?"

"I don't." I sighed. I just didn't like having him this close. "What if someone else comes out of the woodwork, someone just as crazy as Steele or worse?"

"We'll take care of it," Lucca said. "I won't live my life in fear." He noted the dark circles beneath my eyes. "You shouldn't either."

"I'm working on it."

"Well, I'll be around if you need me."

"Let's hope that doesn't happen."

He headed for the door, and I went back to my desk. But he knocked against the jamb. "Hey, Parker, you saved my life. You came back for me. You didn't have to do that. Steele wanted you dead. That stunt you pulled was suicide.

Not a lot of people would do that. You really must be crazy."

"I owed you. I still do."

He tapped on the door. "Take it easy. I'll see you around."

After he left, I stared into the empty hallway. I still had a lot of mistakes to make up for. I just hoped Eddie Lucca's transfer back to the city wouldn't be one of them.

Thick Fog

Don't miss *Warning Signs*, the next novel in the Alexis Parker series.

Sign-up to be notified about the latest release:

http://www.alexisparkerseries.com/newsletter

ABOUT THE AUTHOR

G.K. Parks is the author of the Alexis Parker series. The first novel, *Likely Suspects,* tells the story of Alexis' first foray into the private sector.

G.K. Parks received a Bachelor of Arts in Political Science and History. After spending some time in law school, G.K. changed paths and earned a Master of Arts in Criminology/Criminal Justice. Now all that education is being put to use creating a fictional world based upon years of study and research.

You can find additional information on G.K. Parks and the Alexis Parker series by visiting our website at
www.alexisparkerseries.com